DIAMOND & DAWN

Also by Lyra Selene

Amber & Dusk

DIAMOND & DAWN

BOOK TWO

LYRA SELENE

Scholastic Press · New York

All rights reserved. Published by Scholastic Press, an imprint of Scholastic Inc., *Publishers since 1920.* SCHOLASTIC, SCHOLASTIC PRESS, and associated logos are trademarks and/or registered trademarks of Scholastic Inc.

The publisher does not have any control over and does not assume any responsibility for author or third-party websites or their content.

No part of this publication may be reproduced, stored in a retrieval system, or transmitted in any form or by any means, electronic, mechanical, photocopying, recording, or otherwise, without written permission of the publisher. For information regarding permission, write to Scholastic Inc., Attention: Permissions Department, 557 Broadway, New York, NY 10012.

This book is a work of fiction. Names, characters, places, and incidents are either the product of the author's imagination or are used fictitiously, and any resemblance to actual persons, living or dead, business establishments, events, or locales is entirely coincidental.

Library of Congress Cataloging-in-Publication Data available

ISBN 978-1-338-54759-7

10 9 8 7 6 5 4 3 2 1   19 20 21 22 23

Printed in the U.S.A.   23

First edition, December 2019

Book design by Elizabeth B. Parisi and Mary Claire Cruz

For all the dreams that may change,
but refuse to die

ONE

The moon had not risen on the Amber Empire for a thousand tides. But that didn't mean my people never craved luster.

Or spectacle.

A crowd of silent people lingered in the Marché Cuirasse—mere steps from the orphanage I'd planned to visit. Sunlight raw as uncut ambric sent their shadows sliding along the uneven cobblestones and turned their eyes to mirror glass. They'd heard I was coming—I saw wilted paper sunbursts chased with kembric leaf hung from painted sticks. I also saw a few sharp-nosed masks, red as blood, perched jaunty on children's heads or shoved in back pockets. I saw hard mouths and bruised eyes. I saw fear.

I did not see any smiles.

I swung out of my carrosse, stepping into the ruddy light and fighting unease. In the nearly two spans since defeating Severine, I'd spent barely any time in the city. The first span had been a chaos of fleeing the Skyclad army, marshaling aid from Belsyre, and recapturing a city on the brink of revolution. And in recent weeks, I'd barely left Coeur d'Or—patching a broken government, demilitarizing a vast army, and planning a coronation left me little time for jaunts through my seething capital. But strange whispers had begun to reach the palais, and I knew it was time for me to walk among my people, even if I was not yet Amber Empress.

A platoon of Belsyre's formidable soldats moved to flank me as I approached the staring crowd, their jet-black uniforms darker than the clouds above the Midnight Dominion. Even after a span serving as my honor garde, the Loup-Garou—*the*

Werewolf—still made me nervous. Their booted feet stepped in unison, echoing the hollows between my heartbeats. I almost turned toward them in the dusk—to search their pale impassive faces for a sharp half smile, to seek out a pair of green eyes among their matching emerald signats, to find a trace of familiarity in all this strangeness.

I didn't turn. I clutched the fabric of my golden skirts and looked into the faces of my people, savoring the edge of my own power reflecting in their eyes. A flare of pleasure burst along my spine when I remembered—I was their dauphine. I was their *Sun Heir*.

I sank to my knees before a little girl hiding in her mother's ragged skirts. She must have been about seven, although her small size made her look younger. Hunger etched out her jaw and chiseled her ribs; I could see them jutting through the thin material of her worn frock. She was clutching one of the sunburst kites—handmade, cut from cheap parchment and painted in garish shades of yellow and orange.

"Hello." My voice came out too soft. I cleared my throat. "What's your name?"

She nestled deeper into her mother's skirts, mute. I bit my lip and tried to see myself how she must see me. A girl—a *woman*—not much younger than her mother, gowned in a magnificent dress of kembric and cream, designed to catch the light and amplify it. A woman with ambric gilt dusted around her cheeks and along her collarbone. A woman who was to be her empress.

"My name is Mirage." I leaned closer, conspiratorial. "Although once upon a time my name was Sylvie."

Something flickered in her eyes, then disappeared. An idea coaxed the edge of my mind. I smiled, held out a hand, and made the little girl see something that wasn't there. A ball of flame appeared, blazing red as our static sun. Light poured between my fingertips, splashing the cobbles with kembric and gowning the little girl in radiance.

She gasped, her eyes glazing with awe. Her mother's face softened. The crowd inhaled and leaned a little closer.

My smile grew. This—*this* was my gift. The legacy of illusion—a wash of impossible colors born in the dusk and glittering like sunlight in my veins. This was what drove me out of the shadows and into the light. To the Amber City, to the palais of Coeur d'Or, into this complicated, confusing, remarkable life. This was why I was here.

I made the fantastical sun bigger. But something was wrong— a taint of darkness stained the molten glow an ugly red. Brilliance battled with blight as the orb stuttered on its axis. Horror scorched my throat. My fingers trembled. I clenched my fist. The sun shattered into a thousand pieces, sending a flickering firework of scarlet and shadow bursting into the crowd. Droplets of blood danced on the breeze, then disappeared like a broken promise.

The crowd's scattered, unenthusiastic applause tasted like soured wine. I turned my gaze back to the little girl, suddenly nauseous.

"I'm Cosette," the little girl whispered, at last. "Maman calls me Etty though."

"Etty is a lovely name," I choked out, gesturing to the mass of paper and string clutched in her little palm. "May I see what you're holding?"

Etty nodded, handing over her sunburst kite without protest. I tried not to care when her mother's calloused hands tightened on her daughter's shoulders, but a shadow of resentment caught in my throat. I unfolded the symbol in my lap, smoothing its edges with fingers that came away yellow. I cooed over it, winking at Cosette. I flipped it over.

Drawn on its reverse, in negative space, with charcoal and a decided hand, was an image of the moon. But this was not the silent, serene moon I remembered from the frescoes in the Sisters' Temple where I was raised. This moon had sly, slitted eyes and expectant brows, like she had just awoken from a delicious, devious dream. This moon smiled like she would shatter an empire just to see herself reflected in all its broken pieces. This moon would not forgive a world who had forsaken her.

I breathed a tiny sip of sun-stained air. Sunder had been right after all. I'd barely believed him when he'd said this image was spreading around the city like a secret. The sunburst did not surprise me, for it had long been a symbol claimed by the Sabourin dynasty—the royal line descended from Meridian's mythic blood. That blood flowed through my own veins. But the moon? I didn't understand what it had to do with me.

"Do you know what this is?" I gently waved the kite. "Do you know what these pictures mean?"

"Ye-e-es," said Etty. "The pretty yellow one's supposed to be the sun. And the other one—" She sucked her bottom lip into her mouth and glanced at her mother. The woman darted her eyes to me, then gave a curt nod. "The one with the round white face is supposed to be the moon."

"Why?"

She screwed up her little face. "Why *what?*"

"I didn't—" My hands still trembled. I clutched the kite tighter. "Why did you and your mother draw the moon on the back side of the sun? What's it supposed to mean?"

"It means *you*, of course," said Etty matter-of-factly. "Because you were born in the dark, but you came to the light. Maman says you're not the Sun Heir. She keeps calling you the Du—"

I heard a rough intake of breath from the crowd. The scuffle of bodies colliding—the melee of half-drawn swords and shouting soldats. I turned a half second before a body slammed into me, colliding with my hip and knocking my legs out from under me.

I hit the ground in a chaos of elbows and knees churning against the pavement. My neck bent back, then snapped forward. My head pummeled the cobbles with a jarring wave of pain. Darkness lapped at my vision as hands grabbed my shoulders, grappling for my throat. Panic frothed wild in my chest, and I pushed up, bloody palms on cobbles. I slammed backward into my assailant. He grunted, fingers slipping from my neck as a Loup-Garou soldat grabbed for him. I threw myself forward into a limping run, my vision swimming as I gasped for breath to scream, to flee—

A cool voice sliced through my haze of fear, quiet but demanding: *If you cannot fight*—flee!

No.

If you cannot fight, hide.

My steps slowed as sudden calm descended upon me. My frantic heart stuttered, and my palms itched. Shouts and screams sliced my ears. The churning crowd coughed up a slight figure. A weapon flashed in low sunlight. He headed straight for me.

I'd practiced for this. I knew exactly what I had to do.

I froze, then made myself invisible, a trick I'd learned just spans ago. The world glazed over me like I wasn't there. I took a half step back, replacing myself with an illusory copy. She hitched her skirts around her knees and ran. Her hair spilled out of its braid and flew out behind her like a pennant of shadow.

Footsteps clattered behind me, then stopped. The boy who attacked me stopped in the spot where my fantasy doppelgänger had just stood, close enough for me to count the beads of sweat on his upper lip and smell the stench of fear wafting off him. He was young—barely fifteen, by the looks of it, although death and violence had scrubbed his youth away. A sharp mask dangled around his neck, painted garish red. His fist gripped a blood-stained blade. He stared after the girl in the kembric gown, sprinting toward the shadows at the edge of the Marché Cuirasse, confusion and anger and suspicion giving his face sharp edges.

What had he seen, amid the chaos, to make him look like that? Had he seen his dauphine flicker in and out of existence before fleeing across the market? Or was it enough that when I'd glanced over my shoulder in fear, he'd seen me not as a hated political opponent, but as a person?

He yanked the mask back over his face, tightened his grip on his dagger, and ran after the mirage I'd conjured as my decoy.

A bitter cocktail of fury and fear and relief coated my mouth, and I fought the urge to crumple to my knees. Instead, I blinked back into sight and turned toward the crowd, heart vaulting. Anticipated regret burned my bones, for I already knew what I would see.

The Loup-Garou had subdued the crowd with violence and precision. The damage was bad. Broken vendor stalls listed to the side, shrouded in ripped awnings. An overturned cart spilled fruit onto the pavement—split rinds spewed rich pulp onto cobbles stained with human blood. A child wailed. I saw black-forged swords held to quivering throats; bruised arms and shredded tunics beneath a wall of glowering eyes and tearstained faces.

"Enough!" My voice came out reedy. I cleared my throat and tried again. "That's enough, I said!"

Swords slithered into sheaths. Booted feet kicked through limp paper sunbursts and shattered red masks. The Loup-Garou surrounded me in a loose circle, impassive faces turned outward. All but one—a tall figure detached himself from the platoon and stepped toward me. His black uniform was identical to his fellows' but for a strip of stark argyle at his shoulder and an ambric sunburst above his breast. He pushed back his hood, spilling pale hair over his brow. Dristic-ringed eyes gleamed greener than the emerald signat glinting in his ear.

Sunder.

My heart pummeled my chest when I remembered how close I'd come to losing him. Memories flicked by—the moment I left him behind, bleeding on the steps of the Atrium, and the moment I found him again, festering and feverish, abandoned by the Skyclad when they surrendered the palais.

But that had been weeks ago. He'd survived, as I'd known he must. I leaned toward him, reaching for his stark solid presence. His gloved hand dropped to his sword hilt, but he didn't move toward me.

"Are you hurt?" His voice was soft but sharp, a blade concealed in silk.

"No," I lied. A massive bruise bloomed along my hip and I could taste blood where I'd bit my lip. "I used the feint we practiced. He ran after my decoy."

Sunder's jaw tightened, and his eyes moved toward the shadowy entrance of the marché. I followed his gaze, but the pair of figures had long since disappeared. "Do you want us to pursue him?"

"He tried to kill me," I snarled. "Would you have him get away with it?"

"He's just a boy," Sunder muttered.

Sudden sympathy made me hesitate. Again I saw his smooth boy's face—too young to shave. His skinny arms. The fear slicking his eyes.

"He was no innocent." I closed my eyes against the memory of my face in the dirt. The long sharp mask. That knife, its red hilt stained with the sweat of his fear. "Or did you miss the boot in my back and the knife at my throat?"

"Surely he wasn't the one to plan this."

"And yet, he was the one to carry it out." My tone rang harsh.

"If we catch him—and we will catch him, demoiselle—he will be interrogated. Perhaps worse." Something akin to sorrow razored across the planes of his face before he dropped his head into a posture of deference. The pose fit him like a poorly tailored coat. "I await your command, dauphine. Whatever it may be."

I dared to glance past the Loup-Garou at the scene of destruction beyond. The Amber Citizens—referred to commonly as Ambers—had scattered, leaving behind the wreckage and detritus of the struggle. Despite the bloodstained cobbles, I saw no bodies. No dead.

A throb of pain shot toward my temple from where I'd slammed my head. This was not my fault. Was it? I had come here today with nothing but good intentions. But violence had been done to me, and in my defense. And yet—if I sent these soldats after that boy, he would face the consequence of a man. Was I willing to decide on such a fate?

A chill memory ghosted over me—another dusk, another decision, another brush with death. I remembered swords and soldats in uniform and the brisk tang of fear in the back of my throat. The incandescent thrill of wielding power heightened by a glass-bright need to survive.

Across the market, a scarlet mask looped over a lamppost shifted in the breeze—a long red finger pointed straight at me. I tightened my shoulders and lifted my chin.

"Find him," I commanded. "Find him, but don't kill him. I want to know why he tried to assassinate me."

Sunder nodded, curt, then pulled his hood over his eyes and turned on his heel. As one, the Loup-Garou followed, a sleek machine sprinting dark through the golden streets. Two remained at my shoulders, tall and still.

Indecision churned hot in my stomach as I watched them disappear into the labyrinth of the Mews. I didn't doubt they would find the boy, but I almost wished they wouldn't. A soft part of me cried out for his youth, stolen by poverty and violence and the treacherous allure of misplaced ideals.

Perhaps, once upon a time, we'd been the same, me and that boy. We were both children. We both had a lifetime of choices laid out in front of us. We were both innocent.

Innocence. I turned the word over in my head until it stopped making sense. When had I lost my innocence? Long ago, one forgotten day in that frigid dusk where I was raised, ignored by righteous Sisters and slapped by vicious children. When I too was a child, full of impossible dreams and sunlit wishes. But then I'd discovered the royal, magical blood flowing through my veins. And I'd changed. My magical legacy had changed. *Everything* had changed.

I turned toward my carrosse, gilded and gleaming in the shadow of a tenement building. Above the roofs of the city, Coeur d'Or dazzled like a promise, a vision in kembric and amber. My satin slipper nudged a tattered piece of parchment: a pale face, a winking eye, a sly mouth.

Perhaps we had once been the same, me and that boy. But now he was a half-hearted assassin with a blade in his hand and a dungeon in his future. And I—I was the Sun Heir, dauphine of the Amber Empire and soon-to-be empress.

We were not the same at all.

And I wouldn't change that for the world.

TWO

I stalked through the labyrinth of Coeur d'Or's twisting hallways toward the sick beating heart of the empire—the sanctum where the beast slept. Hanks of hair tumbled out of my elaborate coif and flapped over my shoulder, so I tore jeweled pins from my hair and dropped them to the marble floor to glitter like fallen tears.

Two of Sunder's Loup-Garou trailed me to the Imperial Suite. It was still a shock to see them in the palais instead of the once-familiar Skyclad Garde—where the empress's forces had been shining chips of Prime desert sky, Belsyre's militia looked more like shards of Midnight. But the Skyclad had been too fierce, too unswerving, too loyal—to *her*. Not to me. Never to me.

"You'll wait outside," I commanded, as I'd done each time I'd come here. "Only Dowser and your commandant may enter. No one else."

"Yes, dauphine." The male soldat—Calvet—was a few tides older than me, with flaxen hair and a set of enviable dimples. He moved to open the door.

"Dauphine," echoed the female soldat, his partner—lean and muscular, with a crown of braids and paper-white skin. She posted at the threshold.

Severine's rooms were quiet as a coffin. Despite the empress's outward extravagance at court, her private chambers were almost austere. The white marble walls were free of gilt, the crown molding bare of filigree. No hangings or portraits or landscapes marred the clean walls. And yet, in contrast, papers and books sprawled across a vast ambric desk. In the dressing room, a thousand stained-glass gowns were flung haphazardly over armoires; priceless tiaras and necklaces slung limp across bureaus and between broken high heels. I'd barely begun to sort through the chaos of Severine's affairs—frozen in time on the day I'd launched my insurrection—but already they perplexed me.

Beneath a skylight bleeding red loomed Severine's bed. It was huge, draped in gauzy curtains drifting in an invisible breeze. A slight form occupied its center.

Severine.

I stood at the edge of the bed and regarded my sister. She looked so small and ethereal like this—a lost queen from legend, cursed to a lifetime of sleep. Her face, scrubbed of cosmetics and absent its customary regal mask, looked young—too young to have ruled an empire for seventeen tides, too young to have hurt so many, too young to have earned the fate I dealt her.

Too young to have been murdered.

Almost murdered.

Because Severine wasn't dead. Her body had been recovered by the Skyclad after I fled the city, but it was Dowser who realized she still lived. He'd spirited her here in secret, expecting her to expire quickly from her injuries.

Only she kept living. If you could call this *living.*

She hadn't woken once in the nearly two spans since I'd tried to kill her, even as her heart beat and her lungs pumped air and her wounds knit. Whether she was kept alive by a stolen legacy or the sheer force of her wicked will, we didn't know.

I lifted a hand and circled it around her neck. Her pulse beat a faint rhythm against my palm—frail as a dying bird. Remembered pain sliced up my bare arms, following the path of barely healed nicks and cuts. I tasted blood in the back of my throat, and when I lifted my hand away from her neck, I saw it was slick with the stuff. Sticky fluid glued my fingers to a splinter of mirror glass reflecting my savage eyes back at me. I gasped, but no air filled my lungs. I reeled away from the bed as red flowers bloomed on Severine's pale bedclothes, ruby liquid seeping from her mouth and nose as she choked and frothed and—

A door clicked shut behind me.

"Mirage." Dowser's firm, low voice. Surprise dragged my attention away from the vision of gore before me, and when I glanced back, I knew I'd conjured it involuntarily—Severine lay amid pristine blankets with diaphanous drapes sighing around her.

Dowser brushed past me to the bed, severe as a raven in the bright white room. He loomed over Severine's frail body, and I was reminded of how big my mentor and teacher was—hunched behind a parchment-piled desk in a smoke-dim room, it was easy to forget. He put his fingertips to Severine's wrist, counting heartbeats. Finally, he pursed his lips and released her arm. He polished his glasses on his robe, a sure sign he was perturbed about something.

"Isn't it a bit ghoulish to keep coming here?" he scolded.

"You're here too," I pointed out.

"As one of only a handful of people who knows she's alive, I confess I feel responsible for her." He heaved a sigh. "As I do for you. I heard about what happened at the marché. I'm glad you're all right."

"I suppose you're here to reprimand me for inciting a riot?"

"Those people who got hurt—that wasn't your fault." He paused meaningfully. I knew whose fault he believed it to be— Belsyre's wolves. Dowser had disliked the Loup-Garou's presence since we'd recaptured the city. He didn't like their *optics*.

"Dowser, Sunder's militia is the only thing holding this city together."

"You can't buy peace with weapons of war."

"I'm not trying to buy peace. I'm trying to buy time. Until my coronation—until Ecstatica."

Ecstatica—one of the high holy days of each tide, marking the rapturous moment Meridian caught sight of the Moon's exquisite face and fell from the sky, ushering in the beginning of the longest day and the world as we knew it. We'd celebrated it in the Temple of the Scion where I grew up, but as a purely religious holiday, complete with periods of fasting, three days of silence, and hours of prayer that left me with bruises on my knees. The Amber City celebrated it as a secular holiday—gifts were exchanged, cakes were eaten, and plenty of wine was drunk.

The last three Sabourin rulers—Severine; my father, Sylvain; and his father before him—were crowned at Ecstatica. We hoped following suit would lend an air of legitimacy to my tumultuous rise to power. But the holiday was still nearly a span away. And the city had begun to gnash its teeth.

I decided to change the subject. "Did Sunder find the boy who attacked me?"

"I believe so." Dowser retrieved a package from the door, and laid a blade across the foot of Severine's bed. "He attacked you with this."

Long and slender, the sword was forged of dristic, but a coating of bright red glossed the blade. At first it looked like blood, but when I dragged my fingertip along the balance it flaked away like paint.

"A painted sword?"

"I'm no expert on weaponry," said Dowser, "but I know a few things about history and mythology. You're familiar with the story of Meridian and the beginning of the longest day?"

"Of course." Me and every man, woman, and child in the Amber Empire. The story of a wicked Sun enamored of an uninterested Moon, who tasked a powerful god-king named Meridian to slaughter the object of his affection. He flew across the heavens in a chariot of fire, with a golden net meant to capture the Moon, a silvery spear meant to pierce her heart, and a diamond vial meant to catch her blood. But when he saw the Moon, he could not kill her, and he fell to earth with his terrible tools. The net became kembric; the spear, dristic; and the broken vial, stained with mystical blood, became the ambric bones of an empire. And lost Meridian became the Scion, worshipped in many forms across the daylight world. "What does that have to do with this?"

"The legend didn't spring into being fully formed. Like many stories, it evolved over time—each voice shading its meaning, each telling a new expression on a familiar theme. In a much earlier myth, Meridian did not carry a spear, but a sword. And because it was forged in the bosom of the Sun, the metal was molten—red-hot in Meridian's hand. He was only able to carry it because in payment for his terrible deed, the Sun had promised him his own throne. He had named Meridian the Sun Heir."

"You think this blade is supposed to represent that sword?" My head throbbed as if I'd slammed it on cobblestones again.

"That red mask the assassin wore too."

That made sense—the pointed red nose did resemble a blade.

"But why?"

"I think it is an old image resurrected for a new problem." Dowser hefted the blade. The skylight's amber glow played over its contours. "Whoever these people are, they don't believe you are the rightful Sun Heir. And they're willing to die to try and stop your coronation."

Dowser's words fit sharp teeth around my heart, releasing a trickle of doubt down my ribs. Once upon a time I'd dared to dream of a strange, lovely world where I belonged. Jewels of memory gleamed at me from the dim—a dream of paradise and an empress's sharp smile; a winter jardin and blood-red talons in the dusk; a kiss frozen in ice and a question that never had an answer.

But had that dream been nothing but illusion? I'd fought for that impossible world, but it had come with such steep costs. There had been bloodshed and death, pain and broken promises. The Skyclad banished to sprawling detention camps in the foothills of La Belladonne, replaced by Belsyre's forbidding militia. A city chafing against the shackles of martial law. My own friends, broken and reeling, trying to repair lives shattered like the mirror glass I'd used to kill my own sister.

Almost kill.

Reflexively, I looked at Severine. Her continued existence was a threat to everything I'd fought for, every faint breath an accessory to my creeping doubts. I reached for the bright hope I'd welded to my heart these last spans. All of this would be worth it in the end. I just had to keep fighting for my dream of a more perfect world—a just, glittering world, where the poor had enough to eat, where magic created beauty instead of violence, where the promise of sunlight meant more than a wish.

That dream had once felt impossible. Now I just had to keep it from fading.

"We have to find the other Relics," I said, wrapping my hand around the sunburst ambric pendant hanging from my neck— the only known Relic of the Scion, abandoned with me as a baby in the Dusklands. Dowser had searched for others during my coup against Severine, but had failed to find them. "With the Relics of the Scion, it won't matter where I came from or what I did to seize power. They'll have to accept me as empress, regardless of their red swords and old superstitions."

Dowser nodded. "I'll keep looking. I've been meaning to

explore some old texts Barthet found in the Unitas library—perhaps one of them will give us an idea of what we're looking for."

"If only she had told you," I hissed at my sister's prone form.

"If only she had told me," Dowser echoed. He turned toward the door, then turned abruptly back.

"One more thing—I nearly forgot." He drew a sheaf of parchment from his sleeve. "It's been nearly three weeks since you had me send the emissaries out. We've had some luck in the Dusklands—there was an outpost near Toulet with a few still alive. Near the sand ports in Dura'a too, although I hear more than a few defected to join Zvar corsairs in the desert."

Severine's lost legacies. Hope writhed hot and wild in my chest. "And?"

Wordlessly, he handed me the pages. I thumbed through them with trembling fingers, eyes scanning as fast as my brain could keep up.

Mirabeau.

Alveche.

De Laurion.

I flipped to the last page. "No Montrachet."

"No." Dowser shook his head, spectacles slicing through reflections. "But we'll keep searching for him. Are you sure—?"

I wasn't. All I could remember was that last, horrible moment when I'd found Thibo lying broken and empty in the undergrowth. I'd run for help, but I'd been too late. By the time I'd gotten back, he was *gone.* And now he kept slipping away from me, like water through my fingers—a sweeping feather hat with no face beneath it, laughing words with no voice to speak them, a ruffled silk shirt with no heart beating inside it. These were all the things I had left of my friend.

"His heart was beating, the last I saw him." I handed back the sheaf of papers like they'd scalded my fingers. "Just find him. Find all of them. If it's the only thing I do before—"

I clicked my teeth together, unwilling to finish the sentence. Before *what*? My unspoken doubts roused restless heads. Before another red-masked killer attempted to assassinate me in the street, and succeeded? Before Severine roused from her coma with vengeance in her eyes and violence in her heart to steal my legacy and regain her throne?

"Just do it."

Dowser nodded. His footsteps receded.

I turned to Severine's desk with a sigh. I'd already examined its contents more than once, but I kept hoping to find my sister's secrets—where she'd hidden her Relics, where she'd banished her lost legacies, why she'd ruled her empire with a dristic fist and manipulated her nobles with gilded lies.

I tidied a few books—a heavy treatise on the principles of war by an Aifiri philosopher named Dax Kinza; a tome of translated Lirian death poetry bound in crackling leather that looked enough like human skin to make *my* skin crawl; a collection of famous love letters between my ancestor, Celestine Sabourin, and the beautiful and accomplished courtesan she never got to marry.

A slender volume tucked inside a Cascaran history book fell to the marble with a slap. I picked it up. Bound in suede, it had a simple lacy pattern embossed along its spine, but no title or author to speak of. I flipped it open. Elegant, girlish handwriting looped across the pages, fine as spider silk, and I squinted at the letters. I still wasn't as literate as I'd like, and while I could usually get by with printed words, handwriting always posed a challenge.

. . . *F punished me again today, although I did not deserve it. He knows I never meant to drive her away, but it is a convenient excuse.*

And so he made me watch as he tormented S with the twisted power he dares call legacy. I know my brother will not blame me, as F intends him to. But I blame myself.

A notion dark as the winds out of Dominion chilled me. My eyes cut toward Severine's limp body, motionless in its bed. This was a diary. Could it be—?

I shoved the journal away, as though by increasing its distance from my body I could diminish my desire to read it. But it was no use. I snatched it back up, flipping through pages and pages of looping writing. Just past the halfway mark, the entries abruptly stopped. I thumbed to the last entry, curiosity and a distant kind of inevitability spurring me on. It was a single line, inked in black at the top of a swathe of staring white.

The baby is dead, it read. *My last sister is free. And I am finally alone with my burden.*

Ice crackled along my bones and congealed in my veins. A low buzzing teased at my ears and tingled along my palms. I dropped the book, then picked it up again and shoved it into my pocket. And when I fled Severine's spare, silent chambers, I swore I heard her laugh—a distant sound like chiming bells and anticipated pain.

Lys Wing smelled of crushed lilies and bittersweet memories.

Birdsong echoed through the green-draped courtyard. Clouds seared black lines across a cinnamon sky. It was too quiet. Most of the courtiers who'd fought with me in the coup had returned to their estates, to reconnect with their families and shore up their corners of this teetering empire. The legacies loyal to Severine remained in the palais, confined to their chambers until I decided what should be done with them. I trotted past chambers I no longer slept in toward Lullaby's rooms. No one answered my knock, and I had almost turned away when the door creaked open.

"Yes, lady?" The petite girl who answered was one of Lullaby's handmaidens.

"Is Lullaby at home?"

"No, lady." Camille shifted her weight. A snowflake of dismay brushed my heart. *Again?*

Since I'd returned to the city, my relationship with Lullaby had been strained. Although she'd survived the coup unscathed, she—along with Sunder and a number of other legacies—had been captured and incarcerated by the Skyclad when I fled to Belsyre. While retaking the palais, I'd found her outside her cell, standing over the body of a soldat who should have known beautiful things could still be weapons.

Are you all right? I'd asked, urgent. Fingerprints bruised her arms and violence bruised her eyes.

Fine, she'd whispered.

But when I reached out to embrace her, she held up a shaking hand and turned her face away. Loup-Garou blurred around us, kicking open doors and subduing Skyclad. So I asked about the only person I still hadn't found.

Sunder?

She pointed deeper into the dungeon. *He might still be alive.*

And she'd avoided me ever since.

I gave up trying to catch Camille's lowered eyes. "Will you tell—" I reconsidered. "Will you *ask* your lady to attend her dauphine's next Congrès? I miss her wisdom."

Camille curtsied, then snapped the door closed in my face.

THREE

I jolted in bed, a dream of Midnight and mirror glass shattering on sudden wakefulness. The last somnolent chime of third Nocturne lingered like a secret, and I saw a shadow hunched at the foot of the bed.

My pulse soared, then calmed. A sparking emerald. White-gold slashed over a furrowed brow. I sat up in bed, curling furs around me to fight the chill of Belsyre Wing.

"Sunder," I breathed.

"I have to ask, demoiselle." Sunder's half smile gleamed like a knife. "What have I done to merit a dauphine in my bed?"

Since we'd retaken Coeur d'Or, I'd slept in Belsyre Wing. With the exception of the Imperial Suite, Sunder's rooms were the safest in the palais. His wolves might not be sworn to me, but they were fiercely loyal to Sunder and his twin sister, Oleander. "I couldn't sleep in my room. It's too cold in there."

"It's colder in here."

"You have warmer furs."

"If you don't like the cold, demoiselle, no one's forcing you to share my chambers. Or my bed."

"Who said anything about sharing?" I sniffed, haughty. "The floor looks perfectly comfortable to me."

He did smile then, levering himself heavily off the foot of the bed. He sat beside me, slinging one long leg onto the mattress. A spear of red light slanted in from the skylight and cleaved him in half, rendering his features in the abstract—a fathomless eye ringed in purple shadow, hungry hollow cheekbones, plush lips set in a rigid line.

"Did you eat?" I whispered, leaning toward him.

"No." He lifted a gloved hand and pushed a lock of hair off my cheek. The leather barely brushed my skin, but a pulse of energy coiled toward the base of my skull. I tried not to flinch.

"Why not?"

"I wasn't hungry."

"You have to eat, Sunder."

"My parents died when I was two. It's a little late to be mothering me now."

The comment wasn't designed to sting, but it did anyway. I leaned back against the headboard and wrapped my arms around my chest.

"Did you find him?" I asked, curt. "Did you find the boy who tried to kill me?"

"Yes." Sunder scrubbed pale hair off his forehead. It needed cutting—jagged strands brushed his collar and fell into his eyes. "When he realized your decoy was just that, he fled to the Paper City. We found him hiding in a slag heap outside an illegal ambric refinery. His name is Pierre LaRoche. His mother was Skyclad—she died during the coup. He's the eldest of five siblings—he'd been scrubbing stoops and sweeping trash in Rue de la Soie when the Red Masks recruited him. Sounds like it wasn't hard to talk him into murdering you in public."

"Did he know anything else?" Eagerness blotted out a question growing inside me. "About the Red Masks? Who's leading the movement, where they meet, what they *want*?"

"No. He told us the names of his handlers, where he met with them. The names were fake—aliases. And the warehouse he mentioned, south of the Mews, was empty—cleared out. We won't find the leaders of the Red Masks this way."

"Scion help us. They're like ghosts."

"Worse," Sunder said, grim. "Ghosts can't kill the Duskland Dauphine."

then closed it. I met his keen metal eyes
in their depths—an anticipation of pain
s sea. His hand had moved to his side,
ously to his stomach. Guilt poured cold
f my irritation. I rose onto my knees and
rical buttons lining his uniform.
our coat. Here—let me."
he front of his jacket. Sunder inhaled
He sat motionless on the edge of the
one could hold him together. Gently, I
n, then another. The thick black fabric
e final button opened the stiff collar
ing a white linen undershirt and the
v of his throat. I lifted my eyes to his
vere dark with want. A thrill kissed

me like a warning.
collar and around his neck, twining
ft hair. But he caught the hand in his

't touch me," he rasped. "Remember?"
llowed, but when I spoke my voice
ere's touching, and then there's . . .

d again for his collar, sliding my
n jacket and the soft undershirt
y pulsed against my palms, and
d back and away, so all I could see
the pull of his brows. Slowly, I slid
lders, my hands gliding over his
of his shirt, his skin needled at my

fingertips. But it was a faint sensation—nothing I couldn't ignore. Nothing I didn't *want* to ignore.

The jacket dropped to the ground. I twined a hand with his, then lifted our joined fingers. The suede of his gloves was soft against my lips as I brushed my mouth over his knuckles. He shivered, his eyes drawing lines of cold fire in the air between us.

"See?" I whispered.

He made a noise low in his throat and slid an arm around my waist. He lifted me as he stood, my legs draped around him. His eyes didn't leave my face as he spun me gently and laid me back against the bed. Warmth pooled in my belly. His face hovered over mine, and in our shared breath I tasted his desire, so sharp it was almost acrid—burnt parchment and petrichor, a bitter wasteland of want. His mouth found the seam of silk grazing over my collarbone, and he followed it with his lips—past the pulse throbbing in my throat to brush along the swell of my breasts and then down along the ridges of my ribs. His hand skimmed the curve of my hip and slid behind my knee, painting heat on my skin as he curled my bare leg against him.

I closed my eyes, a gloss of want skimming over a jumbled sea of thoughts and sensations. I could sense how tightly he was holding himself together, yet I could still feel the hectic riot of barely controlled power sizzling within him. My focus narrowed to his touch, halting yet intense, each fingertip a caution, his lips speaking silent warnings to my skin.

A blade of agony sliced me from neck to navel. My body spasmed, my throat making an animal whimper that stopped time. Sunder threw himself away. He groaned and doubled over, bracing his forearms on the mattress and burying his face in the crook of his elbow. A shudder racked his frame, and he fisted hands in the rumpled blankets.

"I'm—I'm sorry." I was on my feet, instinct shoving me away

from him. I forced myself to stand still, to step toward him, to reach a hand toward his shoulder. "Sunder, I didn't mean—"

"*Don't!*" His voice came out guttural. He hurled himself off the bed, stumbling toward the armoire in the corner. He braced one arm against it as he tore at his shirt, shredding the neckline with his fingers until the material ripped jagged to bare his torso.

I stared. His chest heaved with exertion, and the lean muscles in his abdomen flexed, spasmodic. But that wasn't what caught my eye. It was the slab of refined ambric embedded in his side. Dristic staples held it in place. Inflamed skin curled away from its edges as though it was hot to the touch. Veins of red climbed his stomach and slithered beneath the waistband of his trousers, throbbing bloody.

His *timbre.* I hadn't seen it in weeks, but the sight of it brought back a flood of nausea and strangling regret. Dowser had made sure Sunder didn't bleed out in the dungeon—a kindness for which I would never stop thanking him—but there'd been no one willing or able to properly heal him. The wound in his side had festered, racking him with a fever that should have killed him well before I returned.

Vida was among the dissident legacies who were arrested and locked up, and I'd asked her to use her gift to heal Sunder. She'd set her palm against his skin, then jerked her hand away like she'd been scalded. When she turned to me, her cool-dark eyes held equal parts pity and triumph.

There's nothing I can do for him.

Nothing? My stomach dropped. *He's dying.*

She'd hesitated.

There's a practice common in war, where doctors are few and healing legacies fewer, she admitted. *An ambric device known as a timbre.*

I'd never heard of such a thing before. In the Dusklands where I was raised, the only real medicine was prayer. At Coeur d'Or, there had always been at least one legacy in residence with a healing ability—Vida and her brother, Mender, had both possessed the gift of knitting bones and sealing wounds. Besides, the most serious complaints at court were usually bad hangovers and broken hearts.

It keeps a person alive, up to a point. But it's unpredictable for legacies. There tend to be . . . consequences.

Like what?

She shrugged. *Sometimes the cure we need isn't the cure we want.*

For a while, I'd hoped a better solution could be found. But the medics and scholars I'd summoned from the lower city weren't more help. And after a few days of examinations, Sunder had fixed me with a smile like venom and said:

I'm alive, demoiselle. But if you keep letting them poke and prod me, we'll be taking bets on whether they can kill me before I kill them. And my money's on them.

So he'd gotten his timbre and I'd sent them all away. And Sunder was right—he was alive. For now.

"Does it hurt?" I whispered, stupidly.

"Of course it *hurts*," Sunder snarled. He pressed his hand to the timbre and flinched when it pulsed brighter.

Waves of pain radiated from the device, digging grooves along his hip bones and raising the veins on his forearms. He hissed and curled forward. His pupils were blown wide and dark, nearly blotting out the green of his irises. When they met mine, his desperation was like an arrow through my skull.

"Just breathe." I reached for him, but he flinched away. I let the hand drop, guilt and relief souring my stomach. I wasn't going to push it. I'd learned too well what it felt like when a boy whose legacy was pain couldn't control it any longer. Because that's what the timbre had done to him—even as it saved his life, the ambric had attached to his legacy and amplified it, feeding into his own powers yet flooding him with agony. He'd lost nearly all control of his abilities. Instead of being able to deal pain with a thought, he had *become* pain. It was tearing him apart from the inside out.

And it was my fault.

"Just breathe."

He gave a curt nod and took a shaking breath. I inhaled too, counting as I did.

"One . . . two . . . three . . . hold."

He blew out a lungful of air. A whisper of tension slipped off the hard line of his shoulders.

"Again. One . . . two . . . three . . . hold."

I don't know how long we stood like that, face-to-face yet miles apart, counting breaths and tallying regrets. Sunder finally calmed, his muscles unclenching as the livid lines striping his torso slid back to the ambric timbre, which dulled and winked dark. His shoulders slumped, and his hand dropped away from his stomach. I shifted my feet, suddenly awkward.

"Your shirt," I said, to fill the yawning silence. "It's ruined."

"It doesn't matter." He dropped the shredded fabric to the floor. He ran a hand through his sweat-damp hair, and slouched toward the bed. "I'll send for more tomorrow."

He slumped into bed, flinging his head back against the pillows and clenching his eyes shut. I watched him for a long moment; the troubled line between his straight brows, the ragged ends of his too-long hair, the uneven pulse leaping in his throat. I gathered my dressing gown around my shoulders and crept toward the door.

"Rest well," I whispered, with my hand on the knob.

The door had nearly swept shut behind me when Sunder's voice drifted across the room.

"Demoiselle." A long silence made me think I'd dreamed his voice, but then: "Do you want to stay?"

His words brushed my heart with translucent colors. Yes, I wanted to stay. Scion, I wanted to stay so badly it was like a laceration in my chest. I wanted to climb into that bed and fit myself into the circle of his arms. I wanted to touch him without feeling like it might kill us both. I wanted to kiss him and forget.

I had once reviled him for his legacy, for his inborn ability to cause pain with a touch. But it was I, in the end, who had hurt him. It might be the ambric timbre radiating agony through his body, but sometimes it felt like I had held the knife to his stomach and slid the blade home.

"Please?"

The word was barely audible, but it undid me. I crossed the dusk-lit room on quiet footsteps. I slid beside him beneath the mountain of blankets and furs, feeling the feverish heat unspooling off his skin. He used to be so cold. Beneath the familiar crisp bite of genévrier and frost, he smelled like sweat and something else—something dark and metallic that lingered on my tongue. He turned on his side to face me, lifting a hand toward my face. I suppressed the urge to flinch. He laughed, but it rang harsh as a tarnished bell.

"I wouldn't dare touch the Duskland Dauphine without asking permission."

The words lacked malice, but I winced nonetheless. He raised his hand to drift along the contours of my face, his fingers a hairsbreadth from my skin. My skin tingled as though he actually touched me. His eyes skimmed my features, following the path of his fingertips: the arch of my eyebrow; the bow of my lips; the seashell of my ear. Heat climbed my throat, and I searched his eyes for my own reflection—to see what he saw, to feel a hint of what he was feeling. But his eyes were fathomless.

"Sunder?"

A sharp shock of energy passed from his hand to my cheek.

His mouth tightened. He fisted his hand and shoved it beneath the pillow.

"Mirage?"

"Do you regret it?"

"Regret what?" His green eyes flickered. "Do I regret protecting you from Severine when I knew who you were? Do I regret telling you the truth? Do I regret helping you murder your family in order to claim a throne?"

My throat worked. "Yes."

"You dared to dream of a new world—a better world—and I will never regret that. I reserve regret for mistakes and broken promises. And so should you."

When I finally found sleep, I dreamed of glowing faces and shadow mazes and stones bright as sunshine. And when at last I awoke, the bells were chiming for Prime and Sunder was gone.

FOUR

"Reconstruction of the Atrium has commenced," Mathis Barthet droned. "But the original Cascaran marble was mined hundreds of tides ago, and the foreman informs me they're having difficulty matching the rich kembric luster to the beige tone of the modern stone, unless—"

I leaned my head on my hand and tried to focus on the words, not the monotone they were delivered in. I smothered a yawn, conscious of the weight of many sets of eyes watching my every move.

Since we'd recaptured the palais, Dowser had been intent on his self-assigned mission of building a Congrès to guide and advise me. (*Do I really need a council?* I'd asked Dowser. *No,* he'd answered mildly. *Severine didn't bother with one for tides.* I didn't need a mind-reading legacy to intuit his meaning.) And though the Congrès chamber was relatively small—a circular room with a series of curving bay windows overlooking the Concordat—it always seemed crammed full of people. Dowser, my new councillors, a handful of courtiers yawning behind fans, servants scurrying about with refreshments, Sunder and my dedicated pair of black-clad wolves guarding the doors.

Barthet was Dowser's first pick—they'd been friends and colleagues at Unitas, the Amber Empire's most prestigious university. But while Dowser's unique legacy had landed him a coveted role at the Imperial Court serving my father, Barthet had happily remained ensconced in the ancient halls of Unitas, earning the highest honors of scholarship before going on to teach. It had taken strenuous wheedling and promises to rebuild a library before he agreed to join the council, but Dowser assured me he was the foremost scholar of political strategy and post-conflict peace-building.

I found myself wishing he was the foremost scholar of public speaking.

"—which has been further complicated by the matter of Michaël Villaincourt, Vidâme de Cascara." Barthet nervously stroked his long greying beard. "He, along with several other relations of the legacies you have elected to, er, *keep on* at court, are refusing to pay taxes or sanction Imperial trade until the youths have been released."

"Excuse me?" Panic flared in my chest. Scion's teeth, but the parents of Severine's loyal Sinister legacies were revolting? "Why wasn't I told about this earlier? Mutinous nobles seem more important than rebuilding the Atrium."

Barthet tightened his lips and glanced at Marta Iole, the other newly minted member of my Congrès. She shrugged. Dowser sighed, rubbed his temples, and fixed me with a disappointed stare.

"You were told," he said. "The day before yesterday's Congrès, which you were late for. We spoke of it just after the matter of the Skyclad prison camps, and before the issue of religious tithing in the Dusklands."

I fought the heat climbing my cheeks. He was right to chide me. But I'd been meeting with these people once a day for the past span, and with every new piece of information I learned just how far my ignorance stretched. To have an opinion on Cascaran marble, I had to know a place called Cascara existed. To discuss taxation on my nobles, I had to understand tax code. To resolve civil conflicts arising from newly built prison camps in the foothills of La Belladonne, I had to learn the history of ethno-cultural erasure in the wake of the Conquest a hundred tides ago.

And I *wanted* to learn. To sit on Severine's throne and rule her empire, I had to expand my horizons, broaden my knowledge, claw my way up from the depths of my own ignorance. And I'd been trying. I'd been reading (slowly) and listening (badly) and asking questions (when I wasn't too embarrassed to not know the answers). But the harder I worked, the stupider I felt.

"I haven't threatened the Sinister legacies' safety in any way," I argued. "Unlike Severine. But until I'm sure where their loyalties lie, I can't afford to release them back to their estates."

"While holding them hostage may be a deterrent to force, the strategy relies on unequal incentives." Marta Iole's voice was faintly accented—she'd been born and raised in Aifir. She'd fled a life as a concubine and expatriated to the Amber Empire, where she built a mercantile consortium and amassed a great fortune. She was exquisite and composed and—judging by the fact that I understood only one word in five out of her mouth—utterly brilliant. "Setting them free may gain you more goodwill in the long term."

"Setting them free may result in my nobles revolting while I'm weak."

"Keeping them here may do the same."

The door to the Congrès hissed open. Sunder's wolves slid into defensive positions, gauntlets raised and black swords unsheathed. I jolted half out of my chair, turning to glare at whoever dared interrupt my Congrès.

It was Lullaby. The willowy girl wore an unadorned cobalt gown that set off her blue-hued skin and turquoise eyes, and her black silken hair fell straight down her back. Her pert mouth was set. I surged the rest of the way out of my chair, staring at my friend and erstwhile mentor with a thousand questions in my eyes. But she kept her gaze resolutely downturned, walking quickly to stand beside the other Dexter legacies.

I turned back to the table, trying to hide my dismay.

"What's next on the agenda?"

Lady Marta lifted a manicured eyebrow, moistened a finger, and flipped to the next page.

"Ah." Her look of determination made me nervous. "As you already know, the empire's coffers are depleted. The renovation of the palais alone will cost a small fortune. The Skyclad armies need to be paid severance, then discharged. You've asked taxes be lowered on the lowest classes, while increasing levies on your nobles, who are refusing to pay."

I did already know. I remembered what Lady Marta had said the first time she'd explained the crown's finances to me: *It's like you wish your people to eat dreams and be paid in illusions.*

"Yes," I growled. "And though Severine is—*was*—richer than sunlight, because Sylvain never legitimized me as his heir, I have no legal claim to the Sabourin fortune. The town house in Jardinier, the château at Beauvilliers, and Severine's personal accounts are all entailed away from me. I didn't inherit anything. Both the empire and myself are broke. Was there a point?"

"Because of Severine's fondness for *pruning* the family tree, I had a hard time tracking down who did inherit." Lady Marta held up what looked like a letter. "Turns out, he's been living in Aifir."

The floor dissolved beneath my feet like smoke, and I fought to keep my balance.

"Who?"

"His name is Gavin d'Ars," Marta said. "He's your distant cousin."

Jealousy pulsed bloody through my veins, trailed by a curiously blank surge of relief. He was of Sabourin blood. I wasn't the only one left. "Does that make him a Sun Heir?"

Marta hesitated. "Potentially."

"Summon him here." I kept my voice neutral. "I want to know his intentions regarding the fortune that is rightfully mine. And I want to know his intentions regarding the Amber Throne."

"Dauphine," Marta said. "That's what I was trying to tell you."

She passed me the letter across the table. I scanned it with all the concentration I could muster. *Familial trust . . . imagine my surprise to discover . . . all haste.* I looked up.

"Are you telling me he's already on his way?"

"He apparently left Aifir immediately after hearing of Severine's accident."

Accident? Was that what we'd decided to call it? I bit back a desperate laugh.

"When am I to expect my cousin?"

"Any day now, dauphine," Marta said, with a look I couldn't decipher. "Any day."

I extricated myself from my councillors the moment the Congrès drew to a close, only to see Lullaby's dark blue skirts flicking away between the gilded doors. Twin fangs of guilt and irritation gnawed at my chest. I knew she'd been through something awful, locked away in the dungeons. And I'd tried to give her space—to process, to recover her equilibrium, to *heal*. But *space* was beginning to look like *evasion*. I wanted to know why she was avoiding me so diligently.

I missed my friend.

I hiked my heavy dress around my knees and sprinted after Lullaby. She set a fast pace, turning into the wing of the palais that had been all but destroyed during the coup. Luca's Paper City rebels—known as La Discorde—had set off an explosive artifice to coincide with my incendiary performance at the grotto. It was meant to be a diversion, to draw the Skyclad away from the empress so I'd have a chance to defeat her on equal footing. It wasn't supposed to destroy half the palais.

A lot of things hadn't happened the way they were supposed to.

My slippers skittered on broken marble. Crystalline chandeliers listed half-shattered from the ceiling. Gaping windows bared broken teeth to a bloody sky.

"Lullaby?" I ducked through an archway into a forest of pillars wrapped in blackened vines. Muddy streams oozed. Sorrow plucked tight at my throat—I remembered this room. It had once been full of rustling leaves and the cool-quiet rush of clear water. Now, its magic had burned away to ash and grime.

Lullaby waited for me at its center, a shutter of cold hauteur masking her expression. "Yes, dauphine?"

I frowned. Lullaby taught me everything I knew about politesse—I could sense disrespect lurking behind her courtesy.

"I attended your little Congrès, as commanded," she said through her teeth. "What more do you want from me?"

"I didn't *command*, I requested. I wanted to see you. You've been avoiding me."

"You haven't made it difficult."

Confusion and hurt made me direct. "Why are you so angry with me?"

"I'm not angry."

"You're *something*," I snarled. "Ever since I got back from Belsyre and freed you from the Skyclad dungeon you've been treating me like a pariah, avoiding me and talking down to me. Either tell me what's bothering you, or stop acting like I ate your last piece of chocolate and poured kachua all over your favorite dress."

Lullaby went very still, and I knew I'd pushed her too far.

"On my thirteenth name day," she began, so softly I could

barely hear her, "my mother—Colette Courbis—decided to throw me a party. We were still living in Lanaix, the capital of the Sousine, although Colette and my father were already estranged. I loved that house—it had huge glass doors that opened onto a broad lawn sweeping down to the sea. We had a little private cove with hundreds of caves cutting through the red rock, and I used to spend hours splashing through them, finding the faces of my Gorma ancestors carved into the walls."

I knew Lullaby was half Gorma—a race of water-dwelling people indigenous to the Sousine Isles. Among many things, she'd inherited from her father the blue tinge to her skin, the magic in her song, and her soul-deep love of water.

I didn't know why she was telling me this.

"Colette said the party was to celebrate my becoming a woman, but I knew it was because I was finally old enough to field betrothals. She wanted to invite all the great colonial families living in Lanaix—nobles and wealthy merchants and Lirian expatriates—and all the children from my private school. I insisted she invite my extended family on my father's side as well; all my friends from the sea. Grudgingly, she agreed."

Lullaby set her mouth. "I remember going down to the beach on the day of the party. I wore a new gown, and my handmaidens fixed my hair in an elaborate updo and helped me put on cosmetics for the first time. I felt beautiful and grown-up, and even though Colette was using me as always, I felt valued. *Valuable.* I waited for hours for the first guests to show up. But no one ever came. Not my classmates, not their parents, not my friends from the sea. And when the châtelaine came to tell me that my mother had left for Lirias and wouldn't be back for spans, I realized that it wasn't because of *me* that no one came—it wasn't because I was half human and half Gorma, caught between worlds and unwelcome in either of them. It was because Colette had forgotten to invite anyone. She had forgotten about the party. She had forgotten it was even my name day. And I realized that the only thing worse than being hated was being *forgotten*."

She lifted her blue-brindle eyes to mine. I battled sick anticipation.

"Being your friend feels like that name day."

Horror spun threads of hot and cold through my veins. The scars along my arms stung like someone had rubbed salt in them.

"Is this about what happened in the dungeon?" I remembered her bruised arms, her haunted eyes. Remorse crawled up my spine and sank cold teeth into my heart. I should have tried harder to make sure she was all right.

"If you don't already know," Lullaby whispered, "then I suppose it can't be very important, can it?"

She marched away with a dancer's grace and a warrior's resolve. My heart throbbed, but though I wanted to follow her, I didn't. I would find a way to make this right—whatever I had broken, I would find a way to fix.

But no one ever mended a friendship by arguing in a hallway.

FIVE

I paced the Hall of Portraits after the following Matin's Congrès, mulling over my failures and giving my doubts more weight than they probably deserved. I'd argued with Lady Marta again—I'd finally dared to broach the matter of liberating the Sousine, a wealthy Imperial colony and Lullaby's homeland. Marta's words razored through me, harsh:

You want to reform the tax code, dismantle the military, build public schools, and emancipate a colony? I admire your idealism, dauphine, but you have to be realistic. This empire requires capital, especially now the ambric miners are striking in the Dusklands. Freeing the Sousine will ruin us.

I stared at a portrait of a handsome, laughing nobleman and fought despair. Was what I dreamed truly impossible? Or was I just not fighting hard enough to make it real?

Boots on marble rang out behind me, and I forced myself to keep walking—I didn't need anyone to witness me wallowing in a puddle of self-pity.

The footsteps caught up to me in the Rotonde at the center of the palais's façade, where a domed ceiling sent spears of blistering red to score the parquet floor. Vast windows stared out over Coeur d'Or's imposing gate to the Concordat boulevard, then beyond to the tapestry of the city, woven with a thousand bright colors.

"Mirage."

I recognized that drawling tenor. I turned to face Sunder's searing eyes.

"You have vexed me, lord." I gave my chin a haughty twist. "You left this Matin without a word. Again."

"You were snoring. Loudly."

Outrage sparked in my chest a moment before I saw the smile hiding in the corner of his mouth. He laughed at my expression, surging up to catch me around the waist and spin me toward the window. I yelped when he hoisted me onto the broad sill, but I relished the warmth of the sun on my back and the warmth of his regard on my face. He looked good today—his eyes were bright and his color was high.

Maybe too high. Hectic spots of red stained his cheekbones, and his pupils were dilated dark as Midnight.

"Sunder—"

"I like you like this." His gloved hands tangled in my loose curls.

"Like what?" I narrowed my eyes. "Perched inappropriately on a rather public windowsill where anyone might happen by?"

"Well, yes. But that's not what I meant." His laugh burned heat against my throat. "Today in the Congrès—you were passionate, powerful, *fearless*. Marta Iole terrifies me. And yet you oppose her as an equal, a peer. No—you are her empress, and she knows it better than you do."

I swallowed down a flush of pleasure. "I'll take that as a compliment."

"You should." His smile went slow and wide. His hands tightened on my waist. "But you don't need me to tell you this is where you belong."

Belong. The word was a syncopation against the rhythm of my heartbeat. I'd hungered to belong somewhere for as long as I could remember—the very idea of finding my place in this world had become armor against uncertainty, perfume to mask the stench of loneliness. But after all this time yearning to hear those words—*this is where you belong*—I was starting to wonder whether I had earned them. Or if they were even true.

"What's wrong?" Sunder drew back.

"Marta Iole is just one person." Bitterness burst in my throat. "Those Ambers, in the marché. They looked at me like I was an imposter. And those Red Masks—they doubt my legitimacy so deeply they'd risk their lives to kill me. How do I prove to *them*— my people—I'm their rightful empress?"

"Give them time." His thumb brushed my jaw. "Let them see you shine, and they will know you are their Sun Heir."

"How?" I bit my lip. "How do I prove to them I'm more than a fantasy in fine silks and tiaras? I was raised in dusky rags—now I wear Severine's sunlit gowns. I was never loved—how am I supposed to earn the love of an entire city, an entire empire?"

"You do yourself too little credit, demoiselle."

His gaze burned like sunlight through leaf-bare trees. He tilted my chin, his thumb brushing against my lower lip. I leaned into his touch, ignoring the frisson of energy gliding along my jaw. His other arm slipped around my waist and slid my hips against his, molding us together. His lips parted, hovering over mine, and I savored his hope and drank his desire. I hesitated in the bitter-sweet wasteland between fear and want. I squeezed my eyes shut.

Sunder caught sight of something over my shoulder, and abruptly let me go. Cold air drafted between us, slowing my pulse and shriveling my heart. I spun, looking through arching windows toward the palais gates, where a parade marched up the Concordat—

It wasn't a parade. It was . . . a royal procession?

I unclenched my fingernails from my palm, crossed to the glass doors, and stepped out onto the wrought-iron balcony beyond. The music of marching wafted up—shod hooves ringing out on cobblestones, the champagne timpani of laughter and trumpets and song. The cortège was nearly the length of the Concordat: a river of riders in uniform—bright red and pale kembric, metal helms and dancing horses. Children ran beside the retinue, and my breath caught in my throat when I saw the soldats tossing coins to the onlookers. The procession was heading straight for Coeur d'Or's gilded gates, flowing up the shallow steps like a sunlit river.

They finally came close enough for me to make out faces, and that's when I saw *him*.

He rode tall and straight at the head of the procession on a prancing chestnut stallion. Even from here I could tell he was handsome—a bright smile laughed in a golden-tan face. Unlike the rest of the riders—who wore pale surcoats splashed in red— he was clad in kembric armor forged so that the sun hammered sparks off it. His dark mahogany hair seemed to glow, as though woven through with threads of ambric.

He shone so bright it was hard to look at him straight on. He looked like—

He looked like the Sun Heir.

"He's already here," I breathed.

A wave of sickly heat wafted off Sunder, slapping the back of my neck with the stench of bloody snow and icy metal.

"Here to steal your throne," Sunder growled.

"Wait." I spun from the cortège and faced Sunder. "You *know* Gavin d'Ars?"

"Unfortunately. He was at court a few tides ago." His eyes sharpened on my face. "Shall I kill him for you, dauphine?"

The venom in Sunder's tone took me aback.

"You hate him," I realized. "Why?"

His eyes fell away somewhere I couldn't follow. Disgust twisted his plush mouth.

"I can't say," he said finally.

"I've never known you to hold a grudge without good reason, my lord Sunder," I said, sharp. "If there is something I ought to know about my cousin, I command you to tell me."

"It's not my story to tell."

"Then whose is it?"

Sunder hesitated, then smiled like ice crystallizing on the edge of a sword. "My sister's. You will have to ask Oleander if you wish to know more."

My stomach gave a nervous lurch. I turned back to watch my cousin, marching up the Concordat with sunlight sparking off his kembric armor.

Scion, I didn't know this man at all, but he looked so much like a *real* Sun Heir it made my chest ache. Already I could see how they loved him—running beside him, reaching for his stirrup, clasping at his hands. Their cheers rang in my ears.

Another sick surge of relief churned against resentment in my stomach.

"He assumes too much," I said. "If I receive him today, I acquiesce power to his presence."

Sunder's approval was silent.

"Take a platoon of Loup-Garou," I commanded. "Meet him before he reaches the gates and turn him away. I will receive him tomorrow, but with no more than a score of his men at his back. Make sure he knows I will not bow to this kind of display. No matter who he thinks he is."

Sunder cut an angular bow.

"Yes," he said, "my dauphine."

He turned on his heel and strode out of the room, leaving me wondering what in the daylight world I was supposed to do next.

SIX

There was a flurry of activity after Gavin's arrival—messengers pelting around the palais, the handful of remaining courtiers gossiping behind fans, Loup-Garou marching back from the lower city in twos and fours. Dowser, Barthet, and Lady Marta swept me away into a hurried conference, the result of which seemed to be *keep calm; don't panic.* But it was too late—I was already quietly panicking. I paced the palais, wishing I could talk to Lullaby, who currently hated me, or Thibo, who was Scion-knew-where, if not dead.

Instead, I reluctantly sought out Oleander de Vere. Although she and I had spent nearly a span fleeing the city, mustering the Loup-Garou, and planning our offensive against the Skyclad, I had never fully warmed to Sunder's frosty twin sister. And she had certainly never warmed to me.

I found her heading into Belsyre Wing, trailed by servants with their arms full of bolts of cloth—rich satin and shining silks.

"Bane!" Nerves made my voice shrill.

"Bane is the name of a tool and a victim," she said with a pained expression. "I much prefer Oleander."

"Scion, I knew that," I apologized, following her into the sprawling residence. "I'll do better, I promise."

"See that you do." She paused by the door to her room, looking like she wanted to slam it in my face. "Is there something I can help you with?"

"Actually, yes." I straightened my shoulders. "I need to talk to you about Gavin d'Ars."

Her face convulsed with shock before smoothing to brittle porcelain. "Then I guess you'd better come in."

I stepped over the threshold. The door slammed shut, leaving me alone with my second-least-favorite person in the world. I'd never been inside her room—it was as disorderly as her appearance was pristine. Fabrics of all colors and wefts draped over dressing screens; it looked like a couturier's shop had exploded.

"What about Gavin?" She crossed her arms over her chest. As usual, Oleander wore gloves to the elbow to safeguard her volatile legacy of poison. Today's red satin made me think, uncomfortably, of bloodstained hands.

"He's just arrived in the city."

Oleander went so cold and quiet I thought she might break. I wished I hadn't come.

"You knew him."

"Yes."

"Sunder made it sound as though something happened between you two, but refused to elaborate," I said carefully. "I wouldn't normally pry, but I'm trying to make out my cousin's character before I meet him."

"I don't mind," she said, in a way that made me think she minded very much. "I'll tell anyone who cares to listen—Gavin d'Ars is a devious, manipulative, power-hungry thief. Every word out of his mouth is either an empty promise or a lie. I loathe him with my whole heart, which he was determined to break, and if I ever set eyes on him again I might be tempted to kill him."

Her vehemence struck me speechless.

"Does that assuage your curiosity?" Her emerald eyes flashed. "Or must I delve deeper into the lurid details of our unfortunate acquaintance?"

"No, I—" Frankly, I was sorry I'd asked. "Thank you, that was plenty."

Her lacquered mouth worked. "So you're going to meet him?"

"I think I must."

"Are you going to wear that?" She eyed my pale-shimmer gown.

I ran my hand over the glittering outfit. It was part of the wardrobe my Congrès had ordered for me to play the part of Sun Heir for the people—gowns embroidered with kembric thread, bodices studded with crushed ambric, brilliant cloaks that caught the low light and magnified it tenfold. I never much liked these gowns—they felt like costumes stolen from an actress who played a part much better than me. They reminded me of Severine.

Gavin's face seared my memory—sunlit and laughing, his armor molten as he tossed coins to cheering children. Bitterness dug spikes into my throat. Scion knew the crowds had reacted a *bit* differently on my one sojourn out. How was I supposed to compete with that kind of glamour . . . that kind of *glow*?

Unless I didn't try to compete at all. I thought of my unwanted new nickname—*Duskland Dauphine.*

Not all spectacle was sunlit.

"You're the designer." I narrowed my eyes at the spread of cloth and sewing accoutrements clogging her rooms. "Did you have something else in mind?"

Oleander gave me a complicated look as she began to rifle through the swathes of fabric and half-finished dresses that covered her apartment. "Fashion is much like court, Mirage. You would do well to make a study of it. A gown can tell a story or keep a secret, flout rules or flaunt treachery."

"That's actually an excellent segue," I said, suddenly remembering Barthet's report on the Vidâme de Cascara and his little rebellion. Oleander's dynasty was Sinister—surely she was friendly with the legacies I'd put under house arrest. "Several noble families are refusing to pay taxes because they feel their children are being kept at court against their will."

Oleander's eyes glittered. She pinned ribbons onto a half-finished mess of satin. "No one likes being kept prisoner in retaliation for choosing the wrong side in a coup d'etat."

"They're not so much prisoners as insurance."

"Against?"

"Rebellion? The mobilization of personal armies against me?"

"If Sinister parents think you're going to execute their heirs out of spite, that may happen anyway."

"I'm not going to execute them!" I flushed, feeling defensive. "I never intended on keeping them as hostages forever. I'm frankly not sure what to do with them. Should I just let them go home?"

"And give their families the chance to secede while the empire is in flux, and never pay taxes again?" Oleander picked up a gown with its sleeves torn off. "You're right to keep them at court. Truthfully, it's where they're happiest. But you have to understand—they're bored."

"Bored?"

"*Bored*." She arched an eyebrow. "They've been confined to their chambers for weeks now. Some of them can afford apartments with multiple rooms, like Sunder and me, but most of them live in rooms this size, in Gaillarde and Jacinthe wings."

A discomfiting shame crept along my spine. I'd never bothered to wonder what it might be like to be trapped in my room for weeks on end, unable to talk to friends or family, with Belsyre wolves posted at my door.

"Do you remember what this place used to be like?" Oleander went on. "Picnics at Prime, salons during Compline, balls and masques with feasting and dancing well into Nocturne. They don't care about politics—they want their lives back."

"But that was one of the ways Severine controlled her nobles," I hedged. "She kept them distracted with parties and fashions and intrigues so they didn't have time to worry about their estates hemorrhaging money or their fellow legacies disappearing without a trace."

"I know that. It doesn't change the fact that parties are fun."

"So you think I should let them have a party?"

"If that's what you think is best." She licked the end of a thread and pushed it through the eye of a needle.

"Perfect," I said. "Tell them to have a party whenever they want."

"Do I have to explain it to you?" Oleander rolled her perfectly lined eyes. "*You* throw a party for *them*, and then *you* go to it."

"*Why?*"

"Four spans at court and she still behaves like an illiterate Dusklander gamine."

"Won't they have more fun if I'm not there?"

"Inevitably."

I tried to think around the headache beginning to pound at my temples. "You think I should woo them."

"By the Scion, I think she's got it," she drawled. "Their world turned upside down the day you staged your coup. Their empress—who, as you pointed out, controlled everything from their fashion choices to their finances—is dead. The only thing they know about you—the presumed Sun Heir—is that they tormented you relentlessly when you were nobody. Half their friends died in the fighting and the other half are isolated in their own chambers. They're scared and lonely and, yes, *bored.*"

She was right. Maybe I did have an opportunity to woo them to my side—to give them a gesture of good faith, to prove to them and their families this transition of power didn't mean an end to the life they knew. If I gave them a modicum of normalcy, maybe they'd give me a chance.

"Fine," I said. "But my empire is in crisis, people are trying to kill me, and another legitimate heir to the throne just showed up on my doorstep. I'm not exactly flush with time to plan a party. Will you help me?"

"Only because any party you'd plan would just make everyone more miserable than they already were." Oleander shoved a heap of fabric into my arms. "Now try this on."

I shook it out. Billowing silk was dyed in sky-lit colors— ruffled amethyst at the bodice edging toward velveteen blue at the hem. A narrow waist flowed into a skirt like shadow. Cascades of pearls rippled along the trim, lustrous white against a dusky sky.

"Oleander," I breathed. "This is—"

"I know." She gestured toward the dressing screen, impatient.

Obediently, I slipped behind the screen and shucked off my sunny gown, tossing it over the top. The twilight gown sighed against my skin, as soft as it was lovely. It was a touch snug around my waist and shoulders, and pooled heavy around my feet, but I could almost imagine it had been made for me.

"What—?" Oleander's surprised voice jolted me, and I jerked my head around the dressing screen. She was holding a slim volume, bound in suede and stamped in gilt. "A book? I didn't know you could read."

Severine's journal. I knew I shouldn't carry that thing around.

"Why were you going through the pockets of my dress?"

"People keep such interesting things in their pockets." She flipped open the front cover. I bit the inside of my cheek so hard I tasted blood.

"Don't," I pleaded. "Give me that!"

Oleander ignored me, scanning the first few pages.

"This is a diary!" Glee made gems of her eyes. But after a moment her smile fell away, replaced by a line between her perfect brows. "But this isn't your chicken scratch. Who does this belong to?"

I considered lying, then decided against it. I'd intuited it as Severine's after only a few moments. Oleander was many things—few of which I liked—but she wasn't stupid. And there was no real harm in telling her the truth.

"It's Severine's, I think."

Oleander looked faintly impressed. "You stole the personal diary of your half sister and empress just spans after you tried to kill her and take her throne? And here I've been wondering what my brother possibly sees in you."

"I didn't *steal* it." I definitely stole it.

"Have you read it?"

"No."

"Scion's teeth, why not?" Oleander threw herself across the foot of her bed. She sucked her lower lip into her mouth and flipped through the diary. "The sinful and sordid saga of Severine Sabourin? Sounds better than any novel I've ever read."

"Please don't—" I made a grab for it, but Oleander easily dodged me, her eyes still on the pages. "You really shouldn't."

"Wait a minute." She sat bolt upright at the end of the bed, her thumb wedged between the pages of Severine's diary. Her forest-dark gaze fixed on me and her lacquered lips forgot their customary languid smirk. "You really didn't read this?"

I shook my head. "A few lines. That's it."

"Last span, during the coup—you were hoping to find a second Relic, weren't you?"

I lifted both my eyebrows. Only Dowser, Sunder, and I were supposed to know about the Relics.

"Please." She smirked, reading my thoughts. "We tell each other everything. It's a twin thing."

"Yes, all right," I snapped. "We're still looking."

"Well, I think I just found a Relic," Oleander breathed. "It's right here in the diary."

SEVEN

"I knew there was a second Relic!" Dowser cried, his dark eyes shining with triumph.

My heart sang to see Dowser so thrilled. He'd suspected Severine had a second Relic in her possession for tides, but like everything else in her court, the empress kept her secrets in a stranglehold. Not even Dowser—one of her oldest friends and most trusted advisors—had been able to wheedle its location from her. At Carrousel—while I faced Severine—Luca had set a diversion to distract the Skyclad, Sunder had rallied my dissident legacies, and Dowser had broken into her private sanctum in hopes of finding the Relic. But he'd failed, and I knew he blamed himself to some degree for the death and violence that followed.

But neither he nor mystical Relics with unknown powers could have prevented what happened. Once I revealed myself as a Sabourin heir—legitimate or not—and tried to kill Severine, there was no going back.

"What does the passage say, exactly?" Sunder asked.

He'd bathed and changed after sending Gavin away from the gates, but the confrontation had clearly worn on him. His hair, dark with moisture, was pushed away from his face, accentuating the harsh lines of his pain-taut features. I tried to catch his gaze, but his eyes were glazed, pupils so huge and dark I could hardly remember what color his eyes were.

I shook away a creeping shiver and tried to focus on what Oleander was saying.

"*S has given me his Relic, for he knows how I covet it,*" she read out loud. "*It was not even my name day—he simply came into my chambers and handed it to me with one of his strange little smiles. In* that moment I almost wanted to tell him what I've discovered about the Relics, but I did not. *Not because he would change his mind about his gift—but because I did not want to burden him with the truth."*

"She still only mentions one Relic," Sunder pointed out.

"There's more," Oleander snapped. *"But this changes nothing. Just because S gave me his does not mean I want F's any less. I will have them both and then I will find them all."*

Silence hung like a tattered shroud of treachery and deceit. It was Dowser who finally broke it.

"More than two." He plucked his spectacles from his face and ran a hand over his smooth head. "Barthet was right, that stubborn old fool."

"Is anybody else curious," I said slowly, "about who S and F might be?"

"F must be her father," said Dowser. "Sylvain, the dead emperor. For his Relic hung around his neck until the day I hung it around yours and sent you and Madeleine into the dusk."

My throat contracted, as it always did at the mention of my mother. She did nothing wrong but fall pregnant with the wrong man's child. Me. She died to save *me*—another death upon my head.

I swallowed, hard. "And what about S?"

"It's Seneca," said Oleander. "She talks about him with a depth of tenderness usually reserved for siblings."

Sunder snorted. Oleander glared at him.

"I think—" She hesitated. "If you take Severine at her word, Sylvain abused them. With whatever his legacy was."

"What was his legacy?" I asked.

"If I had to make a guess . . ." Dowser polished his spectacles and looked troubled. "I believe he could tease out your greatest desires. And perhaps use that information against you."

"Whatever it was, he'd pick on Seneca specifically, to rile

Severine," Oleander added. "I think her brother was the only thing she really cared about."

Sunder didn't laugh at that. Neither did I—Oleander's interpretation of the family I'd never known had conjured something hot and unyielding in my chest, a bonfire elegy for a life imagined. I'd met my sister—she was corrupt and vengeful and murderous to her core. And everyone I'd met—even Dowser, who once flirted with the Sabourin inner circle—painted a picture of a father wise as he was wild, as loving as he was lusty. Not perfect, by any stretch of the imagination, but *good*.

Good men did not torment their children.

"Maybe she's lying?"

"It's her personal diary," Sunder said, not ungently. "Why would she lie?"

I clenched my eyes against a sudden wave of vertigo, my heart tilting on its axis. My past was like a mirror that had been broken into a thousand pieces, and each time I tried to fit its pieces back together I found them dark and tarnished—a reflection of things better left forgotten.

But I was the one who had to remember. I was the one who had to do better. Because I was the only one left.

Except Gavin.

I looked up to find Dowser pacing.

"Two Relics, at the least," he rumbled. "One for the emperor. One for the Sun Heir. I know the Relics are supposedly tied to Meridian's mythic line, but why? What do they do? Are they baubles, worn by heirs to assert their royalty? Or do they serve some greater purpose?"

I put my hand to my chest, thumbing the timeworn curves of my Relic. Made of pure ambric and shaped into a sunburst, it was pretty in an ungainly way. I'd long wondered whether it possessed some magic properties. Sometimes it glowed warm against my chest, but that was not unheard of—even low-quality ambric contained a spark of alchemical energy capable of powering ambric artifices, from lamps to engines to medical apparatuses.

"We have to find these Relics. They could be the key to everything."

"I must speak to Barthet." Dowser thrust his hands deep into his sleeves and made for the door. "Those esoteric manuscripts he found may hold valuable information, if only we can tease out the threads of truth from the tapestry of legend."

Oleander shot Sunder an unreadable look, slapped the diary into my hands, and left on Dowser's heels. Sunder moved to follow her, but I caught his sleeve.

"Are you all right?" I murmured.

His eyes snapped with frost and pain. "Perfect."

I frowned. "Is this about my cousin?"

"Unsurprisingly, D'Ars is still a prig, but no." He raked a hand through his hair and sighed. "We caught a Red Mask disguised as a palais servant, sneaking through the service corridors. She carried another painted blade. We can only assume her target was you."

Fear spangled white-hot against the back of my eyelids.

"She—?"

"She's dead. She was wounded in the struggle, and then—"

He flexed his fingers and put his hand to his side, gritting his teeth. "I'll redouble the palais perimeter patrols, but we have to assume they're going to keep coming for you. Don't go anywhere without Calvet and Karine—they'll protect you even if I can't."

My fingernails bit into the leather cover of Severine's diary and a spear of sorrow slashed my heart. "Sunder—"

"Don't worry, demoiselle. I won't let them hurt you."

"It's not me who's hurting right now," I breathed.

"I just hoped, once we took the throne—" His eyes went wide and distant, gazing toward something I couldn't see. Then he squeezed them shut and shook his head. "It doesn't matter. I just need to rest."

He bowed, breathed a kiss across my cheek, and walked out.

That Nocturne I struggled to sleep. I stared at my comatose sister's diary, wild with a thousand doubts and questions. Finally, I flipped the book open.

. . . I would take his burden away forever, if I could. But I cannot. So I will bear it for him.

I snapped the diary shut. A creeping certainty wreathed my chest—I'd witnessed a secret never meant for me.

When at last I found sleep, I dreamed I looked into a shattered mirror and saw Severine's face staring back. My hands were covered in my own blood, and that's when I knew I was the one who lay dying.

EIGHT

The Atrium—with its faceted skylights, raised dais, and fluted pillars—had been nearly destroyed during the coup, marooning the Amber Throne amid ruin. The din of hammers and chisels spun hot between my ears as I strode past the hulking throne. Images slid sharp fangs along my memories—Severine presiding over her court while a girl with soaring dreams and uncompromising fierceness demanded a place to belong. She had been so sure of what she deserved, never stopping to see the flaws in her perfect world. Never stopping to see the flaws in herself.

Show me what you dream, when you dream of new worlds.

I squared my shoulders and hurried on.

The antechamber I'd converted into a temporary throne room was lined in narrow windows paned with translucent ambric geometry. Pale statuettes stood in the corners—two male and two female, half draped but mostly nude. Ruby designs fell from the windows, illuminating glittering shapes upon their pale bodies and faces—a sharp-edged heart above a muscular chest, a brittle sword across outstretched hands, a pointed crown resting upon an uplifted head.

I'd only found this room because the blast that destroyed the Atrium shattered its locked doors. Dowser wasn't fond of me receiving supplicants and petitioners here, but I'd insisted on it. Part of me whispered that this room had belonged to my father, and it was Severine who locked it away. But mostly I liked these inexplicable statues with their voiceless gifts stamped on them in amber and dusk. They made me feel less alone.

I took my seat in the simple, straight-backed chair I'd had

placed at the end of the room, spreading my dusky skirts around me. My retinue filed in after me—Dowser, hovering over my left shoulder and whispering facts about Gavin I was too nervous to heed; Lady Marta and Barthet conversing in heated tones by the door; Sunder off to the side, too far to touch yet close enough to miss.

And finally, Gavin d'Ars walked through the doors, flanked by a dozen armed men in surcoats of kembric and red and an older gentleman with a face like the sharp end of a sword.

Gavin looked older than me by a few tides—twenty-one, if I had to make a guess—and tall. His air of boyish mirth belied a forceful, muscular stride that spoke of a lifetime of combat training. His eyes swept the room—I caught him looking askance at my motionless marble companions—but then he caught my gaze and held it, smiling as he walked closer. I maintained eye contact, sweat itching at the collar of my dress.

"Your Grace," said Dowser, stepping forward and gesturing to me. "May I present—"

"Cousin!" Gavin brushed past Dowser and bowed over my hand. His palm was warm. I jumped when his lips grazed my fingers. "You honor me with this audience. I didn't expect you to receive me so soon."

"I saw you arrive, *cousin*," I returned, more tightly than I'd intended. "I only hope you'll forgive me for waiting a whole day."

"I am no stranger to waiting." He grinned, and scanned the room—my silent advisors, a handful of courtiers whispering behind fans, a few black-clad wolves guarding the door and windows. He gave me a blithe look, not seeming to notice my twilight gown or my flat, unwelcoming gaze. "This is awfully formal, isn't it? I wasn't expecting such a regal welcome."

"You made a regal arrival," I said, as serenely as I could manage. "I aimed only to reply in kind."

Gavin laughed with sudden and breathless astonishment, and I felt the entire room laugh with him. I choked on traitorous mirth—I was *determined* to dislike him—and forced my face into neutral lines. But there was something infectious about the way he talked, the way he smiled, the way he breathed—as though sunlight poured off him and made us all the warmer by basking in its presence.

"Touché, lady," he chuckled, lifting his wrist in the attitude of *points awarded*. I noticed he did not call me *dauphine*. "I only meant that though I came to offer my help in these difficult times, you seem to have things well in hand here at the palais."

I sliced my eyes toward Sunder, standing blank and severe between two marble figures frozen forever in contrapposto. The Suicide Twins' collective condemnation echoed in my ears:

Gavin d'Ars is a devious, manipulative, power-hungry thief.

Here to steal your throne.

It seemed hard to believe that this handsome, cheerful gentleman would be inclined to steal anything, not least the Amber Throne. But Coeur d'Or had taught me that courtiers' outward faces rarely matched their inner selves.

That, and *anyone* could be a thief.

"You needn't justify your words to me." I kept my voice light. "Although I do wonder what you mean by *help*?"

Gavin glanced around the room again, discomfort and a creeping air of helplessness in his demeanor.

"Forgive me, cousin. It's been tides since I've been at court, and all these staring faces are making me nervous. Is there somewhere more private where we might get to know each other?"

My sparse court stirred. Beside me, Dowser rose from his chair. Lady Marta clicked her tongue against her teeth. Sunder shifted his weight, amber patterns of light fracturing his face and putting murder in his eyes.

It was an impertinence, if not an affront, and I had no idea how to react to it.

Again I remembered a flower-draped Atrium; stained-glass windows splashing necklaces of gems across a gleaming dais. An ambric throne; a stunning empress; a bouquet of finely scented lords and ladies. And me, in a dirty frock and worn boots, prepared to take what I thought I deserved.

"You read my mind, cousin." I stood. "I never liked these audiences myself. I could use some fresh air. Will you accompany me on a walk?"

Gavin offered his arm. I took it lightly, and fell in step beside him. Standing this close to him, he smelled like a forge—hot metal and the bitter-ash taste of last Nocturne's campfire. As we passed through the doors, Sunder peeled away from the wall and trailed us.

"That's not necessary, commandant," I said. "I'm sure you have more important matters to attend to. Perhaps just—?"

I nodded to my dedicated wolves, severe in their Belsyre black.

Sunder's shoulders looked like they might tear the seams of his jacket. But he motioned for Calvet and Karine to follow us at a distance. A pair of Gavin's soldats joined them, as well as the middle-aged man with the hatchet face.

I turned back to find Gavin looking at me, his emotions a visible vocabulary written on his face. "What is it?"

"Sunder de Vere as your commandant?" Gavin let out a low whistle. "I'd pay good kembric livres to know how that came about."

"You really don't stand on ceremony, do you?" Curiosity burned through me at yet another mention of the mysterious animosity between Gavin and the Suicide Twins, but I bit my tongue. We passed along the corridor through a rose-draped terrace, then beyond to the pillar-lined Esplanade looking out over the gardens.

"From what I heard," he said carefully, "neither did you."

"No, I suppose I didn't." I wasn't oblivious to his use of the past tense. "How quickly things change. And how quickly we fall into the habits of our forebears. Good and bad."

"Did Severine *have* any good habits?"

I stopped, dropping my hand from his arm and turning to look at him straight on. He was smiling broadly, which made me think the quip might have been meant as a joke. But then again, so far I hadn't seen this handsome boy *not* smiling. I met his eyes—a startling shade of blue shot through with veins of kembric—and tried to read the unfamiliar lines of his face.

"I'm afraid you have me at a disadvantage." I let an edge of dristic creep into my tone. "You seem to know much more about me than I you."

"Scion, I'm sorry." He held up an apologetic hand. "I'm terrible at this kind of thing. It's one of the numerous reasons I left court after barely a tide. I couldn't keep up with the gossip or the intrigue, and I was always telling other peoples' secrets by accident or saying exactly the wrong thing. Whatever cachet the Sabourin name lent me ran out extremely quickly. Can we begin again?"

I surprised myself by laughing. I couldn't fault him for his bewilderment at court. "Why not?"

"I'm Gavin." He stuck out a hand and flashed an impish grin. I shook it gingerly, trying to remember the last time someone shook my hand instead of kissing it. "Gavin d'Ars, Duc de Douane. Although everyone just calls me Gav."

I found it hard to believe that any person angling for the throne of an empire would refer to himself as *Gav*.

"That's my first question," I said.

"Well, Gav is short for Gavin."

I shot him a chilly look. He favored me with an exaggerated wink.

"Hah," I managed. "I meant your surname—it's d'Ars, but a minute ago you mentioned the Sabourin name lending you a certain cachet. How are we two related?"

"They haven't told you yet?" He tugged at his sun-shadow hair and looked sheepish. "I confess I don't know much about our genealogy."

"And I know nothing."

He sighed. "The matriarch of my family line, Lise Sabourin, was the half sister of one of Severine's—and your, I suppose— grandfathers or great-grandfathers. It was around the time of the Conquest, if that helps." He screwed up his face. "Great- grandfather, probably. She was older than he was, but he became emperor because of some inheritance scandal."

And hence, Gavin's distant but legitimate claim to the Amber Throne. A whisper of fear tripped along my spine.

"Lise had two sons and a daughter," he continued. "The sons feuded over some ancient dishonor, and the family split in half. One half stayed close to home—most of them are Beaumanoirs and Legardes, these days—and my half, the d'Ars, expatriated to Aifir, where I grew up."

"So that makes us . . . ?"

"Related somehow," he chuckled, "like most aristocrats of the Amber Empire."

I must have looked shocked, because Gavin's smile grew wider.

"You didn't think the notion of us all being descended from Meridian was mere legend, did you? Scion, a few centuries ago it was considered a point of pride if your family was inbred. Some highborn families still take such *purity* fairly seriously."

"Really?" My ghoulish interest was piqued.

"Indeed." A thought or memory ghosted across his face, and his eyebrows tightened. It was the first expression I'd seen him make that wasn't humorous, and it looked almost obscene on his face. "Just ask your friend Sunder."

I tasted the bait, felt its sharp edges in my mouth, and decided not to bite.

"You were at court," I said. "What is your legacy?"

"One of the unlucky Sabourins without one." He shrugged, and grinned. "Or lucky, depending on your point of view."

I narrowed my eyes and tried to decide whether I believed him.

"Tell me about your militia. You came to the city with, what, two hundred soldats?"

"Closer to five," he admitted. "Honestly, I thought you might need help keeping the Amber City under control. But Belsyre's wolves seem to have that well in hand."

Was that judgment? "Are they your household garde? I don't recognize their colors."

"They are Husterri," Gavin said. "It translates to something like *Red Riders*. They're primarily Aifiri, although they recruit from across the daylight world. They were loyal to my mother before she died. I suppose loyalty is something one can inherit."

"As are fortune, property, and position." The words spilled out of me before I had the chance to corral them. An awkward silence stretched between us. "And your man-at-arms. Is he Husterri also?"

Gavin laughed. "He's my godfather. He was like a brother to Papa. He's my advisor, friend, and confidant."

"You seem flush with support." I tried to sound neutral. "One last question, and then I promise to stop interrogating you—why did you travel all the way from Aifir with neither invitation nor summons?"

Gavin looked confused, then flushed dark. "You think I'm trying to position myself as Sun Heir?"

"Am I wrong?"

He faced me. "I know you don't know me, cousin. But when I heard Severine had been dethroned, I was *glad*. You have to understand—your sister was no friend to me. My time at court was fraught. But it made me the man I am today—without the difficulties I faced at Coeur d'Or, I'm not sure I would ever have invited in the Scion's light. In a way, it was Severine who finally inspired me to banish the dusk. I just wanted to share that light with the person brave enough to finally defeat her."

His words thudded with unwelcome familiarity in my ears. They were the Scion's Vow, and I'd heard them a thousand times in the Duskland temple where I was raised.

Have you invited the Scion's light to banish the dusk?

And the answer was always: *I see his light beyond my eyes.*

So Gavin d'Ars was a believer. And he'd come here with his holy light and his unerring faith to tell me how to run the empire I'd stolen with my own sister's blood.

I swallowed the memories of my shadow-smeared childhood, hidden away in the dusk; my soul-deep certainty that I belonged somewhere else and would risk everything to find that place; shattered mirror glass and dim sunlight, grappling fingernails and the splash of blood. The scars along my arms ached.

Why couldn't I remember what it felt like to be *sure*?

My sunburst Relic throbbed against my chest, as if to remind me of everything I'd lost, and everything I had yet to find.

"I apologize, but I'm going to have to cut this meeting short," I ground out.

"That's too bad." Disappointment wafted across Gavin's face, then blew away on a breeze of excitement. "Will I see you again?"

"I'm sure you will. Have you spoken to the palais châtelaine about accommodations? I'm not sure we can house your entire retinue, but perhaps—"

"I'm not staying at the palais," interrupted Gavin.

"Oh." I frowned. "Then where?"

"The Sabourin town house in Jardinier." He named a wealthy district outside the walls of Coeur d'Or. "Haven't you been?"

Of course I hadn't been. I'd only found out about it a few weeks ago, and only to discover it didn't belong to me. I chained sudden resentment behind a carefree smile.

"Afraid not."

"Well, you'll have to come visit. I'll have you over for tea and show you all the family heirlooms."

I forced my creaking knees into a passable curtsy. Then I fled the Esplanade and my distant—but legitimate—cousin's smiling air of grace and innocence.

NINE

I marched back toward the palais, self-loathing and uncertainty churning my stomach. Calvet and Karine peeled away from the Husterri, pacing me. I pushed back into my makeshift throne room, but Sunder and most of my advisors had gone—only Dowser remained, reading a heavy book in the amber light from one of the windows. He looked up when I walked in.

"You weren't gone long." His refined bass filled the room. "Is everything all right?"

"Not really." I felt off-balance and anxious after my little tête-à-tête with Gavin—like I'd stared too long into Dominion shadows and couldn't remember what the staring eye of the Scion looked like. "He has me at every disadvantage. He inherited the fortune that should have been mine. He looks and sounds like the Sun Heir. And he's so certain of himself—of his place in this world."

"It wasn't so long ago that you were that certain," Dowser reminded me. "When you fought for a dream only you could see, and inspired others to fight alongside you. We all still believe in your vision for a better world, child. Gavin's arrival changes nothing."

He put his hand on my shoulder. The touch was meant to calm me—ground me—but instead it made me jump.

"We have to find the Relics," I said. "I need the symbols of this empire to bolster my claim to the throne. I need something Gavin doesn't have. I need to be undeniable come Ecstatica."

"I may be able to help with that." Dowser nodded to the book he held, a heavy tome literally coming apart at the seams.

"Barthet found this at Unitas. We overlooked it before—it's more or less a book of children's stories."

He handed it over, revealing broad pages covered in lush but faded illustrations. I touched a page with gentle fingers that came away dark with the dust of tides. Sudden melancholy struck a silvery note in my heart. Once upon a time, this book had been loved. It would have held a place of honor in a nursery, its pages pored over by generations of faceless, nameless, long-dead children. But it had been relegated to the obscurity of time.

"It dates from before the Conquest—"

"—When the Sabourins ambushed their neighbors, annexed their principalities, centralized the monarchy, and expanded the Amber Empire to its modern borders," I supplied.

"You've been studying." Dowser smiled. "Do you remember the version of the Meridian myth I told you the other day?"

"With the molten sword?"

"Yes. It seems that version diverged from the widely accepted legend just before the Conquest. I'm not sure why. But this book contains a version of it."

He flipped toward the middle. The full-page illustration featured a magnificent sunburst, extravagantly gilded and painted with kembric leaf so it shone like hope. A glittering Meridian floated in an azure sky beneath it, nearly as bright. And on the ground below him were four smaller figures, each holding an object.

"In this story, Meridian doesn't disappear into Dominion," explained Dowser. "He rules as the Sun Heir for many tides before finally growing disillusioned with power. He abdicates his throne, but is unable to choose a new heir from among his four children. Instead, he bestows upon each of them an object: the dristic blade, forged in the heart of the Sun, he gives to his strong-armed daughter Aliette; the crown of kembric, woven from the net he used to capture the Moon, he gives to his crafty son Bastien; the locket of ambric, stained with the Moon's heart-blood, he gives to his compassionate son Raphaël; and—" Dowser shook his head. "It's written in an archaic dialect and I'm afraid I'm not translating this bit correctly. It says he gives his *soul* to his ambitious daughter Liliane, who dreamed always of the stars."

"His soul?" My heart thrummed against my pendant—*locket?* "What happened then? Did they all kill each other for the Relics the moment Meridian left them alone?"

My question seemed to trouble Dowser, and I had to confess it took me aback as well. But I almost felt like some midnight scrap of me already knew this story

"In a way. It's a children's book, so there's no killing—as off-spring of the Scion they were supposedly immortal. But they competed against each other in something called the *Ordeals of the Sun Heir.* In the end, the heir who won the most Relics won them all, and went on to rule the kingdom."

"Who was it?"

"Your ancestor a thousand generations over—Sébastien Sabourin, progenitor of your royal line and fabled son of Meridian himself."

I wrapped a hand around my pendant and closed my eyes. The Sisters of the Scion stuck closely to the teachings of their scripture and denounced all fairy tales as dangerous nonsense— so why this eerie familiarity?

"So we have an idea of *what* we're looking for, at least," I said. "That's good. Now we just need to know where these four Relics are hidden."

"I wonder whether—"

Sunder burst into the antechamber, interrupting Dowser mid-sentence. He stalked close, eyes glittering with triumph.

"The Loup-Garou raided a Red Mask cabal in the Paper City. None of the dissidents were captured, but my wolves confiscated stacks of a pamphlet they meant to distribute."

Fear and anticipation tangled in my chest. "May I see?"

Sunder handed me a slim volume, printed in livid ink on cheap paper. "It's something of a manifesto."

I flipped through it, my throat tightening as my eyes skimmed crude etchings of bloody swords and beaming suns; Meridian's flaming chariot plummeting through a black night. Words jumped out at me, half-familiar and smudged with tallow and dusk: *the light of the Scion . . . with glory thy glave . . . crowns the Sun Heir.*

I dropped the pamphlet like it burned my fingers.

"Tell me the gist." I gritted my teeth.

"The Red Mask leader preaches a new era of peace, light, and piety in the Amber Empire."

Dowser took off his spectacles and polished them on the front of his robe. "What's the catch?"

"This utopia must be ushered in by a true Sun Heir, who will rid the empire of the darkness in its heart with the flaming light of the Scion's molten sword."

"Let me guess," I spat. "I'm the darkness in the empire's heart—the Duskland Dauphine."

"I imagine that's one interpretation."

This couldn't be happening. From the moment I'd known enough about the world to see my place in it, I'd fought against the teachings of the zealots who'd raised me. They had believed in the Scion with an unflinching devotion that had always felt like an affront to me—the child standing before them begging to be loved. And so I'd derided their teachings, seeking out every flaw in their ideology, every chink in their beliefs, every hole in their philosophy. Because if they couldn't be bothered to love me, then maybe I could at least earn their hate.

I'd traveled half the daylight world to escape that doctrine. I'd run away from the dusk toward the light at the heart of an empire. And yet I'd found more fanaticism. And the hate I'd always thought I wanted.

"And this Red Mask leader? Who is he?"

"No one knows. Those who have heard him preach say he wears a red mask—the inspiration for all the others. His followers might know what he looks like, but they have proven incredibly tight-lipped."

"Why don't we destroy all the pamphlets?" I asked. "Send the Loup-Garou through the Paper City, gather the books, publicly denounce his hateful ideas—"

"You can burn paper, but you can't destroy ideas," Dowser said. "You'd just make a martyr of his philosophy."

"He's right," Sunder said. I already knew it was true. "His ideas, though radical, are finding purchase among Ambers whose lives have been upturned these past spans. His philosophy offers a scapegoat for their uncertainty and a bright promise of hope to chase away their despair."

"But false hope!" I protested. "There is no such thing as a *true* Sun Heir. The Sun Heir is just something invented by the Sabourin dynasty to give divine right to royalty."

"But isn't it tempting to believe?" Sunder drawled. "When you have nothing else to believe in?"

"That nothing being me?" I snapped.

"You know that's not what I meant."

Something grotesque squeezed slimy hands around my heart. I turned away.

"The boy—Pierre LaRoche," I said, after a seething moment. "I want to question him myself."

I'd never been inside a dungeon, unless you counted the prison of a temple I was raised in.

I expected mold-black walls and seeping bricks and rusting shackles. Instead—behind the palais, past the courtyard with the stables and kennels, and down two flights of dark steps—Sunder led me to a severe but mostly clean series of caverns carved smooth from solid stone. Light came not from ambric glow-globes but torches, and the scent of tallow and woodsmoke dragged me back into the past so quickly I had to steady myself against a wall.

Unexpected panic pushed frigid water through my veins.

We were just out of sight of the guards when Sunder caught me by the elbow and spun me into a deep alcove. My skirts swirled heavy around our legs. A glass window to nowhere acted as a strange mirror, picking out a reflection of the jewels at my throat and the blue of my eyes. It left Sunder in shadow.

"Are you sure you want to do this?" Sunder stood so close that I could feel the smolder of his fever on my skin. "I already inter-rogated the boy."

I fought to recapture my equilibrium. This place made my teeth ache. "I have other methods of persuasion than you."

"What's that supposed to mean?" His eyes were raw with unease.

"I'm the *Duskland Dauphine*. I'm the woman he tried to kill. He hates me for what I represent—I am an idea to him. He might react more emotionally to a questioning from me. He might let something slip."

"Perhaps." His expression was unfathomable in the dark. "Or he will slip inside your head and show you all your doubts and fears."

"He's just a boy."

"He's a zealot. He's been brainwashed and manipulated, demoiselle—he has lost the skill of nuance. I would protect you from that kind of misplaced certainty."

I swallowed, pine ash and melting snow and gratitude slicking the back of my throat.

"You protect me from many things, Sunder. But you can't protect me from everything."

TEN

Pierre LaRoche looked awful. His hair was matted to his skull in sweat-whorled spirals. His sallow skin puffed with exhaustion-bruised bags beneath his eyes. His tunic was shredded and dirty. Manacles hung loose on his ungainly arms, and I could see where he'd tried to escape his bonds— scrapes and lacerations covered his wrists. He looked up when Sunder and I entered the cell, but it was long moments before he recognized me.

Loathing shaped his face into a livid mask.

I would have had more pity for Pierre LaRoche if he hadn't looked at me like that.

"You," he croaked, then coughed. He spat onto the floor by my slippers. "Scion curse you."

"Scion curse *me*?" I sidestepped spittle. "I imagine he saves much of his wrath for assassins."

"You're one to talk." He sneered, baring several broken teeth. "You murdered your kin for a throne. If I kill, it is because I bring righteous light to the dusk of immorality."

His words conjured a restless familiarity within me, thrusting me back into the dank hallways of my childhood.

"Have you invited the Scion's light," I murmured, "to banish the dusk?"

The boy's eyes widened, like I said the last thing he ever expected.

I glanced at Sunder, a sculpture in marble and onyx at the door, then knelt before the boy. Sunder's boots moved closer.

"I am the sun staring at the twilight," I recited, although the words felt as dusty in my mouth as they had at the Temple of the Scion. "I am the solace that banishes blight. I am—"

"I am the sword that culls with light." Pierre LaRoche's eyes glowed, and he smiled a vicious, broken smile.

My pulse thudded strange in my ears. I'd had the Scion's Vow memorized for as long as I could remember. And the third line was: *I am the moon shining deep in Midnight.* LaRoche's line was *wrong.*

"That's the wrong line," I said out loud.

"No, it's not."

"Who taught it to you?"

LaRoche's eyes gleamed. "He who will crush you with sunlight and feed your bones to Midnight."

Blood burst behind my eyes. I slapped him. His head twisted on his neck and bounced against the stone wall. I lunged for him again, but a pair of hands clamped onto my shoulders and dragged me back.

"I thought you had other methods of persuasion?" Sunder's disapproval was a knife against my throat. "That kind of interrogation is a little more my style."

I wrenched myself out of his grasp and paced to the wall and back, struggling to control my breathing. LaRoche still smiled, although a hand-shaped bruise bloomed on his smooth cheek.

"Your red masks," I said without preamble. "They're supposed to be Meridian's flaming sword, is that it?"

His eyes flickered. *Good.* I knew something I wasn't supposed to know. I leaned closer, pressing my advantage.

"Did you know Sisters of the Scion raised me in a temple on the edge of Dominion?" Pierre sneered, like he thought I was lying. "I have seen the edge of Midnight, Pierre. I have seen bloated red clouds slide away into blackness. I have dreamed the glimmer of impossible stars. I have tasted the smoky shadows creeping into the light to snatch away the living. And I can tell you firsthand—there is no Scion. There is no beacon shining light into dark. There is no solace at the edge of the blight. And there is no molten sword doling out justice."

The smile dropped off his face.

"This prison reminds me of the Dusklands." My voice rang harsh. "Except for one difference—I am here. I am your sun. I am your solace. I am your sword."

"Sacrilege," breathed LaRoche.

"You are the eldest of five children?" Fear blossomed in the boy's eyes. "Living in this city is hard enough as an orphan, without the taint of disgrace that comes with a brother's head mounted on a spike at the city gate." I paused to let my words drip down the cage of his imagination. "Do you see? You have a choice, Pierre. Give me the name of your leader, and I will be merciful. Your siblings will see their brother again. You will not die a traitor. Deny me? Well, I think you've already met my friend."

Sunder's jagged expression could have cracked the world. LaRoche stared from me to Sunder and back again, indecision tangling his features into knots.

"Pierre?" I prompted.

"You'll never find him," he snarled. "None of you preening aristos know the Paper City well enough. And the sooner you kill me, the sooner my soul becomes one with the light. I banish the dusk. I renounce the night."

I rose from my crouch, smoothing my skirts as Pierre LaRoche began to pray. I swept toward the door, pausing beside Sunder.

"Demoiselle?"

"See what more you can learn from him," I ground out.

"I already tried." His voice was hoarse. "And all this? Imprisonment without trial, multiple interrogations, using a suspect's family against them? It doesn't look much like the new world you dreamed of. It looks like everything you claimed to hate about Severine's rule."

Severine. Her name seared my tongue. Sunder was right—everything that happened these past two spans was because I'd dared to dream of a strange, lovely world where I might finally belong. But what had that dream bought but bloodshed and death, pain and broken promises? Pierre's vitriol made me confront what I hadn't wanted to admit to myself—this city *hated* me. But I couldn't begin to rebuild what I'd broken when Red Masks lurked behind corners and spread lies about me. Severine's ways may have been brutal, but they'd kept her on a throne for seventeen tides.

"Try again." I made my voice like stone despite the raging bonfire spinning smoke across my heart. "He can either live for me or die for them. Maybe you can make his choice a little easier."

I didn't wait for his answer before I fled. I clawed up the stairs. And when I abandoned the midnight of the dungeons for the sunlight world above, I still felt cloaked in Duskland shadows.

I forced myself to bathe and eat after I left the dungeon, but something about that place—that *boy*—had settled in my stomach like slow poison. The prison had felt so familiar—it had reminded me of the Scion temple I'd grown up in, but there was something else too, a faded sensation glossed over with memory. Torchlight embossed on smooth dark stone. A crystalline gleam. The creeping feeling of being forgotten.

I shivered, and concentrated on deciphering more of my sister's diary. Each passing page curled sharp-fingered hands around my heart and drew blood. I could not plumb its depths without feeling a pang of sympathy for my fiendish half sister, but nor could I fully square its spider-fine words with my own knowledge of my dead family.

Severine told the story of a brutal father obsessed with power and drunk on lust, and his two heirs, as different as different could be. Seneca—the Sun Heir—was a frail, sweet, strange young man with a legacy of dreams. Dreams that came and went like ebbing tides, frothed with truth but touched with madness. And Severine, a devious but devoted sister who would protect her brother at any cost, pitting herself against a father and emperor who possessed a legacy I could not fully tease out from her writings. Whatever it was, he used it to try to turn Seneca's dreams and Severine's love against each other.

My sister's words rang with truth. After all—as everyone had pointed out—it was her personal diary. Why would she lie? But I couldn't forget how carefully my sister had crafted her appearance, how cunning her sense of spectacle. What if this—this little book that outlived her—was her parting shot, a way to absolve her sins after she could no longer defend herself?

. . . and so I wandered the Oubliettes, haunted like the halls of my memory. As though it would matter where I hid it when F inevitably noticed what I'd stolen.

I sighed and snapped the journal shut. If she had written it to be read, she might have tried to be a little less circumspect. Half the entries were written in a kind of code, the other half wrapped up in metaphor and allusion. Each sentence was a knotted chain of kembric: beautiful to behold but impossible to untangle.

The bell for third Nocturne chimed low, and a moment later, boot steps rang crisp in the hall. They paused at my door. I sat up in bed. But after a moment they moved on. The door beside mine snapped shut.

Sunder. But he hadn't come in. Which meant he'd discovered nothing from Pierre.

Guilt cramped my stomach.

It also meant I'd commanded him to torture that boy for nothing. To use the legacy he loathed for no purpose and to no end. But surely he understood. Somewhere in the Paper City a group of fanatics pursued my bloody death. If that wasn't a reason to deploy the anguish staining his blood, I wasn't sure what was.

I closed my eyes against a memory swirling snowflake-soft against the back of my eyelids.

So you don't mind, I'd said, *if I'm a monster?*

No, Sunder had breathed. *Because I'm a monster too.*

But why did either of us have to be monsters? Was it this tainted blood burning through our veins, this legacy of a long-dead god-king who'd fathered us all? Or was it a burden we'd taken upon ourselves because we didn't know any other way? I'd dreamed of a better world, but I had to wonder if that had been an impossible ideal—an *illusion.*

I opened my palms and waited for colors to spill out, a balm against the shame shrouding me in dusk. But I did not conjure beauty. I conjured the Paper City, crowding close in this freezing room—slums shattered with violence and stained with red. Blood dripped down shopfronts and splattered doors, and each stained windowpane showed my own reflection—a face like wrath.

I chewed away the wash of colors, swallowing them into the vault where my nightmares lived.

The Paper City.

Pierre LaRoche had mentioned the Paper City in his final curse. What had he said?

You'll never find him. None of you preening aristos know the Paper City well enough.

And he was right. I didn't know the Paper City at all.

I jumped to my feet and pulled open the drawer of my vanity. The letter inside was inked on cheap paper and reeked of liquor. I scanned it for the first time in weeks, then shoved myself into clothing and opened the door.

I didn't know the Paper City at all.

But I knew someone who did.

ELEVEN

The lower city rang quiet with all the sounds curfew had quenched.

I ducked from shadowed doorway to darkened storefront, dodging the circles cast by ambric glow-globes. I had honestly forgotten that I'd signed off on a strict curfew for the Amber City, enforced by roving bands of Loup-Garou—they were silent as a secret and shadowy as a curse. I'd nearly run into three different packs as I stumbled my way down the Échelles behind the palais, through Rue de la Soie, toward the edge of the Paper City. I probably shouldn't have snuck out without my dedicated garde, but I didn't want anyone to know where I was going.

Not even Sunder. *Especially* not Sunder.

The person I was going to see disliked Sunder almost as much as Sunder disliked him.

I retreated deeper into the shadow of my cloak, then stepped across a river of mud into the dristic, wood, and stone mountain they called the Paper City. The stench of still water and human refuse seeped into my nostrils, and I fought the urge to cover my nose. I looked at the paper clutched between my stiff hands, but I'd already memorized the address (if you could call it that): Rue Sèche, Porte du Lait. *Dry Street, Milk Gate.*

I strode forward, splashing moisture onto my expensive boots. Dilapidated towers cobbled together from mismatched materials cast a strange gloaming. Garbage covered what might once have been a sidewalk. A set of glowing eyes peered from behind a pile of rubbish before flicking away. Moisture seeped between sheets of corrugated metal, leaving stains like blood.

I caught sight of a bent sign, tagged with graffiti. *Rue Sèche.* A sewer grate gushed dirty water down a narrow alleyway lined with taverns and bordellos.

"The Dry Road," I grumbled. "Hilarious."

I squinted. A sign rocked from the lintel of a three-story house, marked with two pale orbs. *Moons* . . . except they looked like—

Porte du Lait. Milk Gate.

What unholy iconography—?

The door swung open, releasing the sounds of lust and mirth into the Paper City twilight. Two laughing girls shoved past me, arms twined and heads close together. I took the opportunity to slide into the hallway past them. Inside, a fête raged. Drunkenness smeared faces into masks, blurring between parchment circles and opalescent lamps etched with the mysterious Moon.

Of all the places—

"Can I help you?" A tired-looking bartender accosted me.

"I'm looking for someone. A Monsieur Balquinal. He's been boarding here for a week or more."

She narrowed her eyes.

"We're friends," I tried to explain. "His mother's name is Rina—her chartered ore convoy travels from Dura'a to Piana. His little brother's name is Vesh. I need to ask his advice."

She shrugged, and pointed up the stairs. "Luca's lucky with the ladies tonight."

Ladies . . . plural?

I hurried up the stairs and knocked roughly on a narrow door. Luca answered, laughing. His smile fell away when he saw who it was, his kembric eyes widening in his bronze face before narrowing with surprised mirth.

"*You?*" He propped a lean arm against the jamb. "Consider me astonished."

"Were you expecting someone else?"

He laughed, and I smelled alcohol on his breath. "No."

I pushed past him into a tiny garret apartment—little more than a narrow bed, a closet privy, and a bare kitchen. Its only redeeming quality was the view—a fair-sized window looked out across a sea of rooftops. I eyed a half-full bottle of liquor languishing between two chipped glasses.

"I hope I'm not interrupting something."

"You're not."

"A nice place you've got here."

"It's cheap," he said. "And usually no one bothers me."

I held up the letter he'd sent just after the coup. "If you didn't want me to bother you, you shouldn't have included your address."

"Sylvie." My old name in his mouth sounded strange. I noticed he no longer wore his tri-metal signat—the mark of his erstwhile profession as an ore trader. "Did you *read* the letter?"

Of course I'd read it. Luca had managed to escape the ruin of the palais the Nocturne of Carrousel along with Oleander and me. The three of us had fled halfway to Belsyre, where we'd met the first of the Loup-Garou, summoned by Sunder in anticipation of our failure. We'd waited for the rest of the militia to join us before marching on the city. But Luca had never cared for our cause—his group, La Discorde, had been slaughtered in the coup, and he had little love for the aristocracy or the monarchy. Which, these days, meant me. So he'd left without a goodbye sometime during the fighting. A week later, he'd sent me a note:

I hope you will be a better empress than your sister. No matter what happens, I will always be your friend.
Luca.

"So that offer of friendship no longer stands?"

"A Tavendel always keeps his promises." Luca rinsed out

the glasses and plunked them down on the table. "So what do you want?"

"What makes you think I want something?"

"You," Luca said, with something resembling a smile, "always want something."

I tossed my cape over the back of a chair. "I wanted to ask you some questions."

"You don't get to barge into my apartment in the middle of Nocturne demanding answers." Luca sloshed amber liquid into the glasses and pushed one toward me. "And friendship isn't an interrogation. It's a conversation."

The liquor smelled like anise and bitter almond, cheap casks and young hops. I crinkled my nose. "I don't want to drink this."

"It's fourth Nocturne." Luca smiled his broad white smile, but it looked forced. "And you have some catching up to do. How about a game? You aristos seem to love those. You want answers? Fine. But for every question you ask me, I get to ask one of you. And if I don't think the answer you give is true, you have to drink until I believe you."

I frowned. At Coeur d'Or I had a reputation as a notorious lightweight. "Only if it goes both ways. If I think you're lying, *you* drink until I believe *you*."

"Salut." Luca clinked his glass against mine. "You go first."

"Do you know a boy named Pierre LaRoche?"

"Only by name." Bitterness touched his voice. "Everyone knows Sunder's wolves knocked out half his teeth at Maison Creux before dragging him through the Paper City in chains."

Hard not to take that as truth. I nodded at him to go. He considered.

"What did it feel like to kill your sister?"

The question swept my tongue into the back of my throat, and I nearly gagged. *Brittle diamonds of glass strewn across a tile floor; a shattered oculus seeping blood; the livid imprint of my sister's desperate gasps.*

"It felt good."

"Drink."

The liquor burned my throat and scalded my soul. "My heart broke like mirror glass, and that was what I stabbed her with. I dream sometimes that I am her, and I feel the force of my own hatred when the blade breaks my skin. Sometimes I think I died that Nocturne, right along with her, and now I'm a ruthless ghost of the dauphine I hoped to be. Is that what you wanted to hear?"

Luca's bonfire eyes flashed. He downed his portion, then sloshed more booze into both our glasses.

"Does this work if you drink on both our turns?" My voice felt raw.

Luca shrugged. "Your turn."

"Do you know who leads the Red Masks? Who's been trying to kill me?"

"Yes and no." He propped his elbows on the table. "He's a priest of some kind, if his rhetoric is any indication. Calls himself Sainte Sauvage. He showed up out of nowhere after the coup, preaching Scion theology to anyone who would listen."

Sainte Sauvage. That was news. "Why are they listening? I thought Ambers tended toward the secular."

"Tensions are running high, Sylvie. Higher than they were before your coup against Severine. Nobody likes your wolves— they're quiet and fast and they fight too clean. At least with the Skyclad, people could hear them clanking around—you always had time to pack up your stolen goods or pull the shades over your lotus den. And if they did catch you, a nice stash of joie or kembric livres would convince them to look the other way. The Loup-Garou are above all that."

An odd flash of pride warmed my stomach. Although it

might've just been liquor burning its way through my intestines. "Isn't that a good thing?"

"It might be, under different circumstances. But people are scared and isolated and, above all, uncertain. They don't know who you are or what you stand for or what's going to happen next. They're looking for something to believe in—to put their *faith* in. And Sainte Sauvage has given that to many of them."

"Who *is* he?"

"I don't know. I tried following him once, but he lost me in the Paper City after five minutes. I do know he's recruiting. Young people with nothing much to lose. People he can bend to his will. People he can convince to kill."

"Will it end?" The words hurt to speak. "After my coronation at Ecstatica, will they stop trying to kill me?"

Luca clicked his tongue against his teeth. "You asked four questions. My turn."

I bit down a selfish protest.

"Are you—" He downed his drink and cleared his throat. "Are you and Sunder together?"

My mouth opened, but no words came out. Of all the questions, that was what Luca wanted to know? There had been a time when we'd been close, when we'd flirted with the idea of . . . *something*. But that felt like an age ago. Sudden melancholy threw dust against my heart, and I looked at the candy-bright rings on my fingers and my crushed velvet cape. I'd come so far from the pathetic orphan heating scraps of borrowed meat over a cook fire. And Luca? I studied him, his hammered kembric eyes and lean muscles, his three-day stubble and liquor-sharp breath. He wasn't the same boy who'd sung me Tavendel songs and offered me friendship at no cost.

We might as well be strangers to each other.

Luca watched my hesitation, eyes full of candlelight. "Well?"

"I don't know," I said honestly.

"Elaborate, or drink."

I ran my finger around the rim of my glass and decided to be honest. I hadn't shared this with anyone—these days, no one seemed too keen on sharing—but who would Luca tell? He and Sunder barely stood each other's presence, and it wasn't like they ran in the same circles.

"We're trying. He's with me most of the day, every day. I spend most nights in his bed. But there are—" I thought of Sunder's ambric timbre, seeping menace through his veins. I thought of the lexicon of lust scrawled between us in hungry touches, and the constant pain blotting it out. I thought of all the things I owed him; the pressing weights of debts unpaid. "—complications."

"Does it matter?"

I cocked my head and frowned.

"I mean, the man's in love with you," Luca said. "Or didn't you know?"

I laughed. I couldn't help it. Love seemed impossible when my whole life was fear and doubt and uncertainty. "He's not."

Luca's eyes gleamed. "Drink."

I laughed again, and threw back my drink, then held out my glass for another dram. The liquor didn't taste so bad anymore, and my head swam warm and pleasant. "He expects things from me. I've become his symbol for a world that's better—*shinier*—than the one he lives in. It's not me he loves. It's my potential."

"Scion's teeth, Sylvie!" Luca leaned back in his chair and whistled. "That's harsh. And if he did love you for who you are, instead of what you represent?"

"If he truly loved me for me?" I took another sip. "I'm not sure I would deserve it."

Luca went quiet. "You don't believe you deserve his love?"

"I'm not sure either of us deserves it." My chest had gone numb.

"If you don't believe you're worthy of one man's love," Luca murmured, "how can you expect to be worthy of theirs?"

"Theirs?"

"*Ours.* Citizens of the Amber City—of the Amber Empire."

I'd begun to ask myself the same question.

"My turn." My head spun. "Why did you leave? You took off before the fighting ended."

"You didn't need me anymore."

"Why would you think that?" I gripped my glass more tightly. "Luca, you've always been wrapped up in this. You helped open my eyes to Severine's cruelties. You set in motion the assassination attempt that ended with me discovering my true identity. Your revolutionaries destroyed half my palais. We spent a span in the Belsyre foothills—you, me, and Oleander—camping and plotting and mustering troops. You think that all ended the moment we defeated the Skyclad? I needed you then. I need you now."

Something sharp and hot flared in Luca's eyes. "Why?"

"To remind me where I came from. To remind me what I'm fighting for. To help me keep this dream alive."

"You have plenty of people for that."

"Plenty isn't enough. I need you all."

Luca lowered his eyes and rolled his glass over his palm. "How is Oleander?"

"Oleander?" My head lurched trying to keep up with the conversation. Why would Luca be asking about Oleander? The three of us had spent a harried span together when we fled the Amber City, but the two of them had barely spoken. "Same's always. She's makin' me throw a party. She helped me find—"

Did Luca know about the Relics? I clapped a hand over my mouth and tried to swallow the words forcing their way up my throat. Were they words? My head swam, and I staggered out of my chair, reaching for my cape.

"Whoa, whoa!" Luca was at my side, wedging an arm under my shoulder and checking my reeling steps. "Just where do you think you're going?"

"I think . . . have t'go home."

"Home?" Mirth shaded Luca's eyes to bronze. "I lost count of how many of those you had, but you're not going anywhere."

"Can't . . . stay here."

"Better that than the future Amber Empress wandering around the Paper City, blind drunk, past curfew, when there are Red Masks trying to kill her."

He had a point. He half carried me to the bed, then hoisted me onto the mattress and tossed a blanket on me.

"'S your bed," I feebly protested.

He sank to the floor, pillowing his head on his elbow. "I've slept on harder surfaces, Sylvie."

I drifted through the dusk toward Midnight, but an urgent thought flamed across my mind.

"I didn't tell anybody where I was going."

"You idiot." Luca's laugh sounded distant. "Of course you didn't."

"Sunder's gon' be so worried."

The last thing I heard before I surrendered to sweet oblivion was Luca's voice.

"Maybe I got it wrong. Maybe it's you who's in love with him."

TWELVE

I left Luca's apartment after fifth Matin feeling like I'd been kicked in the head by a horse with a grudge.

Luca had woken me fifteen minutes earlier with a glass of lukewarm water in one hand and that Scion-cursed liquor bottle in the other.

"Rehydrate, then take a bite of the beast that rode you." He sloshed the amber liquid. "It might make you feel better."

I nearly gagged. I slurped the water like a greedy child and tried not to look at the alcohol.

"I wanted to let you sleep." Luca seemed annoyingly entertained by my misery. "But they're looking for you."'

"*Who?*" I surged to my feet. The movement made me feel even worse, which I didn't think was possible. My stomach heaved, and I flung out an arm to steady myself against the wall.

Luca had the grace to look sympathetic. "Everybody."

I cursed, and made for the door. Luca *tsk*ed, flopped my cape over my shoulders, and threaded my arm through his.

"Bad enough you came here alone," he said. "But it'll be my head if I let you go back without an escort."

We hurried down the rickety stairs and through the mud-slopped street. The Paper City during Matin was a different place—humanity ebbed and surged around me like a noisy ocean. Light filtered harsh between listing buildings. Odors slapped me in the face, and I breathed through my mouth to keep my nausea at bay.

We were halfway up the winding, terraced streets of the Échelles—spitting distance from the palais—when I heard hoof-beats on cobblestones and saw a pair of riders canter around the corner. It took me a long minute to recognize their livery—I still wasn't used to seeing red and kembric surcoats glinting in the low sunlight. They were Gavin's household garde—what had he called them?

Husterri.

They barely slowed as they approached. My stomach throbbed with acid and guilt, and I hid my face deeper into my cloak. Scion, let them not see me. But Luca waved them down. They reined their steeds, impatient.

"Looking for the dauphine?" He yanked back my hood, cheerful. "I hope there's a reward, because you found her."

The soldat lifted his fingers to his lips and loosed a piercing whistle. I heard more hooves round the corner, and another half dozen riders thundered up. My stomach gathered rocks when I saw cracked-agate eyes beneath waving mahogany hair.

Gavin.

Could this day get any worse?

"Lady Mirage!" He flashed one of his dazzling smiles. "You're safe! Glad we found you at last."

I sniffed with as much dignity as I could muster. "I wasn't lost."

"Perhaps not." He laughed, shooting a glance at Luca. "Still, you had everyone worried. Enough for them to summon me from Jardinier to join the search. Who's your friend?"

"Luca Balquinal." Luca introduced himself before I even opened my mouth. He clasped hands with Gavin before sweeping his palm along the arched neck of the other boy's horse. He whistled. "Long time since I've seen an Aifiri Ashka in the flesh. Is he bred for pleasure or war?"

Gavin looked surprised. "Would you believe me if I said both?"

The stallion stamped a hoof and bannered his tail. Luca and Gavin both laughed.

"Never known an Ashka who didn't love to show off."

"You know your horseflesh." Gavin cocked his head, curious.

"I'm Tavendel," Luca said, by way of explanation.

"You should stop by my stables in Jardinier sometime," Gavin said. "I've got an Alomar mare who'll make a religious man out of you."

"Not to interrupt," I said icily. "But should we be getting back to the palais?"

"Sorry." Gavin looked abashed. He started to swing down from his stallion. "Here, you should ride—"

"I don't know how," I snapped. "I'll just walk."

"That won't do." He gestured to Luca, and together they hauled me up on the horse in front of him. I protested, but Gavin wrapped a strong arm around my waist and angled my legs across the horse's withers. He saluted Luca. "Thanks for the assist!"

And then we were rushing off through the city, and I didn't have the energy to concentrate on anything other than keeping the meager contents of my acid-splattered stomach on the inside.

I bathed and changed quickly, trying to scrub away the cloud of nebulous shame hanging over me. I had nearly reached the Congrès when I heard my name.

"Mirage."

I smelled him before I saw him—genévrier and ice, underlaid with a snap of metal and the bitter tang of masked pain. *Sunder.* A frisson of regret scuttled down my spine when I thought of how I'd ditched him and his wolves to visit the Paper City unescorted.

I spun to face him. He wore his black uniform, the argyle of his house colors slashed stark across his breast. He breathed hard, his hair damp with what looked like sweat. His eyes yawned with vicious disappointment. I looked away, Luca's words weaving bright strings through my haze of memories.

The man's in love with you.

"If you're here to scold me, get it over with."

"I'm not your father." His voice held no expression. "But I did spend the whole of Matin looking for you. I heard *Gavin* found you, wandering up through the Échelles. Did it slip your mind that there are Red Masks trying to kill you? Or did you just want to get drunk with that Tavendel lowlife without supervision?"

"You're neither my father nor my keeper," I lashed out at him. "I don't have to explain myself to you."

"Did you forget asking me to serve as your commandant?" He reached for his side, then clenched his fist and lowered it. "Scion help me, but I thought you'd start acting more like a dauphine and less like a Dusklander brat once we defeated Severine."

The words stung like a slap to the face, but it hurt more to see him like this—cold and unyielding as a glacier. His masklike expression conjured a memory from another time, before I'd learned that a heart beat hot beneath his frigid exterior. Ice slicked my bones and numbed my tongue. *"Excuse me?"*

Dowser poked his head out of the Congrès, irritation marring his usually placid mask. "I thought I heard voices. You're late."

I nailed all my angry words to my ribs. Then I brushed past Sunder's fever-chill into the Congrès.

The room was full of people I barely knew. Besides the core trio—Dowser, Barthet, and Lady Marta—there were a number of legacies. Mostly Dexter, but a few from Sinister stood against the wall—after my conversation with Oleander, I'd loosened their restrictions. Gavin must have lingered in the palais after riding up with me from the Échelles—he lounged, smiling and handsome, beside his severe godfather. But there were also a dozen or more people I'd never seen before in my life, clutching pens and parchment and trying to look important.

Strangely, they made me the most nervous.

I smoothed my cobalt-and-magenta skirt around my chair. "I beg pardon for my tardiness. Shall we begin?"

"Lord Sunder," Dowser said. "You had news?"

"Indeed." Sunder braced his hands and smoldered at the table. "The Loup-Garou have subdued three riots in the last week. The first began when bakers in the Paper City inflated the price of bread higher than it's been in tides, making it impossible for most of the lower classes to afford food. Looters rushed a grain silo, breaking down the door and spilling nearly a tide's worth of wheat into the street. Considering the trade freeze currently in effect on the city, we ought to consider stockpiling what's left, lest we all starve."

"The Imperial stores are kept separately from the city's," Lady Marta cut in. "Based on my accounting, there is no danger of a shortage at the palais."

"Last tide's harvest was good in Aifir," Gavin added. "If you're willing to lift the embargo, I can have a shipment of wheat sent by the end of next span."

He was addressing me. "Oh! I—I see no reason why some trade cannot resume. As long as the trade convoys have proper charters and are vetted by the garde. Lord Sunder, you'll double the gate patrols accordingly."

"I don't have the people for that, dem—*dauphine*." His eyes were metal.

"Find them," I said, a little harsh. "I won't see my people starve. And did I hear you say, Lady Marta, that the palais's grain stores are kept separately from the city's?"

She inclined her head.

"Have half our grain sent down to the city under close guard, then distribute it in the Paper City. Also—issue a decree that bread shall not be sold for more than the standard cost. Subsidize the bakeries, if necessary."

Sunder's fists tightened on the edge of the table. "The second riot occurred in Rue de la Soie."

Surprise sprinted through the room. Rue de la Soie was a commerce district beyond the Échelles—wealthy merchants curated goods from across the daylight world, and skilled artisans sold expensive luxury merchandise.

"Over what?" Barthet asked.

"Religious beliefs," Sunder ground out, "although it was hard to tell over all the shouting. Zealots are targeting the district—rocks through windows, warehouses being set on fire, flaming swords painted across the doors and windows of known atheists. The citizens are demanding more Loup-Garou patrols and an investigation into who's been putting their business at risk."

The Red Masks had moved beyond the Paper City and begun victimizing Ambers who didn't worship the Scion?

Outrage tightened my limbs. *I am the sword that culls with light.*

"Halve the number of wolves in the palais," I growled. "Send them to patrol Rue de la Soie."

Silence slapped me in the face.

"Dauphine, the city is already crawling with wolves," Dowser protested. "An increase in patrols might make this dissidence worse."

"Or they will see you as an easy target here in the palais," Marta said. "Attempts have already been made upon your life."

"Enough," I commanded. "We must preserve rule of law and religious tolerance in this city. My coronation at Ecstatica will hopefully provide much-needed stability, but until then sacrifices must be made. You mentioned three riots, Lord Sunder. Which was the third?"

"Not so much a riot, dauphine, as an altercation." His face tightened with remembered violence. "A group of Red Masks held up a carriage in Jardinier and took a noblewoman hostage. Their terms for her release were simple—they demanded the freedom of Pierre LaRoche, the first boy who tried to kill you in the street."

Ice coated my veins, and I saw the young man's glowering, gloating face: *They will crush you with sunlight and feed your bones to Midnight.*

"And?"

His smile was a wolf's—all teeth. "The Loup-Garou doesn't like demands. The lady was safely returned to her family—albeit a little worse for wear."

"And the Red Masks?" My chest tightened. "Did you manage to capture any of them for questioning?"

"No, dauphine." His eyes glittered with ice. "I did not."

"I think the point is," Dowser interrupted, "that there are powerful factions growing restless with that boy being kept prisoner for so long. This could be an opportunity to show the city you stand for justice."

"Or you stand for mercy," Gavin suggested, from the corner. "You should pardon the boy. Show him the Scion's mercy and the city will love you for it."

"That will only show she is weak," Sunder sneered. "The boy tried to assassinate her in full view of a crowd of bystanders. Such a thing is treason and punishable by death."

"He will stand trial, before the city and the Scion," I said, ignoring the brush of dusk against my heart. "Rotting away in a dungeon or disappearing in the Nocturne—that was how Severine treated her enemies. But rule of law must also be upheld. I will not pardon a traitor on a whim. Does anyone have an argument with that?"

No one did.

"Very well." I laid a hand flat on the table. "Set the trial for this week. I want it somewhere public, so the city can see I have nothing to hide. Barthet—can I rely on you to see this is done?"

The older man nodded.

"Was there anything else?"

"Yes." Marta Iole shuffled a stack of papers. "The crown is still hemorrhaging capital. Your request to emancipate the Sousine has led to even more of your nobles refusing to pay taxes. The Skyclad are still languishing in prison camps near La Belladonne—they must either be rehabilitated under your rule, or disbanded with pay."

"I do not recommend the latter," Dowser murmured. "Unless you wish to have half a million mercenaries roaming the daylight world offering their sword to the highest bidder."

"And now you wish to give crown food reserves away for free." Marta fixed me with a stare that reminded me how she'd rejected her upbringing, escaped a life she'd despised, and turned herself into one of the most celebrated and wealthy Aifiri expatriates in the Amber Empire. "What will you have me do, dauphine?"

Across the room, I caught Gavin giving me a glittering, considering look.

I swallowed a sigh, pushed against the headache beginning to pound at my temples, and clenched my hands in my skirts.

"Shall we review the tax code once more, Lady Marta?"

THIRTEEN

After the Congrès, Gavin d'Ars caught up with me in the halls, smelling exuberantly of soap and hot metal. My gardes moved to block him, but I waved them back.

"Scion, you were amazing in there," he enthused. "If I didn't know any better, I'd have thought you were born into this life."

Suspicion clanged against the flare of pleasure his words conjured. But he seemed to mean what he said. I relaxed.

Despite everything, it was hard not to take to Gavin. With his easy smile and lack of airs, he—under different circumstances—could easily have become a friend, if not an ally. Unlike most of the courtiers at Coeur d'Or, he seemed to have little notion for guile and no head for deception. I hated to admit it to myself, but I *didn't* hate him.

Even if he's angling for your throne? whispered a voice within me.

"Thank you," I said, neutral.

"I'm on my way to the stables," he said. "Will you join me?"

"I've never been," I admitted. "I've also never known a courtier to see to his own horse."

"I suppose you wouldn't, up here in Coeur d'Or." Gavin led me off down a side corridor. "But the d'Ars are all horse fanatics. I practically grew up in a stable. I think I knew how to ride before I could walk. Mother—" A shadow pulsed unfamiliar across his face. "Mother especially loved to race."

"Did something happen to her?"

He hesitated. "My mother never could turn down a challenge. She tried to race an unbroken colt on a dare. He threw her into a fence and broke her neck. She died instantly."

"Gavin, I'm sorry." Shock spangled through me. "I had no idea."

He shrugged. "She was Aifiri, and rode with the Husterri before she became Papa's wife. She died doing the thing she loved best. I suppose we should all be so lucky."

That was one way to look at it.

"Papa loved horses too." That familiar smile crept back over his face; a deep dimple punched his cheek. "He spent a few tides at Coeur d'Or in his youth—just before Sylvain's reign. Apparently he once pulled a massive prank on Cyril Rochelle— he stole all his best horses in the dead of Nocturne, replacing them with identical but inferior steeds. Weeks passed before Rochelle figured out what happened and by then he had no way to prove it was Papa."

"That's—" I was going to say *awful*, but Gavin laughed, and before I knew it I started laughing too.

"Illegal?" Gavin supplied, chuckling. "Wicked? Utterly bad behavior? Yes, yes, and yes. But that's how court used to be, if you heard Papa talk about his glory days. Xavier d'Ars, Remy Legarde, Félix Arsenault, and Sylvain Sabourin—the rogues of the realm, breaking hearts and heads from Matin to Nocturne."

"Wait—your father and my father were *friends*?"

"Great friends," said Gavin. "Until, of course, they weren't."

"What happened?"

"A falling-out." He gave a careless shrug. "Papa never liked to talk about it."

"But—"

We stepped into a courtyard of broad cobbles behind the pal- ais. I glimpsed a square lawn and a cluster of outbuildings—a greenhouse with hothouse flowers pressed against the glass like captive butterflies, a mill or brewery of some kind, and a mag- nificent expanse of stables. I trailed Gavin into one of the barns.

A bar of tangerine light lanced in through the other side and sent our shadows bleeding red across the dusty floor.

Gavin stopped by one of the stalls, reaching in to pet his chestnut's muzzle. "Do you like horses?"

I eyed Gavin's stallion, who stamped a hoof and arched his imperious neck. "I'm afraid I haven't spent much time with them."

"That's too bad." Gavin bent, rummaging for something in a box near his feet. Finally, he handed me a stiff brush. "Here. He needs to be groomed before I saddle him again. Want to help?"

"Why not?" I slipped my gloves into my pocket. "What do I do?"

Gavin showed me how to grip the brush, sweep it firmly against the horse's hide, and place a hand on his rump when I moved behind him. We worked in companionable silence for a few minutes, me brushing the stallion's sleek chestnut neck and Gavin using a sharp implement on his hooves.

"Earlier," Gavin interrupted. "Did you say you didn't know how to ride?"

"Not unless you count the village mule in the Dusklands."

"I'm afraid if we're going to be friends, that won't do." A sly smile creased Gavin's face, as though a delightful scheme had just occurred to him. "Shall I teach you?"

"Um." I backed away. "I don't think so."

"Why not?"

"Because he's a two-thousand-pound beast with sharp hooves and gigantic teeth?"

"Don't listen to her!" Gavin whispered, placing his hand over the stallion's ears. "He's also impeccably trained. It'll be fun, I promise."

"No." I shook my head and glanced down at my gown. "Even if I wanted to, I'm hardly dressed for it."

"That's an easy fix." Gavin's eyes sparked with wicked humor.

He dropped to his knees in the dirt, grasped the hem of my skirt, and pulled. The gown tore past my knees with a rasping pop, exposing silk stockings tied with ribbon and a pair of lacy bloomers. My jaw dropped open and outrage seared my veins with a flare of excruciating heat.

I clenched my fists and glared at Gavin, but he was already laughing, his head thrown back with mirth. A bar of low sunlight caught the threads of kembric in his hair and gave him a radiant halo, and I suddenly couldn't remember what I was so angry about. I began laughing too—laughing so hard I doubled over and clutched my stomach, harder than I'd laughed in what felt like spans.

Gasping, I wiped a kohl-stained tear from the corner of my eye. "Do you know how expensive that dress was?"

"I'll buy you a new one," Gavin promised. "Now get those ruffled legs up onto this horse!"

I shook my head, but Gavin covered my hand with his and showed me how to grasp a handful of mane at the horse's withers. He wrapped one hand around my waist while the other cupped my exposed knee. He lifted me astride the huge stallion. My heart throbbed in panic, and I clutched at the reins looped long around his neck, but the horse didn't so much as shift his weight.

"There." One of Gavin's hands still rested on my stockinged knee, sending a burst of heat singing toward my stomach. "That's not so bad, is it?"

"What am I supposed to do now?" I gritted my teeth.

Gavin grinned. "Try not to fall off."

He grabbed the horse's bridle and led us out into an exercise yard behind the stable. I clutched nervously at the pommel of my saddle, trying to pay attention to Gavin's string of instructions—*elbows in, knees tight, heels down, shoulders back.* But ultimately, the rolling rhythm of the horse's easy gait relaxed me. I settled in, almost beginning to enjoy myself as we looped around the enclosure.

Gavin eased the stallion back toward the barn. "Your seat actually isn't half bad."

"Say that to my face."

His face cracked into its habitual expression of surprised jollity, and I couldn't stop a broad smile of my own.

Scion, were we having *fun*? I'd almost forgotten what that felt like.

"You know, I didn't know what to expect when I first met you," he admitted. "I was fully prepared to be in awe of you."

"Awe?" I cocked my head, trying not to take offense at the implication that he clearly *wasn't* in awe of me. "Why?"

"You stood up to Severine, and won," he said plainly. "The most I ever defied her was refusing to die when she tried to assassinate me."

A tang of metal scraped the back of my throat and kept me quiet. Severine had murdered almost a score of our illegitimate half brothers and sisters after she took power, to consolidate her claim to the throne and prevent any upstart usurpers. Like me. Like *Gavin*. But she'd failed—I'd returned to defeat her, and take from her what she'd sought to prevent any of us ever having. *Power.*

And now Gavin had returned too.

"I'm not sure I deserve anything for murdering my half sister, least of all awe," I finally said. "She tried to have you killed too?"

"Three times. Although I didn't realize the first two were her until much later." The memory couldn't dampen his cheer. "I thought the first two were just courtly pranks gone too far. But it was hard to argue with—well, the person who came for me the third time obviously had their orders directly from Severine."

"How'd you escape?"

"I got lucky." He shrugged. "But I didn't think twice about tucking my tail between my legs and fleeing back home to Aifir, where she didn't have spies everywhere. I don't think I ever would've been able to look her in the eye and face her."

"If that's true, why are you here now?"

"I wanted to shine light into the dark." The low sun sparked veins of kembric in his eyes and turned his expression serious. "I wanted to meet the only kin I have left in this world, and show her this family was capable of good."

His earnestness made me want to believe him, badly. I wanted to believe he had both our best interests at heart. I wanted to believe the promises of righteousness spilling like sunlight from his mouth.

A burst of excruciating relief seared my heart.

Scion, I almost wanted to believe he could do what I hadn't been able to. I wanted to believe he could be the Sun Heir.

We clattered back into the barn. Gavin lifted me down and set me on my feet with a flourish. I was a little out of breath, and I could tell my hair had fallen out of its twisting side braid—dark curls clung to my damp cheeks and kissed the nape of my neck. Gavin grinned, and pushed one of the locks behind my ear, his fingers skimming my cheekbone. I braced myself for a frisson of pain, but of course, it never came. There was just the touch of his skin, sun-warm and smelling of hay and leather. I breathed in that new scent, tasting its complexities, and when I looked up, I found Gavin's startling eyes lingering on my face.

"There," he said softly. "Didn't I keep you safe?"

His hot hands curled around my neck, his fingertips brushing the soft hairs at my nape. His eyes searched my face, more intent than I'd ever seen him, and I shivered. In the dim of the stables, Gavin seemed to radiate an almost-imperceptible glow—the moment just after a candle is blown out, or a memory of sunlight. He looked handsome, with his mahogany hair mussed and his jacket awry and his eyes dark with interest, and I realized with a flash that I was attracted to him.

He tilted his face toward mine, and kissed me.

"Gavin!" I gasped out, alarm unfurling beating wings within me. I pushed against his chest, struggling out of his embrace. For a bare second, he gripped me too tightly. And then he let me go.

"What's wrong?" he asked. "Aren't you attracted to me?"

My skin tingled with discomfort. Was I? Scion, for a moment I'd felt like—I shuddered. Disgust thundered through me, but I didn't know whether it was aimed at him or myself.

"I think," I said, carefully, "that my attraction is spoken for."

Gavin's expression shuttered. "Sunder?"

I nodded.

He sighed, and swung up onto his horse. "Then, my lady, I will bid you a very warm goodbye."

FOURTEEN

Back in Belsyre Wing, I found Sunder in my room. He stood when I slung open the door. His frost-pine eyes rattled my heart in its dusk-bound cage.

"Here to berate me once again?"

"Actually, I came to apologize." His eyes narrowed on my torn gown. The blade of his mouth was whetted on loathing. "Who did that? D'Ars?"

I flushed. "It's not what you think."

"If he so much as touched you—"

"Do you not trust my word?"

Sunder trawled a hand through his bright hair and looked away.

I slid behind the dressing screen, desperate to shuck off the offending gown. I couldn't remember now why I'd found the incident so funny. Gavin had ripped half my gown without asking, for Scion's sake. It had been disrespectful, if not downright predatory. And yet I'd *laughed*—laughed like it didn't matter, laughed like he had a right to my clothes, my body.

Laughed like he had a right to my throne, my city, my *empire*. And why not? Scion knew neither of us had earned it, but at least he looked the part.

I swallowed a hot lump and swiped away a tear. What was wrong with me? I cursed, tugging at my stubborn stays.

"Will you call Elodie for me?" I'd gotten passably good at doing my own corsets, but the thick fabric of this gown made it impossible to take off without help. "I'm having trouble with this dress."

"I'm already here," Sunder said. "Let me help."

"And I suppose you're an expert at corsets?"

"Taking them off, at least," he drawled.

I glared around the edge of the screen.

"That was a joke, demoiselle." A smile coiled in the corner of his mouth, and he crooked a finger at me to come closer. "I grew up with a sister whose own servants refused to touch her. I know how to lace—and unlace—a gown."

I stepped out, clutching the half-laced dress to my waist and shrugging against its sagging shoulders. Sunder's eyes darkened. I turned my back to him, giving him easier access to my laces while hiding the heat flaming at my cheeks. His hands—encased in suede gloves, as usual—slid against my neck, lifting my mass of dark hair and nudging it over one shoulder. I shivered as his fingers gently tugged at my stays.

"Why did Oleander's servants refuse to touch her?" I gasped out, to distract myself from the fire-flush burning a hole in my belly.

Sunder made a noise in his throat.

"No, I mean—" I choked on hesitation. I knew neither Suicide Twin particularly liked talking about their malignant legacies. "She wears gloves to keep her touch from being poisonous. Couldn't they have done the same?"

"The gloves are more warning than safeguard." A shock zinged down my spine from his fingers, as if to corroborate his words. "When Oleander first grew into her powers, there were—accidents. A careless maid ended up with both her hands amputated. A pretty groom in the stables lost his lips and teeth and never spoke again. After a while, she feared to touch them even more than they feared to touch her."

"And so you helped her lace her corsets." Shock and creeping pity sank sharp teeth into my heart. "Weren't you ever afraid she would poison you?"

"She is my sister. I could never fear her. Not when I know

exactly what it feels like to be feared. We are a matched pair—as long as we are together, we feel a little less like monsters." He gave my stays one last tug. "There. You're finished."

His hands lingered at my waist. I turned, met his eyes. An ocean of desire frothed against the icy cliff of his will.

"Where there any accidents?" I knew I shouldn't ask. "When you first came into your powers?"

"Almost too many to count." His gaze writhed with ancient torment and fresh anguish. His hands fell from my waist. He stepped away from me. "I hate that you went to the Paper City without a garde last Nocturne. It was reckless, impetuous, and borderline suicidal. After everything we've all done to secure your place as Sun Heir, we deserve to know you're safe."

"I know." I clutched my loose bodice against my chest. I expected to resent his words, but just felt wretched instead. "I know I haven't lived up to the potential you all saw in me. I know you thought that impossible world I dreamed up would give you all the empress you deserved."

Something fractured in Sunder's face. "That's not what I meant."

"*Deserve.*" I rolled the word around my mouth and tasted its cold contours. "As a child I begged the Sisters to love me. I wrapped my arms around their legs and kissed them as they passed me by, but I had too much dusk inside me for them to love. When I grew old enough to leave, I sought a new world, but all I found were hollow promises of that glittering life I'd dreamed. So I stole what I thought I deserved—I *stole* it, with guile and blood and death. I stole dusk into the light and now you wonder why it's still so dark here."

Sunder's mouth went soft, then hard. "Is this about Gavin?"

My fingernails bit into my palms. Sunlight and golden coins, laughter and ease. I didn't know how to compete with that. Especially when I'd failed to manifest anything from that impossible world I'd once dreamed.

"Is this who I am, Sunder? A mirage of something I might once have become, if only I hadn't reached too high and fallen too far? Will I ever be more than the girl waiting impatiently in the dusk for something she could never earn and would never deserve?"

"You will earn your place." Sunder caught me against him. I could feel how tightly he was holding himself together—his muscles strung hard as bowstrings, his hand tingling strange where it cupped my head. "You will earn their love. Not because of what you deserve, but because of who you *are*. Because of what you dream. Because of how hard you fight for the worlds only you can see."

"How do you know?"

He just smiled, tilting my face toward his.

"I know."

The sound of his voice sifted fire along my bones. He touched me like I was something precious he had lost. Unveiled desire pulsed in his eyes, and for a moment that hurt more than his touch. Scion, how badly he wanted this.

I closed the gap between us, and kissed him.

I tasted my own indecision first—a creeping inhalation of regret transcended by a lingering exhale of resolve. His fingers moved like moths on my neck, then glided along my collarbones, stinging yet soft. His tightly wound muscles held his legacy in check. I shuddered, leaning into him even as I cautioned myself for craving his touch. He buried his hands in my hair, scattering diamond pins on the floor. My mouth opened on his and he deepened the kiss, until all I could taste was my own delirious dread at doing something I knew must end in pain.

I savored his desire and drank his hope.

He nudged the arms of my unlaced gown over my shoulders. The dress gasped to the floor, pooling heavy around my ankles and gusting cool air through my chemise. I sighed into his mouth. His hands dropped to my waist and smoothed over my hips. He lifted me, bracing me against his hard body.

And when he leaned me back against the bed, trailing searing kisses down my throat, I realized how much I wanted this too—this glittering moment looped bright between us. I wanted to taste his kisses and swallow his promises until they were polished hard as diamonds that could never break apart. Maybe then I would be all right.

We would *both* be all right.

FIFTEEN

"Of all the places you could have asked to meet me," remarked Lullaby as she walked up to the door of Severine's chambers, "this one is easily the most macabre."

Even though I'd summoned her, I still jumped a little at the sound of her bell-bright voice. Nerves tangled in my chest as I reached for the doorknob. Lullaby didn't know Severine was still technically alive—I'd had neither the inclination nor the opportunity to tell her. But now I thought I must. I only hoped this shared secret could stitch our friendship back together, not drive us further apart.

"Thanks for coming." My voice sounded stilted, even to my own ears. "There's something I need to tell you. Or maybe I'd better just show you."

I led the way into the chamber to the curtain-shrouded bed and my sister's prone figure.

"What—?" Lullaby's face creased with confusion, then crumpled into horror. Color drained from her skin, leaving her pale and shaking. For a brittle moment, I thought she might faint. But then she flushed, hot and angry, and marched closer to the bed. "A bloody assassination resulting in the deaths of twoscore noble children and countless Paper City rebels. A broken crown with empty coffers, an exiled army encamped in brutal conditions. A city chafing at the bonds of martial law—striking workers, criminals looting businesses, ordinary people rioting in the streets. All that—? Do you mean to tell me all that was for *nothing*?"

The echoes of her words bored holes in my chest.

"Not *nothing*." The word choked me, heavy with the weight of my own doubts. "Dowser says she is unlikely to wake ever again. She will not stand in the way of my coronation."

Lullaby's eyes narrowed. "Who else knows?"

"Dowser. Sunder, so probably Oleander too. And you."

"Do you want me to finish the job?" she asked abruptly. "Do you want me to kill her for you?"

I stared at Lullaby with my mouth open, shocked into silence for once in my life.

"I'll do it, you know. For what she did to Blossom—to all of us. But especially for what she did to Thibo."

"It's not right," I said, without conviction. My palms itched, and the air around us shimmered with all the boundless nightmare deaths I'd never had the guts to inflict on her. "It would be a brutality."

"It would be mercy," Lullaby spat. "After everything she has done? It would almost be a kindness."

"Maybe." I hated that my voice quavered. "But if anyone does it—it has to be me."

"What are you waiting for?"

I hated myself for killing her once. Imagine how I would hate myself for killing her twice. "I think I'm waiting to prove her wrong. To prove I can do better than her. To prove—like you said—that this was all worth it in the end."

"Is this the reason you brought me here?" She gave her head a rough shake. "I'm not sure what good this does us, Mirage."

"I also—" I hesitated. Echoes of what had once been a friendship drifted tenuous between us. An apprehension of loss clutched me, and I knew if I couldn't be vulnerable with Lullaby now, I would lose her forever. And I didn't think I could do any of this without her. "I also wanted to ask for your help."

Caution and disdain played a complicated game across her face. "With what?"

Wordlessly, I took Lullaby's hand, closed my eyes, and dreamed of a world I'd never seen—the world of the ocean.

It was a dream of turquoise deepening to azure. A froth-danced surface blotted out the red sky above: a dark-water womb of salt and sand. Shafts of sunlight painted a silent susurrus against the ocean floor, illuminating blossoms of algae and coral blooming pink between the greening fronds. A school of jeweled fish darted past, shatter-bright and gleaming.

I opened my eyes in time to see the illusion go wrong—ghostly water stained dark as vengeance, cloudy sea-foam frothing spittle along bloody sand, poison tendrils slapping against bloated bodies. I clenched my fists, biting down on the corrupted vision. It hissed away into nothing.

"Your illusions." Her sea-blue eyes met mine with something darker than pity and paler than curiosity. "What's wrong with them?"

"Recently—" I hesitated. I didn't want to admit what I'd known almost since that day in the Marché Cuirasse. Admitting meant it was real. "Ever since I tried to kill Severine, they've all been stained with blood, tainted with Duskland shadows. It's like all my dreams have turned into nightmares."

"Like that Nocturne in the dungeons," she murmured.

I'd been in the dungeons exactly once—two days ago, when I spoke to Pierre. "What Nocturne?"

"It's a tradition in Dexter, a kind of rite of initiation." Lullaby hid her face behind a sweep of midnight hair. "The girls all take the newest legacy down to the dungeons—usually empty in Severine's rule because, well, why waste space on a criminal you can just disappear?—blindfold them, sing a creepy song, snuff out the torches, run away giggling, and leave them in the dark for a while."

"That sounds like hazing." Bewilderment and alarm beat

wings of shadow against my heart. "But it never happened to me."

"It did." Lullaby's face was unreadable. She sat heavily in the chair beside the bed. "Shortly after you got to Coeur d'Or. It wasn't my idea, but I agreed to it. They did it to me, when I first got to court. It was unpleasant, but afterward we all laughed and got wine-drunk. It might sound strange, but I thought you'd feel more at home if you had a common experience with the rest of the Dexter girls—a way to relate to us. You might feel like you belonged."

I sank onto the very edge of the bed, trepidation scratching at the scars along my arms. "But I have no memory of that."

She gave me a bald look. "We got you to the dungeon, and everyone—including you—was laughing and shoving and reveling in the pageantry of the thing. But when we snuffed out the lights and sang the song . . . Mirage, you just about lost your mind. Colors spilled out of you, like they did a moment ago, except none of us had seen anything like it before. It was terrifying. Like a nightmare come to life. And you were screaming, with your hands over your head. We dragged you upstairs, but afterward you were in a daze."

"And then?"

"Dexter closed ranks. You were an outsider—a Dusklander— and I was barely better. Nobody wanted to face consequences for a hazing gone sideways. And I didn't know what to do, so . . . so I asked Thibo to take the memory away. And the next day, you were fine."

A cinder of resentment caught fire and scorched me. "You took my memory away? Without my permission?"

"I did what I thought best. To guard your mind, I betrayed your trust. And I'm not sorry for it. You've been perfectly happy without the memory of a Nocturne that traumatized you."

"But—" Angry words spilled up my throat, but I forced myself to swallow them. That Nocturne was in the past, and it was easier to forgive what I couldn't remember. Lullaby was actually talking to me—that was more important than stirring up old grievances. "You mentioned a song. What song?"

Lullaby opened her primrose lips. It was a haunting melody—an elegy to sunlight, a paean to dusk, a madrigal for the wind at the edge of tomorrow.

Oubliette, oubliette,
Let me down so I may forget,
My hopes, my dreams; the things I regret,
I offer them up to the deathless quartet.
Oubliette, oubliette.

Colors burst out of me with a midnight slap of panic. Darkness pricked with moonlit crystals—dristic swords sheared sharp on diamond helms—crowns of kembric yawning wide as cities—thrones of ambric crumbling away into dust.

Lullaby's hand was a cool comfort against the back of my neck, rubbing soothing circles on my spine and humming her namesake. I shuddered, then clenched my fists and regained my self-control.

"That's exactly what happened last time," Lullaby muttered.

But her song had jangled something loose in my memory. I grabbed Severine's diary out of my pocket, thumbing through the slim volume until I found the line I was looking for:

. . . and so I wandered the Oubliettes, haunted like the halls of my memory.

"The Oubliettes," I whispered, half to myself. "That has to be where she hid the Relics. But where—*what*—are they?"

"What is that?" Lullaby was staring at the book.

"It's . . . Severine's personal journal."

Though I tried to read the emotion in Lullaby's turquoise

eyes, it was like looking into a pool of still water—all I saw was my own face staring back at me.

"You're reading the personal diary of a tyrannical and murdering empress *why*? To understand her better? To learn about your family? To ease your guilt for assassinating her?" Her eyes slashed over to my sister. *"Almost* assassinating."

I swallowed the uncomfortable sensation of being too clearly seen.

"To find the Relics of the Scion," I said. "The people don't yet see me as Sun Heir. But maybe—maybe if I can find my family's mythical Relics, then I'll be one step closer to earning the throne. One step closer to proving I'm the right person to succeed Severine, even if I am the Duskland Dauphine."

Lullaby narrowed her eyes. "What makes you think the things in Severine's diary are true?"

"I asked the same question." Disquiet raised the hair on my neck. "But it's her personal journal. Why would she lie if no one was ever supposed to read it?"

"Everyone thinks they're the hero of their own story, Mirage." I didn't like the ragged edge of Lullaby's smile. "And even those who like the bitter taste of murder know it is more easily swallowed with a dusting of sugar."

"It's the only lead we have." Eagerness knocked my ribs. "I want to investigate. I want to find the Oubliettes. Will you help me?"

"Now?"

I glanced at the clock. I was already late for another Congrès.

"Soon. If you're willing?"

I held my breath for her response.

Her face was like marble and her voice like an unforgiving sea. "We'll see."

SIXTEEN

That Nocturne, I dreamed of stony hallways.

Warm red sunlight spills through narrow windows, lighting my path. Through their illuminated panes, I glimpse perfect cities as I run, fly, *dance*. But there is only one city I wish to find. And here, here it is: glorious and shining, the city on the hill. I reach for it, but my hand strikes glass and the reverberation distorts my reflection until I'm looking at a stranger's face. A singing voice whispers echo-soft in the shadows.

Oubliette, oubliette.

Fear thrums through me. The prelude to a nightmare chills my skin. A frisson of dread makes me gasp suddenly frigid air.

I jolted awake. I wasn't in my bed.

Terror and confusion shook me. I stared around unfamiliar surroundings. After a blank, panicked minute, I recognized where I was—the dungeon alcove Sunder and I had stopped in two days ago, with its strange window to nowhere. The smooth-carved stone seeped chill through my bare feet and the echoes of long-forgotten voices seemed to hollow out my bones. Most of the torches had been snuffed out past Nocturne, but lingering smoke stuck in the back of my throat. My ambric Relic thudded like a second heartbeat against my chest, glowing.

I curled my hand around it and tried to calm my thready breathing. I peered out from the alcove. I heard the clomp of Belsyre boots, the murmur of living voices, the scrape of a metal plate being shoved into a cell.

I took a shuddering breath. This was not normal. This was not *good*. How in the Scion's hell did I get here? Even if I'd sleepwalked across half the palais, there were gardes every-where. Why hadn't anyone stopped me?

I closed my eyes. When I opened them, my reflection stared back at me, with empty shadow eyes above a glowing sun heart. I leaned closer to the pane of glass, tracing its edges with my finger. Behind the glass, I saw only darkness.

Scion, why was I here?

A surreal whisper of inevitability told me I'd been brought here.

But why? I turned in a circle, examining the walls, the ceiling, the floor—

My toes scuffed an indentation in the floor, caked with dust. I fell to my knees and scraped my fingers against a shallow hol-low full of ancient, hardened grime. After a few minutes of work, I'd cleared it enough to see a pinwheel shape. Disbelief flared like a firework in my chest, followed by a weird, calm hope. There was no possible way my Relic would fit, and yet—

If I was still dreaming, it would fit.

Part of me wasn't sure what was real. Part of me didn't want to know.

I inserted the Relic into the divot.

The floor groaned, creaked, and fell out from under me.

I fell through a blackness so absolute I almost thought I'd died. Then I struck solid ground, and pain made me sure I was alive.

Panic thrust hands under my shoulders and levered me into a seated position. My head screamed and my knees ached. I touched my hands to my face, just to make sure my eyes were open. They were. Fear seared my throat. What if I hit my head when I fell and now I was—

Get ahold of yourself.

But I had never experienced darkness like this before. It had a weight and a texture, like smothering velvet. I could taste its infinity: the sweep of shadow at the border of Dominion. It choked me. My hands trembled.

Words spilled into my mind, unbidden—the Scion's Vow. *I am the sun staring at the twilight. I am the solace that banishes blight. I am the moon shining deep in Midnight.*

I almost laughed. I was neither sun nor moon. And I was no one's solace.

Except, perhaps, my own.

What had dragged me out of the dusk toward the light? My legacy. What had gleamed bright as sunlight when I'd doubted my own power? My legacy. And what had driven me to overthrow the darkness lurking in the heart of the empire? My legacy.

I clenched my eyes shut, forcing my awareness inward to the well of colors churning always inside me. Imagining sunlight into the dusk was like trying to imagine hope into despair. I did it anyway.

Violet clouds draped over a livid sun.

Dusk-lit swords and sunlit armor.

Blood on mirror glass.

The bright shining heart of an ambric throne.

I screamed, and thrust my power outward. Blades of brilliance sheared away the black heart of Dominion and cut open the gemstone luster of daylight. The darkness fled, leaving me kneeling on a stone floor in an echoing passageway wreathed in shadow and draped in cobwebs. A damp tomb-chill ate into my flesh.

I stood, willing my heartbeat to slow and my knees to stop trembling. Radiance blurred along the corridor, illuminating the edges of things and casting others in darkness. Looming pillars— or were they petrified trees? Gargoyles whose faces changed as I neared—teeth elongating and eyes widening. Windows—a hundred windows of stained glass and quartz, staring at nothing and echoing my pale looming face. And at the end of the corridor, a door, its edges rounded and its face painted with an all-too-familiar image.

The glowing ambric face of the sun.

Even faded with time and covered in a layer of dust, the door shone magnificent. Crushed ambric was layered over tarnished kembric—a gilt-bright lamina sharpened upon lathes of glittering tesserae. The sun's corona—echoing the symbol at my breast—struck sparks in the dim and splashed me with warmth.

But there was no knob.

I pushed on the door. A pulse of energy jolted me to the elbow. I snatched my hand away, then put it back. Nothing happened. The door stayed resolutely shut.

Damn.

I stepped back from the door. Like I had in the alcove, I ran my eyes and hands over every inch of it, then beyond to the wall it sat in, looking for symbols or indentations or—

My fingers brushed against grooves scored into the wall at waist height. I leaned in, pushing my illusory luster closer to another sunburst. I unlooped my Relic and pushed it against the symbol, but the grooves were far too large. They were more the size of—

Hands.

I put my necklace back on and lifted my palms, joining my wrists and splaying my hands so my middle fingers pointed north and south. I pressed them into the wall.

The door sighed open. Twin pulses of excitement and fear scalded my veins. Beyond, I saw a glimmer of radiance, like sheer sunlight on a perfect city. I braced myself to go through, and lifted my hands from the wall.

The door snapped shut.

I frowned, and repeated my actions. I splayed my palms against the wall—the door opened. I lifted them away—the door closed. Frustration bloomed inside me, fierce and sudden. How was I supposed to go through the door if I had to stand here to hold it open?

I gritted my teeth, slapped the recalcitrant door, and retreated. The moment I gave up, exhaustion swept over me like a heavy blanket. The luminous colors painting the hallway dipped and darkened, and I quickened my steps.

I'd found something miraculous. Something spectacular. Something everyone else had forgotten about.

No—I hadn't *found* it. I gripped my ambric Relic, intuition breathing against my neck. I'd been *led* to it.

Severine's diary had called this place the Oubliettes, which meant a place of forgetting. But as I fit my pendant into the floor and rose back up into Coeur d'Or's dungeons, I thought perhaps it might be a place of finding. I just didn't know whether that would be a Relic, an Amber Throne, or the road map to the world I'd dreamed of, so long ago in the dusk.

SEVENTEEN

If I hadn't awakened to dust-black feet, smears of ancient dirt on my nightgown, and a ragged memory of sneaking invisible into Belsyre Wing, I would have thought the Oubliettes were just a dream. I clutched my ambric pendant and fought to separate the threads of unease and anticipation tangling within me. Part of me wanted to pretend I'd never even heard of the Oubliettes. Another part of me wanted to race back to the dungeons and slide into that impossible Midnight world once more.

Oleander took the decision out of my hands by pushing into my room without knocking, carrying an armful of clothing. She seemed surprised to see me in my bed.

"What are you doing here?"

"Sleeping is the most generally accepted activity," I snapped.

"I mean, don't you usually sleep in my brother's room?"

Rude. "What are *you* doing here, Oleander?"

"Putting these in your wardrobe." She waltzed into my dressing room. I slouched out of bed and followed, in time to see her hanging gowns with hems of thunderous blue and sleeves of roaring violet. All the colors of dusk, picked out in silk thread and staggering skill.

"Did you make all these?" Wonder lit my voice.

"Designed them." Her eyes skimmed a neckline for some invisible imperfection. "I had help with the sewing."

"You really didn't have to—"

"I didn't have anything else to do," she said, brusque. "Besides, these colors suit you much better than your little Sun Heir outfits. Dusk unveils the luster of your eyes."

A laugh escaped me. I didn't think Oleander had ever complimented me before.

"Thanks. Although my Congrès will be furious I'm not dressing the part."

"Compete with Gavin if you want." She made a complicated face. "But when it comes to looking like the Scion's light shines through you, he seems to have more practice."

"What if my dusk serves only to make his light shine brighter?"

"You'll just have to find your own light." She turned abruptly toward me with a revolted expression. "Why are you so dirty?"

"I found the Oubliettes." The words sounded absurd out loud.

"The Oubliettes are a myth. A tale told to frighten credulous young courtiers."

"I've only heard the song. Is there more to the story?"

Oleander sighed. "Hundreds of tides ago, when the Sabourins were provincial kings and the Amber Empire was barely an idea, a smaller château supposedly stood where Coeur d'Or now stands. A citadel, built to withstand siege rather than inspire awe. When the Sabourins gained enough wealth and power, they built a new palais. But instead of razing the old château, they covered it with dirt and rock and built directly on top of it. And the ghosts of Meridian's long-dead heirs haunt those forgotten halls."

"They're real," I said. "I found a door, in the dungeons, leading below the castle. There's a network of tunnels, I think, although I didn't go far—"

"You're serious." Oleander's eyes glittered with excitement. "An old château, lying beneath the new palais! I can't wait to throw a party down there, can you even imagine—"

"Severine's journal implies she hid Relics down there," I reminded her.

"Even better." Oleander's red mouth twisted into a shrewd smile. "So let's go look for Relics. You already have one. Find the others, and you'll be the true Sun Heir. They'll have to accept you as empress then—even Sainte Sauvage and his stupid Red Masks."

"My thoughts exactly."

"What are you waiting for? Get dressed."

I rolled my eyes, but obeyed. Then I remembered: "I told Lullaby I'd explore the Oubliettes with her."

She lifted an eyebrow. "So?"

"So—" Surely this wouldn't come as a surprise. "So Lullaby hates you."

"If people like you and me avoided everyone who hated us, we'd be hermits in the Dusklands." Oleander's eyes gleamed. "And just think how dull that would be."

Lullaby answered her door with a cautious look.

"I found the Oubliettes," I said, without preamble.

"I thought we were supposed to look for them together. Did you forget? Like you forget everything?"

Hurt and guilt writhed through me. "I found them by accident."

"Convenient." Her face was skeptical. She pointed a sharp chin at Oleander, who wasn't even pretending not to eavesdrop. "You're with her. What do you need me for?"

"I don't need you to come. But I do *want* you to come."

Lullaby hesitated a moment longer before grabbing her cloak and stalking off ahead of us.

"Lullaby may hate me," Oleander said to me in an undertone, "but I think she *loathes* you."

"Oleander?" I trotted to keep up with my willowy friend. "Shut up."

Oleander's footsteps echoed behind us as we made our way toward the dungeon. After some casual sneaking, we reached the stone alcove with the impossible window. I slipped the pendant from my neck and held the Relic over the divot in the stone. I lifted my eyes to the two girls—Oleander was aglow with barely contained excitement, but Lullaby still looked skeptical.

"Ready?" I lowered the Relic. "Brace yourselves."

This time, I was prepared for the sudden vertiginous rush of the granite dropping away beneath my feet. Torchlight blinked out as midnight descended. I looped a tight chain around the colors bursting like fireworks in my chest and forced radiance into the dark. The light was like tarnish on an ambric jewel, but it would have to do.

"Ow," Oleander said, before her eyes went wide.

Lullaby didn't say anything, just glided off the pedestal into the murk of the Oubliettes. She performed a slow pirouette.

"This," she breathed. "This is *amazing!*"

Oleander stepped after her, and I followed closely behind, my light pulsing raw against the carven walls. I shuddered at the chilling darkness. But neither Oleander nor Lullaby seemed to share my discontent. Oleander traced a finger along a crooked stone tree and murmured a verse of what I thought might be poetry; Lullaby pressed her face against an aquamarine windowpane as though it might be an impossible shard of sea glass.

I marched to the sunburst door, its reflective light more brilliant than my own ragged illusion. Both Oleander and Lullaby left their exploration and came to flank me.

"This is it?" Oleander looked unimpressed.

"Watch." I fit my hands against the grooves, like I'd done before. The door hissed open, yawning into more darkness. I lifted my hands. The door slid shut again. "I can't open the door and go through it at the same time."

"Let me try." Oleander fit her slender fingers along the grooves. Nothing happened.

"You're wearing gloves," Lullaby pointed out. "Maybe it only works with bare skin."

But even without her gloves, the door remained stubbornly shut. Oleander looked pointedly at Lullaby. Lullaby copied the motion. But her touch was as ineffective as Oleander's. Both girls looked at me.

"It only works . . . for me?"

"Scion save us from stupid Duskland gamines," Oleander drawled. She reached into the laces of her bodice, retrieving a glinting object. "Hold out your hand."

"What—?"

Oleander grabbed my arm. I tried to clench my fist, but she was too fast for me. A blade flashed—pain flared sharp along my forearm—blood burst hot down my wrist.

"Scion's teeth!" I growled, snatching my arm away and cradling it against my chest. "What was that for?"

"Rub the blood on your palms." Lullaby had clearly jumped to a realization before I had the chance. "And try the lock again?"

I stared from her to Oleander and back again.

"The door only responds to you, Mirage." Oleander was impatient. "If this place is truly linked to the Relics, then maybe your Sabourin blood is the key."

I gritted my teeth. She was right. I just wished I'd thought of it before she'd had a chance to slice my arm open. I smeared the sticky blood along my fingers, then slapped both palms onto the wall. Again, the door sighed open. This time, when I moved my hands, they stayed that way.

"Yes!" Oleander's eyes glowed eerie.

"Here." Quickly, Lullaby wrapped a length of cloth around my bleeding wrist—she'd ripped the hem of her dress.

"Thanks." I tried not to sound too surprised.

"Don't mention it," she grunted.

"Shall we?" Oleander prompted, stepping into the dark corridor beyond the sunburst door. Lullaby went after her.

"Will it stay open?" I looked at my blood glowing livid on the wall.

"How should I know?" Oleander flounced ahead. "It's not like we came here because we knew what we were getting ourselves into. Besides, if we're down here too long, someone will fetch us."

"No one else knows we're here," I reminded her.

Lullaby's mouth quirked nervously.

"Since when have you been afraid of anything, Mirage?" Oleander's voice echoed from the dusk swallowing her figure whole. "You may be rude, graceless, self-important, and annoyingly dim-witted, but I never took you for a coward."

I knew it was a dare. But she wasn't wrong. I squared my shoulders, clenched my bloody fists, and followed Oleander and Lullaby into the Oubliettes.

EIGHTEEN

Beyond the entrance, three passageways branched off into darkness.

"Let's go left," Oleander said.

"I prefer right," Lullaby protested.

"Um." I suddenly regretted bringing either girl. "Middle?"

We crept down the middle passageway in uncomfortable silence, red-tinged light following us like a curse. Past the sunburst doorway, the Oubliettes seemed less mystical and slightly more explicable—I could see how the dark stone and narrow passageways might once have been part of a fortress or citadel, meant to house soldats and withstand siege instead of soar over a city and dominate a horizon like Coeur d'Or. Still, it was hard not to jump and shudder at each twist and turn of the corridor— I kept expecting faceless ghosts and impossible monsters to leap out. But there was nothing but grim streaks of ancient mold and the sepulchral hush muffling our footsteps.

After a few minutes of silent walking, Oleander sighed, "I knew we should have taken the left passageway."

"Of course you did." Lullaby's voice held an edge.

"While I appreciate seeing the half-fish songstress grow sharper teeth," Oleander sneered, "you might want to reconsider whetting those fangs on me."

"Why?" Lullaby's eyes narrowed, glittering in the low light. "You've never given me such consideration."

"Haven't I?" Oleander asked, loftily. "You should be lucky I even know your name."

"Seriously?" Lullaby pointed an accusing finger at the tall blond girl, something she usually had too much self-control to do. I noticed her once-buffed nails were bitten nearly to the quick. "When I first came to court you hazed me like it was your Scion-given purpose."

"That doesn't sound like me."

Lullaby gave a high-pitched laugh. "So you don't remember cornering me with all your minions and dumping me into the Weeping Pools in a new ball gown I could barely afford? You shoved my head underwater to see how long the *blue girl* could hold her breath. I nearly drowned, and coughed blood for a week afterward."

"I thought you had gills." Oleander was expressionless. "And if you couldn't afford a wardrobe then you shouldn't have come to court."

"My mother is a baronne. She couldn't afford my gowns without the empress's favor my presence at court bought."

"So sad, your mother being poor. My mother is *dead*."

Both girls lapsed into a quivering silence. I held my breath.

"It wasn't anything personal," Oleander finally breathed. "The Amber Court has always been that way. You have to earn the position you never asked for. And if it helps, what I did to you was nothing compared to what I got when I arrived at Coeur d'Or."

Lullaby's eyebrows winged toward her hairline. "Who had the audacity to haze a Suicide Twin?"

"Everyone." Oleander toyed with a frayed finger on one of her gloves. "Our legacies were already notorious by the time we got to court. It became like a game for the older courtiers—how loud could you make *pain boy* scream? How close to *poison girl* could you get without losing a finger? An eye? Severine encouraged it, I think—she didn't like how beautiful we were. Or how dangerous. But none of that was as bad as what Gavin—"

Oleander broke off, realizing who she was talking to. She shot me a wary glance, and I remembered her words: *I loathe him with my whole heart, which he was determined to break, and if I ever set eyes on him again I might be tempted to kill him.*

"Tell me." I threaded a note of command into my voice.

"He's your cousin."

"You're my friend."

Oleander considered me a moment longer before lifting her lovely chin.

"Sunder and I were fifteen when we came to Coeur d'Or," she began. "Gavin was nineteen, and as a distant Sabourin cousin, one of Sinister's most popular courtiers."

I gave my head a little shake, and quickly did the math. The Suicide Twins were two tides older than me—nineteen themselves now. But that made Gavin . . . *twenty-three*? And his dynasty had been Sinister? I stumbled on a loose pebble, rocking off-balance.

"Like I said—the first few spans at court were misery," Oleander continued. "The hazing was unbearable. A legacy named Bender found out I was immune to most poisons. He held a knife to my throat and forced me to guzzle arsenic until my eyes bled. A girl named Ruin threw acid at my face and cackled with glee until she realized she'd just burned away my clothes while giving me the ability to shoot acid myself.

"Gavin was different. He'd laugh, sometimes, at these public humiliations, but he never participated. So when he started to *woo* me, I thought he must be kind. He wooed us both, in a way. He treated Sunder like a brother—something he'd always longed for but never had—and showed me every condescension. Fancy dinners, carriage rides through the lower city, his gallant companionship at parties and balls. He was handsome, and funny, and mature. I thought the fact that he never even tried to kiss me was because of my legacy. I thought I was in love with him, and when he told me he felt the same way I believed him."

She paused so long that I almost thought that was the end of the story.

"I married him. We snuck down to the Paper City, where he'd found a Scion priest who didn't care about the banns of marriage or the parental consent. I still remember the vows—*I am the solace to banish your blight.* But he was no solace. It turned out he was broke. Penniless. He'd discovered I was the wealthiest bachelorette in the Amber Empire and decided my unfortunate legacy made me an easy mark. Unlike most aristocratic weddings, a Scion-sanctioned marriage made us equals in everything. He planned to steal my fortune, then leave me. He told me five minutes after we left the chapel, and laughed when I cried."

Shock and horror struck me mute. Were we talking about the same Gavin?

"What happened then?" Lullaby's voice rang with a bare note of sympathy.

"I got lucky, I suppose." Oleander shrugged. "Two days after our farce of a wedding, the empress made her third attempt on Gavin's life. He fled back to Aifir and the marriage was eventually annulled. But—"

"But what?" I whispered.

Oleander's throat worked. "That was the first time Sunder worked for the empress. He volunteered to murder Gavin, to avenge my honor or some other male idiocy. It was how Severine found out how to manipulate us both into doing her ugliest deeds: by using our love for each other against us. And it was how I found out that the only thing that comes from love is pain."

A Duskland shadow coiled around my breaking heart and

breathed nightmares toward my fingertips. I clenched my eyes against the sudden push of images—

"Scion help us," Lullaby breathed, the melody of her voice burning off the fog in my head. "There's something down here after all."

NINETEEN

The passageway deposited us into a vast dark cavern. No— I had to keep reminding myself that although we were underground, these Oubliettes weren't caves. They were a château, buried and forgotten by time. With a little effort, I pushed my illusion outward, sending a ruddy dawn cascading toward the ceiling. Dust puffed around us as we stepped slowly into an elaborate ballroom or banqueting hall.

Once upon a time, this place would have been magnificent— although designed to be a fortress, I could nevertheless glimpse the hallmark Sabourin glamour that characterized Coeur d'Or. Reaching trees carved from black stone and veined with kembric took the place of pillars. A stained-glass ceiling arched high above. Ambric tiles beneath our feet ignited as we stepped on them, coiling in complicated spirals toward the center of the room, where a raised dais sat.

"This is where the throne would have stood," Oleander said.

I squinted around the vast hall. "Not to question your interior design aesthetics, but why the center of the room?"

She lifted her eyes from the dais to the ceiling above, and I did the same. Faceted ruby panes picked out the pattern of my family's sunburst emblem on the arching dome. But instead of being centered in the ceiling as I might expect, the sunburst rested nearly on the lip of the dome. And away from the emblem, the tiles grew darker—more opaque—until they disappeared into shadow on the opposite side.

"The sun would have streamed in through the sunburst like an oculus," I realized. "The bar of light would have been like liquid ambric, and it would have landed right on the dais.

But half the court would only have seen the back of the throne."

"None of the court would have been on the floor." Lullaby pointed above the glimmer-black pillars, where she'd noticed what I hadn't—platforms. Or were they tiers? "They would have been up there."

"Watching," said Oleander, a touch darkly.

Watching? I frowned, and pushed my illusions deeper into the shadows. As I stared at the tiers, I was suddenly reminded of Severine's brutal Gauntlet, where she pitted her legacies against one another—there had been stands of seats for her courtiers to spectate. It wasn't a long stretch to imagine this as a kind of *arena.*

Which had to mean—

"The Ordeals of the Sun Heir." My voice filled with wonder, and for a moment I could almost imagine my words echoing through space and time, an infinite reverberation of blood and history and *destiny.* "This is where they chose their next ruler."

"The Ordeals of *what?*" Lullaby asked.

While Oleander brushed dust off the dais, I filled them in on what Dowser had told me about Meridian's heirs.

"Exactly as I thought," Oleander interrupted, triumphant.

Lullaby and I both bent to look at what she'd found. An empty beveled groove scarred the stone platform, long and straight and narrow. It looked like—

"A sword?" Skepticism and excitement warred within me. "One of the other Relics?"

Lullaby ripped off the remaining hem of her dress and began clearing great swathes of grime from the dais. Oleander and I both joined in, until the massive stone platform was cleared. Lullaby was the first to look up, her expression elated.

"Mirage, I found where your Relic goes!"

I leaned close. Yes—I'd know that shape anywhere. I'd worn it on my chest since I was a child.

"I found something too," Oleander added, disappointment chasing excitement across her face. "What did you say Bastien's Relic was supposed to be?"

"A crown."

"This doesn't look much like a crown to me. At least, not a crown I've ever wanted to wear."

She was right—the shape was narrow and pointed, too small for a head. I glided my hands across the table until I found a fourth shape carved into the rock. My pulse leapt, then plummeted as my fingers explored the divot. It was nothing more than a plain circle—one half of a small sphere.

"Mine's just a circle." I looked at the other girls. "Could this be it? Four Relics for four heirs?"

"You said Dowser told you each of Meridian's children represented a quality." Oleander stared around the dais, eyes narrow. She pointed to the sword, then the sunburst. "The sword represented physical strength. The ambric sunburst was passions of the heart. If mine is, in fact, a crown, that stood for Bastien Sabourin's intellect."

"Hand, Heart, and Head," Lullaby said.

Oleander nodded. "Which leaves—"

"*Soul*," I supplied. "But Dowser didn't know what that was supposed to mean. It's just a circle. It could be anything."

"What does Severine have to say about it?"

"How should I know?"

"Please." Oleander rolled perfectly lined eyes. "If I'd found my evil sister's personal diary, I wouldn't let it out of my sight."

Reluctantly, I drew Severine's journal out of my pocket, clutching the slim volume between sweaty palms. Oleander snatched it out of my hands and flipped toward the middle, where I'd found the passage about the Oubliettes.

"Here—this is just after Seneca gives her his Relic as a gift." She read out loud. *"I have found their place, but they cannot stay. So I will keep them with me a little longer. Still, I am glad I finally found it. It reminds me why I must never play F's game—not because my life would be forfeit, but because I know S's would be."*

A chilly memory of a forgotten nightmare laddered my spine.

"You're right—she was here," I said, with a certainty I didn't understand. "She had two Relics—Seneca's after he gave it to her, and the one she had always had, as a Sabourin dauphine."

"What?" Oleander frowned. "That's not right—Sylvain had one as emperor. Seneca had one as Sun Heir. Why would Severine have a third?"

"Don't you see?" I gazed up at the sunburst blazing nothing but darkness into this world. "They've kept playing—fighting—whatever you want to call it. The Ordeals of the Sun Heir. My family has been doing this in secret for a thousand tides—an Ordeal for every generation."

The silence after my words was louder than my heartbeat.

"How do you know?" Lullaby asked.

"Think about it—the twisted lines of succession, all the mysterious deaths and banishments and scandals. They haven't been going by primogeniture or birthright—the Sabourin line is secretly decided by an archaic, half-mythic contest passed down for a thousand tides. Except—" A shadow of understanding lurked at the edge of my mind. "Except Severine didn't want to play. Because she knew Seneca wouldn't survive. So she tried to stop the Ordeals before they began."

"By stealing all four Relics before Sylvain had the chance to die and bequeath his Relic to one of your many half-blood siblings," Oleander added slowly. "But that's still only three Relics. What—and *where*—is the fourth?"

For an echoing moment, we all digested silence.

"What happens if you put your sunburst here, in this marking in the dais?" Lullaby asked

I hesitated. "What if I put my Relic in and can't take it out again?"

"Didn't you hear what Severine said?" Oleander ran her finger along a beveled groove. *"I have found their place, but they cannot stay.* Without an Ordeal, the Relics are probably useless."

"Or they're linked to these Oubliettes," Lullaby argued, "and their magic is stronger here."

The amulet had never done more than glow hot against my chest. But what if Lullaby was right—what if the Relic could interact with this impossible place, this secret arena of royal succession? A flush of anticipation burned my veins. I lifted the chain and set the ambric gem gently into the slot.

I waited for a few moments, but nothing happened. I released a disappointed breath and reached for the Relic. Lullaby caught me by the wrist.

"Wait!" The set of her mouth was urgent. Beside me, Oleander turned her head high on her elegant neck, as though scenting the air. I heard a distant sigh a moment later—a breeze through bare branches, or the prelude to a lover's touch. It grew louder and closer, gathering force as it came, and fear broke out in pinpricks across my skin. I braced myself, reaching for Lullaby's hand—

A gale roared into the chamber. I shielded my face, particles of dust biting into my arm like glass. The wind on my skin felt like the dusk at the edge of Dominion—dark as wine and thick as regret. I turned away, but the air swirled around my face and I smelled the sharp tang of winter—genévrier and frost, ice wine and chilly lips. Sensation thundered down on me—the memories of everything I'd ever desired.

Jewel-bright dreams and bitter-black power.

Hot kisses and cold promises.

Glow-dark thrones and diamond-hard death.

At last, the wind shifted away, leaving me gasping. An ache pounded in my chest—something between sorrow and denial. I opened my eyes to see Lullaby sitting up from where she'd lain on the floor; Oleander stared statuesque into the middle distance.

"I saw the ocean," Lullaby whispered, wistfulness turning her eyes to sea glass. "Or—I didn't so much see it as *feel* it, like a kind of sense memory, or . . ."

"We have been shown our hearts." Tears glittered in Oleander's eyes, bright as the diamonds in her hair.

"A prelude," I agreed. "A warning from the Heart Relic."

"Or, perhaps, a promise." Oleander leveled a lingering glance at Lullaby's shining face. "Although I hope neither of you will begrudge my innermost desires staying a secret."

She stepped to the dais, wedged the Relic out of its slot, and tossed me the pendant.

"Now, does anyone have any objections to getting out of this place? I think I need to wash my hair."

Lullaby trailed Oleander out of the Sun Heir arena. I followed a few steps behind, wondering at the sunburst ambric jewel nestled in my palm. I had always thought it next to useless, even after Sunder told me it was a Relic. But now I thought of how close I'd worn it to my chest—all the times I'd squeezed it between nervous hands—every wish, hope, and prayer I'd rained upon it.

The *Heart* Relic.

And I suddenly knew—this amulet had brought me home. This Relic had mined my heart for everything I'd ever wanted and used that metal to pave a road toward an impossible world. A world both more beautiful and more monstrous than the one I'd been raised in. A world where *I belonged*.

I swallowed those old words, that ancient desire. I hung the Relic back around my neck.

And as we crept through the winding passageways of a château forgotten by anyone but my ancient, bloodthirsty ancestors, I swore I saw their ghosts pass by. Antique armor and flowing tunics—a pastiche from a different era. A quartet of young men laughing in the halls, wine-drunk to hide their fear, but with eyes that spoke of grave intent. Boys screaming with agony, girls laughing with victory. And finally, I saw *her*. A slender maiden no older than me, with auburn hair and violet eyes. Her face was soft with concern and hard with determination—a sheer hint of madness at the edge of resolve.

It was the face of a girl who would sacrifice a thousand tides of tradition to save a brother she loved. Even if that meant murdering countless illegitimate half siblings.

After all, she had never met them. They were nothing but rivals—future enemies in a game not yet played. And he—he was her *heart*.

TWENTY

The moment we snuck back out of the dungeons, Lullaby and Oleander dispersed to their chambers to bathe and change. But my Sabourin blood pulsed a restless rhythm in my veins, and I couldn't bring myself to sink into perfumed waters, dress in a gown I'd bought with money I hadn't earned, and sit patiently in the Congrès while my advisors talked over my head about matters they believed I would never understand.

So I went to the only place where I could think, these days— Severine's chambers. And for the first time since I'd come to the palais, when I walked down the smooth hallway toward her rooms—curving like the inside of a shell—I didn't feel as though I was being lured into the lair of a monster, but like I was entering a sanctum.

A creeping sense of calm descended over me. The stillness rang like the moment after an echo fades—luminous with all the things I couldn't hear. I released my Relic and laid my palm gently on her slender throat, wrapping each of my fingers around her neck. Her skin was cool to the touch, and her pulse fluttered like the wings of an injured bird. And yet there was an unyielding quality to her form, as though she had been carved from something rarer than marble and stronger than dristic.

I squeezed, my hand tightening like a vise. Then I stepped away, my arm falling to my side.

"Who were you?" I asked her still, frail form. "Why did you do all the things you did?"

I imagined her bell-bright laugh pealing off the walls, her voice sliding silky into my head.

If you'd wanted to know that, little sister, you shouldn't have killed me.

But no. If I hadn't killed her, she would inevitably have killed me. Because in the end, the Relics were simply an excuse for the Sabourin dynasty to be where they'd always been—at one another's throats.

The door hissed open behind me. Dowser's pervasive scent of tabak smoke and fresh-brewed kachua was its own introduction.

"I thought I'd find you here." He loomed behind my shoulder. "You do know you're late for yet another Congrès?"

"I do. And I'm sorry. But I'm trying to sort through a mess of secrets my family's been keeping for a thousand tides."

His voice held anticipation. "Did you find what you were looking for? Did you find another Relic?"

"I'm not sure it's what I was looking for." I quickly filled Dowser in on everything we'd discovered underground. He whistled, took off his glasses, and began polishing them on the edge of his robe.

"Scion, I never knew," he admitted. "You must understand— Sylvain brought me on as a chevalier barely a tide after I graduated Unitas. And he only took me into his confidence a few months before his death—he'd grown concerned about Severine in the wake of her brother's untimely passing, and wanted my advice on her state of mind."

"Because you were her lover," I supplied, remembering Sunder's long-ago explanation of their relationship.

"Is that what you were told?" Dowser barked a laugh, and turned to sit on the edge of Severine's bed. The mattress sank beneath his weight, and Severine's hand shifted against the bedspread, opening like a flower. "I suppose that's what most people thought. It's always tempting to believe the most sordid explanation. But the truth is, I was Severine's friend. Perhaps her only friend. Although I'd joined the court in my capacity as spymaster, I was an outsider at Coeur d'Or. I was Zvar-born, Lirian-raised, and Amber-educated. I had traveled farther than Severine had dared to dream. And I didn't know enough of court politics to be anything but kind to her. Kindness without an agenda wasn't something Rina had ever experienced before."

Rina. Shards of mirror glass reflected the darkest corners of my heart back at me.

"What was she like, back then?" I choked out.

"She was a study in contrasts." Dowser's gaze grew wings, and flew where I could not follow. "She was stunning, like a portrait painted from someone's gilded imagination. And yet she was hard to look at, her face an exquisite nightmare because of all the things it hid. She could be soft, and unbelievably hard. Half the people who knew her admired her for her beauty, her fierceness, her inability to keep her mouth shut, her sheer determination. The other half loathed her for the same things. And those who admired her did so from a distance, because to get too close was to glimpse a shadow of the monster living inside us all."

I shuddered, and tried to look away from the empty shell breathing shallowly on the bed.

"She found her mask, after Seneca died," Dowser continued quietly. "I thought it was because murdering her greatest love tore away what goodness was left in her, leaving only that deceitful beauty behind. But now you tell me it wasn't her. It couldn't have been her—not if she was doing everything in her power to win the Ordeals of the Sun Heir before they even began. To prevent them from happening in order to protect her brother."

"What if the two aren't mutually exclusive?" I whispered. I opened Severine's diary to the last entry—*My last sister is free. And I am finally alone with my burden.* "She was willing to kill countless half siblings to ensure there would be no one else to compete in the Ordeals. What if she thought the best way to save Seneca from this cruel world was to—to ease his way out of it?"

"No." Dowser frowned at the words, as though they triggered a memory. "Severine was intense before Seneca's death, but she only became mad after. Sylvain grew afraid for himself, and for his other children—for *you*. He commanded me to spirit you away to the Dusklands *with* his ambric Relic. No—someone found out what she was doing. Someone warned the emperor. Someone else killed Seneca."

My hand clenched around the sunburst Relic. "Who?"

"I don't know." Dowser looked up at me. "Scion, I wish she had taken me into her confidence. Then—or anytime in the seventeen tides I served her. I wish she had told me what she was trying to do, and why she was trying to do it."

"Would that have made her actions redeemable?"

"No," Dowser said. "But perhaps, instead of condemning her to death, I could have found a way to forgive her."

I looked away to hide the tears springing suddenly to my eyes. I had dreamed a thousand different ways Severine's and my story might have ended. I dreamed of both of us flying far above a bloody plain toward Dominion, and dying among the stars. I dreamed of two swords dissolving into diamond dust as we embraced like sisters in the bosom of dusk. I dreamed of killing her, again and again and again.

But I had never dreamed of forgiving her.

TWENTY-ONE

T he next day, I waylaid Gavin just past the palais gate leading out into Jardinier.

The Nocturne before, I hadn't been able to think of
anything besides the Oubliettes, the Relics, and the Ordeals
of the Sun Heir. And when obsessing over Sun Heirs past and
present inevitably led me to thinking about Gavin, I realized
that despite our handful of encounters, I didn't really know my
cousin. He'd given me little reason to doubt his demeanor of
bright humor and cheerful grace. But when I considered
Oleander's damning narrative about the duplicitous boy who
schemed to marry her only to steal her fortune, it was hard not
to wonder whether Gavin might be hiding a side of himself he
didn't want anyone to see. Least of all me.

I had a mind to discover his secrets.

His face betrayed surprise when he saw me waiting for him
on horseback, Calvet and Karine astride their own steeds behind
me. I sat a little straighter in my new split-skirt riding habit—
midnight-blue velvet trimmed in violet satin ribbons, with smart
suede boots and a jaunty hat to match.

It seemed boring Oleander half to death had its advantages.

"I see my lesson stuck!" He laughed, recovering himself.
"Ready for another session?"

"As long as this one doesn't include a ruined dress."

He had the grace to look abashed. "I am sorry about that."

I forced a small smile. "Will you ride into the city with me
today?"

"Really?" His grin slipped away. "Haven't you recently survived several assassination attempts? Are you sure it's safe?"

"Would you have me hide away like a criminal?" I made my voice bland. "Besides, it inspired me to see you ride among the people the other day. Your proximity seems to have earned you their love."

Discomfort soured Gavin's expression.

"Anyway, I'm well guarded." I gestured to my two wolves, then glanced meaningfully at the half dozen Husterri riding at his back.

"All right," he said. "But can we wait a minute? I hope you don't mind—I was supposed to be meeting someone else."

A moment later, Luca came bounding up the sloping avenue, with his shirt buttoned all the way to his throat and pomade in his dark curls. It was my turn to frown. Gavin leaned down from his horse to clasp forearms with my friend, who didn't bother to so much as greet me.

"Well met, sir!"

"And you." Eagerness leapt in Luca's eyes. "Did you bring her?"

"I did." Gavin laughed, and gestured toward his entourage, where one of the Husterri led a spare horse. Luca leapt toward the mare, exclaiming as he ran his hands down her slender legs and patted her gleaming rump.

He whistled. "May I?"

"That's why she's here."

Luca swung up on the steed. The pair performed a complicated set of maneuvers before trotting over to where Gavin and I waited.

"I haven't sat astride an Alomar in years." Luca was breathless with glee. "She's perfect."

"Lady Mirage just invited me to ride with her into the city." Gavin looked torn. "Any objections to postponing our planned jaunt?"

"Only so long as Syl—*Lady Mirage*—has no objections to my joining." Luca looked like he wanted to laugh.

"None." I did, in fact, have several objections. I'd wanted to use this meeting to unearth Gavin's true self behind that laughing, sunlit façade. I supposed I would just have to try to do that *around* Luca. "Shall we?"

We clattered down through the Échelles, the boys easily chatting about horses while I sat wooden on my pony and tried not to fall off. Mercifully, the cobbles flattened out near the Mews, the avenues narrowing. Ambers crowded around us, and I heard both *Sun Heir* and *Duskland Dauphine* whispered in our wake. A few sun-moon banners hung tattered from ambric lampposts and doorframes, but they just made me think of Red Masks. I tightened my legs in the saddle, and my horse shied forward.

"Dauphine." Calvet caught at my mare's bridle. The hard set of his mouth hid his dimples. "Are you sure this is safe?"

"I'm fine," I ground out. "They won't attack me while I'm with *him*."

Calvet nodded and fell back, but I knew he didn't believe me. I wasn't sure I believed me either.

I saw Gavin toss a kembric livre to a child reaching for his stirrup. Behind him, his Husterri also began handing out money. No—they weren't *giving* it away. The riders bent down and exchanged words with the civilians before passing out coins. What were they saying? Casually, I reined in my horse, falling back to eavesdrop. The murmured exchanges came to me fractured, at first, before bursting in my ears with intolerable familiarity.

"Have you invited the Scion's light to banish the dusk?" the Husterri were asking.

Some shook their heads. When they did, the Husterri moved on. But some passed their hands in front of their eyes, whispering:

"I see his light beyond my eyes."

To them, the Husterri handed out coins.

Acid boiled in my gut. They were paying people to utter the Scion's Vow? It had been nearly a tide since I'd left Mother Celeste's Temple, but I'd spent my entire childhood there, and this—this felt like *sacrilege*. My mare sensed my tension and sallied beneath me. I shoved her forward, pushing between Gavin's and Luca's mounts. Luca frowned at me, but I glared at him. He fell back to ride beside Calvet and Karine.

"Your Husterri," I said to Gavin, as casually as I could manage. "I couldn't help but hear them asking the Scion's Vow to passersby."

"You know it?" Gavin seemed surprised. "Then you've banished the dusk as well?"

If I ever did, it had returned with a vengeance. "Not exactly. I was raised by the Sisters of the Scion as an orphan in the Dusklands."

"In a Temple?" Something beatific passed across Gavin's face. "How lucky you are, to have grown up in the light."

"It was the Dusklands." I'd grown up in cold and silence; I'd grown up unloved and misunderstood and miserable. "There wasn't much light to speak of."

I could tell Gavin wasn't convinced.

"The Scion's Vow," I repeated. "Are your men paying people to pledge their faith? Isn't it against your religion to force conversions?"

"*Force* conversions?" He looked affronted. "I would never. We're just doling out a bit of the Scion's charity."

My heart thudded. "You're only giving money to those who respond with the Vow."

"Charity is a funny thing." Gavin shrugged. "Not everyone deserves it. I've given beggars coin only to see them immediately buy liquor or joie with it. Not only was my money wasted, but it only made the tramp's life worse. Asking for the Scion's Vow gives me peace of mind—it assures me my charity helps those who already stand in the Scion's light."

"Not everyone who worships the Scion is without sin," I snarled. "And not all atheists are amoral."

"I can only judge virtue as I see it, cousin." Gavin turned to me with a genuine smile, all warmth and daylight promises. "My worldview may seem too simplistic to you, but I cannot apologize for it. It's all I have to guide me."

My heart thawed, bathed in his certainty. He was so *sure*. Sure of his world. Sure of his place in it. Sure of what made people good, and willing to stand behind that. And I—I *envied* him for it. I hadn't been so certain of anything since the moment I spilled my own kinsblood with a shard of glass and stole an empire I didn't deserve.

Severine's voice echoed in my ears, magnified by a room full of mirrors. *No one deserves anything. The only things worth having are the things you take.*

"Do you think," I asked, half to myself. "Do you think our family deserves that palais? This city? This *empire*?"

"Of course." He sounded shocked.

"Why?"

"Because of our blood," he said immediately. "We've been Sun Heirs for a thousand tides, and we earned the right to rule from Meridian himself. The Scion has favored our family with his perfect light."

"But neither of us has ever *done* anything to earn it."

"We shouldn't have to earn what we were born to," Gavin argued. "Isn't that the definition of legacy? We earn it simply by shouldering our inheritance—the responsibility to something greater than ourselves."

His words thudded toward the base of my skull with a wrongness I didn't have words for. Out of the corner of my eye, I saw Luca listening to our conversation with a strange look on his face. He caught me looking, and flashed me an unsettled smile.

He sounds like you, Luca mouthed, behind Gavin's back.

I expected his words to spark outrage. Instead, I just felt sad. I knew what Luca was referring to—the defining moment of our relationship, when I chose Coeur d'Or over him. He'd offered me everything he had to offer—friendship, love, a world of hard work and harder laughter—but I'd turned him down. I'd turned him down because I'd been so sure of my own exceptionalism. I'd been so sure my bloodline defined me. I'd been so sure I was *owed* something, just by being born.

What had he said? I struggled to remember. *Our blood is nothing without the will that moves it.*

". . . why Papa chose these colors," Gavin was saying. I tuned back in, feeling flustered. "To remind ourselves—and by extension, the world—of where we came from. It's rare, in Aifir, to insist on household colors, but Papa knew we shouldn't compromise on our image."

Shadows crept toward my heart.

"Your image as Sun Heir?" I said sweetly. "But your line has not inherited for what, two hundred tides?"

"The Sabourin succession has not historically been a straight line," he replied equably. "And honestly, Mirage, it's something you might want to consider."

"Beg pardon?"

"I just mean . . ." He gestured at my shadow-blue riding habit.

"What about it?" I snarled.

"You're the Sun Heir, Mirage." He glanced at the Relic around my neck. "Don't you think these dusky colors you wear are disrespectful to the destiny you've assumed?"

I stiffened. My hands tightened on the reins. My mare abruptly reared, tossing her head and lifting onto her hind legs. Panic shoved me forward. I grabbed at her mane and the pommel of the saddle. My thighs throttled her flanks. There was shouting—hands grabbed at her bridle, my reins. Finally, she settled—Luca stood at her head, whispering words I didn't understand into her flaring nostrils. I took a shuddering breath, and moved to slide off her heaving back.

"Don't." Gavin put a gentling hand on the horse's neck. "If you get off, you'll never ride another horse again. Don't let the fear conquer you."

I swallowed jags of terror, and slowly nodded. I gathered the reins in my hand and tried not to think about the distance to the ground.

"D'Ars." Hoofbeats rang up sharp behind us. "I've been looking everywhere for you."

It was Gavin's godfather—the middle-aged gentleman with greying black hair and a face like hewn granite. He wore the colors associated with Gavin's household, in an expensive-looking red duster with gleaming kembric buttons.

"Arsenault! You remember Lady Mirage, and this is her friend—"

"I remember," the man said, brusque. "Apologies, lady, but I'm afraid the duc has business to attend to."

Gavin frowned. "Félix, honestly. I told you to clear my Prime—"

"It's an urgent message from Varek Piers, Gavin."

"Oh. I see." Gavin bowed over my hand, all good humor and grace once more. "Please excuse us, Mirage. I hope you won't hold the interruption against me."

"Please!" I demurred. "Is everything all right?"

"Perfectly." Gavin flashed an easy grin. "Much as I wish my

steward could handle my Aifiri estates in my absence, it never seems to be the case."

He cut a bow over his horse's withers, then cantered off toward Jardinier with his godfather and his Husterri. Luca kicked his horse after Gavin. I caught his eye and glared. He wheeled with a sheepish shrug.

"Sorry!" he called. "But the horse belongs to him."

Leaving me alone with my wolves in a city that loathed me for what I could never be. We rode quickly back up to the palais, Calvet and Karine flanking me with hands on sword hilts. But if any pointed Red Masks stared death at my back from alleyways and dark corners, I was too busy being furious to notice.

Gavin and his godfather might think me a Duskland gamine playing at dauphine, but three spans at court and weeks of near-interminable Congrès meetings had taught me a thing or two about paying attention. And I'd just discovered two very interesting facts.

One—the gentleman in the red coat was Félix Arsenault, one of the men Gavin had said rounded out the wicked quartet that included both our fathers when they were young.

And two—Gavin was lying to me.

I happened to know Varek Piers was an Aifiri high commander. He oversaw most of the ground troops deployed along the Aifir border with Lirias, and commanded several outposts along the southern edge of the Meridian Desert.

There was no chance in the daylight world General Piers was the steward for Gavin's estate. Which meant my cousin didn't want me to know that the only other legitimate Sun Heir was friendly with an Aifiri high commander.

TWENTY-TWO

My conversation with Gavin about light and darkness, charity and sin swirled in my chest. My fingers curled into fists. But by the time we'd ridden back up to the palais, I'd had an idea. I'd had *several* ideas.

I thought of Gavin's sun-bright laughter as he lied through his teeth. My twilight gowns concealing my fear of the dark. Every convenient lie I'd ever told myself like a mask I could interchange with my own face.

"Do you know where I might find Oleander de Vere at this hour?" I asked Calvet as he helped me down from my horse. "I need to speak with her."

"I'm afraid not, dauphine." Calvet brandished his dimples and took the mare's reins. Both my wolves had relaxed once we were safely ensconced beyond the palais walls, and it wasn't hard to see why—the stables neighbored a barracks crawling with fellow Loup-Garou, both on and off duty. "It's my job to know your schedule, not Lady Oleander's. But *he* might know."

He pointed across the courtyard before leading my horse away.

Sunder's uniform strode dark through bars of honeyed light. He was barking orders I couldn't make out to a platoon of Belsyre wolves marching behind him. He looked savagely handsome. My heart beat sudden sharp pinions against the inside of my chest.

I smoothed the front of my twilight dress, and strode across the courtyard toward him.

He caught sight of me and turned, sunlight etching his profile and striking green sparks off his signat. For a moment, his eyes looked like glass, reflecting my own careful elation back at me.

A charge passed between us, too dull for pain but too sharp for pleasure.

The glass broke. Sunder's expression shattered with it, vicious fear warping his mouth into a shout—

I heard the whisper of the blade a moment before its edge found my flesh. Agony sliced through the bodice of my dress and buried teeth into my ribs.

A scream shredded my throat, and I lurched backward. Pain blurred my vision, scraping my surroundings clean of meaning. A figure launched itself at me again. Instinct shoved me to the side, but I wasn't fast enough. They slammed into my hip, rattling my teeth and knocking me off-balance. My knees met cobbles. Weight bore me down. My skull jarred against cobbles and warmth burst over my earlobe.

The edge of a dristic blade scraped the skin of my arm and sent panic shredding my veins. I kicked out as hard as I could.

My heel connected with flesh and I heard a grunt. I thrust myself off the ground and drove my shoulder into the figure's torso. She cried out. Her blade clattered to the floor. I pushed harder, grappling for her throat as she clawed at my face.

A storm of black slammed down around us, and then she was gone. I fell to my knees, reeling. Exertion shaved my breath. I pressed a trembling hand to my heaving chest. My blood surged, then dropped away, leaving my veins chilly and my heart weightless. I fought for consciousness as the edges of my vision curled like burnt paper.

When I finally looked up, I knew I'd lost moments. Amid the thunderous crush of wolves—circling me, gently propping me up, securing the perimeter—I saw Sunder. He stood above the limp and broken body of a young woman, staring down. Her slender neck bent at an almost comical angle and her bright red hair mingled with the scarlet pool spreading beneath her. Sunder pressed an absent hand against the side of his midnight uniform. His gloves were slick with blood.

"Sunder," I choked out.

He turned, and for a moment his face looked like a skull, bare of flesh and empty of mercy. Then his eyes focused on me and his mouth went soft and he dropped to his knees beside me.

"You're hurt." He wrapped gloved hands around my jaw and gently turned my head to look at the wound behind my ear. Even through the stained leather I could feel his legacy spiking—his touch dragged at my nerves and tightened the skin of my face. I recoiled from his grasp.

"I'm fine." I pressed a hand to my ribs, where the blade had shredded my gown and caught on the bones of my corset. My hand came away red. My vision blurred. "You killed the Red Mask."

"She came here to die." In one smooth motion, Sunder slid his arms behind my neck and knees, lifting me like I weighed nothing. My head lolled against his coat, my hair catching on the polished buttons. I managed a grunt of protest.

"I have legs."

"Yes, I'm fond of them." He gripped me tight and stalked toward the palais. "I'm even fonder of all your blood staying inside your body."

"Apparently not everyone shares that opinion." I gasped a harsh laugh. Images tumbled through my head like leaves tossed on a high wind—red swords and scarlet masks, ambric timbres and pain-bright eyes. "What do you mean, she came here to die?"

"If she tried to kill you anywhere else, she wouldn't have gotten within three feet of you—me or Calvet or whoever was guarding you would have stopped her. But here? Where a hundred soldats swarm like ants? We were secure enough to be complacent. To take our eyes off you just long enough—" His hesitation vibrated with guilt. "But even had she succeeded, she never would've made it out alive. That was never part of the plan."

I couldn't read the contours of his voice, and his face was much too far away. "I don't understand."

"She cared less about her own life than ending yours. The Red Masks are escalating."

My head throbbed. I let my eyes flutter shut. "Then maybe it's time to deal with them once and for all."

TWENTY-THREE

The Matin of Pierre LaRoche's trial blew in like one of Midnight's mad winds.

The air smelled like chalk and red sky and all the things we might someday lose. Palais artificers had erected a raised pavilion beside Coeur d'Or's gates. Its silken drapes fluttered wildly in the breeze, like the wings of a great golden beast, and a strange part of me hoped it would fly away. Fly away and carry me back to the dusk—fly me away to the Midnight of my nightmares. But no matter how much the fabric flapped and cracked in the wind, the pavilion stayed where it was, lined with chairs for my advisors and a dais for one young, lonely prisoner.

"Feeling better?"

Sunder's low voice jolted me out of my reverie. I barely remembered the hours after the attempt on my life—I'd ebbed in and out of consciousness as friends and advisors and healers flickered around me. In addition to the cut on my ribs, I'd been concussed—Vida had done her best to undo the damage, but my head still swam when I turned too quickly.

"Yes." I stepped away from the window and looked up into Sunder's dristic-ringed eyes. He'd been silent and distant since the attack—I'd barely seen him for days. If he felt guilty for killing the assassin, he hadn't shown it. Perhaps with so much pain and death already on his hands, one more life didn't make a difference to him. "Where have you been?"

"Hunting Red Masks."

My pulse vaulted. "Any luck?"

He looked out the window, past the elaborate pavilion and the ornate gate to the sweeping boulevard of the Concordat.

Ambers were already arriving, streaming up from the lower city like ants. Black-coated wolves stood guard at intervals, stark against the golden cobbles and golden gate and golden pennants. He shook his head.

"You should know," he muttered, "my wolves have been hearing rumblings. In the Paper City, in the Mews—even along Rue de la Soie. The people are not happy about this trial—no one wants to see a boy of fourteen tides executed in public. Quartiers of the city where Sainte Sauvage has a stronger foothold are especially volatile. Last Nocturne, a number of my soldats reported seeing Red Masks running through the streets, cutting your Proclamation of Justice with red-dyed swords."

"That's not too bad."

"And then they burned you in effigy."

"Oh."

"They're going to try to kill you again. I feel it." Sunder pressed a palm briefly to his side, then turned to face me. His eyes were dark with the anticipation of violence. "That last attack showed me how ruthless they've become. There's nothing stopping them from taking another shot—especially today, when you're in plain sight, in front of half the city, about to execute a boy assassin."

"I don't want to execute him." I *didn't*. But I hadn't wanted to torture him either.

I clenched sweaty palms and tried to ignore the specter of all the things I'd done wrong. All the things I hadn't been able to do.

Sunder's hands lifted toward my shoulders, then fisted to his sides. His need to touch me filled the space between us with palpable weight. "I'm usually the last person in the world to preach mercy for mercy's sake, but if there was ever a time to show clemency, that time is now. His pardon might earn you grace with your people—enough grace to get you to Ecstatica with a head to be crowned."

"He tried to kill me." My voice came out hoarse. The memory of my head bouncing off cobblestones mingled with memories of red swords and broken mirrors and blood. Always *blood*.

"And for that crime I'd kill him myself," Sunder promised. "But there's a bigger picture here."

"If I pardon him out of hand, won't they see me as weak?"

"They will see a future empress pardoning her assassin, and they will know you are fearless."

"But I'd be doing it out of fear."

"Sometimes fear can be a weapon." Quickly, almost helplessly, he brushed an errant curl off my face—his gloved hand skimming my cheek and curling around my ear. Below, a bugle bellowed out from the pavilion, a trio of notes that sounded more like a warning than a summoning. Sunder's hand dropped, his touch gone before I could learn to miss it. "And none of this is worth it if you're dead, demoiselle."

Sudden nerves pummeled my heart. "Will you be there?"

"I'll be as close to you as you'll let me." His smile faded away like a dream. "Look for me on the platform—I'll be with the Loup-Garou guarding LaRoche. If anything happens—well, they'll have to get through me before they can touch you."

He marched away, his spine straight in his Belsyre regalia.

I shivered, racked with too many doubts to count. I hadn't been able to banish Gavin's careless words from our ride into the city: *We earn our place simply by shouldering our inheritance—the responsibility to something greater than ourselves.*

I'd once felt the same way. But that belief had cost me too much. And in the aftermath of the pain, violence, and chaos my entitled actions had caused, I'd finally begun to realize—no one was born deserving anything. *I* hadn't been born deserving anything. Not a place to belong, not the love of a people, and certainly not a throne.

Those were all things that had to be earned.

I looked down at the Ambers gathering along the Concordat. They didn't know who I was, or what I stood for, or what was going to happen next. And unlike me, Sainte Sauvage had given them something to believe in—a vision of a Sun Heir I'd never be able to embody. A Sun Heir who looked a lot like Gavin d'Ars.

But I didn't care what I looked like. I wanted them to put their faith in *me*.

Whether as Duskland Dauphine or Sun Heir, I wanted to earn their love. And maybe I did that by showing them a little of the world I'd dreamed, so long ago in the dusk.

I walked up the steps of the covered platform feeling like I was going to my own execution.

The moment my slippers hit the deck, the crowd quieted. I took a deep breath and smoothed down the front of my gown. I'd chosen to wear the same dress I'd worn that day in the Marché Cuirasse, with a brilliant bodice falling away to a creamy skirt studded in kembric embroidery and ambric gems. Not all of these people would have been there that day—probably only a handful—and many would never have seen me before at all. But it couldn't hurt to remind them that even if they didn't see me as the Sun Heir, I was still a Sabourin.

My one concession to my sobriquet—the *Duskland Dauphine*—was a velvet cape dyed in twilight colors. It whipped around my shoulders in the stiff breeze, flashing smears of amethyst and sapphire at the waiting crowd. I turned my back on them, scanning the rear of the platform, where my advisors and friends sat stiff in painted chairs: Oleander and a rigid-faced Lullaby; Barthet and Lady Marta in hurried conversation; Gavin, golden-faced and smiling with an unreadable Arsenault at his shoulder; and Dowser. My teacher stood when I approached, reaching from his long sleeves to grasp my hands.

"Do you remember what we agreed?" We'd spent hours yesterday practicing my address to the crowd, what I would say to Pierre LaRoche. This was only my second time appearing before a large crowd of Ambers, and the first time I'd been nothing more than a momentary diversion—Severine's captive legacy. "They don't want to be convinced of Pierre's guilt. They want to be convinced of your capacity to judge him."

I released Dowser's hands and stepped to the edge of the platform. I was ready.

"Good citizens of the Amber Empire," I called, casting a simple illusion that carried my voice along the sloping boulevard of the Concordat. I could have used an ambric artifice to magnify my voice, but I liked the way the people near the back of the crowd started, as though I was standing just behind their shoulders. And if my voice sounded a little distorted—a little *dusky*—well, what was the harm in that? "Today you bear witness to something I take seriously as I move toward the day of my coronation—justice. My predecessor, Severine, cared little for these niceties—if your local magistrates couldn't resolve your disputes, then you were either ignored or disappeared in the Nocturne by merciless Skyclad soldiers."

The crowd grumbled like thunder, and I raised my voice.

"But that ends today! I hear your discontent with this city's current circumstances—Belsyre's wolves patrolling the streets, strict curfews, soldiers at the city gates. But the wolves are there to hunt Red Masks. Your curfews are to protect your safety. The soldats at the city gates keep out mercenaries and thieves who would loot your homes and businesses. And know this—even as we speak, I am drawing up plans to expand the role of magistrates in the lower city, to train a civil police force, and to institute a series of appeals courts for your legal issues. By Ecstatica, this city will return to its former glory, rule of law intact. I hold this public trial today to show you I have nothing to hide!"

"Then why've you been hiding up in that palais like a murderess?" someone shouted.

"Duskland monster!" screamed someone else.

The crowd roared.

I clenched my hands, but my palms slipped, slick with sudden sweat.

"The true monster calls himself Sainte Sauvage!" I cried out, my voice hoarse over the sound. I scanned the crowd, and wasn't surprised to see slivers of red hidden beneath coats or tucked into pockets. "And you have seen the *Red Masks* who serve him. Twice in the past span, I have been attacked. Both attempts left me with nothing more than injuries, but I am not the only one who has been targeted. Perhaps you have tasted their harsh judgment for nonbelief in the Scion—extremist graffiti painted on your doors, warehouses set to blaze, children stolen from nurseries, innocent women taken as hostages. Imperial decrees burned to ash because they believe they are above the law. Fanaticism cares nothing for justice—it injures the innocent just as readily as the guilty."

My words rippled through the crowd. Creeping anger dawned on unforgiving faces. I pressed my advantage.

"It is they who perpetrated this crime. They who infiltrated your city and my palais and put poisonous ideas among you. They who seduced and tantalized a boy too young to shave with ideas too big for him to fathom."

I gestured to the platoon of Belsyre wolves standing at the edge of the platform. They lurched Pierre LaRoche onto the dais. Bound and gagged, he looked worse than he had when I'd seen him in the dungeons. His lank hair was twice as greasy, matted with dried blood. The small cuts and bruises had crusted over and grown into discolored continents visible beneath his dirty clothes. I cringed, regret screaming through me—this was not the face I wanted to show to the citizens of the Amber City. Why hadn't I asked about his condition?

The crowd heaved at the sight of him, shouting indistinct, restless curses at the pavilion. Someone threw a piece of rotten fruit—it landed a few feet from where I stood, splatting red and black viscera onto the hem of my dress. I stepped back, fighting against the flood of violent images at the edge of my mind. Control slid like water between my fingers. I glanced over my shoulder, and the mute disapproval of my advisors and friends seemed nearly as loud as that of the muttering crowd. Dowser moved a hand over his forehead, and Gavin looked shocked. Only Sunder looked at me instead of the boy—when his icy gaze caught mine he nodded, minutely.

Ice might be slick to the touch, but right now it was the only thing solid beneath my feet.

"Unbind him," I ground out to the quartet of Loup-Garou hauling him onto the stand. They looked surprised, and one threw a questioning glance at Sunder, but they did as I asked, cutting the rope around his wrists and untying his gag. The boy rubbed his wrists and flexed his jaw, staring quickly around the pavilion. I noticed him mark each garde, each possible escape. But there was nowhere for him to run.

"Hello, Pierre," I said.

"Heretic usurper," he hissed between broken teeth. "The Scion's sword will cut out your tongue and feed it to the dusk."

The crowd went quiet. I turned toward them, slowly, hiding my churn of emotions. Pierre's gardes had informed me that the boy had been aggressively mute since the last time I'd visited him, saying nothing under questioning. I'd expected stoicism, not vocal fanaticism. But what if this new Pierre could work in my favor?

"He curses with the voice of a bitter man of forty, although he is but fourteen!" I called. "Would any of you parents out there let your children speak so to a dauphine, even one born in the dusk?"

I didn't hear a consensus among the cacophony, so I plunged onward.

"What was left of this boy's childhood was cut away by Sainte Sauvage, just as readily as his future was. He was preyed upon by radicals, his grief and loneliness and hardship taken advantage of by those who care for nothing but the harsh, bright light of an unforgiving Scion!" I walked over to Pierre, grabbing his wrists and lofting his hands to the sky. He hissed at my touch and tried to break away, but I went on. "These hands, twisted to violence. This head, exploited by tempting lies. This heart, pulsing with treachery. And his soul—stripped of kindness or empathy and filled only with hate!"

The blood pounding in my ears drowned out any sound the crowd made. Pierre looked at me with such loathing I nearly shrank away from him.

"Pierre LaRoche," I managed. "Did you attack me in the street with intent to assassinate me?"

"Yes," he snarled. "And since you have freed my hands, Dominion demon, I will try again."

TWENTY-FOUR

He launched himself off his stand with startling speed, catching me full in the chest and bearing me to the ground. We hit the boards with a thud, his weight knocking the breath out of my lungs. I gasped at nothing, struggling to make sense of the swirl of light and color blanking my vision. Sound roared in my ears. Fingers scrabbled at my neck. Pain ricocheted from my throat toward the back of my head. Something gave way—whether it was my skin or the fabric of my dress, I didn't know. I struggled against the disorienting blur of motion, flinging my arms out and releasing a hurricane of color with them.

Gasp

I could breathe again.

Gasp

I was weightless without LaRoche upon me.

Gasp

I staggered upright, spooling the mad burst of illusions back toward my center and shaking my head to clear my vision. Sunder clenched a struggling Pierre against his chest, one arm tight around the boy's throat while his other hand ratcheted his elbow into his back.

I brought my hand to my throat, where a hot thread of blood trickled along my clavicle. The stays of my gown had split—the kembric bodice gaped obscene, exposing my corset. A vile burst of fury sent heat raging through my veins and nearly unleashed my illusions again.

Not yet.

I stood shakily. The crowd was wild, seething toward the

platform against a barrier of Loup-Garou. Whether they wanted to help me or Pierre, I didn't know.

"He declares himself traitor in actions as well as words," I rasped. I cleared my throat and projected my voice louder. "And yet, I will be merciful."

The crowd fell back, uncertainty rippling across their upturned faces.

"You forget—Pierre LaRoche is not the one on trial here today. *Sainte Sauvage* is."

Cheers mingled with boos. I saw more than one Red Mask move among the assemblage. Nerves choked me.

"LaRoche—you have tried to kill me twice. To attack a member of the Sabourin line is treason, punishable by death. Do you confess to this sin?"

"Yes," he snarled. He was unwavering in his beliefs, I had to give him that. "All my sins will be banished by the sword of the Scion. But his light will never banish the darkness of your bedamned birth."

The hairs on my arms stood. I swallowed, and motioned to the edge of the platform. Luca appeared from behind a flapping drape, and he wasn't alone—he had a girl with him, towheaded and freckled, younger than twelve. Pierre saw her in the same moment the crowd did. His eyes widened, his own freckled nose wrinkling.

"Annalise?" For the first time since I'd met him, his face crumpled with something like regret, and I saw just how young he was. "What are you doing here?"

"Pierre!" The girl moved toward her brother, but Luca caught her gently and drew her back. His desert-blast eyes snagged on mine, and I read the message in their glittering depths easier than any line of text.

He'd been reluctant when I'd asked him to find the other

LaRoche children. I didn't blame him—I wanted to keep them out of this almost as much as I wanted to find a way to save a brainwashed boy from execution. He'd finally agreed to bring the eldest to the trial, but he'd made me swear an oath.

Promise me this girl will not be witness to her brother's death.

I'd sworn.

"Do you see?" I leaned in until my face was inches from Pierre's. I could smell his stench, and it wasn't all physical—I smelled fear, and hatred, and a creeping note of venom, piercing as a lode of rot in a week-old fruit. "I will set you free—your sister is here to take you home. Your new home, with the rest of your siblings—an orphanage run by the Sisters of the Scion." It was all true—although my stomach churned to think of those fate-poor children growing up in that loveless house of an uncaring god. "Isn't that nice? Every Matin and Compline, they will take you through your Salutations, and you will praise the Scion in all his light."

Pierre sucked in a rattling breath, his eyes fixed on his sister. A tear tracked down his dirty face, and the hope blossoming on his face seemed to surprise him.

I softened my voice. "I will set you free. All will be forgiven. Nothing more will be said of treachery or treason. I just need one thing from you."

Pierre held his breath. The crowd held it with him.

"All I need is the name of Sainte Sauvage."

I watched that precious flower of hope fester and die. His face crumpled. Words formed on his lips: *I don't know.* And then I watched his mouth tighten, his brows clench, his fanaticism roll over him like a cloud.

Say it, I silently pleaded with Pierre—with anyone who would listen. *Say I don't know. Say it so I believe you.*

"Sainte Sauvage is our savior," he hissed through shattered

teeth and a broken life. "I would never speak his name in front of Duskland *trash*."

The word was a clarion—a klaxon crying doom. Pierre heard the sound of his own death knell and laughed madly. A stiff breeze whipped the hilarity from his lips. Out of the corner of my eye, I saw Luca usher a weeping Annalise out of sight.

But I couldn't do it. I couldn't order his execution.

I stared desperately toward my advisors; toward my friends. Pierre kept laughing.

"I don't know what to do." My voice came out ragged. I buried my fists in the skirts of my ruined dress and rounded on the crowd. I scanned their upturned faces—a rainbow of pale to dark, punctuated by the gleaming whites of their eyes—but I couldn't tell what they wanted. "How can I serve justice when Sainte Sauvage flouts all rules? Will no one rid me of these lawless Red Masks?"

I heard the whistle of an arrow. Time slowed. Panic shoved against weird calm and paralyzed me. The wind of its flight kissed my cheek.

Metal and wood—fletched in scarlet feathers—sprouted from Pierre's throat. An arc of blood left his neck and splattered across Sunder's uniform. Pierre gave a choking death rasp.

How had I become so familiar with the sound of death?

"No," I whispered. Shadows clutched at the corners of my mind and juddered at my fingertips. Still I couldn't move. I *promised*— "He wasn't supposed to die today."

"You did this!" The voice rang out, masculine and smooth as sunlight through honey.

Gavin.

He rose from his simple chair like they said the Sun had once risen over the horizon, and I fought the urge to shield my face from his light. He was *resplendent*, although he wore nothing but his kembric regalia over a pale doublet. His bare head shone glitter-black in the low sunlight, and his face was alight with hot righteous fire.

I *loved* him in that moment, like a child loves its mother or a flower loves the rain.

Love.

But I didn't love anyone. Especially not Gavin.

I dredged my eyes away from his glittering perfection and down to the shadows churning violet from my fingertips. When I looked back, he was simply *Gav*. Handsome, imperfect, ungainly Gavin.

But I was clearly the only one who thought so. The crowd was staring at him like they'd witnessed a miracle, and they were crooning words I could barely hear—words that crawled into my ears and spread ice down my spine. It sounded like . . .

Sun Heir.

Adrenaline sprinted through my veins and blotted out one simple thought: *How was he doing that?*

"Sunder!" I shouted, panic shattering my composure. "The Red Masks are here. Find them!"

For a moment, I thought Sunder's hesitation was born of whatever magical glamour Gavin was spreading. But his gaze was fixed on me. His expression was unreadable, eyes flat and colorless as a frozen lake.

"Find them!" I screamed. "Kill them!"

Sunder released Pierre to the ground and dived into the crowd, a pack of wolves at his heels.

"You did this!" Gavin marched toward me, his footfalls like the trumpets of a returning king. "This was a miscarriage of justice. The boy had done wrong, but he did not deserve to die!"

Cheers rattled the pavilion; boos made a bass for their symphony.

"Me?" Disbelief shoved me toward him. "What have I done wrong?"

His eyes shone. "You called for that boy's death."

"Are you mad?" I cried. "I was trying to save him from execution!"

"By calling on someone else to do the deed?"

"How dare you?" I shoved him, hard, on his gleaming chest. He staggered back a step, shock registering on his face. "The Red Masks did this!"

"Why would they kill their own?" His voice was grave. "You condemned that boy to death with your words."

Everyone was listening to us. Gavin took my moment of indecision to push by me toward Pierre. He knelt where the boy slumped over the boards, eyes glazed and expression almost peaceful in death. When Gavin turned back toward the crowd, his face was riven with unspeakable sorrow—impossible hurt. I couldn't ignore the words they were chanting.

Sun

Heir

Sun

Heir

And that's when I saw the sword hanging from Gavin's waist. At first glance, there was nothing special about the blade—a normal piece of formal regalia. But where its hilt usually would have been forged of dristic, I saw it was pure kembric. I knew by the way the low sunlight purred along its edges and settled in its grooves. And its shape—that beveled edge ground against my memories; those pointed tips sank teeth into my heart.

I knew that shape.

No—I knew the *absence* of that shape. A form in negative, bit into ancient, dust-streaked stone. A dim, echoing room. Oleander's voice as she swirled her finger against the silhouette:

This doesn't look much like a crown to me. At least, not a crown I've ever wanted to wear.

But it wasn't a crown for a head. It was a crown for a *sword.*

Gavin had a Relic.

My neck burned, and it wasn't from the still-warm blood trickling down my neck. I pulled my ambric Relic into my palm. It was hot to the touch, a spark that set my veins alight. And I suddenly knew—knew in a way that made my heart throb—that this was my answer. This was the way to earn their admiration, their trust, their *love.* This was the way to prove I was the rightful heir—I was the true Sun Heir.

Words bubbled up inside me—words written in blood, words echoing across a millennium, words that tasted like the edge of an ancient, molten sword.

"I challenge you," I said, but I sounded like I was speaking underwater.

Gavin turned to me, frowning. "What?"

I clenched my fist, pulling until the chain around my neck snapped. I held my ambric Relic up. It spun ruddy sunlight through the crowd; a helix of light, a kaleidoscope of brilliance. For a moment, it shone even brighter than Gavin.

"I, Sylvie Sabourin, dauphine of the Amber Empire, challenge you, Gavin d'Ars, to the Ordeals of the Sun Heir!"

TWENTY-FIVE

For a long, excruciating moment, Gavin genuinely seemed to have no idea what I was talking about. Then his face gathered lines, stringing sharp between spikes of memory—realization, regret, trepidation, resolve. He crossed the distance between us in three long strides, and caught my hand with his, grinding my palm hard against the ambric Relic. Glimmers of amber streamed between the cracks in our fingers, and I bled my tainted power into those bars of light until a scarlet halo crowned us both.

"Have you gone mad?" The red light clashed upon his golden face. "Don't do this."

"Two heirs," I whispered back. "Two Relics. Has not this ever been the way of our family?"

"How do you even know—?" He slashed his free hand between us. "You don't know what you're doing. You don't know what you're *asking*. We can still do this the easy way."

"None of this has ever been *easy*."

I broke away from Gavin and stepped closer to the crowd, who were rabid with confusion and curiosity. Again I lofted my Relic, and sent light laddering toward the sky. Brilliance struck the gold off the pavilion and shattered diamonds across the crowd. Gavin shook his head, mute. I fought a burst of resentment. I didn't know what trickery he'd used to make himself look like a Sun Heir. But I was the fantast—illusion was in my blood. I could give them a better show than he ever could.

"For a thousand tides, your rulers have kept a secret from you!" My voice tolled like a bell down the boulevard. "The lineage of the Sabourin crown is decided by neither primogeniture nor merit, but by conflict! In the dubious tradition of our founding father, Meridian himself, once a generation the Sun Heir of the Sabourin dynasty is chosen from among four contenders. I hold in my hand a Relic of the Scion himself—the ancient god-king whose light shines upon us all—one of a quartet that decides your ruler, and therefore, your fate."

But as I looked out across the crowd, my gaze latched onto a splinter of stillness—*Sunder*. He stared back at me from the crowd, and his eyes snapped with frost and unexpected hurt. My heart backflipped in my chest and my Relic gave a responding pulse.

In all the mayhem and confusion of the last few days, I had completely forgotten to tell Sunder about what Oleander, Lullaby, and I had found in the Oubliettes. He didn't know about the Ordeals. I looked away before his condemnation paralyzed me.

"I know you have never seen me as your Sun Heir!" I shouted. "And I don't blame you—I came out of the dusk and snatched power before you had a chance to see the face behind the shadows. But my blood is true—as is my claim to the Amber Throne."

Waves of encouragement crashed against waves of outrage.

"But neither would I deny the claim of my cousin, Gavin d'Ars. Though he is half Aifiri—" I waited for the jolt of noise to settle. Gavin's eyes flashed molten across the pavilion. "Though he is half Aifiri, Sabourin blood flows in his veins as it does in mine. So let this conflict be decided the old way—by the Relics, gifted to us by Meridian himself and passed king to queen, empress to emperor, for as long as the daylight world can remember."

Cheers rang in my ears.

"I would drag what has been hidden—the dirt beneath marble, the secret behind the throne—out into the light of the Scion! If I am to face my cousin on equal footing in the Ordeals of the Sun Heir, I would not hide it from you, the people who will someday pay our taxes, serve in our armies, and obey our laws! I would have you be witness to what should always have been partially yours—the decision about who would rule you."

Eagerness touched their faces, like foam on a cresting wave, and I knew I had them.

"Gavin?" I held out a hand. Reluctantly, he stepped forward and slapped his palm against mine. An unpleasant shiver stung my fingers where they gripped the ambric Relic, shuddered through my chest, and traveled down my arm toward our shared hands. Gavin winced at the tremor, and put an involuntary hand to the sparking hilt of his sword.

"Let the true Sun Heir win!" I cried, and raised our joined hands. I sent an illusion of light sparking from our fingertips—brilliance lanced away toward the dusk.

Spectacle.

The crowd went wild. And as Gavin reluctantly repeated my words, I heard them echo along the Concordat, like sunlight piercing through dusk. But as we turned away, Gavin's hand tightened, until his nails bit into my palm and his fingers crushed mine.

"Mark my words, Mirage," he growled, his voice more menacing than I'd ever heard it before. "Today you have cursed us both. You have brought to the light what should have stayed in shadows. And we will both pay."

TWENTY-SIX

My Congrès was chaos. Everyone kept asking questions and jumping on to new questions before hearing the answers, if there were any. And anyone who did have salient information was promptly ignored in favor of wild speculation and stressful arguments.

I put a palm to my throbbing head and tried to ignore the glaring eyes staring accusingly at me from around the room.

"That's enough!" Dowser slammed a hand on the table, his usually quiet bass resounding. He rose up to his full height, and his deceptive bulk had its intended effect—strangers and friends shied away or sat, unused to my advisor's rarely deployed physicality. "The dauphine has surprised some of you—I understand. That does not give you the right to behave like ignorant savages. We will go about this discourse like the educated lords and ladies we are!"

My council subsided, but if anything, I caught more accusing eyes staring at me. I quelled the urge to glare back.

"Better." Quickly and succinctly, he summarized everything I'd discovered over the past week or so—my discovery of Severine's diary (which he referred to as a *previously unknown primary source*), the lost myth regarding Meridian and his children, and my exploration of the Oubliettes. His explanation finished, he stared over the tops of his spectacles at me and cleared his throat. "None of which explains, I might point out, how you intend to go forward with the Ordeals when there are only two heirs and two Relics."

I squirmed uncomfortably. I hadn't given the matter much thought before challenging Gavin.

"Two is enough," said an unfamiliar voice from the corner, "although if the Relics have imprinted upon their heirs, it will likely end in a tie."

I rose half out of my seat and spun to face the voice, the rest of the courtiers turning with me. Shock spiraled through me when I saw it was Gavin's taciturn and haggard godfather.

"Arsenault!" Gavin snapped, anger suffusing his features. Since our confrontation before the Concordat, I noticed Gavin looked slightly less . . . *splendid*. He pushed dusty hair out of wan eyes and glared at his godfather.

"It's fine, Gavin." Félix Arsenault stepped forward, stiff and wary, as though he wasn't used to speaking in front of crowds. "The only requirement for the Ordeals is that there be at least as many Relics as Sabourin-blooded heirs. The magic will decide the rest."

The mention of Sabourin heirs pulled my hands into fists and hammered unexpected guilt through me. Severine was in no position to compete, and yet—had things been different, these would have been her generation's Ordeals. *Our* generation's Ordeals.

"I'm sorry, monsieur," Barthet said reasonably. "But how in the daylight world do you know?"

Arsenault looked sidelong at Gavin, who sighed and stood. His eyes fell on me.

"Last week you asked how our fathers' close friendship ended," Gavin began. "This is how—the Ordeals of the Sun Heir tore their amity apart and burned their brotherhood to ash. The light of the Scion is blinding and unflinching—it does not distinguish between idle games and mortal conflict."

"They were playing," I breathed. Triumph burst hot in my chest. *I knew it.* "Your father and mine—Sylvain Sabourin and Xavier d'Ars."

"And a third cousin of the blood—Remy Legarde," Arsenault rasped.

"How do you fit into all of this?" Lady Marta was skeptical.

Again, a glance passed between Gavin and Arsenault. I narrowed my eyes. I remembered how they'd tried to pass talk of an Aifiri general off as idle chatter about estates and stewards. I didn't trust either one of them, especially now I'd set myself explicitly against Gavin.

"In Aifiri culture," Gavin slowly explained, "it is customary for young men and women of high birth to take a kind of platonic mate, usually of the same gender—a friend, a comrade, a confidant, although none of those words fully embody the concept."

Across the room, Marta Iole's eyes went deep and wistful. Arsenault's mouth worked.

"Félix was my father's partner. When Sylvain invited Xavier d'Ars to court, my godfather went with him." Gavin looked grim. "Apparently the Ordeals had been *discouraged* since around the time of the Conquest. There was a massive scandal between the heirs at the time—the matriarch of my family line, and your grandfather several times over. Although it was hushed up, the event had ripples, and the Ordeals were more or less banned in favor of traditional parent-to-child succession."

"But Sylvain got it into his head to revive the Ordeals, and convinced Xavier and Remy to join," Arsenault grated out, impatient. "They were five and seven tides younger than him, respectively. They had no idea what they were getting into. Sylvain easily won, although not without cost. Xavier was banished from the Amber Court for life. Remy—well, Remy Legarde has been dead for nearly forty tides."

The words jolted through me, casting shadows across my heart. *Dead?*

"You said something about imprinting." Dowser's scholarly curiosity made his tone eager. "Do the heirs bond with Relics in their possession?"

"The reverse, I believe," Arsenault corrected him. "Xavier used to say his Relic fed off him, like a parasite does a host. Feeding on his power, his life force, the magic in his Sabourin blood. He felt it left a kind of *signature* upon his psyche."

The heat of the ambric pendant against my chest felt suddenly invasive, instead of comforting. I pushed away the idea that it was marking my thoughts and prompting my actions. *No.* I was in control—of my life, of my ambitions, of *everything*. Including this narrative that seemed like it was being twisted to suit an angle. Whose angle, and for what reason? I didn't know.

Yet.

"If Sylvain won his generation's Ordeals," I said slowly, "then why, Gavin, do you have the kembric Relic?"

"When Remy died, my father realized the Ordeals were much more than a game." Gavin's cracked-agate eyes narrowed. "He felt that Sylvain had tricked him—challenged him to the Ordeals under false pretenses. When he refused to give up his Relic, Sylvain turned on Xavier—his best friend. His *brother*. Papa fled back to Aifir with the Relic, an exile from a court and a family he'd never truly belonged to."

"And when he died, he passed the Relic to you," I guessed.

"Yes," Gavin growled. "But Papa never intended for the Ordeals to resume. He *hated* your father for what he'd made him do, what he'd put him through, and all of it for nothing more than an archaic charade of royal succession. He gave me the Relic as a reminder that all power corrupts."

"And yet, here you are at Coeur d'Or, undermining my legitimacy and parading yourself around as the true Sun Heir!"

"I never said that!" Gavin cried.

"You didn't have to," I snarled. "You accused me of murder, incited a riot, tricked them into hating me!"

He flinched. "I didn't need to *trick* them."

"Enough!" Dowser's voice boomed around the Congrès, shocking us both into silence. He rubbed a hand over his smooth brown head, then turned briskly to Arsenault. "All of this is to say, Mirage's challenge stands? The Ordeals may go forward with two Relics and two heirs of Sabourin blood?"

Arsenault stood still and quiet, as though he was thinking hard about some great silent thing he'd thought about many times before. Then he flipped a hand over his head and drew out a blade from a sheath concealed beneath the billowing red coat. I jerked back, and my council shied with me, but Arsenault just laid the sword gently at the center of the table and gazed at it with a level of warmth I'd never seen in his face before. I barely glanced at the blade before I knew what it was—the dristic Relic, representing *hand*, or physical strength.

"A third Relic?" I breathed, out loud. "But how—?"

"Godfather?" Gavin was staring at Arsenault, surprise blurring toward betrayal. "What is that?"

"It's a Relic, godson, as your cousin intuits." Arsenault gave Gavin a look I couldn't read, then turned his chalk-ash gaze to me. "Your father may have been complacent in his middle age, but he wasn't stupid. When Severine murdered her brother for his Relic, Sylvain realized his daughter was hungry for the Relics—hungrier even than he had been in his youth. But she wasn't doing things the *right* way—she wasn't playing the game Sylvain loved so much. So he sent his remaining Relics far away—far enough away so Severine could never find them."

I frowned. All these narratives—of Severine, and Sylvain, and the barbarous games they played—had tangled in my head until I couldn't sort the truth from the lie, the embellishment from the bias. Was this the story of a wicked, twisted princess hungry for power? Or was it the story of a girl who loved her brother too much and went too far to save him from a world too cruel for them both? I didn't know if I'd ever truly find out.

"Ambric, he sent with his last bastard." Arsenault dropped me an unkind nod. "Dristic, he sent to his greatest enemy, a man who had once been like his brother—the man who already held the kembric Relic in his possession. Xavier d'Ars. I suppose he had more faith in his old rival than his grasping daughter. But Xavier was done with all the Sun Heir business. He had fallen in love with an Aifiri noblewoman. He had a young son." He gave Gavin a small smile. "So Xavier gave the blade to me, for safe-keeping. He knew my loyalty to him transcended everything else, and he trusted me to do with the Relic what he would want done."

The court held its breath.

"But now I offer it up as the tiebreaker of this generation's Ordeals of the Sun Heir." Arsenault touched the edge of the blade, almost reverently. "*Not* because I believe in these ancient, dangerous games that killed my old friend and tore my comrades apart. But because I believe to my core that Gavin—as the son of Xavier, who was cheated out of his rightful place by your scheming and ambitious father—is the rightful Sun Heir. He has been ordained by the Scion and shines with his light. And if you will not step aside, lady . . ." The greying man glared at me, and I quelled a shudder. "Then the Ordeals must go forward."

The door opened into the choking silence following Arsenault's words. Sunder stepped into the Congrès, flanked by a few of his wolves. His hair was wild and his eyes shone with weird light. I gave him a questioning look. He gave his head a stiff shake.

He hadn't caught the Red Masks who had killed LaRoche. I swallowed a hot blur of guilt and rage.

"We can still do this the easy way," Gavin said. I frowned—he'd said the same thing when I challenged him. But when I glanced toward him, he wasn't looking at me. He had his eyes fixed on Sunder.

"And what's that?"

"We could get married," Gavin suggested.

"*What?*" My thoughts scattered like bits of broken glass, reflecting apprehension and distaste and a sudden shadow of regret. A memory curled around me: his hands in my hair, his mouth on mine. Had I given him the wrong idea, had I—?

"You ended Severine's rule, but I legally inherited the Sabourin fortune. You are Sylvain's daughter, but bastard-born. My lineage is distant, but unassailable." His voice was too serious for me to think he was joking. "Neither of our claims to the throne is without flaw, but if we were wed? You would earn your rightful half of the fortune you deserve. No one from outside our Scion-blessed bloodline would dilute the purity of the throne. Our children would be undeniably Sabourin and could rule with impunity. And neither of us would have to descend into darkness and yield our destinies to the Ordeals of the Sun Heir."

It was a long, aching moment before I funneled fury and confusion and impossible hilarity into three calmly stated words:

"Everyone. Outside. *Now.*"

TWENTY-SEVEN

Fury and panic beat wings about my ears as my Congrès slowly rose to leave. Papers shuffled. Silk and leather rustled as they rose from plush chairs. Footsteps clomped toward the exit. The door hissed shut.

But not everyone had left. Sunder stood glowering in the empty space, and if ice could burn, we would all be on fire.

"Sunder." Gavin's mouth lifted into a grin, but it wasn't the kind of smile that made me want to join in. "Never met a marriage proposal he liked."

Sunder stalked across the room toward Gavin. His movements were spare—almost careless—as he lifted an elbow, jammed it into Gavin's throat, and shoved him toward the opposite wall. Gavin's arms came up, grappling with Sunder's, but though both boys were strong, Sunder had the advantage of height. Gavin's back slammed against the hard surface, his head jarring and his breath knocking out of his lungs. Pebbles of plaster rained onto the marble floor.

"What in the Scion's hell are you still doing here, d'Ars?" Sunder's tone was almost conversational. His face was very, very close to Gavin's, and his lips were bared over his teeth. "I thought you'd have already run from court with your tail between your legs like you did four tides ago."

"What can I say?" Gavin choked out. "I enjoy the company."

Sunder ratcheted up his choke hold on the other boy, and Gavin groaned, the tips of his boots scrabbling on the floor.

"Sunder!" I shouted, picking up my skirts and dashing across the room. "That's enough. You're hurting him!"

"Good," Sunder growled, without looking at me. His eyes

narrowed to knives of green. "This is between me and d'Ars, Mirage. We have unfinished business."

"That's right—you never did manage to kill me." Gavin swallowed hard against the forearm at his throat. "What was it you threatened to do? Crack every one of my ribs and crush my heart?"

"I've learned a few tricks since then." Sunder's smile was a jagged blade forged for torture. "Recently I've been dying to see what happens when I pull a man's spine out through his mouth."

A froth of fear surfaced in Gavin's gaze, although he tried to hide it. "It would ruin that pretty outfit of yours."

"I've got spares."

"Will both of you stop it?" I snarled, to mask my unease. I'd never seen that look in Sunder's eyes, not even when he—

I swallowed against the blood-hot memories of snapping bones and screaming faces, crooked necks and viscera on marble. I tried not to think too often about how many people Sunder had hurt or killed. But now, with murder in his eyes and vengeance on his breath, I wondered where his lines were drawn.

"Tell me, d'Ars," Sunder whispered, so softly I barely caught the words. "First, you seduced and illegally wed my sister for a fortune she hadn't even inherited yet. Now you propose marriage to my—my *paramour*, in a half-hearted grab for a throne that will never belong to you. What is it about the women I love that so appeals to your grasping, hoarding aspirations?"

Love. The word was a jewel, unpolished and unfaceted yet gleaming with its own light. I reached for it, but it was cold to the touch, wrenched from a place of pain instead of given in peace. I watched it fade, even as I longed to clutch it to my chest.

"Perhaps it's a testament to you, de Vere—your ability to surround yourself with scintillating, ambitious women." Gavin smiled, suddenly—his white teeth stained with blood where he'd bit his tongue. "Wait—did you just call her your *paramour*?

You know that to love a woman you have to be able to touch her, right? Perhaps even kiss her. Otherwise it's just unrequited lust. Or maybe idolatry."

"Shut up."

"Or were you imagining *you'd* get to marry her?" Gavin's smile was honed sharp on malice. "You, Sunder? You raised an unknown orphan from the dusk, named her Sun Heir without any proof, and put her on the path to a throne before anyone could so much as protest. You marry this future empress, and voilà! The man goes from provincial marquis to emperor while barely lifting a finger."

"Gavin!" I pushed the words around the apprehension gluing my teeth together. "That's not—"

"And we've all heard—whether by torture or seduction—just how persuasive Lord Sunder can be."

He laughed, bright and sharp. My own cheeks tightened as my lips curled upward, and I felt humor building in my belly. I giggled too—a strained bubble of hilarity bursting unexpected in my throat.

And I suddenly knew what Gavin's legacy was.

I swallowed the laugh almost instantly, but it was too late— Sunder had heard it. He tensed, and his timbre pulsed bright red, with a force that made my ears pop. He gritted his teeth around a scream, nearly doubling over as a wave of pain rippled along his torso. His grip on Gavin loosened. The other boy thrust forward with a cry, tackling Sunder and toppling them both onto the ground.

For a tortuous minute, all I saw was flailing limbs and swinging fists. A kick. Two swift punches to someone's stomach. Glittering eyes above a bloody smile. Sunder rolled on top of Gavin, his legs clamped around the other boy's chest, his hair a pale gyre above. Gloved fingers circled Gavin's neck. Gavin coughed, then gagged. Lines of ambric edged in black crawled along Gavin's throat, pulsing from Sunder's fingertips. Gavin's eyes rolled back into his head.

"Stop!" I screamed, flinging myself between them. My hand found Sunder's shoulder. He reached out, reflexively. His open palm struck the center of my chest, beside my heart. Agony shrieked through me, a flaming blade in the dusk. I jerked away from his touch, lurching back and losing my balance. I fell to the floor, my knee cracking into the tile.

When I looked up, Sunder's face had shattered, his eyes a chasm into a bleak, unending despair.

"Mirage," he whispered, "I'm so sorry."

He threw himself away from Gavin and reached for me, hands trembling. Behind him, Gavin rolled to his feet, found purchase on Sunder's collar, cranked his head back, and swiftly punched him in the face. *Once. Twice.* Gavin reeled back his elbow for a third strike, but he staggered, dizzy. I found my footing and shoved in between them, planting my hands on Gavin's chest and pushing him back. He stumbled and lifted his hands in a gesture of surrender. Relief sprinted across his face.

"Enough!" I commanded. I glared between them. Both boys were breathing hard. Gavin rubbed at his throat and coughed. Sunder levered himself slowly off the floor, a gash below his eye oozing blood against what would soon be a livid bruise. "That's enough from both of you."

"Mirage—" Sunder's voice held a note of pleading.

"No." I thrust the word between my teeth and met his eyes. The unspoken horror of what had just happened passed between us like a curse—although it had been an accident, he'd used the full brunt of his legacy against me. He'd *hurt* me. Part of me had already forgiven him, and yet—"I can't look at you right now. Just go."

Sunder's mouth flattened. He yanked his ripped collar away from his throat, dragged a hand through sweat-dark hair, and stalked out of the room. The door shut behind him with a sound like the end of the world. Heat filled my throat. I swallowed, and forced myself to face Gavin. He looked down at me, triumph shining in his eyes.

"That was nothing to be proud of," I snarled. His face fell. I looked him over—the blood trickling from the corner of his mouth, the finger-shaped bruises blooming on his neck. "Are you all right?"

"I will be." He shrugged, then winced. "Not the worst beating I've had. And probably not the last."

I folded my arms across my chest. "You deserved it."

"Is the idea of becoming my wife to save an empire really so disgusting?"

"That's not what I meant."

"Oh. Oleander." Gavin scrubbed a hand over his face, sat back against the windowsill, and sighed. I smothered a fizz of sympathy, arming myself with the new intuition shoving hard against the back of my mind. How had it taken me so long to realize—?

"Look, I'm not proud of it. But we were both young. Too young to get married—I know that now. But all's well that ends well, right? She had the marriage annulled when I returned to Aifir—turns out it wasn't strictly legal—and we haven't spoken since. Besides, Sunder already took his shot back then. Why stir things up now?"

"Because even if it happened four tides ago, you still seduced his twin sister and tried to steal their family fortune?"

Gavin straightened. "Yes, I was broke. But so were other courtiers. And we did what poor nobles have always done—live off the fat of the empress and the largesse of our wealthier friends. My only crime with Oleander was asking her to elope without the blessing of her family or friends. If she thought there was something else going on . . ." He trailed off, clicking his tongue against his teeth.

I wanted to believe him—even spattered in his own blood and exhausted, he was so handsome and earnest. Repentant, as if there could possibly be anything wrong with trying to run away with your first love.

Oleander's voice echoed up from the Oubliettes, dim and dark and ringed in shadow: *He told me five minutes after we left the chapel, and laughed when I cried.*

I closed my eyes, sifting through memories. Gavin shining like the sun on the Concordat. Gavin tearing my favorite dress without asking—when he'd laughed, I'd laughed with him. Gavin stealing a kiss—he'd been so surprised when I hadn't returned it. Gavin inspiring a froth of impossible, improbable adoration from me, from *everyone*.

I swallowed sudden nausea.

"I know what your legacy is, Gavin."

Doubt warred against creeping suspicion in his eyes. "I told you—I don't have a legacy."

"I create illusions, but a person has only to close their eyes to escape them." My voice scraped my throat. "*You* though—you climb inside a person's mind and alter the way they perceive you, their world, their own emotions. You've made me see things that weren't there, laugh at things I didn't find funny, believe things that weren't true. But worst of all—you made me doubt my own heart, my own mind."

He stood very still.

"How many times have people done things for you they didn't want to do?" I hissed. "How many of those loyal to you have been forced into it? How many women have found them-selves in your bed without explicit consent?"

His hands curled into fists. "That's an atrocious accusation."

"Tell me I'm wrong."

He shook dark hair out of his eyes. "I wasn't always perfect, Mirage. I know that. Yes—I resented being a poor relation to the powerful empress. Yes—I envied how easy the twins had it, with their beauty and their strength and their money. Maybe, when I eloped with Oleander, I wanted a little of that—a little of that grace. But then I found the light of the Scion, and all that noise was cut away. I'm free of all those shadows now. I know what truly matters. And I won't let you saddle me with blame I haven't earned and do not deserve."

"You deny your legacy?"

"Deny I'm a monster who warps perceptions for his own advantage?" He gave a short laugh. "I do indeed."

He turned curtly to the door. "You'll regret this, cousin. You'll regret challenging me to the Ordeals."

"Why? Because we might die, or lose our minds?"

"Because I'll win." Weariness stretched his voice and dimmed his light. "You should know—I didn't come here to steal your throne. But now   now I'll have to."

He turned on his heel and left me alone. Sudden trepidation gripped me, cold as death foretold. All the adrenaline and fury and excitement I'd felt during the last few hours dropped away, leaving me gasping.

What have you done? The words spun through me, untethered. And their answer was a hopeless prayer from another time, a broken promise from my forefathers.

You were always going to challenge him. Because this is how you earn what you were born to.

I clenched my fist around my Relic and fought the urge to throw it to the ground. *I am the master of my fate.* All of this was still up to me. I had choices—I had *options*. None of this was written. My actions still mattered.

They had to matter.

If I heard a distant laugh—which I *didn't*—it rang bell-bright and blood-dark, like the voice of the sister I'd never had.

TWENTY-EIGHT

I threaded through a bustling palais full of painted courtiers and black-clad wolves and servants running around with the news that *the Duskland Dauphine challenged the Sun Heir for the Amber Throne!* I found Oleander in her bedroom, trying on a gown that made her look like the mythic Moon. A luminous bodice fell away to sheer panels of midnight blue, a dark diaphanous skirt twinkling with diamond shards.

"Do you like it?" She gave it a twirl. "I designed it myself."

"It's stunning," I said honestly. "Do you mind if I ask you a question?"

"Is it, *Did Vida agree to heal the nasty bruise that makes my boyfriend look like a common brawler?*" Oleander guessed. "Because the answer to that is *no.*"

"I didn't—" Her words thudded through my roil of thoughts and slapped heat onto my cheeks. "He's not my—not that I don't want but "

"Scion save me from the garbled ramblings of dusk-addled dauphines," grumbled Oleander, unlacing her gown. "Just when I thought we were making progress."

I shoved thoughts of Sunder far, far away. "I wanted to ask—do you know what Gavin's legacy is?"

Oleander's fingers froze on her stays. Her eyes, bright as beryls, met mine. "Supposedly, he doesn't have one."

"*Supposedly?*"

Her mouth twisted, shrewd. "Severine wasn't the first Sabourin to make a secret of her legacy. I don't know whether they hid their powers to disguise strength or conceal weakness.

Either way, we mere mortals have never been deemed worthy to glimpse the god-given glory of Meridian's perfect children."

Her words made sense. I remembered my first day at court—I'd dared ask Severine what her legacy was. Lullaby had chided me for it, and I'd barely thought of it again until I'd faced off against my sister. Then she'd used several powers in a row before trying to *steal* mine. And Sylvain—what had Dowser said, the other day? *If I had to make a guess at his legacy*—

"I know what Gavin's legacy is." I tamped down the fizz of uncertainty his denial had churned up. "He alters perceptions, emotions. He can make you laugh when you're not amused. He can seem to shine like a god when he is just a man. He can make you adore him when you barely like him."

"Why are you telling me this?" Oleander stepped out of her dress and stood before me in her elegant silken underthings.

"I—I thought it might make you feel better."

"To know my love for him was not just seduced, but coerced?" Oleander's face barely changed. "Falling for a weak man's weak legacy just makes me weak too."

"You are not weak, Oleander."

"Losing control makes everyone weak." She hung the midnight luster gown, then sat at her vanity and began removing her cosmetics. "The source of that loss makes no difference."

I heard the dismissal in her tone. I moved toward the door.

"Mirage?"

I turned, and caught her eye in the mirror. Without her rouge and kohl, her face looked vulnerable, almost wistful. "Yes?"

"Be gentle with him."

"Gavin?"

"You know who." She turned fully, her loose hair falling like snow around her shoulders. "You will never be able to punish him as much as he punishes himself. So forgive him instead."

A shadow unfurled from my heart and climbed into my throat. "I want to."

Oleander's alpine eyes went flat as dusk-lit ice. "I kissed a boy, once. Or he kissed me. It's hard to remember now. His lips—they shriveled up and away, so he could never kiss anyone again. His teeth blackened and crumbled out of his mouth. He'll never eat anything but broth for the rest of his life. And yet, when I went to his house and stared into that ruin of a face and asked his family how much money their son's mouth was worth, he didn't scream or weep. He just pressed a note into my hand, a note he'd written. It read, *This wasn't your fault.*"

My throat burned with all the tears she should have been crying. "Oleander—"

"Shut up," she breathed. "Our power is pain. Our only constant is consequence. Our vigil is unending. And yet—for the first time in forever, my brother has hope. For a world we believed to be impossible—a world where we can be loved by anyone other than each other. A world more radiant than our own—a world where even if we're monsters, we can still deserve love. *You* gave him that hope. Don't you dare take it away from him."

She turned back to her mirror without another word. And I turned back to the door, mourning for the hundredth—*thousandth*—time, that spectacular, impossible world I'd dreamed up.

What if that world had always been out of reach? What if monsters couldn't ever be loved?

Not even by each other?

I didn't sleep that Nocturne. All my feelings felt too raw, too confusing. Pierre's death. Challenging Gavin; his misplaced proposal. Sunder's legacy, slicing through me like a blade.

I imagined him—there, on the other side of the wall—his pillow near my pillow, his head near my head. When I closed my eyes, I could see him—sharp cheekbones and soft mouth, snow-drift hair and sooty eyelashes. His scent, like the winds off the mountains, bracing and fierce.

His touch, like icicles and frozen knives and brittle mirror glass.

His hurt, singing true as an arrow to sink into my heart.

His love, monstrous and imperfect and beautiful.

His love.

I wasn't ready to talk to him yet.

TWENTY-NINE

I battered on Lullaby's door, the sound louder than necessary in the hush of Lys Wing.

"Mirage?" Lullaby's voice sounded strange through her cracked door. "It's third Nocturne. Is everything all right?"

"Not really," I choked out.

Lullaby pushed the door wider. She glanced around and raised a quizzical eyebrow. "No Suicide Twin entourage today? Did you assume the Red Masks would stop trying to kill you now you challenged their favored Sun Heir to a glorified duel?"

"You're still angry with me."

"Less than I was." Lullaby cracked a half-hearted smile. "Why aren't you exploring the Oubliettes, before they're overrun by advisors and courtiers and commoners and *Gavin*? It's soon to be a badly kept secret."

"I was about to," I admitted, "except that place scares the stuffing out of me. Will you join me?"

"Are you sure you want me to?"

I thought I heard a bare hint of pleading in her voice.

"Of course I do," I said, vehement. "Don't you know how much I've missed you?"

She relented, and we trotted down the hall in silence for a few minutes. There was only one wolf guarding the dungeons. I cast a ragged but passable illusion of invisibility over the pair of us so we could sneak to the entrance.

Lullaby waited until we were through the portal in the Oubliettes before speaking again.

"When you challenged Gavin—I was surprised."

"You didn't think I'd do it?"

"Not so soon, at least. I think I knew it would eventually happen—these Ordeals sing a song that sounds like destiny."

My Relic throbbed.

"Do you believe Arsenault?" she asked. "About Severine going mad over the Ordeals and killing Seneca for his Relic?"

"I don't know." Our voices echoed strangely in the halls. My arm smarted as I reopened Oleander's wound and smeared my blood on the sunburst door. It hissed open, and we reentered the labyrinth. "The story he tells is the one I believed a week ago. But it contradicts Severine's own explanation. And part of me—" I gnawed on a lip. "I know it doesn't make sense, but I *want* to believe Severine. She killed our father, she killed countless half siblings, she tried to kill *me*. And yet, I want to believe she had a reason beyond pure power to do the things she did. It doesn't excuse her crimes—not by a mile—but if she did what she did for Seneca, for the love of a brother? I want to believe that kind of love exists."

Unexpectedly, Lullaby nodded. "Sometimes I feel that way about Colette—about my mother. If I can find an explanation for the things she does, the ways she uses me, that will soften the hurt. If I can understand *why*—why the things that I am traded for are so important to her—that might make her actions acceptable."

Her voice wavered on the last word, and I remembered her awful story: *Being your friend feels like that name day.*

"Oh, Lullaby," I whispered. "You're not talking about Colette anymore, are you?"

Her face fell like shatterglass. My heart twisted hot and dark in my chest.

"Why *him*?" she asked violently. "Why did you choose Sunder over me?"

"I—" Her words knocked me off-balance. I realized with an

uncomfortable pang that I had to ask a follow-up question to her accusation. "Which time?"

Lullaby barked a laugh. "Every time! You ran off to Belsyre—with *him*—without even telling me where you were *going*! Do you know how worried I was? Thibo had barely been gone a few days, and Mender a week before that, and Scion if I didn't hate myself for worrying about you, but I was sick with it. I didn't know if you were—" She swallowed, hard. "But I forgave you for all that, when you told me what happened, when you told me about everything. And yet, mere days later, you abandoned me again. You sent me away—out into an exploding, battle-torn palais with Skyclad patrols around every corner, to look for a healer for *him*. While you crouched on the marble and embraced him."

"He was dying." I knew it was no excuse.

"We all could have died." Lullaby looked at me with hollow eyes. "You made choices, that day. Hard choices, I'm sure. But choices nonetheless. And that's how I found out that I wasn't a lead character in my own story, but a supporting one in yours."

"Lullaby—"

"So just tell me why. Why him?"

"Because—" That all seemed so far away now. I *had* made hard choices, but now they seemed flimsy, translucent—as though it wouldn't have mattered if I'd chosen differently. As though everything that had happened was always going to happen, no matter what I chose. "You may not believe me, but I never actually considered that I was making a choice. We were all on the same side. We all risked death to defeat Severine. We all risked death for each other. It never occurred to me that to you, it must have looked like a choice."

"Is that supposed to make me feel better?"

"I am sorry, Lullaby." I took a deep breath. "Whether I meant to or not, I hurt you. And for that, I'm truly sorry. Please forgive me."

"*Sorry* is the word of a liar or a changed woman." Lullaby shrugged. "So I guess we'll see. Let's keep walking."

I trailed her down the passageway in silence.

"I thought you might say you chose him over me because you're in love with him," Lullaby said baldly. "Are you?"

"How should I know?" I sounded a little desperate. "I've never been in love before. Have you?"

"No."

I cast my memory back over all the conversations I'd had with her and Thibo. I could have sworn— "What about Blossom?"

Lullaby's shoulders stiffened. "What about her?"

"I thought you said—well, Thibo *implied*—"

"I just liked spending time with her. We didn't kiss, or really touch. I didn't want to, even though it . . . came up, sometimes."

"Oh." I mulled over her words. "Maybe you don't like girls that way? Maybe a boy—?"

"You're not listening." Lullaby was curt. "I'm not interested in anyone that way. I love my friends—Scion help me, I even love my family. But I don't love anyone the way the rest of you seem to be *in love*. The way Thibo loved Mender. The way you love Sunder."

I held my tongue at her last comment. "Does that bother you?"

She considered this. "Not really. Does it bother you?"

I smiled at her. "Why should it?"

"It bothered Thibo." She lifted her slender eyebrows. "He couldn't fathom why anyone wouldn't want to constantly be kissing someone else."

"I mean—" I made a helpless gesture and hoped we were back

to being able to joke with each other. "He's not wrong. I kind of want to kiss you right now."

"Shut up!" She shoved me, playful, but a moment later her face grew sad. "I miss him."

"So do I," I whispered.

A struggle warped Lullaby's face. "You barely knew him."

"I know. I didn't know him as well as I wanted. I didn't treat him as well as I should have. I didn't protect him like I ought to. But I still miss him."

Slowly, Lullaby nodded.

"I'm looking for him, you know. If he's out there, I'll find him. I promise."

Surprise played across her fine features. "You think he's still alive?"

"His heart was still beating, the last time I saw him," I managed, around a sudden lump in my throat. "Which means I can hope."

Impulsively, Lullaby reached out and clasped her slender fingers in mine. Then she danced ahead, her lambent voice lilting off the walls. "Hurry up! These tunnels aren't going to explore themselves!"

I followed her with my eyes, brimming with gratitude and the warm rush of being forgiven. But strangely, as she whirled and spun down the corridor, I saw a pale glow just past the next turn in the hallway. I frowned. I knew my illusions like I knew my own heart—I knew their bright contours as well as the shadows hiding in their valleys. This light was different—a pale shimmer of ice-chased glass, or a memory of a chilly Nocturne. I quickened my footsteps. The light waxed brighter, casting my friend in silhouette.

"Lullaby!" I shouted.

But she had already stumbled to a halt, her hand braced

against the wall. I heaved up beside her, breathing hard. My breath stopped when I saw what Lullaby had found.

The passageway fell away from our feet into a sawtooth chasm. Dark pebbles skittered into a blaze of impossible light—light I barely had words for. Our world was scorched red and black—this light was luminous ice to its dim fire. It cut through me like paper, slicing through skin and bone until it tossed my heart open and laid the whole of me bare. It made me wild and wondrous and worshipful. And I knew it for what it was—*moonlight.*

I shielded my eyes until they could adjust. When I looked back down, I saw an army.

Fear shot through me, and for a panicky moment I thought we had been ambushed by Skyclad gardes. But no—these soldats were impossible and beautiful and eerily still. And they were all *women.*

"Mirage!" Lullaby's breathless voice was nearly inaudible. Her hand clutched my bicep. "What—*who* are they?"

"I have no idea," I admitted.

For a long time, we both gazed into the enormous, echoing chamber. There were hundreds—*thousands*—of them, marching in clean bright crystalline rows. They were translucent and strikingly realistic, as if each woman had been transformed from flesh and blood to flawless diamond. Each figure was unique, each face a map of histories—an atlas of emotion—beyond the scope of even the most talented sculptor. But that was all they were—statues.

"Lullaby." I was loath to break the hymnlike hush. "When this château was first filled in—hundreds of tides ago—what if these Ordeals used to be more serious? More formalized? Not a game for bored or ambitious royals, but a ritual death match."

She shivered. "We'll never know, will we?"

"No, what I meant was—" I searched for the right words. "The trophy for the winner would have needed to be more than a title. *Sun Heir* wouldn't have been enough to tempt them into this arena. There would have needed to be spoils."

She looked askance at the glittering horde. "What use is a diamond army?"

I didn't know.

But I wanted to.

THIRTY

I shivered in the cool air outside Sunder's door, scented with genévrier and snowfall, and dared myself to knock. The door swung open. I wrapped my arms around my chest, stepped inside, and looked into Sunder's eyes.

His black-wolf shoulders were tight as a strung bow; the set of his mouth was like purgatory. He clearly hadn't slept—he still wore his Loup-Garou uniform, although the black-and-white argyle sash had fallen askew and I saw mud—or was that still Pierre's blood?—spattered on his usually polished boots. A savage bruise drowned his right eye in mottled purple and green, and I almost had to smother a laugh. Only a Suicide Twin could manage to make a swollen black eye look fashionable.

"More trouble in the city?" I asked, skirting awkwardness.

"They're throwing Sun Heir parties—impromptu masques filled with pantomimes and gambling and too much drinking. But everyone's also taking sides, which means fights are breaking out in every single quartier. I had to break up a brawl in Jardinier— two satin-clad courtesans had come to blows over who they thought was going to win the Ordeals. I'm not sure which was worse—the wine bottle one kept using as a bludgeon, or the makeshift blade the other had fashioned out of her high heel."

"Isn't it a little early to be celebrating? Or brawling?"

"I expect it will get worse before it gets better."

"Your eye. Vida couldn't fix that for you?"

"Wouldn't," he clarified. "Doesn't matter—I deserved it."

"For what?"

"For losing control." His words were strangely distant, as though he'd rehearsed them—or thought of them so many times they'd lost their meaning. "For letting my emotions get the better of me. For hurting you."

Oleander's voice echoed in my ears: *Be gentle with him.*

I sat on the edge of his bed. "That was an accident."

"I don't get to have accidents." Roughly, he undid the buttons on his asymmetrical jacket and ripped it open. A wave of sickly heat rolled off him, smelling less of genévrier and ice than burnt wood and singed metal. His ambric timbre glowed like a furnace beneath his undershirt. His eyes, when they met mine, were glazed with fear or fever. "I think—I think I shouldn't touch you again without being sure I won't hurt you."

"When will that be?" My voice came out raw.

"I don't know." Both his eyes looked bruised in the low light, exhaustion and regret clinging to his stark features.

"It's getting worse?"

Sunder said nothing, but the timbre's angry throb was its own caustic assent.

"Sunder," I said, reaching for him. "Come here."

But when I kissed him, all I could taste were my doubts and his anguish and the helpless sensation of falling—falling like Meridian, away from the luster of moonlight back into the perilous dusk.

He pulled away first. "You shouldn't let me do that."

"Why would I punish you for something I did to you?"

"You didn't do this."

"Didn't I?"

He lifted piercing green eyes to my face. I gazed into them, glimpsing the edge of that seething abyss where he hid all his pain. He always seemed so hard, so sharp—a blade honed on ice and violence. But this Nocturne he seemed forged from broken metal—when I looked hard enough, I could see all the cracks where the pieces didn't fit. "Do you really want to do this now?"

Trepidation chilled me. "Do what?"

He looked away, shuddering with blank dread. I watched him put himself back together again, bricking away his want and his hurt and his fear with painstaking care, until all that was left was a veneer of composure, slick as ice. He jerked his jacket more tightly across his stiff shoulders and buttoned it quickly over his heaving chest. When he looked at me again, it was his courtly mask I saw. I swallowed a froth of dismay.

"Do you mean to go through with it?"

"What do you mean?" I shivered.

"This Sun Heir business."

I made my voice colder than his face. "Do you think I should let Gavin become Sun Heir? Do you think I should let him have the throne? Is that what you want?"

For a long moment, silence was a purgatory between us.

"Don't you understand?" Sunder's voice was slick with strain. "We have all done terrible things. The Nocturne of the coup, I saw Oleander breathe tangerine fire on a platoon of Skyclad soldats and watch as their faces melted off. Lullaby sang a man to *death*, Mirage. And I—I *mauled* a half-dozen legacies I'd once called friends before one of them shoved an iron spike through my liver. Their names will be a shadow in my throat until the day I die.

"You yourself drove a sharp pane of glass into your half sister's chest and watched her bleed out. But we did these bad things for a good reason, a reason everyone seems to have forgotten about—to put *you* on the Amber Throne. And every moment we hesitate—every moment we equivocate about what we should and shouldn't be doing *now*, about who we should let edge in on our dubious triumph—takes away from the things we already did. The longer we wait to see you crowned, the more likely it becomes that all of this was for nothing. And the only thing worse than doing what we did . . . would be having done it for nothing."

Anguish choked me. "What are you saying?"

"I'm saying *screw* Gavin. Screw these Ordeals. My wolves hold this city together with their bare teeth, but *they* hold it. It's less than a span until Ecstatica—until your coronation. Then you'll be empress, without competing against an undeserving cousin or sacrificing any of the things you've already earned."

"Earned?" I repeated, chilly. "What have I earned but the city's loathing? I have to prove I'm worth their love."

"You think these Ordeals will make them love you?" His laughter cut me. "Everything I've done—every sacrifice I made—was because I believed in that strange, beautiful world you dreamed of so long ago in the dusk. You should be showing them that, not competing in some archaic farce of a competition with a man who would never be Sun Heir if you weren't handing him the opportunity!"

"I'm continuing a tradition stretching back a thousand tides," I argued, spiky.

"Don't you remember railing against the world the Sabourins built? A world that spawned Severine, and Coeur d'Or? A world full of dangerous deceits?" His words carved out a hollow in my chest. "These Ordeals—they are the epitome of that world. Violence and death. Siblings pitted against each other. Blood-drenched thrones. You swore to me you would break that world to see it remade into the world you dreamed of. Even if it made you a monster."

I choked on memories that seemed impossibly far away. "That world was an illusion."

"It must have been." His forced sarcasm slithered toward sadness. "At Pierre's trial you demanded the deaths of Sainte Sauvage and his Red Masks. A boy died, and you called for more blood—you screamed at me to hunt them down in the street like dogs."

Guilt punched me in the stomach—I'd barely thought of Pierre since he'd collapsed, lifeless, to the boards of the pavilion. But now it came rushing at me like a gale—his broken body, small in life and smaller in death, ended with all the gravitas of a twig snapping underfoot.

"That wasn't my fault." The edge of my voice winged up like a question and I knew I was done for.

"You gambled with his life and his loyalty, and you both lost," Sunder said, grim.

"I was so sure." A note of desperation curdled my voice, and I folded my arms tighter around myself. "I was so sure he would turn on Sainte Sauvage."

"But he didn't."

"He tried to kill me. Twice. Didn't he deserve to die?"

"Death for death is a monster's parade." Sunder pushed himself off the bedpost and stepped close. His gloved hand skimmed my neck and whispered against my chin, urging my gaze toward his. I resisted for a long moment, then met his eyes. They were pain-scored and almost pitying, and part of me cried out as I fell toward a shattered sea of fragile hopes. Cried out for him, for all the agony he'd borne; cried out for me, and all the promises I'd broken. "But do you know what the worst of it is?"

I shook my head, not because I didn't know, but because I didn't want him to tell me.

His voice, when it came, was an elegy for innocence. "You screamed at me to hunt down people just like Pierre—boys and girls sucked in by zealotry—and *kill* them. Not catch them. Not even interrogate them. Just kill them."

"One of them shot that arrow."

"One of them. The rest? Their greatest crime is searching for something to believe in. And I *have* killed them. Their blood is on my hands. But it was you who smeared it there."

"You never showed me you cared." I hated myself for all the excuses climbing my throat. "I mean, isn't it—?"

"Isn't it what I do?" Irony made a knife of his mouth. "Isn't that who I am? Perhaps it is. But I thought you, at least, might pretend to hesitate before using me like the tool—like the weapon—I am."

"I just thought—" I grasped for something to shield me against the cold fingers of self-loathing creeping quiet around my heart. "I thought, after everything you'd already done—"

"—That I would be immune to the horror of killing? That I could be inured to the feeling of a life bleeding away between my fingertips, just by doing it often enough? Then you truly must think me a monster."

"I *don't*."

"Then you'd be the only one."

"I never meant to be your pain," I said, around the tears choking me. "You must know that."

"I do," he said. "But it only makes it worse that you used me thoughtlessly. You couldn't be bothered to think about my wants, my feelings, because you knew I would do whatever you wanted, whatever you asked. Because of the way I feel about you."

"Forgive me," I pleaded. "I only asked you to be my commandant because I thought you wanted it—because I thought you wanted to protect me."

"I did," he growled. "I do. But I don't think I can do *this* too. I cannot be both your consort and your commandant. I cannot be both your knight and your lover. And it only makes sense for me to sacrifice one."

I shuddered around a sob. "Sunder, no."

"I know you have never felt comfortable in my arms—not that I blame you." His eyes held a yawning abyss of longing stark as blood on a new-forged sword. "Isn't this what you want?"

I reached for him, forlorn. "Of course it's not."

"Then give me something." He caught my outstretched arm and drew me close—too close, his mouth a hairsbreadth from mine. "Give me something other than illusion, demoiselle."

I sipped at our shared breath and measured the weight behind his words. I knew what he wanted me to say. But I couldn't—not here, not now. Not after the accusations he'd laid on my head. Not when it felt like the only thing that might save us.

I wouldn't be his pain.

We were cut from different cloth and sewn together by conflict—how long until we came apart at the seams anyway?

I shook my head, roughly. He released me, turned toward the door. His shoulders stooped, then straightened.

"Do you know what they're calling me, in the lower city?"

Misery made me mute. He half turned, the light from the ambric glow-globes turning his profile to hammered metal.

"*The Butcher of Belsyre.*" A coil of decaying humor lifted his cold mouth. "They used to call me *Severine's Dog.* But she never had the audacity to name her leash *love.*"

THIRTY-ONE

The next Matin, I took my time getting dressed, struggling against emotions violent as bloodstained shards of mirror glass. How had everything gotten so mixed up, so *wrong*? The impossible world I'd reached for had turned to ash in my hands; the beauty I'd longed for had smeared away, like tarnished gilt on rotten wood. I'd thought I was fighting for something perfect, but all I'd done was alienate friends, make new enemies, and lose some bright part of myself that I stupidly thought would keep shining forever.

I cast my mind back—back as far as I could remember, to the dusk where I'd grown up. The Temple of the Scion, lit by cheap stinking tapers, heavy with the dust of hundreds of tides, echoing with the prayers of a thousand generations of sanctimonious Sisters. I'd barely had the chance to be a child, but Scion help me, I'd tried. I remembered dancing through the drafty halls, humming songs I'd overheard the villagers singing, working songs and drinking songs and songs long as stories—songs about amber cities and dristic mountains and impossible diamond skies over kembric sands. But Sister Cathe had caught me. Her bony fingers closed over my elbow and she dragged me into the fane, where icons of the Scion stared at me with heavy, glittering eyes.

Dreaming does not belong in these halls, she'd snapped. *Such sins only breed misfortune. Think on that while you pray.*

And so I'd thought on it. I'd traced out the shapes of mountains in the dust and murmured half-familiar names to myself, and *thought*. I'd closed my eyes and dreamed of impossible, incandescent colors, and *thought*.

And finally, I knew—if dreams did not belong in that Temple, then neither did I.

I'd spent the last tide of my life searching for an eloquent, radiant world where I would finally belong. I thought I'd found it here, in Coeur d'Or, until a forgotten family and a bitter destiny came hurtling out of the dusk of my past. And then I thought perhaps—*perhaps*—if I could break that world apart, and replace it with a world I dreamed of, *that* would be where I belonged. So I broke it. But I was beginning to see I had only broken myself and those around me.

And for the first time in my life, I had to ask myself: What if the Sisters had been *right* all along? What if dreaming just led to selfishness, and believing in a world only you could see just led to pride?

A soft knock at my door dragged me out of my bitter reverie. Dread dragged sharp fingers through my composure when I remembered my altercation with Sunder last Nocturne. Scion, I didn't want to believe all the things he'd laid upon me, but an unflinching part of me knew what he'd said was true. I'd lost my vision of that impossible world, and in doing so started using him the same way I'd hated Severine for using him. I'd taken the things he hated most about himself and *used* them.

I stood, squared my shoulders, and marched toward the door, hoping I could manage to apologize for once in my life instead of sounding off at the mouth.

It wasn't Sunder.

"Dowser?" Surprise made my voice strangely high. My teacher never came to my rooms—he always sent a note, or, more frequently, I had to find him when he lost track of time.

"Do you have a moment?" His hands were tucked deep in the sleeves of his robe and his gaze was grave. Worry unspooled inside me.

"Of course." I led the way to one of Belsyre Wing's luxurious sitting areas—this one was tucked behind a flowering terrarium. Weightless birdsong struck a jarring chord against the dirge humming dark between my ribs. "What's the matter?"

Dowser sighed, heavily. "The first Ordeal is set for three days from now. According to Arsenault, it is customary to begin with Head, then move on to Hand and Heart. Soul would come last, if we had the requisite Relic."

Head. So, the kembric crown Relic would be the first I had to win. A thrill pulsed through me. I leaned forward.

"What can I expect from the first Ordeal?"

"I don't know." Dowser put two fingers to the corners of his eyes. "Arsenault claims he doesn't know the details, and even if he did, the Ordeals are different for each contestant."

"How does that work?"

"The magic of the Oubliettes is . . ." Dowser searched for the right word. "*Old.* Listen, after yesterday's Congrès, Barthet and I visited the libraries at Unitas to look for clues about the Ordeals, the Oubliettes, the Heirs—everything. What little we found was disturbing."

Unease tripped down my spine. "How so?"

"Meridian might have existed," Dowser said. "But whether he was a god, a king, or a man whose legend outgrew him, no one really knows. His children, the Heirs of the Scion, are equally shrouded in myth—your progenitor, Sébastien Sabourin, included. Were they really children of Meridian? Did they truly inherit these Relics from him? There is little actual *history* about your ancestors until just a few hundred tides ago. But the legends tell of a family with arcane, *powerful* magic—magic they would do almost anything to protect."

I frowned. "I don't understand."

"The château that stood where Coeur d'Or stands now—in

the lore, it's referred to as La Citadelle. The texts speak of armies laying siege, hoping to loot its riches, only to find its gates wide open. The soldats who went inside never came out again. There are legends of monsters, of madness, of deathless magic. One author even suggested that the old château was not filled in and built over to make way for a new, bigger palais, but . . . to *hide* a place that couldn't be allowed to exist any longer."

I made myself laugh. "That sounds like a bedtime story for naughty children."

"Does it?" Dowser pinned me with canny eyes. "You're the only person I know who's been down there."

I suppressed a shudder against images of bloodstained sunbursts and moonlit diamond armies and the echoing voices of long-dead Heirs.

"As ridiculous as it sounds," Dowser went on, "Arsenault seemed to think no two Ordeals are the same. That the Oubliettes would tailor each Ordeal to you and Gavin."

"So?"

"So I want you to know . . . if you decide to give up, I won't blame you."

"*What?*"

Dowser shook his head. "I know you are proud. I know you never listen, not when you've set yourself against something. But my conscience will not be easy unless I tell you—you've gone far enough."

"I thought you believed in my claim to the Amber Throne. I thought you wanted to see me as empress."

"Your claim is true, Mirage," Dowser said. "I know better than anyone—you are Sylvain's daughter, and therefore dauphine and heir. But none of that matters if you're mad or dead." Dowser surged to his feet and paced to the wall and back. "These Ordeals are dangerous, Mirage. The first Ordeal is predicated on skills of the *head*—intelligence, problem solving, intuition—but the second Ordeal will test the physical. Strength, agility, resilience. You know you are no warrior, child."

"Not all forms of strength are physical," I pointed out, my voice chilly. "There is strength in beauty, agility in the mind, resilience in peace. I am not without my own power."

"I know that." Dowser sat back down, uneasy. "I just meant that the Oubliettes will test you."

I thought about Sunder, about Lullaby, about all the ways I'd failed my friends. "Perhaps I deserve to be tested."

"And if it's a test you can only fail?"

"Then everything will be a lot more clear, won't it?"

"This isn't a joke, Mirage."

"Sorry." I put a hand on his arm, and tried to articulate all the thoughts that had plagued me since my fight with Sunder. "I just meant, I'm not afraid of what's going to happen. I asked for this—in a way, it's the first thing I've done right in a long time. I've made too many wrong decisions lately. I don't know if I'm the true Sun Heir or not, but I'm tired of arguing about it. Maybe it's right to let the magic of the Relics decide."

"What do you mean?"

"When I first came to the palais," I began, "I believed I was owed something. I believed the accident of my birth meant I deserved a place in this glittering world. And when that dream turned into a nightmare, I blamed everyone else, never considering that perhaps I was the one at fault. But I finally feel like I have a path toward *earning* what I was born to do. I don't want it given to me. I want to work for it. I want to be tested. It will make the winning all the sweeter."

"Spoken like a true Sabourin." Dowser folded me into a brief, gruff hug. I inhaled the aggressive perfume of tabak smoke and old leather; ink-splattered robes and too much worry. He stood, wiping at his brow and heading for the door. "Prepare yourself, Mirage. I have a feeling the next few days are going to get complicated."

I watched him go, then slowly pulled my ambric Relic from the bodice of my dress. Its familiar planes glowed skin-warm and sun-hot, and I stared at it for a long, curious moment. Much as I'd tried to think of it as I always had—as a slightly ugly antique with mysterious origins—I'd begun to attribute thoughts, *intentions* to the hunk of ambric. Did it want me to face Gavin in the Ordeals? Did it want me to reunite it with its fellow Relics and win my place as Sun Heir? Or was it simply a tool, a vessel—for unknown magic, for power untold?

I slipped it back into my dress. I didn't think the next few days were going to be complicated at all.

Beat Gavin in the Ordeals. Win the Relics. Earn my place as Sun Heir.

Or walk away from this world—this *impossible* dream—forever.

THIRTY-TWO

T he day of the first Ordeal arrived with a glossy, effervescent sort of calm.

I posted myself beside an arching window looking out over the rear courtyard of the palais, to watch the crowds file in through the dungeons, stamping careless feet down new-built ladders and through artificially braced doors. Dowser told me they'd held a lottery throughout the city for the limited space in the Oubliettes—apparently there'd been so many entries, Sunder's already overtaxed wolves had had to wheel them up to the palais in wagons. The official list had been posted yesterday, and now what looked like hundreds of people filed in through the Échelles gate, of all ages, genders, skin colors, and styles of clothing.

"The first—and last—time any of us will ever see so many people willingly walking into a dungeon," lilted a high, sophisticated voice.

I turned to see Oleander, Lullaby, and Sunder lingering near the door. I gaped, for a moment—I thought it was also the first and last time I'd see these three willingly spending time with one another.

"You found me." I sounded a little breathless.

"How are you feeling?" Lullaby asked.

"Strange," I admitted.

"So, normal," Oleander said, without inflection.

I laughed. Something giddy was rising up inside me—pale effortless wings lifting me toward an inevitable hour. Sunder's cool-burn eyes touched my face, but I forced myself not to look at him. We hadn't spoken privately since our fight. His brusque, businesslike demeanor and cold haughty mask made me think we never would.

I tried not to think too hard about how that made me feel.

"I brought you this." Oleander stepped forward and held out a top of some kind. "It's armor."

"*Sort of* armor," Sunder clarified.

"*Sort of* armor," Oleander agreed, with a roll of her eyes. "Belsyre women all learn weaponry, but I could never stand that horrid dristic chain mail the Loup-Garou wear under their uniforms. It chafed my skin and hid my lovely figure. So I designed this."

I ran my fingers over the long-sleeved jacket. It was tooled in rigid leather the color of midnight. It didn't look like any armor I'd ever seen.

"The first Ordeal is kembric—*Head*. I'm not sure I need—"

"Wear it," Lullaby commanded. Sunder inclined his bright head in agreement.

"Fine," I grumbled, and Oleander helped me into it. It was surprisingly soft and light, with snug sleeves and a tapered cut.

"It's reinforced throughout." Oleander fastened a series of straps across my bust and waist. "But it's lightweight enough to move in. See?"

Swiftly, she punched me in the gut. Reflexively, I doubled over, but it took me only a moment to realize I wasn't in any pain. I'd felt the impact of her fist, but distantly—diffuse.

"That's—Oleander, this is amazing!"

"I know." She preened.

"Did you know some people consider modesty a virtue?" Lullaby asked.

"Really?" Oleander looked genuinely surprised. "Who?"

"Let's get you to the Oubliettes." Lullaby looped her arm through mine and tugged me toward the door, whispering,

"While you still have any goodwill at all left toward Oleander."

I let my friend lead me out. Sunder and Oleander trailed us through the palais toward the courtyards and the dungeon beyond. I stopped at the door, extracting my arm from Lullaby's.

"You all go on without me." Sudden gravity hammered down. "I'm supposed to meet Gavin here. We're going in together."

Lullaby gave me a sudden, fierce hug. *"Win."*

"Please do." Oleander inspected one of the leather straps on my armor, and I chose to read affection into the cursory gesture. "Don't let that bastard steal any more of what doesn't belong to him."

And then I was alone with Sunder. He reached for my hand, and swiftly brought it to his mouth. His lips slid along my knuckles, cool and sharp—a kiss of hesitation, a wasteland of yearning. I tightened my fingers on his—I reached for him—but he'd already let my hand drop.

"Sunder." I couldn't let him go. He was the only person who knew my fears. He was the only person who told me the truth. "Sunder, I'm afraid."

His green eyes flickered, gathering shadows.

"There was one Belsyre seneschal when Oleander and I were young." His voice was a coil of smoke, dark as Dominion and bad dreams. "He had a taste for wicked things. He used to corner me in hallways and stairwells, touching my arms without asking and demanding things I didn't want to give him. I was terrified of him. I begged one of the butlers, Bertan, to put locks on all my doors, but it wasn't good enough. He just went to the chambers beside mine, to Oleander's rooms. I was too afraid to stop him, to confront him, even though it was me he was after. I listened, mute and powerless, as she yelled at him to leave her alone, to stop watching her sleep, to stop touching her hair."

I bit my lip. A tear slid down my cheek.

"The next day I went to the blacksmith's forge and gathered

all the scrap metal I could find. I borrowed a whetstone and sharpened the dristic until my fingers bled. Oleander helped me sew each piece into my jacket, on the inside where it couldn't be seen. I wore that jacket for days, even though the metal cut through my shirts until my arms bled. But it was worth it—the next time that man touched me without asking, he nearly lost his fingers. Scion, I can still hear his screams, the blood running down his arms and painting the floor red. But he never came near me or my sister again."

"Are you saying," I whispered, "that I shouldn't be afraid?"

"Demoiselle, you should be very afraid." He reached out and softly brushed a tear off my cheek. "But you can choose to let your fear ride you until you're so weak you loathe yourself. Or you can choose to turn it into a weapon."

He disappeared into the dungeon stairwell, his pale kembric hair a torch against the dim.

I waited beneath a sky etched with bloody tears for my rival to appear. And when at last Gavin strode through the Échelles gate, I was glad to have accepted Oleander's gift. Because Gavin had come dressed as the Sun Heir—a blazing silhouette of a man, armored in kembric and haloed in amber light from the sun at his back. And for a moment, as I watched him approach, I *loved* him—I loved the honesty shining on his face, I loved the strong lines of his powerful shoulders, I loved the light that poured off him like the Scion's blessing. Then I saw Arsenault stalking beside him, a frown on his hatchet face and the kembric Relic held before him like a prize to be won.

And Gavin's glamour slipped away like water down a drain.

I squared my shoulders, shaking off the lingering effects of his legacy.

"Ready?" I put on a brilliant smile. Gavin wasn't the only one who could create an illusion.

"Are you?" asked Gavin, with a flash of the young man I'd first met.

"Depends." I nodded at Arsenault. "Is he going to make me do long division? Because I'm terrible at math."

"I won't have anything to do with it," Arsenault growled, with a glimmer of something like disgust in his eyes. "But let's get on with it, shall we?"

With one last glance at the Coeur d'Or, gilded in kembric and domed in ambric, a dristic promise at the heart of everything I'd ever fought for—I descended into the waiting darkness of the Oubliettes.

I just wished I knew whether I would find destiny or doom.

The main cavern of the Oubliettes blared with unnatural light— hundreds of firelit torches ringed the massive chamber. The spectator seating had shouldered an air of grim revelry—I glimpsed livid leering faces in those high tiers, and heard the echoing chink of bottles being passed mouth to mouth, livres and écu passing hand to hand.

My giddy, glossy calm frayed at the edges, leaving me jittering with nerves.

The moment Gavin, Arsenault, and I passed into the Relic arena, the crowd surged to its feet and roared. There was something barbaric in the sound—as though the moment we stepped into this chamber we went from powerful nobles to *prey*. As though this had been the spectacle they wanted all along— danger and mayhem, dueling crowns and the prospect of death. The thunder of their chanting—*Sun Heir, Sun Heir, Sun Heir*— wormed its way between my ears and ate into my heart.

My teeth clenched tight and I quickly scanned the spectators for familiar faces. There were *so* many people, and for a hideous searching moment I couldn't find my friends. But there—two diamond heads bent close in discussion; a gleaming dark pate; shining seafoam eyes in an exquisite blue face.

I loosed a breath. Of course they'd come.

I looked for Luca, and when I saw him, I was barely surprised to see him with Gavin's entourage.

Arsenault stepped into the middle of the room, by the stone dais. He seemed to have absorbed some of the room's frenzy—a fevered light shone in his copper eyes, and his customary scowl seemed exultant. He held up the kembric Relic for all to see. It caught the torchlight and sent sharp blades of sunlight into the shadows.

"Behold the first Relic of the Scion—a crown of kembric forged from the net Meridian used to capture the Moon." The cavern took Arsenault's voice and flung it against the arching glass ceiling. "The first Ordeal of the Scion will test these Heirs' mental agility— their wits, their quick thinking, their problem-solving. But most of all, it will test their intuition. Do you witness this Ordeal?"

The crowd's response was the rumble of distant mountains.

"Then let the first Ordeal of the Sun Heir begin!"

Slowly, Arsenault lowered the misshapen crown toward the dais. The kembric Relic settled into its hollow with a dull thunk. For a tortuous moment, the only sound was a thousand breathing mouths and my own uneven heartbeat.

Every single light in the grand chamber went out at once. Panic sent thready feelers through the crowd, and I felt the answering thunder of my own blood. Then radiance blossomed above the dais—light like the sharp heart of a bonfire, blinding and merciless. Lines of fire exploded along the floor, illuminating the chamber in golden glow, until they too dimmed and disappeared.

All but two.

The light nearest me brightened the moment my boot stepped onto it, a pulse of energy flinging itself toward the deepest parts of the cavern. I followed. At last, the golden light resolved itself into an object hanging several feet in front of me. It was a crown—not the kembric Relic; this crown was large enough to sit upon my head—hanging in midair in front of my face. I swallowed, glancing quickly over my shoulder, but the rest of the chamber had faded away into the dim.

I grabbed the crown. A firework in champagne and sunlight flung itself out of the shadows toward the ceiling, arcing along the painted glass and loosing trailers as it went. A shimmering kembric dome encompassed the space above me, blurring the audience away.

The floor fell out from beneath me.

I fell to my knees, bracing myself against the chilly stone. But it wasn't the floor that was falling down. It was the walls that were falling *up*. I found my balance.

Impossible golden stones screamed up from the floor, glowing like molten metal and thick as ironstone slabs. They shifted in complex, vertiginous patterns before slamming into a tight corridor around me. The floor shuddered with the force of their arrangement. I shuddered too, trepidation and fear tangling ragged threads around my heart.

At last, the motion ceased, leaving behind a soft, endless silence. I looked up into the shimmering dome. I could still see the crowds watching, but I couldn't make out their faces, and what should have been a full-throated roar of entertainment was nothing more than a whisper.

I clenched suddenly sweaty palms and lowered my eyes. Better not to be distracted, anyway.

I shoved myself toward the looming walls and placed a

hesitant palm against the nearest glowing slab. I nearly snatched my hand away. It felt like human flesh. I buried a visceral burst of disgust, and pressed harder. The material pressed back, with an impact that jarred me to my elbow. I curled a lip, and scrubbed my too-hot palm against the skirt of my dress.

So I couldn't pass through the stones. I lifted my gaze to their towering heights—I definitely couldn't go *over*.

The only way out was *through*.

A labyrinth? Whatever it was, I had to to solve it quickly—on the other side lay the plinth with its Relic to be won. I couldn't let Gavin get there first.

I took a deep breath, and stepped between the golden slabs. My footsteps rang like wind chimes on the floor, and I noticed patterns etched into the tiles below my feet—circle, blade, crown, sun. *Soul, Hand, Head, Heart.* The symbols of the Relics flashed by as I sped along the corridor, and I loosed a breathless laugh around the shreds of fear and excitement tangling within me.

Scion, but this was really happening. I was competing in the Ordeals of the Sun Heir, to beat my cousin and prove once and for all I could *do* this. I could be the heir the Amber Empire not only needed, but *wanted*. An echo of inevitability glanced off the walls and reverberated like the footsteps of long-dead ancestors and forgotten family. Somehow—some*time*—I was always here, always running toward that light, that power, that destiny.

The tunnel ended abruptly in a circular chamber. I slammed to a halt, my glee melting away like a dream. Four doors stared out of blank, shimmering walls. I stepped closer to the left-most door. It had a large circle etched in the spot where a knob ought to have been, and above that, in the center of the door, were two other symbols: a blade and a crown.

I frowned, and looked to the other doors. The second door had the symbol of a blade in place of its knob, and on its face it wore two other symbols—circle and sun. The third door had a crown at its knob and a crown at its heart. The fourth door had a sun at its knob, and all three other symbols marked on its face.

What in the Scion's name . . . ?

I moved closer, and my boot scuffed against a raised plaque in the floor. I dropped to my knees before it, hoping for a clue or hint. The metal shifted at my touch, a few lines of verse appearing in raised letters. I gritted my teeth, and sounded out the words as quickly as I could.

To find your way you must be bold,
There is just one way through.
Only one of these doors has a truth to be told,
The others' falseness is the clue.

I read it twice just to make sure I had all the words right. But there was no mistaking the verse—it was a riddle.

There is just one way through. That could have only one meaning: Just one of the doors was the correct choice. I reexamined the symbols etched into each door. The Relic symbols at the knobs must identify each door: circle, blade, crown, sun. The marking above must be hints to which door was correct.

I repeated the second half of the verse. *Only one of these doors has a truth to be told.* Only one of the doors was giving the correct clue; the others were lying. I ran through the clues again. The first door hinted the correct doors were two and three. Two hinted at one and four. Three's hint was . . . itself. And the fourth door indicated it was any door *but* itself.

Slowly, my hand strayed toward the third door—the crown door. A crown at the knob. A crown on its face. This was the Head Ordeal, after all. It made so much sense. But I forced myself to think it over just a moment longer. If I was wrong, this would be the first and last Ordeal. The sudden end to my nonexistent rule as Amber Empress.

I couldn't afford to be wrong. I had to do this the right way. And that meant going with my wit instead of my gut.

Four doors. Three lies. One truth. There was no way to be sure if any door was lying or telling the truth. Which meant the only way to solve this was to work backward from each possible correct answer.

My breath carved out a space between my clenching ribs, and started with the first door. If that were the correct path, then both two and four would have to be telling the truth. Which was impossible.

My chest loosened. *I could do this.*

Door two. If that were the correct path, then both one and four would have to be true. Also impossible.

My heart vaulted, and I crept toward the third door—the crown door. Yet again, I reached for its tempting symbol, but I knew it was meant to fool, to foil. When I looked over the doors, yet again, I saw that crown symbol marked on door one, door four, and, of course, door three. Which meant that if this were the correct door, all three would be telling the truth.

My hand fell to my side. Fevered excitement pulsed within me. If door one, two, and three were all impossible, then the only one that remained was . . .

I closed my eyes, hard, and ran through the logic once again. I couldn't afford to be wrong.

Swiftly, before I could change my mind, I chose the fourth door. My fingers brushed the spoked sun, its contours familiar in their inverse. With a click and a groan, the door swung upon onto another narrow passageway curving away into the glow.

THIRTY-THREE

Relief turned my bones to liquid. I shoved my way into a corridor. The door's edges glowed faintly for a moment, then smoothed away into the glow of the kembric slabs behind me. I shuddered, and turned my gaze forward.

I followed the passageway until it abruptly split in two. I looked around for a clue. Nothing.

I cast my mind back to the handful of times I'd stumbled my way through the hedge labyrinth in Coeur d'Or's manicured gardens. It had been more trysting site than intellectual challenge, but Thibo had been fond of the privacy behind its high green walls. I'd been amazed when he'd easily found his way to the sparkling fountain at its heart. He'd laughed at my surprise.

Follow the left-hand wall until you find your way, he'd explained. *It might take you forever, but you'll get through eventually. And once you know, you know.*

I didn't have time for *eventually.* But it wasn't bad advice. Each path in a maze had only two outcomes—correct and incorrect. And both gave me the information I needed.

I chose the left path at random, and dashed down it as quickly as I could.

Left.

Right.

Dead end.

I turned on my heel and ran back the way I'd come. When I reached the original intersection, I paused. I needed a way to mark the path, to ensure I didn't go wandering in circles. But I hadn't brought anything with me, no ink or paint or—

I might not have ink, but I had something better—my *legacy.*

I fumbled over images and symbols, before finally settling on the only thing that might show up against the incessant shine of the maze: *Duskland shadow.* I threw a scrap of midnight against the floor.

This way, it said. *Remember you went this way.*

I left it with a scrap of attention—intention—scraped from my soul, and prayed to the Scion it would stay after I'd gone. I took off along the other path.

The next intersection split into three hallways. Another plaque rested at its nexus, with another riddle. Irritation bloomed around my heart, but I quelled my anxious desire for speed and read the words as quickly as I could.

The Sun must now darken,
The Moon must not shine her light,
No bright swords,
One bright crown,
To guide you through this endless night.

An involuntary shiver went through me. I stared into the forking passageways, but each glittered, urgent. There wasn't even a suggestion of night, other than the scrap of darkness I'd left three turns back. I didn't know what the riddle meant.

Unease weakened my muscles. I didn't have time to linger. For all I knew, Gavin was speeding through the maze, drawing ever closer to the kembric Relic and with it, the throne. I read through the riddle once more, committing it to memory in case I needed it later. I tossed another scrap of shadow toward the floor and kept moving.

The labyrinth was littered with more puzzles and riddles— some so simple I doubted my own instincts, some so challenging they took longer than I could afford. And at each new puzzle and riddle and twist and turn, I scraped shadow from my heart to remind myself where I'd come from.

A room floored with the same tiles as the entrance to the maze—tiles etched with the Relic symbols. When I stepped on the first tile—a crown—it fell away into a molten heart of a distant sun, and I nearly fell with it. Then I remembered the order of those first tiles I'd stepped on—circle, sword, crown, sun. I followed those symbols precisely across the vast floor and made it to the far side.

A wall studded with pairs of colored lights. Each light brightened when a line was drawn to its pair, but if the line was broken or crossed, the light dimmed once more. I unraveled a tapestry of colored lines across the wall. The wall split in half to let me through.

And *riddles*. Riddles on doors. Riddles to reveal passageways. Riddles to reveal more riddles. Every riddle felt personal—as though the Oubliettes had stared into my heart and stolen my secrets.

> *I am a warning you wish to shun,*
> *I touch you and you come undone.*

Ghostly fingers gloved in suede brushed my cheek, and I scented frost and pine on the air. The answer was *pain*.

> *I am nothing but a thief,*
> *My price is joy; you pay in grief.*

A voice I thought I'd forgotten spoke the answer to that riddle; a once mirthful voice made bitter with sorrow. *We are all thieves here.* And I felt what Thibo had felt when he'd lost Mender, what we'd all felt when we lost Thibo—*loss*.

You seek me though I weigh you down,
My burden lies upon your crown.

The answer was a hole in my chest long before I had the courage to answer it. *Power.*

I stepped through the door, exhaustion pulling at my footsteps. I stared at yet another identical wall of shimmering kembric before I saw the flaw, the shred of *wrongness* souring my stomach.

A sliver of night. A scrap of shadow.

My glitter-numb mind caught up. *No.*

I squeezed my eyes shut, as though I might wish away the nightmare. But I knew that shadow like I knew my own mind—it was one of the illusions I'd left behind to mark my way.

Anger boiled up inside me. I'd been trying to solve this maze for what felt like *hours.* I loosed a strangled scream of frustration, lashing out to punch the living wall. The slab punched back. The impact jolted my arm and flung me backward. I landed in a heap a stone's throw away, the wind knocking out of my lungs in a *whoosh.* For a long moment, I lay on the floor and gasped for air. And when I finally levered myself onto my hands, I was staring at a plaque set into the floor. A riddle—*the* riddle, the one I hadn't been able to solve.

The Sun must now darken,
The Moon must not shine her light,
No bright swords,
One bright crown,
To guide you through this endless night.

Scion help me—what if I'd strolled right past the key to the entire maze? I rolled the words over my mind, but they made no more sense than before. *Endless night*—how could there be any kind of night in this incessant shine? There was nothing but *light* here.

I sat up. Maybe that was it. Maybe I was supposed to create my own night.

Quickly, I conjured an illusion, dark as the shreds of shadow I'd scattered in my wake. But this one was huge, encompassing the maze intersection and trailing down the corridors. I turned in a slow circle, staring into the darkness. But kembric still glowed incessantly at its boundaries.

I sighed, and released the illusion.

I squeezed my eyes shut. But I could still see the maze's light—a red glow against the backs of my eyelids.

Desperate, I crouched, wrapped my hands around the hem of my dress, and tore. The fabric ripped ragged, but I kept at it, until I had a length of fine-dyed cotton in my hands. I folded it thickly, then wrapped it around my face. I yanked it tight, the makeshift blindfold scratching my cheeks. I tried to open my eyes.

Darkness—darkness, at last—fell soft and thick around me. I lifted my hands in front of my face, but I might as well have been blind. Again, I turned in a slow circle, hope chasing despair across my heart.

And then I saw the glimmer in the dusk. For a moment, all I could think of was the Scion's Vow I'd known since childhood: *I am the sun staring at the twilight. I am the solace that banishes blight. I am the moon shining deep in Midnight.*

But it was neither sun nor moon. The distant shine was the same color as these living stones, except now it was isolated by darkness. Haltingly, I walked toward it. My brain screamed at me that I was about to walk into a wall, but I ignored it. Two steps. Three. I shivered, because I should already have bounced off those hateful kembric slabs. But I just kept walking. I could almost imagine I'd left the physical world behind, because nothing stopped me as I strode through the midnight of my mind. I walked straight on, following that glittering metallic gleam, which was slowly resolving itself into—

A crown.

My steps sped; I flew forward. My rational mind kept insisting I would trip, I would run into something, I'd wind up on the ground with missing teeth or a black eye. But I just kept moving, focused on that perfect light, my hands flailing through the blindness for its touch.

The sound of a crowd roaring crashed over me like a clamorous wave. I knew in that instant I'd cleared the maze, and without breaking stride I ripped the sweat-slicked blindfold off my face. Light screamed into my eyes. The racket of the cheering crowd slammed into my ears and disoriented me. I flung myself toward the dais at the center of the Oubliettes as if by memory, my fingers reaching—

I saw Gavin—one more shining thing amid the tumult of light. He barreled toward the dais from the opposite side of the cavern. He caught sight of me a moment after I did him, and our eyes met across the plinth. He blinked.

My legs crumpled, as if some force had swept them clean out from under me. I collapsed onto the floor, wheezing. My fingers found the lip of the dais. I dragged myself forward, my nails scrabbling against stone. I reached—

The kembric crown Relic leapt the last few inches from its granite hollow to fit itself into Gavin's palm.

The crowd exploded into frantic noise. Gavin lofted the Relic, pumping his fists toward the sky and roaring triumph. And if I screamed from my place on the floor—screamed from rage and frustration and exhaustion—no one heard me.

I clawed my way into a standing position and stared into

Gavin's smug, bleating face. And I knew I'd never be able to forgive myself for two things that happened today.

I'd never forgive myself for losing the first Ordeal.

And I'd never forgive myself for being weak enough to let Gavin *cheat*.

THIRTY-FOUR

G uests had been told to arrive at Oleander's party in a costume that either concealed or contradicted their true nature.

The palais still echoed hollow with the celebrations of Gavin's victory. I'd put on a brave face in those aching moments after he'd won the first Relic—clasping his hand and congratulating him around bared teeth—but I'd taken the first opportunity to leave. My friends had caught up to me quicker than I'd wanted, and I couldn't shake the looks on their faces as they watched me scrub angry tears from my eyes. They'd pitied me—pitied me for solving the maze too slowly, pitied me for losing the Relic to Gavin.

But most galling of all, they pitied me for future loss. Because no one thought I could win the Hand Ordeal, scheduled just two days from now. And if Gavin won the second Ordeal, this competition would be over. And I would have lost without ever getting the chance to win back the ambric Relic, the Heart Relic—*my* Relic.

Only Oleander treated me the same. She'd helped me out of the leather armor she'd made me, and casually said, *I scheduled your party for the day after tomorrow.*

I choked on confusion. *My party?*

Yes, your party. That you asked me to plan?

Helpless anger made me rude. *Cancel it. I'm in the middle of the Ordeals.*

Scion give us strength to endure the fickle whims of the dreamy dauphine, said Oleander, to no one in particular. *Our lives didn't stop because you challenged your cousin to an archaic underground death match. I'm not canceling. And you still need to choose a theme.*

And I remembered—I'd already thought of a theme. Days ago, after a sun-bright Gavin had lied to me through his teeth. After all the dreams I'd fought for had begun to feel like lies. Still—I didn't know if being honest about deception would earn me trust, or yet more condemnation.

Surely it didn't matter now.

The theme for the party should be hidden selves, I said.

She'd seemed impressed. But the party couldn't stop me from obsessing over the darkness behind that blindfold, the shadows I'd scattered behind me that had warned me too late—*too late*—of the mistake I'd made. Scion, if I'd been mere moments faster, if he hadn't caught sight of me in those spare seconds before I'd reached the dais—

I tried to relax my clenching jaw as I climbed into my costume. I'd asked Oleander to design a kembric dress much like the one I'd worn to defeat Severine. Sharp blades of mirror glass traced the scars on my arms when I put it on, but I knew that with a flick of the wrist, the bodice and skirt would fall away in an ombré train to reveal a sleek dusk-lit gown splashed with opalescent gems. I'd commissioned a handheld mask to match— on one side was the sunburst face of the Sabourin sigil, and on the other was the pale staring face of the moon.

I shivered as my handmaiden Elodie laced it, forcing away my creeping doubts.

You will never be their Sun Heir. So why not become their Duskland Dauphine?

Oleander swept into my room without knocking, elaborately gowned in crimson and vermilion. Her costume was magnificent—a tapered red bodice climbed into translucent flames blazing against her throat. The skirt hugged her hips, then fell away in sheer ruched panels that showed off all eighteen miles of her slender legs.

"Scion!" I gasped. "What are you supposed to be?"

"Sunder and I were *supposed* to go as *fire and ice*," Oleander spat. "But *someone* thinks it's *childish* to play at *fancy dress*. So now I'm just *fire*, which doesn't make any sense. It's an absolute disaster!"

"I think you look magnificent," I said honestly. "Besides, with your pale skin and hair, *you* could be the ice, and the dress could be the fire."

"Hmph." Oleander pursed her lips, but looked slightly mollified. "I suppose that's not the worst idea."

"And the apartment looks amazing. Is everything ready?"

"You mean the little twist we decided on?" Oleander favored me with a blood-freezing smile. "Everything's set."

"Thank you."

"Oh—I almost forgot." Oleander reached into her reticule and drew out a flat box the length of my hand. "This came for you."

I reached for it, curious. "Really?"

Oleander turned to the mirror, smoothing her already-perfect hair. "One of the servants thought it was for me and left it in my room. But the note has your name on it."

"Has it ever occurred to you to learn their names?" I fiddled with the clasp on the box.

"The servants?" Oleander snorted. "I pay them extremely well to do a fairly simple job. Their names are irrelevant."

I opened my mouth to argue, but the box snapped open in my palm, flinging prisms against my face. It was a necklace—an ornate dristic choker studded with beryls, emeralds, and chips of diamond. It wasn't hard to guess why the servant had thought it was meant for Oleander—the palette of silver and green was much more suited to her than me. But she was right—the small note nestled in the box had my name on one side and a brief, curious note on the other: *With light.*

A tingle of foreboding glided along my spine. I turned, holding the box out for Oleander to see.

"Who is this from?"

"How should I know? Imagine you with a secret admirer." She inspected the jewelry with an expert eye. "This is expensive— the emeralds especially are exceptional. But I'm not familiar with the craftsmanship. I doubt this was purchased in the Amber City."

"It's not from—" I choked on the name, remembering our awful fight, and stared mute at the green gems.

"Sunder?" Oleander's eyes sharpened on my face. "I think you'll find my brother has better taste. And usually has the good manners to present a gift of expensive jewelry in person."

A whisper of memory sailed across my mind—a winter jardin and a cabochon of ambric; enchanted frost and red dye like blood on snow. I remembered Sunder's last gift of jewelry all too well.

"Well, I'm not wearing it." I set it on my vanity. "It doesn't go with my costume."

"Nothing much does," Oleander said obliquely. "Come on. The party's starting."

Oleander had transformed Belsyre Wing into a world bright to look at, yet dark to behold. Had she somehow caught a glimpse of my own heart and made it manifest in silks and sensation? Shimmering drapes hung from columns of quartz, sparking widening gyres of light across the suite of rooms. Yet when I moved between the curtains I saw their reverses gleamed dark, spangled with glittering diamonds bright as mythical stars. Giant tabak pipes with sinuous necks smoldered between layers of diaphanous gauze, sending sylphs of fragrant smoke to blur the senses and tease the eyes. A troop of ethereal dancers flitted between the pillars, their steps whisper-soft and light as air. When I looked closely, their bodies seemed to blur into the gossamer shrouds. They had no faces.

I forced my gaze away from the gilded splendor. For once, this illusion hadn't been created by me, and I couldn't afford to get lost inside it. Not this Nocturne.

Fifty or so courtiers mingled between the gauzy drapes, clutching goblets of shimmering Belsyre ice wine and darting glances at me. Most of them were Sinister, but invitations had been sent to remaining courtiers in both dynasties—I glimpsed a few Dexter faces as well. Everyone watched as I approached with Oleander, and I saw doubt harden into malice when their eyes fell on my gown, so similar to the one I wore the Nocturne I fought Severine. A niggle of worry clenched at my brow.

Scion, let this evening of illusion warm them to me instead of making them hate me more.

"Lords and ladies, I welcome you!" I called, spreading my arms. "We have been divided too long. Let us put aside our differences and partake in a Nocturne of fantasy and delight."

I saw a few scornful smiles hidden behind fans, and I knew I should have practiced a better speech.

"Tonight's theme is *hidden selves*." I lifted a glass of piercingly green liquid from the table, catching Oleander's gaze and lifting a questioning eyebrow. Her eyes flashed with arch glee. "These drinks have all been spiked with one of two mild poisons."

A few mouths opened in alarm, but I plunged ahead.

"The first poison forces you to tell the absolute truth. The second poison allows you to tell only lies. You won't know which is in your glass until after you drink it." A few curious whispers scampered around the room. Belsyre servants moved through the crowd, offering glasses. I didn't see any of the courtiers turn them down. "The poisons will last until fourth Nocturne. But once they fade, you will be left with no memory of which poison you drank, only the things you have said and done. So, whether you choose to be careful or careless with your words, they will be all that remain when this Nocturne is through."

A thrill throbbed through the crowd, an elusive heartbeat of excitement. My own blood rose to meet it, my stomach tightening beneath its layers of silk and boning. I licked my lips, then held my glass to the light to spit emeralds against the floor. My captive legacies' eyes were heavy with judgment, and I knew that if I did not drink first, I would lose them all.

I put the crystal to my lips and drained my glass in one long slug. As I did, I threw out one arm, releasing the mechanism holding the outer layer of my gown. Kembric fabric cascaded from my bodice in a shimmering waterfall and dusk descended over me—amethyst and sheer blue blurring toward midnight at my hem. Diamonds and pearls gleamed like the moon and stars of myth. I waited until I heard their murmurs of appreciation and the chiming of toasting goblets before I lowered my glass. I wiped my mouth to hide the fact that no liquid had crossed my lips.

Because my drink had no taste, no poison, no substance at all. It had been an illusion, and no one knew it but me. Not even Oleander—who'd helped me plan this deceptive evening—knew I never had any intention of drinking either poison.

I had questions I wanted to ask. But I had no intention of giving any answers.

Ghostly words drifted out of a memory of steam and ice, frost and red flowers, cold hands and molten words. *Perhaps you have deceit in your soul. Or perhaps you want to show the world something only you see . . .*

An air of revelry had already gripped the partygoers—they were reaching for more drinks and retreating into the labyrinth of illusion in groups, to watch the dancers or smoke from the giant tabak pipes while they waited for the poisons to kick in. I forced a smile, flicked my long golden train behind me.

And then I went in search of answers.

THIRTY-FIVE

Nerves sharp as fingernails dug into my heart and twisted when I spotted two Sinister courtiers muttering to each other in the corner. I recognized them, distantly—they were leaders of fashion at court. After the Suicide Twins, of course. I threw back my shoulders and smiled, lifting my chin as I gave a shallow curtsy.

"Billow." I named the brown-skinned beauty with her hair dyed in a rainbow of colors. I turned my eyes to her friend, a strapping lord I'd met once when Sunder was sparring for the Gauntlet. "Haze. Are you having a good time?"

"Are you?" A decision of some kind crossed Billow's face, and she flicked vibrant hair over her shoulder. "Can we ask you some questions?"

From the way she'd phrased her question I guessed she'd already discovered the easiest way to prevent someone from guessing whether you were telling the truth or lying—it was not to make any statements at all.

Haze looked surprised by her aggressive move, but nodded in agreement.

"Isn't that what this Nocturne is for?" I spread my arms, trying to look magnanimous and inwardly cringing. I respected Billow for her impulse to put me on my back foot—but if I was honest, I'd been trying to do the same to her. Quickly, I thought of the Nocturne I spent in Luca's garret apartment. An idea struck. "But shall we make a little game out of it?"

"I like games!" said Haze, nervously but enthusiastically. So presumably he had drunk the truth poison. Billow saw the realization in my eyes and glared at her friend.

"Sorry," he said, chastised.

"What do you propose?" Billow asked.

"How about for every question you ask me, I get to ask one in return? But every question must be answered with a statement."

Billow hesitated, chewing on her lip.

Haze blurted, "Are you planning on executing the courtiers who allied with Severine?"

"No," I said smoothly.

"Haze!" Billow snarled, tensing. "Do we know whether she's telling the truth yet?"

"No," he said, sheepish.

"Then will you please stop talking?"

I hid a smile. If anything, Haze had just endeared himself to me by showing me his greatest fear. Fear, I could use. Fear was a weapon, whether it was my fear or someone else's. I cleared my throat.

"Are either you or your parents plotting anything that might warrant an execution?"

They both hesitated.

"You want us both to answer?" asked Billow. "Is that fair?"

I smiled again. "Billow, if I ask Haze that question, what will his answer be?"

Her expression didn't change. "It will be *yes*."

Haze jumped, and his eyes widened. Tendrils of black vapor squeezed out of his fists, and I remembered his legacy was smoke. "That's not true!"

Billow's mouth twisted, and I knew I had my answer. Sinister wasn't plotting against me.

Yet.

"Would you like to ask me another question?" I offered.

Billow's stare was so malignant that for a moment I recoiled from her.

"What do you want from us, *dauphine?*"

I considered my answer. I wasn't under the power of either poison—I could say whatever I wanted. But if I wanted them to believe that I wasn't planning on executing them, then I needed to say something else they would believe to be true.

"I want your loyalty. Whether I have to beg, borrow, or steal it."

I waited to see unease bloom on both their faces before I plucked two tiny diamonds glittering from the ombré hem of my gown. I pressed one into each of their hands.

"Enjoy the party." I kept my voice low. "I mean you no harm. And whether or not I win these Ordeals, know that I offer you my favor."

I turned on my heel and strode away, uncertainty burning my throat like bile.

I found Gavin near a pergola draped in foliage beneath a prism-fretted chandelier. The area was open to the sky, and a cinnamon sun chased with burnt-black clouds smeared rubies and shadow across a gleaming marble floor. A few of Oleander's gauzy veils drifted like specters between strands of ambric lights.

Do you mind if I invite Gavin? I'd asked Oleander, the Nocturne before the party.

Her expression didn't change. *Why?*

I hadn't told anyone about my soul-deep certainty—Gavin had cheated. It somehow felt wrong to say it out loud when I had no proof. But I also knew I couldn't ask Oleander to invite the man who'd seduced and abandoned her into her home without good reason.

He cheated in the first Ordeal, I said. *I want to know how, and I want to know why.*

Slowly, she'd nodded. *As long as I don't have to look at his preening face.*

Gavin wasn't alone. He was talking animatedly to a young man about his height and build, with his head tilted close in interest. Something about the stranger's stance smoldered with familiarity. He wore an outlandish scarlet frock coat with a braided hem, and his throat and wrists sprayed ruffled lace. An extravagant hat with looping feathers sat jaunty atop his curls.

I froze. A sick blossom of desperate hope ignited in my chest. *Could it be—?* I took a few halting steps forward.

But then I realized—it was *Luca.*

I stopped in my tracks and loosed a breath, sour with shattered expectation and bitter disappointment.

"Who did you think he was?" asked a soft, impenetrable voice by the ice gate.

I whirled. It was Lullaby, nursing a wineglass on a bench. She was gowned in blue and aquamarine, embroidered in dristic thread and studded with turquoise. Her pale blue skin had been painted all over with teal pigment and flakes of metal, so that she shimmered in the light like she had fish scales. She was a creature caught between sea and sky, and I could almost imagine the tears glittering in her eyes were just another affectation.

"Is he wearing Thibo's clothes?" I asked quietly.

"Yes."

"Where did he get them?"

"I gave them to him."

"Why?"

"He didn't have a costume. And I thought—I thought Thibo, wherever he might be, might find it amusing."

A hand clapped on my shoulder and Luca pulled me into an embrace.

I hugged him back, fighting a cascade of dueling emotions.

Over his shoulder, I saw Lullaby look down and scrub at her eyes. I drew back, holding Luca at arm's length. Although he wore Thibo's fine clothes, his costume was clearly meant as a mockery of court fashion—his face was heavily painted a few shades too pale, and bright spots of rouge stood out on his cheeks. His lips were drawn in an exaggerated bow, and his naturally curly hair had been heat-tonged into curlicues.

"Rude." I hid a smile.

He cocked one nattily-stockinged calf and I saw he had on courtly heeled shoes he would normally never wear. "Do I fit in yet?"

Behind Luca, Gavin held a hand over his mouth, his shoulders shaking. As usual, I couldn't resist a rising bubble of laughter in response. I fought it, but Luca put his hand on his hip and began an exaggerated courtly promenade around the pergola. Before long, Gavin and Lullaby were doubled over cackling. I couldn't help cracking a smile.

"Come for the drinks, stay for the comedy?" laughed Gavin.

"I can get behind that." Luca slung a familiar arm around Gavin, who threw him a cheeky salute. "Maybe you were right about this place all along, Mirage."

A flare of envy curdled my mirth. I knew Gavin and Luca's friendship had progressed past equine adoration, but it hurt to see them so close. I knew one Nocturne of drinking games couldn't patch all the holes in my relationship with Luca, but now I wasn't sure I'd ever get the chance to patch the rest. My cousin had managed to charm Luca as he did everyone else.

"Did either of you get one of Oleander's special drinks?" I asked.

"Were they in these glasses?" Gavin held one of the crystal flutes the poisons had been served in.

"I didn't." A distant thrill strung the lines of Luca's painted face at eager angles. He disentangled himself from my cousin and reached a hand toward Lullaby. "Your glass is empty, my lady. Would you care to stroll with me in search of libations?"

Lullaby caught my eye, then shot a questioning look at Gavin. I slowly nodded, grateful for her concern. She shrugged, grasped Luca's hand, and walked out with him.

"Did you mean to be late?" I asked Gavin.

"Yes." He grinned back. "Would you rather I came early?"

"What's your costume meant to be?"

"Did you tell me I was supposed to wear one?"

"Did you read the invitation?"

"Yes." He laughed, but this time a shadow of annoyance crossed his jolly features. "Did it mention you'd be dosing all your guests and interrogating them?"

So he'd already learned the game. I'd hoped to catch him before he learned the trap I set, but for someone who claimed to hate court, he was no stranger to guile. I rolled words around my tongue, searching for the right phrasing to make him admit what I really wanted to know. But did it matter, in the end? I could never be completely sure whether he was telling the truth or not.

"Did you cheat in the first Ordeal?"

"No." He smiled all the way to his cracked-topaz eyes. I couldn't not smile with him, and I hated myself for it. "Did you?"

"Gavin—"

"Didn't the note you wrote me say, *rivals, not enemies*?" He reached out, impulsive, and took my hand. I jolted at his touch. "If we're not enemies, then shouldn't we be dancing?"

"I don't really—"

"She doesn't ride," he complained to the ceiling, "*and* she doesn't dance? What did they do for fun out in the Dusklands?"

"Nothing much," I admitted. "Unless you count paying obeisance to an absent Scion multiple times a day *fun*."

He gave another laugh and tugged me out into the hallway. I followed, half-reluctant. I didn't want to dance. But I had more questions for Gavin now I knew he'd drunk the truthful poison.

Hadn't he?

In my head, I tallied Gavin's answers against my own questions. He'd been evasive, sure. But so had everyone, this Nocturne. No one wanted to tell their hearts.

We burst out into the parlor, glitter-black and churning with bodies. A lively gavotte was underway, although from the raucous laughter and missed steps I didn't think choreography was top of mind. Gavin pulled me forward, sliding an arm around my waist so that we stood in position to join the staggering line of dancers.

"Let's not!" I protested, shouting to be heard above the music. "My dress will get ruined!"

Gavin brandished a salute before bending at the waist and sweeping up the train of my gown. We plunged into the boisterous dance, my dress swirling in a breathless flurry of twilight colors. I clutched his arm, unwilling to lose myself in the tipsy frenzy of the movement. Couples whirled around us, a dizzying kaleidoscope of wild costumes and fanciful disguises—I glimpsed a wolf's fangs dripping kembric blood; a cygni's pale wings stretched above a dristic blade of a neck; a diamond soldat and a mask red as ambric—

My eyes flew wide. I froze, fear pulsing through me. Gavin slammed into my motionless figure—stumbled—caught himself on the dancer next to him. Both boys went down, and Gavin's hand on my skirt pulled me off-balance too. I floundered to my knees, still searching wildly through the crowd for that scrap of red, that fearsome mask. A girl shouted—fabric ripped with a loud wet pop—a crystal goblet smashed on the floor, spilling wine over my slippers. A heavy hand on my shoulder dragged me backward. Terror spangled white-hot through my chest. I flung wild fists toward the figure.

It was just Gavin—he caught my forearms and half carried me out of the chaos, deftly moving between reeling drunks and a few couples still trying to dance despite the confusion I'd caused. I craned my neck over my shoulder, still looking for that Red Mask, but all I saw was the aftermath of someone running into a servant carrying a tray of drinks. The harried boy was on his knees in a pool of green liquid, cleaning up shattered crystal as laughing courtiers half-heartedly tried to help. Shards of broken glass winked at me.

"Mirage." Gavin set me in the shadow of a darkened hallway, his eyes keen with concern. "Are you all right?"

"What do you care?" Already the wild thrust of fear had faded, leaving me choked and shuddering and *ashamed*. I could have sworn I'd seen a Red Mask, but that wasn't possible. Not here, in the palais, at a party I'd personally organized. I'd seen the guest list, signed the invitations. The servants were loyal to Belsyre, the guards at the door Loup-Garou. This was the safest place in the world for me. "Why are you even here?"

"You invited me, remember? Rivals, not enemies?"

"I had an agenda," I snarled. "Surely you had one too."

His face hardened. "I came to ask you to cede."

I fought a choking wave of numb fury. "Why in the daylight world would I do a thing like that?"

"You thought you were going to win the Head Ordeal." Gavin's voice was blunt. "But you didn't. And I'm going to—was *always* going to—win the Hand Ordeal. Without either of the first two Relics, it won't even matter if you win the Heart Ordeal and earn back your ambric Relic. I will have already earned my place as Sun Heir."

"You might not win the Hand Ordeal." Terror made my voice cold.

"I'll win."

"My will was forged in the dusk and tempered in kinsblood," I hissed. "I am not without strength."

"Scion, Mirage, I'm not trying to insult you." His eyes blazed. "You're one of the strongest people I know. But if you think the Oubliettes won't test you with sharp edges and cold dristic . . ."

"So? If I must prove myself worthy, like every Sabourin before me, then I'll do it."

"And die in the doing?" He rose to his full height, looming above me. "Why put yourself through a dangerous, potentially life-threatening Ordeal when you know you cannot win? You don't want to do that. Even you're not that reckless."

"So you want me to, what? Just let you win?" The tears in the back of my throat stung like betrayal.

"Forfeit this ridiculous competition before it kills you. What's the point of a crown if you don't have a head to rest it on?"

"If I hand you the throne that should be mine, this empire will have a zealot as its monarch. An emperor with no tolerance for religious freedom. An emperor who had to cheat his way to a throne. And I will be nothing."

"Please, cousin, I'm not without mercy." His smile wasn't kind. "My offer still stands. Marry me, and our Sabourin children will never have to fight for anything."

Silence stretched hard and flat between us. Finally, I stood, gathering my rage around me like a cloak.

"I would rather stand in the sunlight and rail against the dusk than peer at the sun from the shadows and call that living. I will conquer the dusk and breathe light into shadow. I will remind them who I am."

Gavin gave me a long look. "Then I will see you at the second Ordeal, cousin."

THIRTY-SIX

I shoved away from Gavin through the shadow-bright drapes, desperate to find somewhere to breathe, to be alone, to sort through the tangle of emotions surging sour in my throat. But the party was in full swing. I fought my way through a crowd of revelers who'd decided that dancing was much more fun than lying to one another. I stumbled free, and slid down one of the hallways. I found the ice gate to Sunder's winter jardin and pushed it open. False snow sifted between desolate trees, and illusory frost hid a pale marble floor.

At the center of it all was Sunder.

He sprawled on the floor, half-covered in drifting snow and drinking from the narrow neck of a bottle half-full of green liquor.

Even from here, I could tell he was drunk.

I nearly turned on my heel and left. I knew we had to talk eventually, but I didn't relish a rehash of the charges he'd laid upon my head. Not tonight. Not after my encounter with Gavin. And certainly not when he'd been drinking.

But then I glimpsed a second, broken bottle in the shadow of a slender black tree. Only a few green drops clung to its shards.

He was *extremely* drunk.

Concern rippled through me. I crossed to where he sprawled and dropped to the ground beside him.

"What's all this?"

"Just a little something," he drawled, "to numb the pain."

Drunk, and excruciatingly honest. "Oleander said you wouldn't wear your half of the costume?"

"One of these days my sister will learn my primary purpose isn't as her fashion accessory."

I looked at his black wolf breeches, his black boots smudging the pristine tile, his pale shirt rolled to the elbow and open at the throat. "Then what is your costume?"

Sunder's smile was like the end of the world. "Pleasure."

I swallowed bile. "Looks a little more like hedonism."

"Is there a difference?"

I didn't think the chill climbing my spine was from the eddy of snowflakes bursting against my neck. "Did you take one of Oleander's poisoned drinks?"

"Yes. Although I should warn you, I'm mostly immune to my sister's gifts."

"Really? How?"

"Practice."

"Does that mean you're not telling me the truth right now?"

"Does it matter?" Sunder's head lolled back on his shoulder. He gave a ragged laugh. His eyes lifted to mine, but instead of being glazed with alcohol, they were feverish—pupils blown wide around glittering irises. "You seem to prefer when I lie to you, demoiselle."

"Sunder." I caught his hands in my own, twining them together and brushing my lips against our joined fingers. I couldn't ignore the burst of agony lancing through my skull. "I'm so sorry."

He tore his hand from mine and pressed it hard against his side. The gesture had become achingly familiar.

"As am I," he groaned. "I would die a thousand deaths to keep you from my pain."

"And yet," I whispered, "I have already become a part of it."

I would not be his pain.

"Do you want to know a secret?"

I bit my lip. "You're very drunk."

"Yes." He slumped back against the tree. "Sometimes I feel so used up, Mirage. Severine used me to hunt and torture and kill.

Oleander uses me to soothe her conscience, ease her pain, complement her fashion choices. You use me to hide all the things you don't want to look at. But most of all, this magic living inside me *uses* me. Everything—*everyone*—I hurt chips away at my sense of self and transforms me into a man I *hate*. My loathing feeds upon itself and turns into more pain. And I don't know whether I asked for this, in some impossible way. But it's nothing but a burden."

"It's your legacy," I whispered, clinging to all the fading ideals I'd brought with me out of the dusk. "It makes you who you are."

"It makes me the worst of myself."

"It makes you strong."

"It makes me a monster. And I would give anything to have it go away."

For a long moment, we sat in silence. His words rang like a curse in my ears, and I couldn't help but think of Severine's diary—*I would take his burden away forever, if I could. But I cannot. So I will bear it for him.*

His head drooped. His limp fingers slipped on the neck of the bottle. I caught the carafe before it shattered to the floor.

He'd passed out. His eyes were shut, black lashes streaking lines of soot against his cheek. His tousled head lolled between drifts of snow. He looked too young to be so broken.

I stood, stoppering the bottle so I didn't have to patch the cracks in my heart. There was a fur throw beside the ice gate—I picked it up and draped it over his prone figure, brushing his hair out of his eyes.

"I'd take it away," I whispered, "if I could."

I left him to his nightmares and went to find mine.

THIRTY-SEVEN

I stumbled to my room in Belsyre Wing and immediately kicked off my slippers, shucking away my jewelry as though the touch of it burned. Scion, but I'd been an idiot. How could I have possibly thought I could stay in control of a Nocturne whose very purpose was deception? How—

A sound like paper being crumpled dragged me away from my self-pity. I froze, then turned on my heel. The suite was as I'd eft it—the bed unmade, my Matin dress flung over the dressing screen, cosmetics and jewelry strewn across the vanity. Only . . . the skylight was still open, bloodstained light streaking the bed. It was well past second Nocturne. Usually the staff closed the shutters after Compline.

Again, that sound—like wet fabric being torn.

Trepidation shoved me toward the noise. The door to the commode yawned open, and I fumbled for the ambric globe. It blossomed. The ripping sound came again, from my right. On the floor. I turned, shoved the dressing screen open, and stared down at the thrashing figure of a dying girl.

I knew her. It was Elodie—one of my handmaids. She flailed against the tile, her hands scrabbling at her throat. The sound I'd heard was her heels pounding into a mountain of chiffon and tulle lumped on the floor. Her mouth silently worked as blood-tinged froth spilled over her cheeks. And around her neck—a choker in dristic and diamond, studded with beryls and emeralds.

"No," I rasped. I fell to my knees beside her, then pushed myself back up. I shoved myself toward the door to my rooms, stumbling on my hem and knocking over a chair. Glass shattered.

"Help!" I screamed, dristic and poison shredding my throat. "Somebody help!"

I flung myself back toward Elodie. Time slipped and jolted—my hands at her throat, my fingernails stained red with blood as I pulled and pulled at the choker while she silently screamed and screamed. Her head in my lap—her hair a bright splash against the dusk of my gown, her frothing mouth scattering stars through the night. Her eyes on mine, pleading and desperate and full of hope—hope—how could she *hope*?—

"Mirage, what's—?"

It was Oleander who burst into the room, long blond hair undone and a char of worry in her eyes. She measured the scene in one glance before striding toward us, nightgown flaring and determination forging her expression into dristic. She dropped to her knees, shoved me bodily out of the way, and cradled Elodie's still-thrashing figure against her chest.

"This is poison," Oleander said, curt. "How long has she been like this?"

"I don't know." Tears clogged my throat and turned the words to mush. "I just got back—she was already on the ground—"

Oleander didn't wait for me to continue. She bent her head to Elodie's, and kissed the other girl. No—not *kissed*. Her mouth closed over hers, and she pinched the other girl's nose shut. Bloody foam frothed around their lips, and nausea rose in my stomach. I turned away, fighting the churn of bile. When I looked back, Oleander was—*sucking*.

Scion, Oleander was trying to *suck the poison* out of her. I pressed a fist to my mouth, but I couldn't look away. Both girls shuddered. Oleander's palm slapped onto Elodie's chest, exposed above the neckline of her gown. The girl groaned. Lines of black spiderwebbed away from her mouth, pulling the contours of her face tight against her bones. Her veins stood out like ink on parchment, pulsing toward her chest. And I—I sat frozen and helpless beside them, unable even to pray to a Scion who had forsaken me.

I didn't know whether it had been minutes or hours when Oleander finally lifted her head from Elodie's mouth. The handmaid was limp in her lap—her mouth had gone slack. Blood and spittle and vomit streaked her cheeks and stained the floor. Her eyes stared unseeing toward the skylight.

"She's gone," Oleander croaked. She looked like she'd aged twenty tides in a minute—her pristine skin was sallow and discolored. Livid bags carved out her eyes and wrinkles stretched toward the corners of her eyes. "The poison—there was too much of it."

Tiredly, Oleander lifted the girl's head, reached behind her, and unclasped the poisoned necklace. It came away with a slurping pop—metal flanges had dug themselves deep into the skin, gripping Elodie's throat as they delivered poison into her veins. The necklace splattered blood and bile onto the floor. I stared in horror at the brutal device.

It had never been a piece of jewelry. It had always been a weapon.

"You realize this was meant for you?" Oleander's voice echoed my own sickening thoughts. If I'd worn another dress, if the jewels had been a different color, if I'd been in a different mood . . . *if, if, if.* The thoughts circled, vicious. In any number of scenarios, it was me—me wearing that necklace, me flailing helpless on the floor, me dying.

"Why was she wearing it?" I cried.

"I'm sure your girls try on your clothes and jewelry all the time." Oleander lifted a blood-streaked hand to shut Elodie's staring eyes. Already, the blond girl's color was returning, her eyes brightening. "I know mine do. It was bad luck."

"It should have been me."

"No," Oleander said dispassionately. "It shouldn't have."

She stood, wiped her hands on her nightgown, and surveyed the destruction with eyes that grew cooler and cooler, until she was encased in ice—haughty, distant, *familiar*. I could almost forget what she'd just done.

"I'll summon someone to clean this up. You should sleep in Sunder's room this Nocturne."

I gasped against the wave of mixed emotions thundering through me. "I don't think—"

"The poison on that necklace was hemlock. Powerful, and illegal. Someone's trying very hard to kill you." She shrugged. "It's probably best if I act as a second bodyguard from now on. I'll taste your food, test your jewelry. That kind of thing."

I climbed to my feet, my breathing ragged. "Won't that hurt you?"

"I'm immune." It was true—already the effects of the poison were nearly indiscernible. Only a faint shadow remained around her eyes. "Hemlock, joie, even alcohol. None of it affects me—it just makes me stronger."

She turned for the door. I waited until her hand was on the knob before daring to ask the question burning holes in my heart.

"Why?" I managed.

"Why what?"

"Why offer yourself as my bodyguard? Oleander, why would you do that for me?"

She hesitated. When she finally turned, the look she leveled over her shoulder was unfathomable.

"My brother fancies himself in love with you. So I suppose that makes us something like—something like sisters."

A whiff of her ice-wine perfume trailed her like snowflakes as she swept from the room.

I bathed. Then I wept, until my chest was hollow and my eyelids scratched my eyes. Finally, I slid open Sunder's door and climbed between sheets that reeked of genévrier and scorched ice. But I found his bed cold and empty as a long-forgotten dusk.

When I eventually found sleep, I dreamed of star-shine soldats in the blurred dusk beyond the violet edge of Midnight. Their eyes were wide with fear and their lips were parted in warning. And each face was *my* face—a reverberation in space, like the sound of a bell in an echoing chamber. And I suddenly knew—knew down to my diamond bones—that I would *die in this darkness.*

THIRTY-EIGHT

The Matin of the second Ordeal came too soon, shrouded in a cold red fog that filled my lungs with bad memories and worse doubts. I dressed and ate quickly, but anxiety made my fine clothes feel like sandpaper against my skin. The tasty fruits and pastries sat like ash in my stomach. So I stole out of Belsyre Wing without anyone seeing me, and made my way to the Oubliettes alone.

After the first Ordeal, the central cavern had reverted to its original appearance—echoing and dark, save for my bloom of illusory light. I lofted the glow, and stared around. Hard to imagine that just a few days ago, it had been incandescent with false sunlight; a playground of kembric puzzles and midnight riddles. Those eerie words stamped heavy on my heart, reminding me of the friends I'd lost, the mistakes I'd made, the monstrous specter of misplaced love I couldn't bear to look at.

I paced that room. I paced its still, silent floor as though it might give me a hint, a clue as to what I was about to face. What ordeal I was soon to live through. Because if Gavin was right about one thing, I knew it was this:

This Ordeal would be unlike anything I'd faced before. And I was frightened.

But the Oubliettes remained stubbornly silent, and if there was a Scion, he had little interest in my prayers.

I paced until the crowds began to file in, laughing and shouting and drinking and gambling. I lingered near the entrance, hoping and dreading that each footfall would bring Gavin and Arsenault and the moment of my apprehension that much closer.

My friends found me first.

"I told you she'd be down here," Oleander snapped at Lullaby. Brusquely, she adjusted the straps of the armored shirt she'd made me. This time, I had a feeling I might need it.

"I applaud your ability to predict her every movement," Lullaby hissed at the towering blond, before putting a soothing hand over mine. "I'm sure you're going to do great."

I glanced away from their bickering to see Sunder examining me from the shadows. Heat burst along the column of my neck. Had he been sober enough to remember what he'd said to me the other Nocturne? "What?"

"You're wearing a dress." Disapproval was written on his face.

I was—it was one of Oleander's gowns, a silk manteau rippling with sky-lit colors: amethyst and topaz glittering against a sapphire twilight. Let Gavin play out his Sun Heir spectacle. With my ultramarine armored jacket, I was just as striking as the Duskland Dauphine.

"Would you rather she go in her underthings?" Oleander made a face like she'd forgotten who she was talking to. "Never mind."

Sunder flushed dark. "I meant, wouldn't trousers be more appropriate for the physical Ordeal?"

"Why does everyone assume the Hand Ordeal is physical?" I snarled. "There are other kinds of strength, you know. And I'm perfectly capable of moving in a dress."

"Preach," said Lullaby.

"And if she's anything like me, she can also run in heels." Oleander quirked an eyebrow. "On second thought, that probably means she can't."

"Oleander," I growled.

"Pardon me for trying to lighten the mood." She threw up her hands. "I'm going to find a seat while I still have a head that hasn't been bitten off."

"Honestly." Lullaby gripped my hand tighter as Oleander flounced off. "Are you going to be all right?"

"I don't know." I could hear how grim I sounded, so I fought for a note of levity. "Is Arsenault going to hand us both a sword and make us fight to the death?"

"You can do this," she whispered. "The Oubliettes wouldn't set you an Ordeal you couldn't survive."

I returned her wan smile. But as she walked away after Oleander, I didn't think either of us believed her words. I stared at her receding back, unwilling—or unable—to face Sunder once more.

"Mirage." His hand whispered around my wrist. His bittersweet touch was a lure pulling me toward him. He twisted me into the shadows, away from prying eyes, and kissed me— swiftly, fiercely. His lips were flint to my tinder, and I sparked.

"Mirage," he said again, intent. "You have to forfeit this Ordeal."

"What?" I pulled away from him. Regret warred with vicious worry on his stark features, and I suddenly wished I could slow time, reel it in like a spool of thread and spin it backward. Stop it, in the moment our lips still touched, so I never had to hear his doubt.

"These Ordeals are dangerous." He spoke quickly, as though he wanted to get all the words out before I had the chance to interrupt. "They're cursed, like everything else the Sabourins touch. Forfeit, before Gavin has the chance to win. Or worse— *you* win, and become just like them."

"You know it's too late for that."

"It's not," he insisted. "Run away with me. We can go anywhere. Belsyre, if you like. Or the Sousine, with Lullaby. *Anywhere but here.*"

"Sunder—" My voice cracked. "I can't."

"Don't do this." Desperation clung to the edges of his voice. "I could barely watch the first Ordeal. I fear the second will kill me."

I would not be his pain.

I drew away, stiff. "Then don't watch."

"Please. I'm *begging* you—"

"Don't." I gripped his bicep, flexed through the material of his uniform. "Don't drag me back into the dusk."

He stilled at my touch. His harsh regard was a blade tempered from ice, or a diamond forged not from pressure, but from pain. I cringed away from it.

"You have always stood in the light, demoiselle." He scraped jagged hair off his face and bowed, tightly. "Conquer the dusk and breathe light into shadow. Remind them who you are."

And then he was gone. I stared after him, tallying my doubts and regretting my words.

"Are you ready?"

I spun. Dowser emerged from the shadows of the Oubliettes, grave and severe.

"I like to think I am. What are you doing here?"

"I'll be mediating this Ordeal."

"Good."

"You know I won't be able to do anything, if—" He swallowed. "If—"

"Don't jinx it!" I forced a laugh. I stood on my tiptoes and brushed a kiss against his smooth cheek. "I'll be fine."

He smiled at me, but the expression didn't reach his eyes, which were clogged with dread. I looked away, not wanting to see my own fear reflected onto his face.

Gavin strode out of the shadows, blazing like the Scion. We marched into the main cavern together, and this time the applause was so thunderous my head felt like it might split in half. I chose to believe they were cheering for both of us, but I knew in my heart it was Gavin they loved, Gavin they admired, Gavin they wanted to win. He waved, buoyant with his recent victory, the crown Relic at his belt once more.

I knitted my bitterness and fear around my heart and willed it to give me strength.

Dowser drew the dristic Relic from its sheath. The irrelevant pieces of it—the hilt and pommel—had been removed, so it was just the red blade. He held it up for everyone to see.

"Behold the second Relic of the Scion—a blade of dristic forged in the molten heart of the Sun and given to Meridian's daughter, Aliette, as a celebration of her strength," Dowser cried. "The second Ordeal of the Scion will test these Heirs' strength, both physical and mental. It will test their mettle, their bravery, their resolve. But most of all, it will test their resilience. Do you witness this Ordeal?"

The crowd's screams hurt my head.

"Then let the second Ordeal of the Sun Heir begin!"

Dowser lowered the blade toward the dais. The dristic Relic settled into its hollow with a hiss of metal against stone.

This time, when every single light in the grand chamber exploded into darkness, I was ready. My heart throbbed a warning, but I stood perfectly still until pale light bloomed above the dais. It was like candlelight on a moving sword, or liquid ice.

As before, lines of dristic fire wove a frozen tapestry along the floor before narrowing to two lines of silver. I didn't look at Gavin before taking off along my path.

The silver light resolved itself into an object hanging several feet in front of me. It was a sword—not the dristic Relic; this blade was slimmer and new-forged—hanging in midair in front of my face. I swallowed, and regretted my joking words: *Is Arsenault going to hand us both a sword and make us fight to the death?* The last thing I needed was for this ancient mystical death chamber to have a sense of humor about its Ordeals.

I grabbed the hilt of the sword. It was cool to the touch, and grooved to fit perfectly against my palm. I pulled. The blade released, its weight grinding my wrist bones together. I lowered into a crouch as icy white light flung itself to the ceiling. A silvery dome encompassed the space.

The floor fell out from beneath me without warning. Vast blocks of iron-grey stone surged up with a sound like blades screaming against each other. I pitched to my knees as I dropped, fighting nausea as my stomach turned inside out. Although part of me wanted to close my eyes, I forced them wider. I clutched at the sword and scrabbled for purchase on the slick stone beneath my fingers.

The mechanism ground to a halt, jolting me onto my hip across two flagstones. I stared up at the ceiling, but the tiers of spectators seemed impossibly far away—nothing more than dots of silver amid a sea of grey. If they made sound, I couldn't hear it over the throb of low continuous noise emanating from all around me. Already the buzzing was eating into my ears like a worm with teeth. I put a hand to my head, and climbed to my feet.

Panic spackled my heart when I lifted my eyes to the Ordeal. My gaze went up, and up, and still my eyes didn't touch the top of a dristic-and-stone mountain lofting toward a distant silver gleam. No, not a mountain. Scion, not a mountain at all. A tower of whirling mechanisms and glowering barriers and glittering metal, operating in a monstrous symphony of noise and motion.

It was an obstacle course.

All Dowser's and Gavin's admonitions slammed down on me like a curse, and for a long moment I couldn't move. *If you think the Oubliettes won't test you with sharp edges and cold dristic . . .*

The flagstone beneath my feet groaned, then fell away without warning.

THIRTY-NINE

I would have fallen to my death, if I hadn't been standing with one foot on its neighbor. My boot tasted air, and I pitched to the side, my arms flailing. My knee struck granite and instinct plunged my sword arm down. The impact sent numbness coursing to my elbow, but the tip of the blade stuck into the stone. I hauled on the hilt, dragging my weight away from the edge. I gasped, stars dancing against the backs of my eyelids and my fingers cramping.

The Oubliettes were much too fond of dropping the floor out from beneath me.

The flagstone beneath me groaned.

I barely had time to think. I wrenched the blade from the stone and flung myself toward the next block. The one I'd been standing on sighed away into the dusk. I sent my gaze dancing over my surroundings. A sea of square blocks rose like steps toward the mountain of impediments looming before me. And they were all beginning to complain.

I ran.

I barreled over the field of boulders, my skirt tangling around my legs and the heavy sword banging against my hip. The groaning of the blocks was a poor warning—some fell away immediately while others clung on long enough for me to catch my breath. Still, I never stopped moving for long, leaping from stone to stone. They fell away like rotten teeth in a savage mouth, and I dodged each gaping smile with a curse, climbing higher as my thighs burned. I was close now to the first level of the mountain, where glinting metal doors slammed up and down.

I threw myself forward, sucking air into my flaming lungs.

But I'd made a mistake—the rock fell out from under me as my foot struck stone. A terrible, deadly *whoosh* of air caught the hem of my dress. Blackness yawned.

My arms caught the lip of the neighboring stone. My body slammed into its side, impact jarring my elbows and pushing a shout from my throat. I poured every ounce of my strength into my arms, dragging myself bodily over the edge. But I didn't have time to rest. The stone below me growled a warning. I plowed forward, shoving trembling legs until I collapsed onto the steps at the bottom of the mountain.

The last of the stones fell away into a sea of shadows. My breath was a knife in my chest. I clutched my will to my thrumming heart like a talisman, and turned to face the next obstacle.

A narrow passageway skirted the base of the hill. Four burnished doors studded its length. *Four doors.* If I'd been in the mood to smile, I might have appreciated the Oubliettes' sense of parallel. They opened and closed seemingly at random: sleek, heavy doors screaming down before gliding gently up.

The objective seemed oh so simple: Pass each door without losing a limb.

I approached the first, counting its rhythm in my head.

DOWN. Two, three, four.

UP. Two.

DOWN. Two, three, four.

I swallowed my nerves. I sidled up to the door, so close I could sense its menace, and waited for it to lift. *Step.* It hissed down behind me, the force of its slamming lifting the hair off my neck.

I ducked beneath the next. Leapt through the third.

But the fourth sent metallic fear to grip my bones. Different from the others, it opened only halfway, then slid down into the floor to bare its other half. I could crouch and roll, and risk being pinioned to the floor, or I could try to jump over the top, and risk being sliced in half. Several times, I readied myself to do one or the other, only to lose my nerve at the last second.

My eyes flitted toward the top of the mountain. Where was Gavin? How much faster than me was he moving?

An idea struck. What if I could wedge the door open? I hefted the blade hanging from my hand. I hated the idea of sacrificing a tool so early in the Ordeal, but I also had to be honest with myself. What good was a sword to me, of all people? Already, my hand cramped around the hilt and its weight dragged at my footsteps. I was frankly astonished I hadn't cut myself on it yet.

I lifted the sword in a two-handed grip, and waited for the door to slide down. I thrust it into the gap, fitting the blade against the sliding door and the hilt against the frame. The door jerked up. I snatched my hands away. The blade shrieked, bent, and miraculously held. The door shuddered, caged. But not for long. Hurriedly, I clambered through the gap.

The blade snapped with a sound like glass breaking.

The door screamed.

I snatched my foot away. The whisper of swift metal stroked my ankle, too close for comfort.

I stood, relief making my limbs watery. But when I tried to move, I saw the hem of my gown was caught beneath the dristic door, pulling the fabric taut over my legs.

Sunder had been right.

I shouldn't have worn a dress.

A sudden gleam of memory slapped me—Gavin tearing my favorite gown with his bare hands, me laughing like it was a great joke. I picked up a metal shard from the broken sword and sawed at the gown. It fell away in ribbons, until I stood in nothing but my stockings and bloomers. If only Oleander had made armored leggings to go along with my vest. I took a deep, grounding breath, and climbed to the next level of the mountain.

Each trial was its own flavor of misery. I shivered through a claustrophobic tunnel that inhaled and exhaled with me—when I held my breath in fear, it contracted, squeezing my ribs until I thought I would suffocate. A wall of razored rocks sliced my fingers when I tried to climb. Moving barriers shot mirrored javelins at my head and knees.

Finally, I was high enough to see how far I'd come and how far I still had to go. A flat expanse of tile stretched before me. Beyond rose a steep incline of narrow steps, and above that—*nothing*. I wiped sweat out of my eyes and allowed myself to hope. That had to be the top. This had to be the end.

Eagerness pushed me onto the tile. I heard the thunder of sharp footfalls. The wail of a sword leaving its scabbard. Bright sharp motion caught my peripheral vision. I ducked as a gleaming blade whistled above me. I slammed to the ground and rolled, panic twisting my vision into spirals. I struggled back up. Looked wildly for the figure who attacked.

Recognition pulsed through me. It was a statue, etched out of gleaming crystal—a soldat from the vast army Lullaby and I had seen before the Ordeals began. But she'd *moved*. She'd *attacked me*. She was *alive*.

I stared. Now that I'd stepped off the expanse of tile, the crystal soldat stood perfectly still, sword back in its sheath, gazing in the direction of where I'd been standing.

I tried to think around the fear frothing in my stomach. She'd attacked the moment she'd seen me, but had stood down when I moved outside her direct vision. Carefully, I stepped behind her, steeling myself for her to turn and attack once more. But she did nothing.

I licked my lips, and took careful stock of my surroundings. The tiles were laid out in a grid pattern. Two rows down, another fierce crystalline warrior—this time with a spear on her shoulder—faced me. And another, a few columns to the side of her, facing in a different direction. I counted more, scattered across the tile.

Understanding shuddered through me.

I had to find a safe path around these impossible warriors, without one of them catching sight of me and slaying me on the spot. Nerves twisted around my heart. I looked toward the steep staircase. I could feel how close the Relic was. But I could also feel how close Gavin was. Did I have time to solve this puzzle without sacrificing my last chance at being crowned Sun Heir?

Or did I only have time to do something incredibly stupid?

Nothing worth having was ever given . . . only taken.

Before I could change my mind, I hurtled onto the board. The first warrior caught sight of me immediately, unsheathing her sword and charging at me. I dashed along the row, praying I wasn't about to meet a sharp and grisly end. I halted. Two columns down, another soldat powered up at the sight of me, her steps a growing thunder. They barreled toward me. I forced myself to stand my ground.

Three . . . two . . . *one.*

I threw myself into the next row, banging my hip and elbow against the tile floor. The warriors collided with a sound like the world breaking. An explosion of sharp crystals rained around me, flinging pale light and rainbow shards into my eyes. I forced myself to my feet, barely dodging the serrated gauntlet of another automaton.

I ran and dodged and ducked and spun. I led the soldats into each other's paths with ruthless intent. Each slaughter was a firework of violence and pain. It was a dance of death, and even as the air scored my lungs and crystal splinters sliced my cheeks, its rhythm whetted my bones and put a vicious smile on my face.

Was this what war felt like?

Finally, there was only one warrior remaining. She blocked the staircase at the end of the mountain. Adrenaline pulsed through my veins, making me invincible.

I could do this.

I bent, retrieving a crystal spear that had survived its owner's demise intact. It was heavy—so heavy it pulled at my biceps and cranked my elbow. But I just grinned, wrapped my hand around its shaft, and stepped into the last diamond warrior's path.

Her head snapped up. Her twin swords flew off her back. She plowed toward me.

I planted the spear's butt on the tile. But both were slick—the javelin slid backward, dragging my arm as its tip dipped. I tried to release it, to step out of the path of the charging soldat, but it was like my hand had melded to the crystal weapon. Terror spangled through me, chasing away my bravado. I stared into her blind eyes, glittering and unfeeling, closer . . . closer . . . *closer.*

Nothing worth having was ever given.

I bit down a scream, planted my foot against the shaft of the spear, and hauled the sharp point up with both hands. The warrior launched herself at me. The blade shrieked against her breastplate, skittering on the surface. It plunged through her throat. Both spearhead and warrior head exploded.

Diamond shards sliced my face and neck. The heavy crystalline body kept careening forward. It caught my side and dragged me down, slamming me against the tile. My shoulder dislocated with a sick wet pop. I screamed. A wave of blackness threatened to carry me away. I bit into my cheek, trying to focus on the sharp metal taste of my own blood. I heaved at the dead weight on top of me and managed to slide out from under it.

Blood slicked my fingertips. I stared at my right arm hanging limp and useless at my side.

I choked on a sob, pulled myself into a crouch. The staircase loomed beyond, too steep and too high, lined in shining mirror glass. I was never going to make it.

Nothing worth having . . .

I gritted my teeth. One-handed, I unbuckled two of the straps on Oleander's armored vest, and shoved my limp, aching wrist into the gap. I cinched it tight, lashing my bad arm across my chest.

And then I climbed.

Every step was tortured, each step its own mountain. I struggled up the mirrored staircase, and as the panes of reflective glass passed me by, I saw the faces of everyone I'd ever hurt. Horror flared in my chest when I met their accusing eyes, and their whispers followed me up the stairs long after I passed them by.

Luca, with assassination on his breath. *An empress's crown is death and corruption. How could you think you're any different?*

Lullaby, tearstained, her fingers fractured at each knuckle. *You left me behind when I needed you the most.*

Thibo, broken and empty. *You let me go.*

Sunder, *Sunder.* Bloody lines climbed his throat like vines, choking him with pain. *The thing that hurts the most is you.*

I closed my eyes, tried to close my ears. This wasn't real. The Oubliettes were trying to distract me from my end goal, the thing I'd been fighting for—the dristic Relic. Nothing it showed me was true. I slogged upward, one step at a time, the curses of old friends and new enemies ringing false in my ears.

At last, I stood before one final mirror. No, not a mirror—it was a window, its surface reflective enough to see my own face swimming before me, but transparent enough that I could see through it. Out . . . and *down.*

Dismay and sick fear roiled in my stomach. The mountain of obstacles hadn't led me up to the dais, as I'd thought—it had led me to a cliff above it. I leaned my head against the glass, trying to estimate the drop. Twenty feet, at least. Maybe more. I looked up. A twin cliff stared back at me from across the dais, and Gavin was climbing down it.

No. Horror pushed me away from the glass, and I glimpsed my own reflection. Disheveled hair around a lacerated face. The remnants of a ripped skirt over stained petticoats. A dislocated shoulder shoved haphazardly into shredded armor. I watched my eyes narrow, my mouth harden.

I'd given too much to this Ordeal to watch him win without a fight.

I slammed my fist against the glass, shoved at its boundaries. There had to be a way through—it had to be some kind of door. Frustration boiled within me, and I shouted as I pushed and kicked and—

I am not without strength, mocked a silken voice. I froze. The words were mine, but the voice was not. Scorn dripped from every ringing syllable. Slowly, I returned my gaze to the mirror. It wasn't my reflection anymore. My ashen lips were red, my dark hair was auburn, my blue eyes were violet.

It was Severine.

I squeezed my eyes shut and pounded a fist against the glass. "This isn't happening. This isn't real. This is just an illusion."

But when I opened my eyes, she was still there.

Tell me, little sister, she purred. *Are you pleased to have resurrected this archaic death match? You must have known—it wasn't designed for runts to win.*

"She's not really there," I snarled at myself, running my fingertips along the edge of the window, looking for a latch or mechanism to set me free. Outside, I could see Gavin making his painstaking descent down the cliff, his muscles flexing and his armor shining. "Just get through the door before it's too late."

You should have let me relieve this burden for you, as I did the others, Severine mused.

"By killing me?" I snapped. "You're insane."

Think of all the pain it would have prevented. She smiled. *Is this really worth it to you? How much do you want this? Be honest.*

I was quiet.

Some people are willing to die for the people and things they love. And some people aren't. There's no shame in being the latter.

Below, Gavin swung down another few feet. I looked up—up into the hovering tiers of spectators above, their wide blotchy faces impossible to make out in the silvery glow. But somewhere, my people were there. Watching, cheering me on, hoping I'd win. Not just this Ordeal, but this competition—the crown, the throne, everything. Because they believed in me—they believed in my dream of an impossible world, my dream of a world just a little more radiant than our own.

Dowser, who'd fought addiction for me.

Lullaby, who survived weeks in a dungeon for me.

Thibo, who was *gone* because of me.

Oleander, who offered her hated legacy to me.

Sunder—oh, Sunder, who I'd caused so much pain and given nothing in return—who loved me, even if he hated these Ordeals.

I choked on a sob.

Nothing worth having is ever given, Severine said.

Below, Gavin's foot touched stone.

It must be taken, she hissed.

"No." I turned my back on the mirror, turned my back on Severine. "It must be *earned.*"

I took three giant steps back. I turned on my heel, and started to run. I leapt.

Mirror glass shattered into dristic stars. Noise exploded around me, and for a moment I was weightless. Buoyant. I could sail through this night and never meet another day. But then I fell, plummeting like Meridian through a riot of sound and color and ecstatic fear.

I landed on the dais with an impact that shredded my senses. For a dizzy moment I felt nothing. Then pain blazed along my bones. A roar forced my eyes open.

Relic.

I dragged myself along the ridge of stone, stretching useless fingers toward an austere blade. It did not leap to my hand. I curled fingers around its blade and dredged it from its hollow, slicing my hand open.

If the crowds cheered, the ringing in my ears drowned it out. Slowly—excruciatingly—I climbed to my feet. My left leg howled, and nearly gave out. A shard of bone pierced the skin. I reeled—staggered—balanced. I lifted the Relic. Blood slipped from my palm and painted runnels along the blade. The light turned the metal molten.

I must have collapsed. The next thing I knew, someone was prying the sharp blade out of my hand, and strong hands were lifting me up and arms were wrapped around me and people were shouting too loudly.

Then blackness rushed in and I knew—I had earned that too.

FORTY

I was dragged unceremoniously awake by loud arguing.

"*You* did this," said a voice like wolves. "If you hadn't cheated in the first Ordeal she never would have gone so far—"

"*Cheated?!*" A bell of outrage sang out. "I never cheated, not even when—"

"That's not the point!" someone else bellowed. "We can all agree it's gone too far—"

I opened my eyes, or tried to. They were tight and crusted, and the low red light felt like knives. I struggled to sit up, but pain flared the length of my body. I gasped and fisted my hands in the blankets, my body rebelling against consciousness.

"She's awake." A girl's figure swam into view. *Vida*. Cool hands on my shoulders guided me back onto the mattress. She pressed a warm mug into my free hand. "Drink this."

I obeyed. The bitter liquid burned a path down my throat before blooming hot in my chest. My pain faded away, replaced with a numb throb. A pain potion, then.

"Better?" Vida asked. I nodded. "Good. Now, you were pretty banged up. I fixed the leg first, but it'll need time to set—walking on a bad break can lame a person for life. The shoulder will be sore for a bit. The lacerations—well, you know from before. I can heal them, but if I do they're more likely to scar. I closed up a few that were bleeding badly, but I think you should let the ones on your face heal by themselves."

I nodded again. Scion, I'd walked away from that fall with nothing more than a broken leg and a few scratches?

"And . . ." Vida threw a glance at Dowser. He nodded, grave, and she turned back to me. "When you destroyed that last crystal soldat, you were caught in the explosion. Some of the shards— Well, you'd better see for yourself."

She handed me a mirror. Dull dread was a stone in my stomach, but the pain potion made my thoughts slow. I lifted the mirror. At first, I didn't see anything. Then the low light glinted off my neck, where a spray of tiny diamond shards shone like mythic stars. My hand flew up. Raised fragments sparked a jagged pattern down one cheek, over my jaw, and along my neck toward my collarbone. Prickles of bright pain told me more were hidden below the sleeves of my nightgown.

"Your armor protected you from the worst of it." Vida looked unhappy. "I tried to remove them while you slept, but they self-cauterized when they embedded in your skin. Pulling them out might be *more* painful than just leaving them."

I turned my head, slowly. The splinters glittered viciously, turning the low red light to droplets of blood spattering my throat. I looked . . . *savage*.

"Let's worry about it later," I murmured. "Thank you, for everything."

Vida nodded, but she looked rattled.

"I need to rest, and so do you." She turned a pointed gaze to the rest of the room. "Ten minutes, and don't crowd her or upset her. Understand?"

Murmurs of assent followed her out. Eyes turned to me, and I cringed my way into something resembling a seated position. I didn't want to face my friends lying on my back. I focused my swimming vision on each of them in turn. They all wore matching expressions of worry. All except Sunder, who had his arm braced against the doorjamb and his gaze on the floor.

"What happened? After."

"Gavin caught you when you fell from the dais," Oleander

offered, with an expression that indicated she wouldn't have been such a gracious loser. "He helped carry you out."

Sunder looked like he wanted to be sick.

"Thanks." I nodded at Gavin, who shoved his hands in his pockets and looked like he wished he were somewhere else. Beside him, Luca put a hand on his shoulder. "But you don't have to stay, you know."

Gavin looked relieved. But instead of sprinting from the room like I might have done, he came around the bed, clasped my hand gently, and shook it.

"Congratulations," he whispered. "You deserved it."

I narrowed my eyes at him, but he didn't seem facetious.

Luca tipped me a salute. "Remind me never to get between you and a mirror."

They slipped from the room, leaving me alone with a group of people who looked like they might just kill me for almost dying. For a long, excruciating moment, silence rang louder than words.

"I'll go first," Sunder growled. He kept his gaze glued to the floor, but I saw a vein pulse at his temple. He clenched a fist. "Of all the stupid, reckless, insane, *irresponsible*—"

"You could have died, Mirage," Lullaby cut in, her musical voice harsh. "Even after you escaped the crystal warriors, a shard of broken mirror glass could easily have nicked an artery, or the impact of the fall could have broken your back."

"We'd all really prefer if you pursued your obvious death wish in private," added Oleander.

Dowser came and sank onto the edge of the bed. He took one of my hands, frail-looking against his much larger grip.

"This Ordeal was hard for all of us to watch, Mirage," he sighed. "None of us wants to see you injured or killed in your pursuit of the Amber Throne."

"That's not fair," I hissed, up through the numb flatlands of the pain potion. I wished I hadn't taken it—I could barely string a thought together. "This isn't the first time my life has been in danger. I've seen battle. I've faced assassination—by blade and poison alike. That never made you caution me from this path before. If anything, you just urged me on. How is this different?"

"Because you threw yourself in front of it like a madwoman!" Sunder burst out. Anguish and lingering terror lurked behind the ice-bright edge of fever. "What were you trying to prove, out there? That you were brave? That you were invincible? That you were willing to die for a throne?"

"Sunder—"

"Scion, Mirage, I begged you to forfeit the second Ordeal. I don't know how else to tell you that—"

He broke off with a muffled cry. He turned on his heel and slammed his fist into the wall. Plaster flaked away like blood-stained snow. Beside him, Oleander put her hand on his shoulder.

"The point, Mirage," Dowser continued, removing his spectacles, "is that it's time to reconsider. The Ordeals of the Sun Heir have tested you to the brink of death. When I spoke to Arsenault, he implied they only grow more difficult. We cannot let you face the third Ordeal."

"Let me?" I laughed, incredulous, to mask the squeeze of acid tears in my eyes.

Lullaby leveled a warning glance at me, a glance I recognized—it was the look she always wore when she knew I was about to do or say something I might regret. Silently, she begged me to consider my next words.

I bit my tongue. My bones ached and my head swirled muzzy with pain potion and my heart throbbed hot with all the things

I wanted but might never have. All the things I once thought I deserved but never thought to earn. I teetered on the edge of something big—something greater than myself, something greater than my mundane desires or fickle wants. A great, grand, monstrous parade of legend and tradition and blood and power stretching behind me a thousand tides.

Even if I wanted to, I couldn't stop now.

And I didn't want to.

I opened my eyes and set my jaw.

"I know I went too far in the last Ordeal," I said slowly. "And I apologize if I've caused any of you undue pain or worry. The fact is, I owe you all so much, not least in these past few spans. You guided me toward the light when all I wanted was to drown in darkness." I squeezed Dowser's palm. His eyes gleamed. "You challenged me to face my mistakes, admit my failings, and then try harder—be better." Lullaby's gaze shifted toward what I hoped was pride. "You offered me friendship I hadn't earned and didn't always want." Oleander's mouth twitched toward a smile. "You—"

But I couldn't say the words. *You taught me that even a monster could be loved.* Sunder's shoulders hardened to the metal of his eyes. I didn't dare look at him.

"I value each of you more than I can say, and I wish for your support in all I do," I continued carefully. "But this is no longer a group effort. I chose this path. These Ordeals belong to me— were meant for me—in a way that nothing else in this palais has ever been. If I were to forfeit the throne to Gavin now, after winning the second Ordeal—I would be giving a piece of myself away. The piece of me that knows this is where I belong. Not because of the accident of my birth, or the secret of my blood— but because I'm willing to fight for it. I *want* to fight for it. I used to think I deserved this. Now I want to earn it."

Dowser laughed, although his eyes were impossibly sad. "I

should have expected nothing less from the true Sun Heir."

Lullaby sank onto the other side of the bed, a little stiff. Her palm in mine was slight and cool. "I know better than to talk you out of anything. I'll see this through with you, until the end."

"No," groaned Sunder from the shadow of the doorway. Oleander tightened her grip on his arm, like she was trying to hold him back. Or just hold him together. "No! This is insane."

I looked up. Our gazes collided, and I saw something crumble in his eyes. That icy, endless wall of endurance came crashing down, and with it, every promise he'd ever made himself, every wish he'd never dared to hope might come true.

"I can't do this," he said abruptly. "If you're set on going through with the third Ordeal, I won't stop you. But I won't stay to watch you destroy yourself. I can't." He passed a hand over his eyes. "Say you'll forfeit, Mirage. Forfeit, or I'll be gone by Matin. And every single Belsyre soldat goes with me."

A chill kissed my spine, but it only made my back more rigid.

"Lord Sunder," I spat. "Are you giving me an ultimatum?"

"Yes, demoiselle," he whispered. "For I would rather look away from your light than watch you die in darkness."

The air between us snapped with sharp fangs of tension. Beside me, Lullaby cringed.

"Then go." My voice sounded careless. My stomach cramped in knots. "Rest easy—once I am empress, both you and your wolves will be remunerated handsomely for your loyalty."

His face shattered in the moment before he stalked from the room.

For the space of a breath, I saw Oleander hesitate. Her usually smooth gaze rasped like uncut marble on mine. The unspoken question in her eyes took me by surprise.

"You do me honor," I whispered. "But no. Go with him. He needs you more than I do."

She shot me a brief, grateful look before sweeping from the room after her twin. I waited until the door clicked behind her before turning and burying my head against Lullaby's shoulder. She stiffened, then relaxed, smoothing my hair from my face and beginning to hum a strange, sweet tune. Dowser's large strong hand drew patterns between my shoulderblades. And as the haze of pain potion and Lullaby's song blurred away my tears, I sent a wish flinging away into the dim:

I wished that in the end, this was all worth it.

Because it was too late now to give up.

It must have been well past Nocturne when I woke up, surfacing with a groan from the twilight blur of pain potion. Every inch of me hurt, but the trail of diamond splinters embedded in my skin from ear to collarbone hurt the worst. I put a ginger hand to the shards—my fingers came away bloody. I pushed myself up against the headboard, lifting sweat-damp hair off my neck and looking around.

Both Dowser and Lullaby had stayed—Dowser was sprawled sleeping in a too-small armchair, and Lullaby curled at the foot of the bed, her deep breaths even. My heart throbbed—for all it made me glad to see them, they also reminded me of all the people I'd lost. Sunder, Oleander. Luca. *Thibo.*

How long until I was as alone as Severine had been?

My gaze found my sister's diary, lying faceup and open near the edge of the bed. Dowser or Lullaby must have been reading it while I slept. Something dull and riotous shoved sludge through my veins, and before I knew it I was crawling out of bed, sliding the journal into my palm, and creeping silent toward the door. Lullaby stirred, but didn't wake.

I slid out into Belsyre's chilly halls. I looked for Calvet and Karine standing sentinel by my door, before remembering they were gone. Of course they were gone. Sunder had left. Notes of anger and sorrow and guilt struck a grating chord in my chest. My nerves jangled. I limped through the palais in the Nocturne hush.

Severine's chambers were as quiet and pristine as ever. But as I approached the bed, they felt strangely tainted, like everything else in this palais—this world of tarnished promises and gilded lies. Tainted like the jewels embedded in my neck. Tainted like my reflection in the cold honest mirror in the corner. Tainted like the devious little book I held in my hands.

Finally, I stood over my sister. Her face was placid, her lips parted as if she had some secret to tell. My hand closed over her slender throat, where a pulse still beat. My fingertips squeezed, testing the limits of her unyielding form. Lullaby's voice echoed in my ears:

What are you waiting for?

What had I told her? *I'm waiting to prove her wrong.*

I sighed, lifted my palm from her throat, and slid her diary gently beneath the hands folded across her stomach. Her fingers, nondescript without their trademark red varnish, seemed to convulse around the little book. For a moment, I fancied I could sense all my sister's forgotten desires, sweet as honey and bitter as death. I sat heavily on the edge of the bed.

"It would have been us." My voice rang strangely in the silence. "If things had been different, it would have been you and me in that arena, battling over ancient Relics and vying for our father's throne."

My hand brushed against my chest, my thumb fitting against the spot where the pendant usually rested. They'd taken it from me for the third Ordeal, and its absence was like a hole in my heart.

"I believe you, you know. About Seneca. About how hard you

fought to save the brother you loved. He must have meant so much to you, for you to risk so much."

Silence was my only response. I sighed.

"When I first came to the palais, I told Dowser I didn't care about my parentage. I didn't care about my family. And I meant it." I ran a fingernail along the seam of the quilt. I'd never told anyone this before. Not even myself. "But it wasn't always true. When I was very little, I used to beg the Sisters of the Scion to tell me where I came from. Sometimes, the younger Sisters relented. I was the child of a star and a sunbeam, they said. I was a Dominion shadow who got lost in the Dusklands. I was a dream of the Scion come to life.

"Later, I realized those were just stories—fairy tales to mollify a child. So I concocted my own fantasies. I was abandoned by poor miners. I was a terrible monster whose powers might blot out the sun. I was the secret daughter of a dead emperor." I smiled a self-mocking smile. It hurt my bruised face. "But nothing I thought up was as brutal and heartbreaking as the truth—that I'd once had a family, but they'd all driven each other mad or slaughtered each other before I was even born."

I leaned down, so my mouth was very close to Severine's auburn-ringed ear.

"I hate you for many things, sister. I hate you for being wicked. I hate you for being cruel. I hate you for all the pain you caused to the people I care about." Air stabbed into my lungs, a keen lament for never. "But most of all, I hate you for loving him when you never even tried to love me."

FORTY-ONE

The day of the third Ordeal dawned like a curse, all blood-streaked skies and shadow-black clouds. I left my chambers feeling raw and blank, as though the rage of painful emotions I'd felt over the past few days had scrubbed me clean and empty. Gavin had agreed to postpone the third Ordeal until I had time to heal, but even after a week my body felt strange to me; my movements unfamiliar, each step a question mark. And I couldn't stop touching the diamond shards lodged along my throat and cheek—my palm bore score marks where their brittle edges sliced my skin.

I marched toward the Oubliettes, but Coeur d'Or's shimmering halls looked strange without Belsyre's black wolves patrolling the corridors. I'd grown accustomed to their upright forms standing guard outside doorways and between pillars, their strict uniforms like scraps of Duskland shadow, their emerald signats like memories of evergreen kisses.

Gavin's Husterri had already moved into their role. Dowser assured me it had been an organic transition—the palais needed guarding, after all, and neither Skyclad nor Loup-Garou were available—but the sight of their vermilion-and-ivory uniforms set my teeth on edge. I scanned their faces for emotion—sympathy, loyalty, even loathing—but they were sun-burnished and Scion-blank and if they felt anything, they hid it well.

Dowser and Lullaby came to wish me luck before the Ordeal began, but their gestures were cursory, almost rehearsed. We all knew that everything that needed to be said had already been said. Luca crossed over from Gavin's contingent of well-wishers to clasp me in a swift hug.

"Be careful." His hazel eyes gleamed like he wanted to say something else. But then he turned and climbed up into the stands with his new friends.

Leaving me and Gavin alone on the floor. By now, the introduction to the Ordeals felt like a dance I'd learned the steps to. Arsenault lofted the ambric Heart Relic—*my Relic*—and spoke about truth, integrity, righteousness. My fingers itched with the force of some desire I couldn't name, and I lifted my hand to my chest, where the Relic's absence was a kind of weight. My heart throbbed with the promise I had etched onto it: *win, win, win.*

The Relic fell into its slot. Amber light whispered over the edge of the dais and oozed onto the floor. It pulsed its way across the room in rivulets—veins, arteries—and I swallowed against the metallic tang hanging in the air. The light was darker than I'd expected—red as sunlight, red as blood. It slipped beneath my boots and led me away into the labyrinth of the Oubliettes.

As with the first two Ordeals, an emblem appeared—a gleaming sun. I quickened my steps, preparing to reach for it, but it grew no closer. It just hung somewhere in the distance, a seething eye in a dusky sky. I broke into a run, keeping my arms loose in case the floor fell out from under me or a crystal warrior came lurching around a corner. But I wasn't getting any nearer. Uncertainty struck through me, and I slowed. I spun on my heel, staring back the way I'd come. But I only saw unyielding darkness, glowering like the heart of Midnight.

"Sister Sylvie!"

The voice clanged into my ears with a wrongness I couldn't name. I turned back. The light from the distant sun scalded my vision. A figure resolved through the glare, striding toward me across a dust-swept courtyard. She wore a greying, threadbare habit, and her colorless hair was pulled back into a bun beneath her fraying veil. After a long moment, I recognized her—Sister Cathe, from the Temple of the Scion.

"Do not stare so hard into the darkness, Sister," she scolded. "Dominion shadows will seek you out if you look away from the Scion's light for too long."

"I—" My heart thudded strange and dull in the cavern of my chest. I too wore a threadbare habit, too tight at the shoulders and gaping at the waist. "What am I doing here?"

"You were supposed to be sweeping the courtyard." Sister Cathe nodded at the broom gripped in my hand. "But now you're late for Salutations. Come along."

Bewildered, I followed her into the Temple. Dusty, crumbling walls bore faded frescoes of familiar scenes: the Scion in his kembric chariot, resplendent with his Relics and his holy fire; the dusk-cloaked Moon, turning her face away from the light; the hounds of Meridian, named Dexter and Sinister. I'd passed by these walls every day for as long as I could remember, but now their ancient pigments and decaying varnishes caught my eye with inexplicable precision. What was it about today—?

"Sister Sylvie!" Cathe hissed. She gestured brusquely toward the fane. I hurried my footsteps, sliding into the vaulted space behind her.

The scent of cheap tallow candles slapped me in the face. Amber light blossomed against a cobwebbed ceiling. Voices raised in benediction followed a ritual cadence that was as familiar to me as my own heartbeat. I bowed my head and joined in, my lips mouthing long-memorized prayers as I racked my brain for the error in this tableau. It was the feeling of walking into a room with a purpose, only to have it slip out of your mind the moment you crossed the threshold.

I remembered darkness—yes, shadows thick as Midnight.

And the sun—yes! the sun!—hanging low and still and distant—and I had to *do* something, I was meant to be earning—

"Sister Sylvie?" Sister Anouk jolted me out of my reverie with an elbow to the ribs.

"Ow." I rubbed the spot she'd struck me. "What was that for?"

"Did you forget we're on supper detail? Scion, you've been far away today."

I trailed her to the kitchen, where a few huge pots were already bubbling away at the hearth.

"Idle fingers spin shadows." Anouk shoved the metal handle of a large spoon into my hands. The impact buzzed along my palms, and I stared at my rough fingers, my split cuticles and cracked nails. I frowned. My fingers weren't usually idle. And they *did* spin shadows—shadows, and glittering cities, and impossible sunlight, and—

"Sylvie!" Anouk snapped, irritation staining her voice. "Don't make me tell Mother Celeste you've gone lazy."

I stirred while she chopped, making sure the stew didn't clump or burn.

"Sister," I said. The word tasted wrong, metallic and slick, but I clamped my teeth around it. A faint memory fluttered against my neck—a cracked plate, the flavors of rot and dust. "Sister, are you afraid of me?"

"Afraid?" She sliced an onion in half and smiled. "Of you? Why would I be afraid?"

"Because—" I scrabbled for memories I wasn't sure belonged to me. My fingers found no purchase. "Because I'm an orphan?"

Anouk put down her knife and turned to face me. "Are you dusk-touched, Sister Sylvie? You know you are no orphan."

"I'm not?"

"Of course not." She snorted, and turned back to her chopping. "Your parents gave you to us—a tithe to the Scion."

No—no, my mother wanted me, she ran with me into the Dusklands to get away from—

I put my head in my hands. "Why?"

She gave me another strange look. "You were their third child. Too many mouths to feed on a miner's sparse salary."

"So they didn't love me?"

"Of course they love you! They'll be here for your name day, you silly girl." She ruffled my hair, affectionate. "They just don't love you as much as we do."

Name day? My heart thundered in my chest, hot as a raging sun.

"Sister Sylvie!" A fluting voice called down the steps to the kitchen, followed closely by a tiny, wrinkled woman. Her bones looked nearly as frail as the jet-black bird clinging to her shoulder and blinking beady eyes at me. A lively smile creased her face when she saw me. I dredged her name out of my confusion. *Mother Celeste.* "There you are. I've been looking all over for you."

"Why?" I asked stupidly.

"Well, I know it's not your name day until tomorrow," she said. "But I wanted to be the first to give you a present. I know it's nothing fancy, but since you don't have any jewelry—"

Don't have any jewelry. My hand flew to my chest, but of course, she was right. I didn't own any jewelry. I stared at the simple necklace she took from her pocket—bits of string and colored glass, simple but pretty. A Dusklander's treasure. I should have been thrilled—instead, I felt nothing. No, I felt . . . *angry, lonely, neglected—*

"No," I said. "I don't have a name day."

"Of course you do, child."

"No," I repeated, louder. I stood, grasping desperately for the memories stirring at the base of my skull. "You said I was born outside the Scion's light and—and my name was nothing but a curse. I begged, *begged*—all the other children got to celebrate their name days, with cake and gifts—but you refused. You said we'd just be inviting Dominion shadows into our hearts."

Mother Celeste looked shocked. "Sylvie, I would *never*—"

"But you did!" I put my hands on my throbbing temples. "I know you did."

Anouk and Celeste shared a loaded glance. Anouk slowly approached me. I noticed she hadn't put down her knife.

"No—this isn't *right*." Panic shredded my composure. "I'm not supposed to *be* here."

"Sister—"

I turned on my heel and sprinted up the stairs. My too-long habit clung to my legs and threatened to trip me. Anouk and Celeste followed. I thrust out onto the main floor, beneath the disapproving eye of the painted Scion. I hurtled down the corridor, through the main door, and out into the courtyard. I skidded to a halt. A group of figures blocked my path—Sisters, mostly, although I spotted a few strangers in the mix.

"Let me through," I commanded.

A woman detached herself from the group. She was older than me, and lovely to behold, with auburn ringlets and sparking eyes the color of the horizon. She pulled me into an embrace. She smelled like flowery perfume and nail varnish and old blood. I cringed away, but she held me tight.

"Dear sister," Severine crooned, in a voice like the moment before glass shatters. "How I've missed you."

"This isn't real," I whispered to myself, my stomach cramping. "This can't be real."

"Am I real enough for you?" boomed an unfamiliar voice. A greying ginger beard and a jolly smile. A pair of strong arms enfolded both of us. He smelled like everything a father ought to smell like—tabak smoke and ink and leather. Over his shoulder,

I saw my mother—a pretty middle-aged woman with silver sparking in her hair—and my brother, a slender boy with my father's coloring and my sister's shrewd eyes. They both joined the embrace, laughing.

Tears spilled down my face: brittle hopes I'd ignored so long I'd almost forgotten they existed. I lingered at the edge of that dream a moment too long. Over the clustered heads of my family, the sun began to slip toward the horizon.

I jerked myself out of the embrace. Severine's smile slid from her face. My father looked hurt. I swallowed the ache in my throat and gazed at this family—*my* family. I memorized their faces, etching them into a shadowed corner of my heart where I might visit them again someday. I turned my face toward the horizon, where the sun slowly—inexorably—impossibly—slipped below the horizon.

"Where are you going?" my father demanded. "This is your home."

"We love you too much to let you go," Mother Celeste pleaded.

"This is where you belong," chimed Severine.

"No." I turned, meeting her violet eyes. "It isn't."

But there, over her shoulder—a light in the darkness stole my gaze. I squinted toward the edge of Dominion. The wall of blackness shivered with ripples of radiance. A gleam—a glow. The moon began to rise, sailing into Midnight with a billow of perfect light.

I stood transfixed. She was magnificent. Exquisite. Utterly impossible. Behind me, sunlight's warmth faded away, like a hand dropping away from my shoulder. But I hardly cared. I gazed at the moon, reverent, worshipful—there was something about her shape that called to me. Her light, bright as mirror glass and cold as ice, like—

My hand jerked to my throat. My palm came away slick with my own blood. My eyes flew open.

I lay facedown on hard, unforgiving stone. Diffuse amber light stained my vision. Tears left crusted trails on my cheeks, dripping away like the dream—nightmare—*hallucination*. Scion, it had felt so real.

I heard the whisper of a sword being drawn from its sheath a bare second before I heard the whisper of a voice:

"With light."

And then the whistle of a blade shearing down toward my throat.

FORTY-TWO

he blade sang down. Instinct shoved me out of the way.
Sharp dristic bit into the stone a few inches from my face,
flinging splinters of rock at my cheek. I stared at the
embedded sword—blood smeared its length with gory red. For a
panicky moment, I imagined the blood was my own.

No—I wasn't hurt. It wasn't blood.

It was *paint*.

My assailant hauled on the hilt of the sword. I rolled onto my
back and kicked out as hard as I could. My toe connected with
the tip of the blade and jerked it out of my attacker's grip. It skittered away into the shadows. He went after it, unhurried. I
scrambled to my feet, adrenaline spiking my veins. The figure
bent to retrieve the weapon, and when he turned I saw—

He wore a red mask.

No—he wore *the* Red Mask.

Fear turned my blood to water. It was *awful*, far worse than
the disturbing Red Masks in the city. Its shape screamed violence
and its color shrieked murder. Dead eyes stared out over a razor-
sharp bladed nose.

He lifted his red sword. He charged me.

A shadow detached itself from the wall and hurtled at the Red
Mask, catching my attacker at a perpendicular and knocking
him off-balance. They slammed into the wall with a thunk of
bone against stone. The Red Mask reeled, stumbled, fell hard.
The second figure rolled off him, lithe as a desert cat, and dashed
toward me.

Fear and panic made me cry out. Strong hands gripped my
wrists, but they were gentle. Who—?

Black curls. Hazel eyes. A laughing face set in deadly serious lines.

"Sylvie," Luca said. "*Mirage*. It's just me."

I shook. If Luca hadn't been holding me up, I might have fallen.

"Scion, Luca, it's *him*," I rasped. "Saint Sauvage. Just look at his mask."

But Luca was already hauling me down the passageway.

"Luca, stop!" I jerked my hands out of his grip. "We have to find out who he is. We have to unmask him."

"He won't stay down long," Luca hissed. He was right—already the figure on the floor was stirring. "I'm unarmed. My only weapon was surprise, but that's gone now. If we don't leave *now* he will kill us both. Do you understand?"

I stared longingly at the blood-red blade. "You should have taken his sword."

"Were you trained in swordplay?" Luca snapped. "Because I wasn't. Anyway, it's too late now. We need to *go*."

The Red Mask rolled onto his knees and wrapped his fingers around the hilt of the sword. I turned on my heel, gripped Luca's wrist, and fled.

Darkness churned around us as we ran. I knew the Oubliettes barely better than Luca. We took hallways at random, hoping to shake our pursuer. But if Sainte Sauvage trailed us, I couldn't hear his footsteps over the rasp of my own breath, the thunder of blood in my ears, our feet slapping stone.

At last, I recognized a crabbed metal tree; the edge of a sunburst; the whiff of freedom. Luca saw it a moment after I did, and hauled me toward the exit.

"Wait!" I dug in my heels and wrenched my wrist out of his grasp. Sudden doubt muddied my thought processes. "Wait. If I leave, I forfeit. Gavin wins the Ordeal."

"If you stay, you die," Luca snarled. "Besides, I'm—I'm fairly sure Gavin already won."

"What?" My heart throbbed, and I thought suddenly—painfully—of the ambric Relic. *My* Relic. "But I won, I—"

My voice died in my throat. Had I won? I cast my thoughts back over the Ordeal, already dimming like a half-remembered dream. I'd won, hadn't I? I'd rejected the impossible world the Oubliettes had invented for me. I'd walked into the light.

Horror tiptoed into my heart. Scion, what if I'd gone the wrong way? What if I was meant to follow my heart toward the sun, toward the Amber City, toward the destiny waiting for me in Coeur d'Or? Instead, I'd walked into *the moon's* light. But it had felt so . . . *right.* It had felt like home. It had felt like a place I finally, miraculously belonged.

"Sylvie," interrupted Luca, impatient. "The Ordeals don't matter anymore. Listen to me—every entrance and exit into this place was guarded by Husterri. Every single person who came into this place submitted to a weapons check. Including me, and Gavin considers me a friend."

Realization thudded into my skull. "Which means—"

"—Someone let that Red Mask in on purpose. The Husterri are fiercely loyal to Gavin. His word is their law."

"You think Gavin plotted to have me killed in the middle of the Ordeal?" Shock made my voice shrill. "Aren't you his *friend?*"

"He seemed a nice enough fellow in the beginning," Luca admitted. "But no, I'm not his friend."

I stared at Luca blankly.

"Scion, Sylvie, I've been *spying* on him." He shot a nervous glance over his shoulder. "Look, I'll explain everything later. But we need to leave. Leave the Oubliettes, leave the palais, leave the city."

"And go where?"

"Belsyre. It's the only place you'll be safe."

I barked a laugh. "Luca, you and Sunder hate each other. Where is this coming from?"

"First we run," he growled. "Then we talk."

He dragged me toward the exit. I followed, my head spinning. Gavin, in league with Sainte Sauvage and the Red Masks? Luca, spying on Gavin? Luca, advising me to leave for Belsyre—

I was leaving. Without telling anyone. Just like last time.

"We'll leave after Nocturne." Resolve made my voice hard. "But first, I have to do something."

Coeur d'Or's halls were mercifully empty once we left the Oubliettes, but I still cast a haphazard invisibility illusion to hide us from unseen eyes. We made it to Belsyre Wing unaccosted. The residence itself was deserted—the staff had all returned to the estate with Sunder and Oleander. The only attendants left were my own handmaidens, who were either watching the Ordeals in the Oubliettes or taking time off for personal errands. Quickly, I shoved into my room and packed a few belongings— gloves and a fur from the last time I visited Belsyre, a sturdy pair of boots, jewelry and cash for bribes.

"Now can we go?" Luca hissed, impatient. "The longer we wait, the more likely the Husterri will catch us."

"I'm sure they're still combing the Oubliettes for me. Heirs aren't supposed to just disappear."

"All the more reason we should leave while we can."

"Just one more stop," I promised.

I found the entrance the servants used to come and go unseen, and Luca picked the lock. Beyond, the servants' quarters were even more circuitous than the palais's labyrinthine halls. Corridors and stairways branched away between food stations and racks of clothing and sleeping cots.

Luca's hand was a vise on my bicep. "Where are you trying to go?"

"Lys Wing. Lullaby's rooms."

"This way." Luca trotted along a corridor stacked with crates of wine. I followed as he navigated the warren of rooms and entranceways. He didn't hesitate once. Finally, we burst out of a hidden doorway into a foyer draped in gardenias and opals.

"Lys Wing, as requested." Luca bowed.

"Thanks," I said, impressed. We snuck into Lullaby's unlocked chambers, but she hadn't yet returned from the Oubliettes.

"Now what?" Luca shoved his hands into his pockets.

I stared at the blue drapes, rumpled bed, and half-eaten boxes of chocolate truffles. "We wait for Lullaby to come home."

"Why?"

"I can't explain." My feet suddenly felt like two rocks attacked to my legs. I sank onto a divan. "It's just something I have to do."

Luca paced around the room, unease written plain on his face.

"Do you want to tell me why you've been pretending to be Gavin's friend, and how you knew your way around the servants' quarters like that?"

Luca pulled a face. "Let's just say, when Gavin first showed up in the city, it wasn't the first time I'd heard his name. I didn't trust him or his intentions. So I resolved to get close to him—to become his friend, and learn his secrets."

"And?"

"He's—careful." Luca looked at the ground. "And he has a way of earning your trust. When you're around him, it's almost like—like you're incapable of suspicion. Sometimes I'd ask leading questions only to forget what I was trying to discover until hours later. I'd tail him into the city only to wind up laughing and drinking with him at a party."

"His legacy," I said. "He glamours you."

"I guessed something similar." Luca frowned. "And there's some connection between him and Sainte Sauvage. After today, I'm beginning to think he orchestrated this entire thing from the beginning."

I shook my head, slightly awed. "I had no idea you were spying on him for me."

Luca flushed a dull red and looked at the floor.

"It wasn't for me?" I narrowed my eyes. What did he just say? *It wasn't the first time I heard Gavin's name.* The only other person I knew who had serious dirt on Gavin was— "Scion's teeth, Luca. *Oleander?*"

Luca's eyes flashed bright. "It's not like that."

"I didn't say it was like anything!" But maybe it was. I suddenly remembered two empty glasses in his apartment. How he'd lit up when I'd said Oleander's name at the *hidden selves* party. How well he knew the route through the servants' quarters from Belsyre Wing. I clamped my teeth on an incredulous laugh bubbling in my chest. Honestly—were any two people in the daylight world more different than Luca and Oleander?

The chime of high-heeled footsteps stopped me from pushing further. I put a hand on Luca's arm as Lullaby stepped into her room. She took one look at us both, and loudly yelped. She threw the bolt on the door, then flung herself at me. She smelled like fear and fury and the close, caustic scent of the Oubliettes.

"Scion, Mirage! Dowser and I were sick with worry when you never finished the Ordeal!" She was holding back tears, and I loved her for it. "After Gavin won, we all waited for you to return to the dais, but you never came. They organized search parties—

half the palais is still searching for you. Or what's left of you."

I shuddered, and bit back a surge of bitter envy. *Gavin won.* Of course I'd known he must, but still—the thought of my Relic around his neck brought bile to my throat.

"Listen, I don't have much time to explain. I was attacked in the Oubliettes by a Red Mask. The only way he could have gotten past the Husterri with a weapon is if Gavin ordered it. We think Gavin is in league with Sainte Sauvage. Which means I'm not safe here anymore."

Doubt chased shock across Lullaby's face. "Why would Gavin want to kill you if he already won the Ordeals?"

"I believe he cheated in the first Ordeal. And I know he cheated in the third. He won't want me around to taint his victory. And if he's anything like the rest of my family . . . well, historically we haven't been especially fond of loose ends."

Lullaby nodded. "So you're fleeing the city. Where?"

"Belsyre."

"And you're here because . . . ?"

"I'm not abandoning you again, not like last time," I said fiercely. "You should come with us."

Lullaby's soft face gathered hard lines of resolve.

"I can do more here. I'll let Dowser know where you went, and together we can plan for your return."

"Return?" I swallowed against a sudden hot lump in my throat. "Lullaby, I might not be able to come back."

"You'll be back."

I wasn't sure I shared her certainty.

"What about you? Will you be safe?"

"Gavin's not a monster—I doubt he'll throw me in the dungeon just for being your friend."

"But—"

"Go," she insisted. "Get your man. Get your army. Then

march back here and get your throne. We'll be waiting for you."

She stood, brusque, and crossed to her bed, reached under the mattress, and extricated a heavy purse filled with jewelry and money. Rings and necklaces and bronze écu and kembric livres. I shoved it back at her.

"I can't take this."

"You can." Her mouth quirked up. "You can pay me back when you're empress."

"You're a good friend." I hugged her, tight. Unfamiliar words marched up my throat, hot and sharp and unexpected. I let myself speak them. "I love you, Lullaby Courbis."

She cocked her head, surprised, then smiled bright as sunlight on water. "I love you too, Mirage Sabourin."

She watched as we snuck from the room. And then it was just me and Luca and a glittering world full of empty promises and lurking danger.

FORTY-THREE

My first trip to Belsyre had been inarguably unpleasant—
I'd been racked with fever and chills as I detoxed from
one of Oleander's *gentler* poisons. My second had been
little better—I'd been injured and exhausted, numb with grief
and guilt after defeating my sister and losing Sunder and Lullaby
to the Skyclad. My third journey to Belsyre did not buck the
trend.

We never would have gotten out of the Amber City if Luca
didn't have contacts throughout the lower city. Soon after we left
Lullaby's chambers, it became clear the Husterri had abandoned
their search in the Oubliettes and had begun looking for me elsewhere. The city was crawling with their vermilion uniforms,
interspersed with massive street parties celebrating the victory
of the true Sun Heir. My heart jolted more than once when my
boot kicked against discarded moon emblems crumpled like
trash in the street.

I was *Duskland Dauphine* no more. I was nobody.

We quickly abandoned the main streets. Husterri were stopping people at random and demanding identification and avowals
of belief and loyalty. Besides, the streets were too choked with
passersby to stay invisible for long. We made our way to the
Mews, where a warehouse comptroller with greedy eyes and
unscrupulous morals accepted a priceless emerald necklace in
exchange for false papers and the secret compartment in a smelly
charcoal cart. We rattled beneath the gates, and as the city faded
away a horrible sense of loss settled over me, as though I'd just
sacrificed some part of myself that hadn't been mine to give
away. A bright, glittering spark—a shard of ambric in a diamond

sky. A kembric dream of an impossible world. A promise of a perfect life I'd forged from the dristic of my will.

You'll be back, Lullaby had promised. I hoped—hoped—she was right. I didn't want this story to be over yet.

We crawled out of the charcoal cart at the next outpost, hours later. If Luca noticed the tear tracks cutting across my soot-blackened face, he didn't say anything. Instead, he bartered for horses with an innkeeper in an unfamiliar dialect while I lingered in the shadows. The woman sensed our urgency, and charged us twice the going rate. We paid her triple and bought her silence as well as steeds.

We rode north.

My short jaunts in the saddle with Gavin had not transformed me into a horsewoman. My legs ached after the first day, and by the third I thought I might never be able to sit down again. But that was nothing compared to the cold. The moment we climbed into the foothills the air thinned, sucking the warmth from our lungs and leaching the color from our cheeks. Soon, sheer snow-draped peaks loomed above us like stone castles, forbidding against the roiling sky. Luca and I had no camping gear to speak of, so we barely slept, only stopping to rest the horses. Then we huddled together beneath my fur cloak, sharing body warmth and forgoing speech, because the wind just stole our words and wailed them around the mountaintops.

But the horses weren't bred for this terrain. Their thin coats stood no chance against the frigid winds; their shod hooves slipped and slid on steep icy paths. At last, Luca reined his mount to the edge of the path and began untacking her.

"What are you doing?" I shouted through the sheeting snow.

"Sending her home!" he hollered back. He unloaded the saddle and his near-empty pack. "One more day of this, and she'll be nothing but tiger food. Or worse, she'll slip off a cliff and kill us both."

The vapor of my curse turned to ice on my lips. He was right. I slid out of the saddle, ungainly, and began tugging at my gelding's bridle. Before long, both horses were disappearing into the white blur down the mountain. Part of me wished I could go with them.

"What now?"

Luca looked up from fashioning a kind of cloak out of the horses' saddle blankets. His hair and stubble were frosted white. He pointed a finger into the blizzard. "We go that way."

I squinted up. "How can you tell?"

"Once I've been somewhere once, I always know how to get back." Luca shrugged, and hoisted his pack. "Bit of Tavendel magic, I suppose."

After that, we didn't talk. Luca led, and I followed. There was something resembling a road, for a bit, but that fell away into a jumble of knife-sharp boulders that sliced the soles of my boots. The blizzard blew itself out at last, leaving drifts of thigh-deep snow piled beneath a clear ruby sky. The cold that fell after drove blades into my chest and made me forget I had fingers.

That's when I got scared.

I wished I could say I looked death in the face, and smiled. I didn't. I begged the elements. I pleaded with nature. I made promises I couldn't keep to gods I didn't believe in.

And when the endless waves of white finally broke around a platoon of black-cloaked soldats on huge black horses, it felt like salvation.

They saw us before we saw them. Their heavy chargers bore down on us, clouds of vapor blooming from their noses. Pale faces behind ruffs of fur; metal eyes and emerald signats and naked dristic swords. I pushed my hood back with shaking, frozen fingers, and coughed frigid air into my aching throat.

"My lady?" One of the soldats nudged his mount forward. I recognized his grey eyes and boyish dimples. *Calvet.* I sagged with relief.

The captain cocked her head. "You recognize her?"

"She's the Duskland Dauphine." Calvet's voice shifted from surprise to urgency. He reined his horse toward me, then leaned down and clasped my numb forearm. "Hurry—let's get them out of the cold. Or the commandant will have our emeralds."

I waited to see Luca lifted up behind the captain before I surrendered to Calvet's grasp. He dragged me onto the saddle in front of him and wrapped his fur cloak around me. For a moment, I sagged into the blissful warmth. Then every nerve in each of my numb extremities woke up. Pain vaulted up my arms and needled my legs. And as we swept away across the colorless plain, I suffered in excruciating silence, because I knew—I knew this was the price of being alive.

White snow, black mountains, red sky—a hypnotic rhythm of color flashing by in time to the broad muffled hoof-falls of the horses. I must have slept, because when I woke it was to sounds and smells I hadn't learned to miss this past tide: the shriek of metal machinery, the clang of tools, the bitter-black scent of smelting fires running hot on coal, men's dank voices echoing from the earth.

The Loup-Garou had brought us to a mine.

I sat straighter as we cantered through a rough, semi-permanent camp. Snow had been cleared away for rows of canvas tents and shanties of ice bricks and shale. A huge bonfire glowered at the center of camp; the smell of roasting meat made my mouth water. Beyond, a gaping hole had been blasted into a looming rock face. Metal rails led away into the shadows with the rattle and ring of distant contraptions.

The platoon reined to a halt in front of the pit.

"My lord!" Calvet called out.

A blot of darkness at the mouth of the cavern moved. My chest contracted. Sunder stepped out into the ruddy light. Although he wore thick furs, his head was bare—his pale hair was a knife against the darkness yawning at his back. As always, he was more fathomable here, in the mountains of his birth; as though he had been crushed beneath the weight of stone and ice and been transformed into something stronger, harder, brighter.

"Yes, Calvet?" His eyes slicked over us without much care—he seemed far away. "What is it?"

"Lord, it's—" Calvet swallowed nervously.

"It's me," I finished, pushing out of Calvet's furs and sitting straighter. Part of me didn't want Sunder to see me like this—chapped and windblown and frozen half to death—but another part of me reveled in it. Let him see my strength. Let him see my resilience. Let him see *me*. "I come to beg sanctuary of Belsyre."

His eyes stuttered on mine. He froze, then strode quickly toward us. I threw my leg over the pommel of the saddle, trying to look haughty as I slid to the ground.

"My lady—" Calvet cautioned.

"Demoiselle—"

My legs crumpled beneath me, pitching me into the dreck of half-melted snow and soot and slag. Sunder caught me around the shoulders, then slid an arm beneath my numb knees and hoisted me like I weighed nothing.

"Bissot, send for the medic!" Sunder commanded. "Calvet, have the seneschal fetch water—hot water—and blankets from the cache! Armand, prepare a tent for the boy—"

But his orders were fading away beneath the persistent hum in my ears; the weight of my eyelids heralded a wave of blackness. I leaned my head against his shoulder. His soft fur kissed my cheek—it smelled like genévrier and ice. It smelled like him.

I closed my eyes.

I awoke on a hard cot to the creeping sensation that someone was watching me sleep.

I sat up too quickly—my head swam, dizziness threatening to pitch me back onto the cot. I closed my eyes, waiting for the feeling to pass, then slowly tried again.

A single candle blurred the interior of a low, narrow tent. A shadow hunched on the cot across from mine. His eyes caught the light from the flame and glowed unfathomable—*Sunder*. He no longer wore the emerald signat of the Loup-Garou.

"Where am I?"

"You mean to tell me," Sunder drawled, "that you climbed a mountain without knowing where you were going?"

A flash of annoyance robbed me of my calm. "You know what I mean."

His laugh carried an edge. "They're calling it the Wolf's Mouth. A mine—half a day's ride from Belsyre."

"What are you mining?"

"Diamond." Sunder reached into his pocket and pulled out a lump of raw mineral. He tossed it to me. I caught it, but the impact jarred my palm strangely, and it fell away between my limp fingers. I shook out my hand, and picked it up. It didn't look like anything special. Gingerly, I handed it back to Sunder.

"Keep it," he said. "Consider it a welcome gift."

I rolled it between my palms. My fingers tingled. I set it aside.

"The commune isn't big." The mining community outside of Piana had stretched as far as the eye could see, and the ambric lode had only been medium-sized. "The mine must either be very old or very new."

"The latter," confirmed Sunder. "The mineral is extremely rare—there hasn't been a seam this big in centuries. My surveyor discovered the lode while I was still at court."

"Is that why you really left?" My voice came out sharp.

"You know why I left. You seemed intent on pursuing a most fervent death wish." Sunder's smile cut like condemnation. "Something you seem no less bent on now."

I took a deep breath. "Gavin—"

"I know," he interrupted, careless. "Luca's been awake for a few hours now. He told me what happened."

"So—?"

"So we'll leave for Belsyre at first Matin." Sunder stood, his fur cloak sweeping around his boots, and lifted the door to the tent. "You begged for sanctuary. So sanctuary I will give. In the meantime, you should get some more rest."

"Sunder—" I began.

But the tent flap had already whispered shut behind him, leaving me alone with creeping regret and a fading dream of what it felt like to be wanted.

FORTY-FOUR

Returning to Belsyre was like waking up into a dream I'd almost forgotten.

I remembered it—of course I did. But I'd secreted those memories away, into a still, silent corner of my heart—a frozen flower pressed between two panes of glass. Firelit revelations and chilled wine, red-vined pillars and ice-chased kisses—these were memories from another life. It had only been two spans, but I could almost imagine it was another girl who came here, and another girl again who left.

But seeing it now brought all those thoughts and feelings flooding back. The twin mountains looming dark against the vermeil sky were my own fears staring down at me. The pluming cascades of icy water were all my shattered dreams, and I stood on the slender bridge above them. And the château—those glittering towers clawing toward the sky were my own lofting ambitions, sharp and high and impossible to reach.

A host of blank-faced servants in Belsyre livery bowed us into the foyer. As always, the château's stark elegance made me nervous, and I hunched deeper into my borrowed furs. Yet for once the stronghold almost felt . . . *lived in*. Ambric chandeliers and roaring hearths lent a quality of warmth. Furniture gleamed, free of dust or protective white cloths. Tapestries in luxurious tones warmed the walls, instead of being rolled to protect the dyes.

Heeled slippers chimed on the stairs as Oleander hurtled toward us. She flew past Sunder and flung herself into Luca's arms. He wrapped his hands around her waist and buried his face in her hair.

"Luca." Her voice was muffled against his coat. "You made it. I knew you would."

"Where you go, I follow," he promised, with a laugh. "Eventually, at least."

She took his hand in both her gloved palms and led him away. "Tell me everything—about Gavin, about the final Ordeal—"

I watched them leave with my jaw practically unhinged. I'd suspected *something*, but this?

Sunder stared after them with his jaw set. He lifted an expressive eyebrow when he saw me looking.

"Jealous?" he purred.

"Of Luca?" I laughed. "Not even a little. But don't try to tell me you're happy about this."

A muscle leapt in his jaw, but all he said was: "My sister knows her own mind. And her heart. We should all be so lucky."

Heat crept up my throat. "What's that supposed to mean?"

Sunder looked away. "You should bathe, and dress. We dine at second Compline."

And he too disappeared into the cold, pale château, leaving me alone.

Supper was a livelier affair than the first time I'd been at Belsyre.

I dressed in a gown with a pale lace bodice that fell away into a weightless expanse of midnight tulle. The four of us ate at that same impossibly long banqueting table, scattered with spotless crystal goblets and gleaming silverware and candles sparking with the scents of evergreen and captive frost. We ate escargot with shallot butter and brioche; tarragon-spiced rabbit with whipped potatoes and wilted spinach; lavender-scented croquembouche swirled with snowflake sugarwork. I thought it all a bit much—none of us were royalty.

Anymore.

Still, I was hungry, so I greedily shoveled food into my mouth while Oleander and Luca carried the conversation.

"How did you know that Red Mask was going to try to kill Mirage?" Oleander wasn't eating—instead, she had her chin on her hand and was watching Luca with a weird glow in her eyes. I frowned. Was that what people in love looked like? I glanced at Sunder. His eyes glittered over the rim of his wineglass. I looked away.

"I didn't," Luca said around a mouthful of potatoes. He might have won Oleander's affection, but he hadn't picked up any table manners along the way. "The third Ordeal was frankly boring. The two heirs went off into the Oubliettes, and that was it. There was nothing to see. The spectators were getting restless— drinking too much and gambling on who was going to win. Someone started a fight up front—now I see it was probably meant as a distraction. That's when I saw the Red Mask slip away into the Oubliettes after Mirage. I didn't think, just followed."

She touched his hand. "You were brave."

He flushed. "It was nothing."

Sunder rolled his eyes so hard I thought his skull might split. He pushed back his chair, sloshed more wine into his glass, and stood.

"I'm finished." I waited for him to stalk off, but he held out a hand to me instead. "Lady Mirage, do you wish to accompany me on a tour of the château? I think, perhaps, you have not seen much of it before."

I'd done little but wander its halls for three days straight the first time I'd been here. But he didn't know that. Besides, my only other option was to stay here and watch Oleander and Luca try to make babies with their eyeballs. I stood, and took his arm.

"Please," I whispered. "In case whatever they have is catching."

He smiled tightly. I watched him out of the corner of my eye as he led me across the foyer and down through an annex toward another wing of the château. His words and movements seemed automatic, as though he was playing out a script someone else had written. His gloved hands sketched against the outlines of the château, and his mouth moved around words I thought I recognized: *balustrade*, *cornice*, and *arabesque*.

Finally, he dropped my hand and turned to face me. His mouth coiled with pale amusement.

"You don't really care, do you?"

"It's just walls and marble and tile," I said, a little helplessly. "Those may be the building materials of a house, but they aren't the things homes are made of."

He considered this. "If that's true, then this place is built from the bricks of forgotten lives."

I frowned. "Surely you don't believe that."

"Look at this place." I followed his gaze to a vaulting crystal ceiling. "Some ancestor built this château a thousand tides ago, and then died. Generations of my family have lived here. Hundreds of children were born beneath this roof. Someone has died in every room. I inherited their property, their fortune, their lands, and yet I don't know their names. I don't know what they lived for—what they dreamed of, who they loved, why they died. It's just a palais built from memories, with no one to live in it."

"Must we be remembered, for our lives to have meaning?"

"I think perhaps it is the only way," he whispered. "The bits and pieces that linger on, in the broken glass of other people's memories."

"Then we must be sure to tell each other's stories, when we are gone."

Sunder's face hardened with some kind of decision. He caught my wrist and pulled me down a series of corridors before stopping in front of a door. He unlocked it, rested a hesitant hand on the knob, then swiftly pushed it open.

The room beyond stole my breath and my gaze. It was a room, and yet, an entire impossible world held within four walls. Sky painted an arching ceiling with azure. No—not paint. For the pigment had depth and distance that tore at the horizons of my mind. A perilous shining eye stared from the blue, its light like warmth on my face.

And below—Scion, *below*.

The floor plummeted away into endless blackness studded with a million glittering lights. Vertigo swept over me, and for a moment I fell—fell like a bright point of light through the glimmering dark. But then I saw her—the moon, sailing full-bellied and pristine through the night, and I found my balance. I gazed at her as she turned, spinning through her phases in an eternal dance.

The room was more fantastic than any of my wildest illusions. Envy and admiration and an infinite, aching longing burned through me in quick succession.

"My father had this room enchanted." Sunder's soft voice echoed through time and space. He led me out onto the dizzying floor, and spun me once, gently, so my gown floated around my legs. "There was a story he heard as a child, about the Sun and the Moon, and it stuck with him his whole life. He spent half his life studying the lore of the Midnight Dominion—it was his greatest wish to travel there someday. My mother, of course, had no intention of ever letting him." He caught me around the waist, and threaded his gloved fingers through mine. His gaze was far away. "This is my only real memory of him. I was so young when he died. But I remember this room. And I remember his voice, telling me his favorite story. I've kept it locked away for so long. But perhaps—perhaps it's finally time to share it."

With me. I swallowed, and lifted my eyes to his. "Will you tell me the story?"

"I'll see how well I remember it." His mouth was by my ear, and somehow we were dancing—a dance without steps or music. "In a time before time, there was a she-wolf, whose belly grew with a litter of pups. She was hungry, but the snow lay deep and she had grown too large to hunt. She began to eye the moon, hanging fat and lazy in the sky. *Just a taste*, she thought. She took a bite of the moon. But she was still hungry, so she ate a little more. Bite after bite, she tore away slivers, until there was nothing left in the sky but darkness. Soon, her pups were born, but instead of fur and flesh, they were hard and sharp and bright— they were made of moon-stuff. Ashamed, she buried them where no one could see them. She turned herself into a mountain, to watch over them. And the sun—the sun was so furious the she-wolf had eaten the soul of the world, that he sat where he could keep an eye on her for the rest of time."

I shivered, the eerie story striking a chord of familiarity somewhere in my chest. Sunder's hands tightened on my waist.

"Are you planning on going back?"

FORTY-FIVE

The question rocked me off-balance and drove the story out of my head. "What?"

"To Coeur d'Or. You still want the throne."

It wasn't really a question. I answered honestly. "I don't know."

"You asked for sanctuary, demoiselle. I would offer you solace as well." He ran his fingers along the diamond shards embedded in my throat, then cupped my cheek and kissed me. The kiss was fleeting as starlight, the length of time splitting day from night. I knew it was all he dared—as always, it ached when he touched me. It ached more when he drew away. "Would it be so terrible to stay here? With me?"

"No," I whispered.

"Gavin once joked about me marrying you—"

"Sunder," I interrupted. "I wouldn't dwell overlong on any of the things Gavin has said."

"Trust me, I don't." He laughed low. "But it seemed perhaps like you thought it was a joke too."

I stilled. I remembered that day—I'd laughed at Sunder and finally realized what Gavin's legacy was. Guilt writhed through me—had Sunder spent all this time thinking I'd been laughing at the idea of us being married?

"Sunder, *no*." I gripped his biceps and met his eyes. "That was Gavin's legacy—a persuasion, a *glamour*. I could never laugh at you."

His eyes thawed. "And here I thought I had a rather winning sense of humor."

Anticipation laid bare all the spaces between us.

"Would you consider it?" He mouthed the words as though

he wasn't sure he was actually saying them out loud. "You would not be an empress, Mirage. But I can promise—whatever else you dream will be yours. If you wish to be the sun, you will rise in glory. If you wish to be the moon, you will set in perfect darkness and stars will shine in your eyes. Because I will always be the man—or the monster—who falls from the sky at the sight of you."

My breath ratcheted in my chest, and my heart flung jags of hot liquid toward my face. The diamond shards embedded in my arms and throat rippled sharp light toward my fingertips.

"Sunder de Vere." I lifted myself toward him, even as I fell toward the sheer expanse of everlasting sky. "Are you asking me to be your wife?"

"I'm telling you I love you." He said it simply. He said it like a secret. "And I'm asking if you could ever feel the same."

I tasted the words on my tongue—tasted the bright peaks and shadowed valleys of the memories behind them. Moments strung like jewels on a chain—a cold, handsome boy with anguish in his eyes and razors in his mouth—snow on my tongue and the chilly promise of something I hadn't known I'd wanted— the burn of bright green liquor and pain-racked condemnation.

You use me to hide all the things you don't want to look at.

But I wasn't looking away now. And the path behind me churned with red masks and savage saints. A city in the grip of fanaticism, beliefs driven home with flaming swords and violence. And above it all loomed a weak man with the gift of coercion, a man who would cheat to win a throne he'd never earned.

Could I use Sunder to hide all those things? And if I did, would we ever forgive each other for it?

"I hated growing up in the Dusklands," I said. "The darkness was like death—creeping and inexorable. If you tried not to think about it, maybe you wouldn't notice it sneaking up on you. But I didn't want to ignore it. I wanted to escape it. And when I got to Coeur d'Or I tried to leave those shadows behind. I tried to leave that girl who grew up there—*Sylvie*—behind."

I made a memory of that discontent. "So I became Mirage. But she was just as obsessed with possessing the light as Sylvie was with escaping the dark. And I have to wonder if I can still become someone else—someone who lives in both places, who embraces both radiance and shadow in kind."

His eyes reflected sun shards and night. "Demoiselle, what are you saying?"

"I do love you," I whispered. "But I am not yet whole. And I cannot answer your question until I am."

He sighed. His hands fanned across my face and swept back my loose hair.

"How can it be," he whispered, "that it is in the darkness your light shines the brightest?"

I smiled to hide my tears. "I am too acquainted with the dusk to be afraid of the night."

We swayed together in that space between night and day, my hands on his shoulders, his hands at my waist. Soft words and scorching kisses fell between us like stars, and I caught them against the mirror of my mind and crushed them so tightly they became diamonds. So long as they shone, I thought, this moment would last forever.

FORTY-SIX

The somnolent bell for second Nocturne gonged, but still I couldn't find sleep.

Standing at the window, a length of fur wrapped around my shoulders, with snow-heavy clouds and an ice-draped gorge in the distance, I could almost imagine the sun had set, leaving behind an inky sky scattered with diamonds. How strange it must have been, long ago, to split one's day between such wildly different extremes—sun and moon, day and night.

I took the chunk of raw diamond Sunder had given me out of the pocket of my nightgown. I ran my thumb over its contours, frowning. Something about the mineral troubled me, but I wasn't sure exactly what. It felt cold against my fingertips. I knew it had been mined from the depths of Belsyre's mountains, but there was something else too—a numb shock of desensitization that left my hand stinging. It almost felt like touching Sunder.

Sunder.

I polished the diamond of memory once more: *I will always be the man—or monster—who falls from the sky at the sight of you.*

Part of me wanted what he offered me. But did I want it because I never thought to dream it? Did I want it because I never thought I could have it? What if the foundation of our love was simply that it could never be complete? Forever longing, forever aching, never touching. What would happen if we got what we wanted? Would we find that our common ground had only ever been hunger?

I thought suddenly of Sunder's myth, about the wolf who ate the moon. Its cadence had wormed its way between my ribs, a heart beating beside my own. Her insatiable hunger. Her diamond pups. The sun watching her forever, in punishment for eating the soul of the world.

The soul of the world.

The *soul.*

My heart stopped. The floor tilted. I tightened my grip on my composure.

It was a coincidence. Plenty of stories had the word *soul* in them. But I sat hard on the window seat. My thoughts spun back to when Dowser first told me the story of the Relics from that old storybook—the story of Meridian's four children. How had it gone? The dristic sword, to strong Aliette. The kembric crown, to clever Bastien. The ambric Sun, to passionate Raphaël. And—

I struggled to remember the exact words. Dowser had been confused by the translation, he'd said—

Meridian gave his soul to his ambitious daughter Liliane, who dreamed always of the stars.

I remembered laying my hand against a circle cut into a stone dais and wondering what might fit there. I remembered crystalline warriors marching in still, silent rows, lighting the cavern with a twilight glow. And I remembered turning my face away from an illusory setting sun in order to chase a cool, quiet moon.

A moon that felt like a bit of my soul mirrored before me.

I grabbed the raw diamond out of my pocket and clutched it tight. Scion, I knew it was a stretch, but what if the fourth Relic—the Soul Relic, the lost Relic—was the *Moon* Relic? And what if—like that she-wolf's shameful pups—it was made out of *moon-stuff*?

What if it was made out of diamond?

Excitement pulsed hot in my veins, followed swiftly by cool certainty. I stood.

My guess about the Soul Relic might be wrong. It didn't

matter—the Relic was still lost. Knowing what it was got me no closer to finding it. What did matter was this:

I suddenly knew how to beat Gavin and win back my throne.

Sunder, Bane, and Luca gathered in the slick, chilly dining room and looked at me like I might be mad. But I burst with exhilaration I had to share—exhilaration and triumph and a hundred fantastical dreams of a thousand impossible worlds.

"Scion's teeth," Oleander said, not unpleasantly. "It's nearly third Nocturne. What's this about?"

She'd still been fully dressed when I hammered on her door, and hadn't been sleeping—the room behind her blazed with candlelight and perfume. The streaks of high color on her pale cheeks hinted she'd been drinking. When I'd told her I had news to share, she'd opened the door and beckoned to Luca lounging shirtless on one of her couches.

Sunder had also willingly come, but he looked weary and wary. His hand lurked by his side, where his timbre burned sullen through the fabric of his shirt.

"I've given too much power to Gavin's ability to manipulate perceptions," I began, "while half forgetting my own imperfect legacy—*wonder.* Gavin might be able to glamour everyone into feeling what he wants them to feel, but I have something better. I can conjure luster and imagine light. I have only to unleash the wild colors caged around my heart."

"I thought your illusions weren't working," Oleander said, blunt as ever.

"I think that's because I didn't know what to use them for."

"And now you do." Sunder's voice was tired.

"The Amber City didn't want me as their Sun Heir. But I can

show them what a true Duskland Dauphine looks like."

Quickly, I told them about my theory—how the missing Relic, the Soul Relic, was made of diamond carved to look like the moon. I told them about my plan to discredit Gavin—to prove he'd won the Ordeals in bad faith, had allied himself with Sainte Sauvage and the Red Masks. Everyone looked dubious at first, but as I spoke Oleander's lovely face ignited with a hard, sharp light. By the time I finished, she was smiling in a way I hoped never to be on the wrong side of.

"Excellent."

Luca nodded slowly. "It might work."

Sunder bowed his head. When he lifted it, I barely recognized the grim set of his mouth.

"Do you two mind," he asked, "if I speak to Mirage alone?"

Oleander and Luca shared a loaded glance as they wandered toward the other end of the room. Sunder didn't rise from his chair, but reached for me to join him. He caught my hand and twined our fingers together. Heat blazed against my palm through his leather gloves.

"This?" His voice fractured. "This is what will make you whole?"

"Do you doubt it?"

"No." He smiled, brittle and brilliant, and a piece of my heart broke off. "You said you were no longer Sylvie nor Mirage. I believe you are both girls, and yet you are neither. There is strength in transformation—the things that bring us the most pain brings us the deepest perspective. Diamonds are not born— they are made."

"And if this transformation demands I return to the city and fight for my throne?"

"It would be no less than I expected." Sunder lowered his eyes. "Although it is not what I hoped."

"What did you hope?"

Voicelessly, he buried his head against my waist. His hands circled my back, so softly I could barely feel them.

My voice was a caged moth in my chest. I stared in shock at his bright, bowed head. It was hard to think of Sunder as anything but a *man*, but in that moment I remembered he was barely out of boyhood. We were both barely more than children, and yet we had both been thrust into a world where we were expected to behave like adults. This rare moment of vulnerability felt almost childlike, and I hardly knew what to do with it. Slowly, I let my hands fall, my fingers sifting soft weightless strands of blond hair.

His voice, when it came, was barely more than a vibration against my stomach. "I hoped for an end to this pain. I hoped for an end to this bloodshed. I hoped for peace."

I drew his head up, my palms against his jaw and my fingertips in his hair. Pain spangled up my arms, but I didn't let go. I caught his gaze, full of alpine dreams and more love than I could fathom.

"Then you will have it."

"How?"

"I'm not asking you to come with me," I told him. "In fact, I insist you stay."

His eyes yawned with anguish and savage hope.

"It took me too long to realize I was using you," I whispered. "You, and the legacy you loathe. Just by making you my commandant I was asking you for violence, yet willfully ignoring the things you would have to do on my behalf. You carried the burden of all that sin alone, never asking me for redemption."

He made a noise. "I *wanted* to protect you. You never took anything from me I wasn't willing to give."

"I know. But now I want to protect you." I took a deep breath.

"I won't ask you to hurt or kill for me again. I won't be your pain. I release you from my service. I set you free."

The relief in his eyes was the knife I needed to cut me from him. I took one—two—gasping steps backward. He stood and bowed, piercingly formal. And then he clasped me to him, brief and tight.

"I will be there for your coronation, dauphine." His lips were in my hair. "I will be there at Ecstatica. I will see you in victory. I will see the dawn of your reign."

And then his sharp footfalls carried him away from me.

I scraped tears off my face and mastered my breathing. Then I walked to the end of the hall, where Oleander and Luca were sipping wine and pretending like they hadn't been trying to eavesdrop.

"What happened to Sunder?" Oleander asked.

"He won't be joining us this time," I replied, wooden.

Her red mouth opened in surprise. "Why in the daylight world not?"

"Because for once . . ." I murmured, echoing what I'd told Sunder. "For once I want to protect him, instead of the other way around."

She gave me a weird look that almost looked like respect.

"If that means you don't want to help me," I said, "I understand."

"Are you kidding?" She grinned. "I can't wait to see that fanatic imposter get what he deserves. I'm going to enjoy every minute of it."

I looked at Luca. "Luca?"

"She took the words right out of my mouth," he said, with a glint in his hazel eyes.

And so the three of us began to plan. We planned the clothes, the illusions, the words, like directors of a play where the actors had no idea they were onstage. And when at last we were satisfied, I stared away to the east, where I imagined that eternal seething border of Midnight.

Once upon a time, not so long ago, I'd run from that darkness at the edge of nowhere, toward the light at the heart of the empire. This time, I was winging back toward the dusk—in mind, if not in body. And I would earn back what was stolen from me, even if it meant chasing away sunlight with shadow, and finding the luster that lived inside the dark.

FORTY-SEVEN

W e left Belsyre two weeks after arriving.
Sunder returned to the mine at Wolf's Mouth the Matin after our conversation. He didn't say goodbye. He didn't need to.

Still, two weeks was barely enough time. Luca and I rested and regained our strength, while Oleander arranged the bulk of the preparations. She stockpiled food, weapons, and other supplies from Belsyre's well-stocked stores. She convinced twoscore Loup-Garou loyal to her to return to Coeur d'Or with us. She sketched countless designs for clothing, then sewed through the Nocturnes with a dozen Belsyre tailors, making sure each stitch was a vision, each seam like a knife. When I discreetly asked whether she was paying them overtime, one of them overheard.

"We are simply returning a lifetime of favors," the woman piped up. "Last tide I sent my eldest to Unitas, and it was Lady de Vere who paid his tuition."

"My husband and I just expanded our home," added a younger fellow. "We never would have been able to afford it without my lady's steady stream of commissions."

Oleander raised her eyebrow at me, as if to say, *Does that appease your tender sensibilities?*

I had to confess, it did.

Properly attired and well-supplied, the journey back to the Amber City was marginally more pleasant than Luca's and my mad trek. Belsyre's sturdy horses knew the passes well, and Oleander's sleigh glided over the thick snow. Luca and I mostly rode with her while she sewed, although I did brave the elements on horseback when their company grew too cloying.

The snowy steeps gave way to evergreen forests and rolling foothills dotted with scrubland. We camped a league outside the city. Oleander rubbed a paste of roots and herbs into her bright hair, temporarily dying it an alarming shade of red. Personally, I thought it made her look even more conspicuous than before, but I decided to hold my tongue. Luca and I tucked our hair into peddler's caps, and dressed in cheap clothing we'd bartered for in a foothill village. The forty-odd Belsyre wolves who elected to join us wore simple chain mail and kept their black swords hidden.

But sneaking back into the city was easier than I anticipated.

We needn't have tried so hard to keep our identities secret. With less than a week until Ecstatica, the Amber City was teeming with people of every nationality, race, and religion. The main gates were thrown wide open, but I only noticed people moving inward. When I discreetly glanced at the Husterri station beyond the gate, I saw a family of five being violently detained as they tried to leave—their packs were roughly hauled off their shoulders and dumped into the street, and a donkey cart had been overturned, scattering pots and pans and household goods to the ground.

I looked away before anyone recognized my face. But the sight of free citizens being prevented from leaving the city had ignited a spark of fury in my chest, tempered with growing resolve. I hadn't been the perfect Sun Heir, I knew that now—I'd listened to my councillors when they suggested martial law, never argued with curfews and travel bans and Scion knew what else—but it was time for that to change. The people who lived in this city—in this empire—had been without a voice for too long.

It was time for the voiceless to be heard.

Luca led us on a circuitous path through the city, winding through the marchés of the Mews and taking a detour through the Paper City before finally climbing the Échelles toward the palais. But again, we needn't have bothered. The Husterri waved us into the service courtyard without even double-checking our falsified papers.

"All this for Ecstatica?" I grunted when a middle-aged Huster flipped through my merchant's charters.

"The coronation of the Sun Heir, mostly," she said, without looking up.

"That's a lot for you to handle."

"You're telling me." She handed back the papers. "New platoons of Husterri arriving every day too. New recruits never seem to realize the barracks aren't *in* the palais. If I have to give one more soldat directions through the lower city . . ."

She mimed slitting her own throat. I laughed, saluted, and turned away before she could see my smile.

New platoons of Husterri streaming into the city might seem like a bad thing. But it was exactly what I'd hoped for. It meant no one would think anything of a few more unfamiliar faces.

Inside, the stables and storehouses were utter mayhem. Artificers and tradespeople and soldats and artisans crowded around in confusion, shouting for supplies and mounts and who knew what else. I was glad we'd boarded the distinctive Belsyre horses at the last inn—there wouldn't have been any space for them here.

In the chaos, it wasn't hard to duck behind an outbuilding and quickly shuck off our cloaks. Beneath our disguises, Oleander, Luca, and I all wore replicas of servants' livery. The two-score Loup-Garou all wore Husterri uniforms, although the real Husterri might be surprised by certain hidden design elements. Most of them, like Oleander, had elected to dye their distinctive Belsyre blond hair in varying shades of red and brown and black.

"Everyone clear on the plan?" I whispered to the wolves. "You're on your own till we rendezvous at the coronation. Try to split up into pairs and blend in. There are plenty of new gardes in the city, but in case you get caught—"

"Beg pardon, dauphine." Calvet had begged to be included on this mission, and I was loath to refuse those dimples. Besides—by now I owed him my life several times over. "But a soldat's a soldat. We all speak the same language: drinking and whoring."

A few of the other wolves laughed. Calvet flushed.

"Sorry, dauphine—"

I brushed away his apology. "I thank you all. Your service will be rewarded, I promise you."

In twos and threes, they swaggered out and blended with the crowd. Within moments, it was impossible to distinguish them from the other Husterri. I whistled, quelled my nerves, and turned to Luca and Oleander.

"Ready?"

"To watch you ask people who hate you for massive favors?" Oleander flashed a sardonic smile that reminded me rather desperately of her brother. "It's my one true wish in the daylight world."

We ducked into the servants' entrance and moved through the palais. I vaguely recognized some of the corridors and service stations along the way, but if it hadn't been for Luca I would have been deeply lost. We stopped by Lys Wing first.

Lullaby barely looked up from a stack of official-looking documents when I walked in, her mouth full of macarons.

"Do you mind?" she snapped. "I told Camille I wanted quiet."

"Sorry," I said. "But I'm always regrettably loud."

She nearly spat out her cookies. "Mirage!"

I laughed, and we embraced. Quickly, I updated her on everything that had happened since I'd left the palais. Her eyes grew wide when I told her about the diamond, the Moon, and my theories about the missing Relic.

"But what if you can't find it?"

"I'm not even going to try," I admitted. "All that matters it that Gavin thinks I have it. Speaking of which . . ."

"It's been mayhem," Lullaby said. "I didn't think it was possible for things to be less organized than when you were Sun Heir—*sorry*—but the whole city has been in upheaval. Barthet quit immediately after the Ordeals. Lady Marta stayed about a week—I think she wanted to give Gavin a chance, since he's half Aifiri. Dowser's been head-to-head with Arsenault since you disappeared. He's stood against Gavin's new religious edicts."

Horror jolted me. "Tell me."

"He's been using his Husterri to force conversions everywhere. If you don't swear the Scion's Vow, you're liable to be roughed up, exiled, or even jailed."

"You—?"

Lullaby shrugged. "I'm a survivor. My father's people believe in the wind and the tide and the sound of the water—it's no skin off my back to swear faith to a god I don't believe in."

"Will you—?" I swallowed. I wanted Lullaby's help, but I didn't want her to end up in another dungeon because of choices I'd made on my own. "You should protect yourself. If my plan goes sideways, I don't want you getting caught on the wrong side."

"You're an idiot," Lullaby laughed. "You'd have to beat me away from this plan with a stick. But thank you for offering."

FORTY-EIGHT

My next conversation didn't go so smoothly.

"You want us to do *what?*" Billow asked sharply.

I gritted my teeth. While I'd been talking to Lullaby, Oleander had gathered all the remaining Sinister courtiers in the abandoned Belsyre Wing—about a dozen legacies, all told. They glowered at me, seated very close together on sheet-draped furniture.

I unfolded my hands on my knees. When I'd brought this up with Oleander, she'd been sure they'd want to cooperate with me.

"What you call *loyalty to Severine*," she'd argued, "I call survival. We were all her pawns—her tools. We were loyal to her because anything else meant death. She dangled her favor between us like a bone before hounds, then made us fight our friends and family for it. You never understood what it meant to be subjugated—think on that before you call them blindly loyal to a wicked empress."

So I had. I'd thought about it during the whole journey from Belsyre. I thought about it when Calvet was willing—no, *asked*—to risk his life yet again for *me*, someone who'd never done anything for him besides exist. I thought about everything Dowser had tried to teach me about leadership, about hope. About being both who you wanted the people to see, and who they wanted to see *in you*.

I'd thought the people wanted spectacle. But spectacle wasn't the same thing as *inspiration*.

"Let me start again." I looked calmly at the Sinister legacies who led the group. "Billow, Haze, Shade, Tangle—I *want* your help. But even if I were in a position to command it, I wouldn't."

Haze shot a bemused glance at Billow.

"I know what it means to have your dreams held captive," I continued. "The women who raised me told me that to want was unholy, that to dream was a sin. Because they didn't have the power to stop me, I rebelled against them. But I was alone. I had no friends, no family. I could afford to be selfish because there was no one but myself to look after." I took a breath. "It's different when someone owns you, at the cost of the people you love. Severine manipulated your families by holding you hostage, and vice versa. And when I gained power, I did the same thing. I held you here like prisoners, because I couldn't trust what you or your families would do. That's all over.

"I know I'm no longer dauphine. And if you don't help me, it probably won't be my head that crown sits on come Ecstatica. But I want you to know—regardless of which heir you choose, whom you swear loyalty to—I consider you free. You won't lose anything by refusing me. In fact, you're more likely to lose something by helping. You're free to choose, as your conscience and instinct demands."

Haze stared at me, then burst out, "That bastard made me swear the Scion's Vow, or lose my title and fortune! My family estates were annexed during the Conquest, but we have always worshipped the Zvar gods."

"He's right," Tangle said, through her teeth. "Severine made us do awful things in her name, but it's easier to justify violence when you're just trying to protect yourself, your family. Forcing someone to go against their beliefs? That's too far."

Billow still looked unconvinced. She looked hard at Oleander.

"You and Sunder were always the best of us, loved and feared in equal measure," she said. "Why are you helping her?"

"If you thought you loved us, you didn't know us," Oleander

said. "And if you feared us, it was because you had been taught to do so. Mirage may be a fantast, but she has never been anything but authentic. She told us what she wanted, and we hated her for it; she told us the world she dreamed of, and we told her she couldn't build it without all the trappings of power we loathed about our previous monarchs. Don't get me wrong—she's just as flawed as the rest of us. But at least she's not pretending otherwise."

"If it's good enough for you, it's good enough for me," Billow sighed. "I'll do as you ask. Everyone else is free to choose as they will."

After a beat, every other Sinister courtier raised their hand or nodded in agreement.

It was unanimous.

Sinister stood with me.

And as pride and doubt and anticipation swelled within me, I only wished we weren't missing one.

I went to see Dowser alone.

He sat in his study by himself, poring over some antiquated document. When he saw me he surged to his feet. His smile was a kind of validation.

"Lullaby told me you survived the third Ordeal," he said. "But part of me wasn't sure you'd be back. I thought you might accept your—your happy ending with Sunder."

"I don't want any more endings," I said. "I want a new beginning."

Swiftly, I told Dowser about my theories, my plans, and what this coronation might look like. He slowly polished his spectacles on his robe.

"You were right. That old dream of yours is dead. But only because you've found a new one."

He kissed my forehead, and I hugged him as long as I dared.

"Dowser." I drew back. "Can I ask you to stay behind, tomorrow? To stay in the palais."

"You want me to sit this one out?"

"I want you as a last resort. I'll be sending nonessential legacies and soldats back to you. If anything goes wrong—in a worst-case scenario—"

I couldn't tell whether my teacher looked rueful or grateful. Either way, he nodded.

"It won't go wrong." Even though I knew it wasn't his promise to make, the words soothed me. "But no matter what happens, child, know that I will always be your first and last resort."

FORTY-NINE

The coronation procession proceeded up the Concordat, and we all waited and watched from the crowd, breathless with suspense.

Spectators lined the grand boulevard, decked out in Ecstatica finery. The ban on luxury goods had been lifted for the occasion, and it showed—the wealthy dressed in sparkling silks and luxurious satins, bright colors burning hotter than the honey-blush sky. Vendors moved amongst the crowds, offering up traditional Ecstatica fare: sugary demi-coquilles and decanters of crémant, the latter of which were being drunk at an alarming rate. The mood of the crowd seemed festive, with an edge—as though one wrong step or false word would set them to rioting.

It made me nervous.

It wasn't long before Gavin drew close enough for me to see his face. If I'd thought he'd looked like the Sun Heir before, his costume today put everything else to shame. He wore a suit of armor that didn't so much reflect the sunlight as expand it, shooting spears of incandescence into watching eyes. He had all three Relics on him—the blade hanging at his waist, the crown looped safely around his belt, and—

My chest contracted when I saw my ambric pendant dangling from his throat.

He proceeded slowly up the avenue, shaking hands and greeting people as he went. Arsenault stood at his shoulder, and a parade of Husterri marched up the Concordat behind him. For a moment, I was dazzled by Gavin's light and his smile and the sense of goodness oozing off him. I shouldn't be doing this. Who was I to question the outcome of the Ordeals? I wasn't *positive* he cheated—

"Scion, what a rat," Oleander snarled, from my shoulder.

Surprise jerked my gaze from Gavin, and when I looked back, the glamour had faded. Although he stood straight and smiled, his gaiety seemed forced and he looked strained. I noticed he greeted every person with a question I couldn't hear—their voiceless response turned my stomach. They passed their hands in front of their eyes, as though wiping away a vision they couldn't unsee. A Huster behind him passed out glittering gold écu to those who correctly completed the gesture.

Have you invited the Scion's light to banish the dusk?

I see his light beyond my eyes.

I clenched my hands. Today, of all days—on Ecstatica, the high holy day marking a new tide—he was still forcing conversions. My bejeweled nails pushed against my palm, flaking paint from my skin. I forced myself to relax. This would all be over soon, one way or another.

The tenor of the crowd grew louder the closer Gavin came to the palais. A grand platform had been erected by the gates—uncomfortably similar to the one where Pierre LaRoche had been ruthlessly executed by his own compatriots—adorned in all the garish symbolism of my family line. Shining sunbursts adorned the corners; pennants of kembric whipped in the breeze; flowers tumbled in cascades from polished urns. And upon it sat Severine's ambric throne.

Something ugly twisted in my stomach at the sight of it. Even after all this time, the ambric throne still felt like *hers*. But here it was, removed from the Atrium in all its erstwhile glory, plunked into the center of this pantomime like the symbol it was.

Gavin reached the steps leading to the dais. He took them slowly—the crowd roared. Arsenault followed close behind, with a half dozen Husterri. Gavin turned, lifted his hands. He was about to make a speech.

I turned to my people. I made eye contact with them each in turn—Oleander, Luca, Lullaby; Billow and Haze and the few Sinister courtiers I could see planted among the crowd.

"Now," I said.

Haze and Shade joined hands and bowed their heads. Shadows immediately poured out of their joined palms, unspooling like liquid vapor through the crowd. Fingers of darkness curled into crevices and brushed along cobblestones, reaching and coalescing all along the Concordat. A wave of black crested over the crowd. Cries of fear mixed with cries of wonderment. The shadows curled upward, blotting out the sun, and I reached toward the edges of the vapor with my own power, tweaking the borders of the false night and making them go on forever. A haunting melody lifted up above the crowd, a dreamlike lullaby that muffled my doubts in an eerie serenity.

In the black calm that fell, I shucked off my cloak. Gloved hands touched my shoulders—Oleander, helping me adjust my gown by sight alone. Cloth sighed around my legs. Metal boning cut into my ribs and shoulders, painful but necessary. Heavy jewels weighted my steps. I looked toward Billow, nearly invisible in the dusk, and nodded.

My feet lifted off the ground and my stomach did a somersault as I rose up. And up. And *up*.

In the darkness, I couldn't judge distance, and fear pulsed hot between my ribs. I squeezed my eyes shut and tried to remember all the times we'd practiced this. It had felt the same—the breeze whistling in my ears, my body lifting weightless as a feather, my balance focused on the corset clamped around my waist. Finally, I slowed, and I knew Billow had lifted me as high as she was able.

I opened my eyes, and straightened my spine. Below, the crowd was halfway to panic, wails of terror mixing with murmurs of confusion. I didn't have much time before chaos broke out.

I rubbed my hands together, then filled the artificial darkness with stars. Specks of light appeared in the seemingly endless darkness, bright as diamond and just as perfect. Wails turned to exclamations; muttering to excited chatter. For a long moment, I let the stars glitter, distant and icy and pristine. Then I drew the light back into myself. It pulsed above my heart, once. Twice. And on the third heartbeat, I let it go.

Pure radiance cascaded down the front of my gown and beyond, illuminating a bright corona of moonlight around my figure. The dress itself was sewn from velvet the precise color of Haze and Shade's false night, and decorated with constellations of diamonds. The jewels caught the pale light and magnified it against the dark, making it seem as though I floated among the stars. My hair was dusted with dristic and the diamonds embedded in my flesh sang. I hung, motionless and luminous, until everyone in the crowd had caught sight of me.

And then I opened my palm and showed the crowd something that wasn't there—the lost Relic. I imagined it nearly as big as my palm, an enormous diamond of impossible beauty. It caught a lingering shard of moonlight and sparked with white light. Rainbow prisms danced across its face and scattered across the Concordat. It glowed, bright and brighter, until the entire space was pure luster.

The crowd's jubilation was a crescendo in my heart. I drifted down among a cacophony of noise, and though the words *Duskland Dauphine* were repeated more than once, I couldn't tell whether the intonation was favorable or murderous.

I hoped I had time to find out. Already the shadow illusion was breaking apart at the edges—Haze and Shade had agreed they wouldn't be able to make something so big last for more than a few minutes. I had to hope it was enough.

I alit at the base of the podium. I pushed the radius of my

moonlight wider, until it encompassed the coronation dais, Gavin and his men, and the first few rows of spectators. In the light of my illusion, Gavin looked wan and bewildered. It was Arsenault who frightened me—his face was pinched almost to breaking, his eyes flaring with unnatural light. I swallowed, and looked away from them both toward the crowd.

"For those of you who have not yet recognized me, I introduce myself!" I called out, pitching my voice and carrying it to those beyond the radius of my light. "You know me as the *Duskland Dauphine*, but I have many names. Some of those names are ugly: *assassin, usurper, kinslayer.* When I joined the court of Coeur d'Or they named me Mirage, but though it is a name I have carried for months now, it no longer describes me. I am no faint illusion bound to disappear, but a desire you did not know you held, a promise of something better, and a dream of a world that might just be impossible. I am Sylvie Sabourin, daughter of Sylvain, sister of Severine, and true Sun Heir!"

The cacophony of sound was a jumble of cheers and boos and confusion.

"The Ordeals of the Sun Heir are not yet finished!" I threw my hands up to silence the crowd. My illusion of the Soul Relic glittered. "Many of you watched the Ordeals. You watched me lose one, then win another. But you must have wondered when I disappeared. Perhaps you thought I quietly ceded the throne to the so-called true Sun Heir, my distant cousin Gavin d'Ars. Perhaps you thought I grew afraid of losing, and fled. Perhaps you thought I succumbed to the third Ordeal, and died without witness in the Oubliettes. But none of those things are what truly happened. The truth is much more dire."

I turned on my heel and pointed a glittering, trembling finger at Gavin. "I accuse your so-called Sun Heir of treachery most foul! Not only did he cheat in the most holy Ordeals with a nefarious legacy he kept hidden from the world, but he sent an assassin to dispatch me while I lingered in the third Ordeal. An assassin masked in red and armed with a blasphemous sword—Sainte Sauvage himself! These Red Masks who for a span have terrorized your city, destroyed your homes and businesses, radicalized your youth, and pressured your conversions? They are in league with this pretender, this usurper—this treacherous Gavin d'Ars of Aifir."

Gavin mouthed something to a furious Arsenault, but I couldn't hear him over the sound of the crowd beginning to jostle against the line of Husterri at the base of the rostrum. He ran a thumb over the crown Relic looped onto his belt, then his hand went to the hilt of the sword Relic. My ambric Relic pulsed over his heart, but he didn't touch it. He crossed the stage and grabbed my arm, roughly. I dug my heels in and yanked, but he had the advantage of height and strength.

"Scion's teeth, Mirage, what are you playing at?"

"This is no game." I pulsed my illusory moonlight as bright as I could. It clashed against his kembric armor and blinded us both. His hand slackened—I flung myself away from him, silver paint flaking away from my skin.

"But the Ordeals aren't over," I cried, loud enough for the crowd to hear. "There is still one Relic left to be won—Meridian's lost Soul Relic!"

Again Gavin's hand lingered at the sword Relic, but my words made him falter. "You lost the Ordeals—you *disappeared*—"

"I was afraid for my life!" I screamed. "But I tell you now—I will run no longer. Just as the mythic Moon grew weary of her perilous flight from the wicked Sun, so too will I turn and face you in the dim." I threw my arms back, exposing the expanse of my bare, glittering chest. Scraps of darkness drifted around me, kissing my arms and teasing my hair. "This is the only way to claim your misbegotten place as Sun Heir. Do not hide behind masked assassins and shadowed hallways. Bear the burden of your crown and follow the impulse of your soul. *Earn* the last Relic, so you may rule in glory."

Fury and confusion tangled on my cousin's face. He licked his lips and narrowed his eyes. I shuddered with his indecision. If he refused my challenge to return to the Ordeals, he'd lose his legitimate claim—he'd lose the *people*. But if he agreed to return to the Oubliettes for the final Ordeal . . . well, then I'd have to admit I didn't really have the diamond Relic. And I'd be finished.

"Kill her." Arsenault's voice croaked over Gavin's shoulder. "And be done with this upstart bastard for good."

I heard the *shink* of metal leaving its sheath. An inch of red dristic showed above leather. Gavin's hand trembled. He took a shuddering breath, then loosed it. His shoulder slumped. He half turned toward Arsenault, a look of desperation blundering across his face.

"I can't do it," he whispered, almost plaintive.

Arsenault's expression turned livid. He made a sudden sweeping motion with his hands, as though he was gathering moonlight and shadows into his arms. The air twisted in a sudden stranglehold. For a frantic moment, I couldn't breathe.

When I shot a panicked glance out into the crowd, I almost wished I couldn't.

I saw upturned faces frozen in a multitude of expressions: bewilderment, anger, excitement, fear. Limbs caught in impossible angles: gripping fists and lofted hands and stomping feet. Scraps of fading moonlight danced with broken spears of sunlight. And silence.

Silence like death. Silence like emptiness.

Silence like time itself had stopped.

FIFTY

"How—?" I jerked my hands in front of my face just to prove I could. I slashed my eyes to Gavin, who gazed at the crowd with a mixture of terror and awe. We both turned to Arsenault at the same time, and the older man stood taller beneath our regard.

"*You?*" I breathed.

"Godfather?" Gavin said at the same time.

Arsenault stalked forward, batted Gavin's boneless hand away from his belt, and jerked the dristic Relic out of its scabbard. Arsenault smiled, brittle and piercing. The blade sang, inscribing a shining arc of red in the air. I stepped away a moment too late—the point came to rest at the base of my throat. Its kiss was sharp.

"Félix!" Gavin shouted, outrage heating his voice. "What are you doing?"

He launched himself at his godfather, grappling at his arms and trying to wrench the blade from his grip. Arsenault barely blinked as he incapacitated Gavin—two sharp blows to his throat, a well-aimed kick to his stomach, a foot hooked around his ankle. Gavin went sprawling to the floor, clutching at his neck and gagging. The sword barely wavered from my neck.

"You idiot," Arsenault said to me, grim. "You couldn't just leave well enough alone, could you?"

"It was you." Bile burst hot in my chest and climbed my working throat. He had a *legacy*—he had the power to *stop time*. "Scion, it was you who made me lose the first Ordeal. It was you who tried to kill me in the Oubliettes. Are you Sainte Sauvage too?"

"No!" Gavin coughed from the ground. "That's not possible."

I dared to take a shuddering step back. Arsenault easily paced me, keeping the blade pointed at my chest.

"Why did you have to come back?" he snarled. "I let you escape, you stupid girl. I knew you'd run straight to Belsyre. And I was willing to let you have your happy ending. I was willing to let you live out your days in miserable peace. All you had to do was let Gavin *win*. Win the Ordeals, win the Relics, win the Amber Throne. But you just couldn't leave well enough alone."

"*Leave well enough alone?*" I echoed. I didn't know whether I wanted to laugh or cry. "You mean forfeit my rightful place to a grasping cousin being puppeted by a religious zealot with delusions of grandeur?"

"I'm no puppet," rasped Gavin, getting to his feet.

"Of course you aren't, Gavin," Arsenault assured him. "You're the rightful Sun Heir. I've merely been ensuring you got what you deserved."

"So she's right?" Gavin demanded. "You cheated in the Ordeals? To make sure I won?"

"I may have bent rules. I'm not the first, and I won't be the last. The Ordeals were designed to be manipulated."

"I never asked you to do that!"

"You just never imagined you might lose." Arsenault made an exasperated noise. "Will I never be free of Sabourin folly? You all think you're Meridian's gift to the daylight world. Half of you stride forth into the light without imagining anyone would dare look away from your glory, and the other half plot and connive and coerce because you imagine you deserve everything and anything your heart desires, no matter the cost. Some of you do both."

He looked at me, then through me, and I knew his eyes were looking into a past I couldn't see.

"You're doing this because of my father, aren't you?" I guessed.

"Because of how he treated Xavier during his generation's Ordeals."

Arsenault turned his head and spat on the ground. I took the opportunity to edge away from the blade, moving closer to Gavin's bulk.

"Sylvain was a loathsome lying fraud, and as you can see his blood ran true." Hatred flashed in his eyes. "He wouldn't have won the Ordeals if he hadn't cheated and schemed at every turn. Remy Legarde never would have—" He clicked his teeth together, biting the words to pieces. "I'm just trying to make sure that this time, the true Sun Heir sits upon the Amber Throne. So—hand over the diamond Relic so we can end this once and for all."

"This is ridiculous," Gavin snarled. "Ever since I was a child, Papa warned me against these stupid, archaic Ordeals. He *told* me they would only corrupt me. And you, Arsenault—you were supposed to protect me from them. Instead, you encouraged me to come to this city I loathe, to this palais that only brings back terrible memories. You told me we were following the light of the Scion. But if this is what the Scion's light looks like—violence, betrayal, vengeance, and death—then I want no part of it."

Gavin reached for the ambric sunburst Relic hanging from his throat, and snapped the chain.

"Gavin!" Arsenault's eyes widened. *"No."*

Gavin handed the Relic to me. It pulsed hot in my palm, sending a thrill of blood leaping toward my heart. Amber light spilled between my fingertips. Arsenault lunged for me. I dodged, but he caught my elbow and threw me off-balance. I fell to the ground with a cry, banging my knees on the platform. Weight bore down on me—a hand on my shoulder, a knee in my chest. My back struck the ground. The wind blew out of me in a rush, leaving me gasping.

Fingers scrabbled around mine. I wrenched my arm up and out. Arsenault grabbed for the Relic.

Gavin slammed into his godfather with a yell, knocking him off me. I rolled onto my side, sucking lungfuls of air. I still had the ambric Relic—its dull points dug grooves into my palm. I shoved the sunburst into my bodice and levered myself to my feet.

Arsenault and Gavin faced off a few paces away. Gavin had his back to me, arms spread to protect me even though he didn't have any weapons. A sharp burst of regret speared my heart— regret for having misjudged him, regret for having allowed myself to hate him. He had never been my adversary. He had never been wicked.

He had just been blind and weak and easily led.

"I *refuse*, Félix," Gavin was saying. "You can't force me to accept something I don't want."

"Oh, my boy." Arsenault looked momentarily sad. "Neither you nor Xavier ever really knew what you wanted. I could never trust either of you to make the right decisions."

Gavin tensed all over. "You were Papa's confidant. How can you say such things about him?"

"Your father never treated me as anything except a servant," Arsenault spat.

"Papa thought of you as a brother."

"A brother?" Arsenault barked a guttural laugh. "You Sabourins are all so blind. Now move out of the way, and let me finish what I started."

He tried to lunge past Gavin, but my cousin stepped in his way and lifted his arms. Arsenault collided with his gauntlets with a resounding clang, and stumbled back. Again he tried to rush past Gavin, but the younger man was stronger and lighter on his feet. And unlike before—when Arsenault had disarmed him—he knew what he was up against.

They grappled through that timeless world of staring faces and empty eyes. I scrambled away while they were distracted, looking for something to *do*, something to use, some weapon—

A Husterri lieutenant stood paralyzed on the top step of the podium, mouth open in a shout, one arm lifted and the other reaching for his sword. *A weapon.* I crept toward him, unsure whether I'd be able to take his blade if it was frozen in time along with its owner. I lifted my hand and glanced at his face.

His mouth moved—slowly, so slowly. His finger twitched. I jerked my hand back and made sure I wasn't imagining things. No—he was *moving.* The freeze was no longer perfect. Stutters of movement ripped through the crowd—whispers of low, elongated sounds; prisms of sharp light; bright eyes shining like beacons.

I whipped my head toward Gavin and Arsenault, both intent on their fight. Sweat streamed down Arsenault's face, and though Gavin struck another sound blow to his jaw, the older man seemed loath to use the blade on his godson. I allowed myself a small smile, and glanced back at the slowly awakening crowd. Arsenault didn't want to kill Gavin. But the effort was making him exhausted and distracted. His legacy was slipping—his power over time was beginning to escape him.

Every legacy had limits. I just had to find Arsenault's.

When Arsenault's back turned to me, I quickly turned myself invisible, then sent a decoy of myself sprinting toward him. It was an old trick, but it had never led me wrong so far.

"Looking for this?" She dangled the ambric Relic in Arsenault's face.

He jerked his head to the side, and grabbed for it. Gavin nailed him with a right hook. Arsenault's head snapped. He reeled backward.

Time stuttered forward.

"Too slow," my decoy taunted from his other side, dancing within reach.

Arsenault grabbed for her, but she leapt away. He screamed in frustration, throwing himself after her. But she was already too far away—halfway to the edge of the platform. Something ugly spasmed across Arsenault's face. Oozing time slid again to a halt. Slick determination hardened his features. He ratcheted his grip up the sword's hilt. He drew it back over his shoulder, and quickly took aim. His arm flexed. He threw the sword.

The blade arced toward my double. Too slowly, I saw Gavin launch himself after her.

Horror tore through me. I burst back into sight. Already the illusion of me was disintegrating like impossible moonlight, but Gavin didn't notice. He had his eyes trained on Arsenault—on the sword flying toward him like winged death.

"Gavin, *no!*" I screamed.

I tried to run. But a nightmare clogged my steps—as though it was I who was frozen in time, instead of the multitudes. I pumped my arms, dug my heels into the platform, but everything around me seemed to be speeding up, racing toward the inevitable.

Arsenault saw Gavin a moment after the sword left his palm.

Gavin turned his head toward my decoy, evanescing into the dusk. He turned back, eyes narrowing in determination.

Arsenault cried out.

The sword caught the edge of Gavin's throat. Blood sprayed in a brief, bright fountain. Gore splattered the front of his sun-bright armor. He fell to his knees. He groped at his neck. He choked.

He toppled to the ground like a felled tree.

FIFTY-ONE

T
ime blurred by us, rushing forward like a dammed river set free. Motion and noise shredded my senses—shouts and boos and cries, Husterri rushing up the steps toward us in confusion, scraps of moonlight and darkness and filtering sunlight making a chaos of the sky. What must they have seen, in those slivers of time when Arsenault's power failed?

I couldn't imagine.

Again, Arsenault gestured, as though gathering spare moments toward him. And again, time froze around us. But this time, it seemed more labored—sweat drenched his hair and beard as he ran toward Gavin's butchered body. He reached him moments before I did, bending over the dark-haired boy. Arsenault heaved Gavin over onto his back, putting a hand to his ruined throat.

I ground to a halt and stared at my cousin. It was too late. The blood spreading in a vast pool beneath his body no longer pumped with the beat of a heart. His eyes had gone hard and glassy. Even from where I stood, I knew—Gavin was dead.

He'd died trying to protect me. Except it hadn't really been me—it had been an *illusion*. I took one—two—gasping steps backward. Why had he tried to *save* the girl who would have cost him everything? And why hadn't he guessed it wasn't me?

Arsenault looked up at me, his eyes almost wondering. "Do you know what you've done?"

"Me?" Shock shredded my throat. "*You* did this."

Arsenault stood, his motions mechanical. He paced to where the dristic Relic had fallen, red now with Gavin's lifeblood. He picked it up and he knelt once more beside his godson. Shock spangled through me when I saw what he was doing. He reached for the kembric crown Relic, gleaming through its jacket of blood. He unthreaded it from Gavin's belt.

"How dare you—" I snarled, stalking toward him.

In one swift moment, Arsenault put the hilt of the sword Relic beneath his heel and snapped it off. He lifted the hilt-less blade, fitted the angular crown Relic against the crest of the blade, and shoved.

The two Relics came together with a sound like mayhem. Light roared from the sword, bright as sunlight and vital as heartblood. I closed my eyes against the brilliance, but that didn't lessen its impact. It burned against my eyelids with the light of everything I'd once dared to dream of—power and prestige, untethered from the dirt of reality, the grime of politics. It called to me, perfect and pure.

I clenched my fists and forced my eyes open.

"You've ruined everything." Arsenault flashed a glittering grin, an expression at odds with the sweat pouring down his face and the blood all over his hands and his dead godson at his feet. "But then again, perhaps now everything is as it should be."

A Duskland shadow fluttered against my heart, and I took a step away from Arsenault. I dragged my eyes away from the two joined Relics—they set my teeth on edge, in a way that made me want to touch them for myself, take them for myself, conquer the world with them.

"As it should be?" I kept my eyes locked on him, but reached my attention toward the world frozen around us. He'd nearly lost control of his legacy, when Gavin died—I'd *felt* it. He was fallible. He wasn't completely in control. I just had to find a way— "Why did you really come here, Arsenault?"

"To crown the true Sun Heir."

"Please," I scoffed. "Gavin's dead. There's no need to lie to me now."

"Gavin?" Arsenault cocked his head to one side and laughed. "I loved him, but the boy was weak. He was no more true Sun Heir than you are. Did you know he truly believed he had no legacy? He used it without thinking, without any intent whatsoever. It made him so easy to manipulate. All I had to do was tell him to shine—and he *shone.*

"No—he was no true Sun Heir. I might have allowed him a tide or so on the throne, for appearances' sake. But I'm here to finish what your deceitful, treacherous, conniving father started."

"You still think Xavier—" A diamond-bright shard of realization sliced through the wasteland of my confusion. "Not Xavier. *You.*"

Arsenault slapped the blade against his palm in a mockery of applause. Droplets of blood spattered the front of his clothes.

"But—" My mind raced forward and backward, gathering everything I thought I knew and scattering it over the ashes of what I was coming to realize. "Xavier was Sylvain's cousin. Remy Legarde was from another branching line of Sabourins. And you—you weren't just Xavier's *confidant,* were you?"

"D'Ars, *Arsenault,*" he growled. "It's amazing to me how few people pick up on the similarity."

"His illegitimate brother," I guessed.

"Bastard-born," Arsenault agreed. "Just like you."

Just like you. I fought against a sudden whirlpool of similarity threatening to suck me under. Half-siblings, locked in conflict for a throne. An accident of birth pitting people who ought to have loved each other *against* each other. A Sabourin legacy of blood and death and treachery.

"I'm nothing like you," I snarled, backing away from him, closer to the edge of the platform.

"No," Arsenault agreed. "When you challenged Gavin to the

Ordeals, I thought you might be a worthy opponent. But you're weak, just like him. Just like your wretch of a sister."

"Severine?" Something caught in my throat. "What did she ever do to you?"

Ancient fury surfaced in his crackling eyes. The sword in his hand pulsed light across the motionless crowd. Again, time stuttered forward, then stopped once more. My heart throbbed with the ebb and flow.

"She wanted all the Relics for herself, didn't she?" he rasped. "But not to win the Ordeals, no. She didn't want to do it the *right* way. She didn't want to *play*. She was just as treacherous as Sylvain. She went behind everyone's back, trying to gather up the scattered Relics in order to *hide* them, to *destroy* them. Just so she wouldn't have to face off against that weird, feeble weakling of a brother."

My chest pulsed tighter. "Did you kill him?"

"Of course I did," he said. "I needed his Relic so Severine couldn't take it. I needed his Relic so I'd be able to play in the next Ordeals. So I could finally *win*. Sylvain cheated me out of being Sun Heir once. Not this time. Not ever again."

"You're a monster," I ground out. "How many more Sabourins have to die because of these archaic Ordeals? Because you fancy yourself Sun Heir?"

"Ideally?" Arsenault smiled. "Just one more."

He lunged toward me. I sidestepped away, breathing hard, and reached into my bodice. The ambric Relic dangled from my hand, glowing faintly. Arsenault stopped dead when he saw it, desire slicking his manic eyes. I slid my gaze to the side, and was rewarded with the sight of the crowd faintly stirring, the deep elongated sound of sluggish voices. Scion, I just had to keep him talking. I just had to make him angry, knock him off-balance.

"I'll give you this," I promised. "If you spare my life."

Gloating self-satisfaction painted Arsenault's face. His shoulders relaxed, and he lowered the sword.

"Or," I said, "I could just do this."

I dropped the Relic to the ground, lifted my skirts, and stomped on the sunburst as hard as I could. My high heel crushed its center, then split it apart. It shattered with a sound like a heart breaking, sending ambric shards skittering over the platform.

"No," Arsenault whispered. Disbelief shattered his face, and behind him the crowd stirred. Achingly slow, like they were moving through honey. Arsenault dropped to his knees by the glittering ambric shards, the sword dangling from his fingers.

I stepped backward, smiling in satisfaction even as I mentally slid my attention down the front of my dress—toward where the real Relic rested snug against my ribs. It sent an answering surge of energy toward my heart, a syncopation to my own heartbeat. I stepped toward the edge of the platform, nervousness stitching my spine as I prepared my maneuver.

I wasn't going to have more than one shot at this.

Arsenault reached for one of the ambric shards. His fingers slid through it, and wisps of color swirled away. He shuddered in relief, then looked up at me, livid. But I was ready.

I lifted my hand and showed him the Soul Relic. A moon-shaped diamond, as big as my palm, pale and sparking and *perfect.*

I held my breath. I'd never seen the lost Relic. But he had.

I prayed it would be good enough.

Wonder transformed Arsenault's face into something incandescent—a portrait of hunger, a wasteland of wanting. Beyond the circle of light, the crowd rumbled. I used every last shred of my legacy to dampen the sound, so the only thing that existed was me, Arsenault, and the Moon Relic.

"Give it to me." He staggered upright, reached for its impossible light.

I stepped away from my decoy and her false Relic. Invisible, I kicked the joined sword and crown Relics out of Arsenault's hand. Surprise jerked his head to the side. I lowered my shoulder and rammed into him. The impact jolted me to my bones. But it was enough. Arsenault stumbled. Time stuttered forward. I slammed into him again. This time he fell. He reached for my decoy as he toppled, then tumbled through her illusory form. His mouth opened. His hands grabbed at nothing.

The steps of the platform rose up to meet him. He slammed face-first into gilded boards. Bounced once. Then fell still at the feet of the crowd.

Time rushed forward in a river of color and sound.

Scraps of light and shadow scattered away like fireworks.

The Husterri lieutenant put his hand on his sword and shouted at something that had long since happened.

The crowd screamed in confusion.

And I ran.

FIFTY-TWO

I flung myself off the podium and shoved through the crowd.
"Now!" I screamed, the sound like raw metal in my throat.
Scion, was anybody listening? And would they be able to hear
me over the roar of the crowd? "Now, now, *now!*"

One of the Husterri standing close to the podium bent down
as though to tie his boot. When he stood back up, he no longer
wore the red-and-cream uniform of the enemy—he wore a shining breastplate studded with glittering diamonds, and a sweeping
pale cloak that shone like the moon. He caught my eye and
grinned, flashing dimples. *Calvet.* And then he laid into the soldats around him, striking one across the temple with the hilt of
his sword before he could so much as raise an eyebrow, then
grabbing him around the throat and using him as a shield against
his compatriots.

I turned away, quickening my footsteps. Dotted through the
crowd, more of Belsyre's wolves transformed their replica
Husterri uniforms into regalia of Oleander's design. I'd known if
things didn't go to plan, we'd need reinforcements. But my heart
rose in my throat when I glanced over my shoulder. The Husterri
lieutenant was helping Arsenault to his limping feet. Scion, but
what if he still had the strength to use his legacy? He could hunt
me down in the crowd simply by freezing me along with everyone else. I'd never know until a knife pierced my throat.

Panic shoved me faster. Lullaby appeared through the crowd,
frantic, gesturing at something behind her as she pushed toward
me. I focused on her mouth, but couldn't hear her words. *Dead?*
Dead *something?* I gritted my teeth in frustration and shoved a
gawking youth out of my path.

"Stop her!"

The voice thundered down from the podium. Arsenault had climbed the steps. I sensed time slip—I saw Arsenault stutter a half step forward, then fall to his knees in exhaustion. Relief pounded through me, even as stranger's hands reached out and grabbed at my arms, my dress. If he needed others to stop me, he couldn't do it himself. His legacy was spent.

"Murderess!" he howled. "She killed the Sun Heir, just like she did her sister, the empress!"

A spiderweb of Ambers caught me and held me tight. Sharp fingernails bit into my arms. Vicious eyes turned on me. Sparks of diamond shoved through the crowd toward me—bared teeth and flashing blades—but scraps of red and cream rose up to meet them. Pockets of violence raged around me. I looked to Arsenault, shuddering on the stage. Blood streamed down his broken nose and turned his teeth red. His arm looked broken—he cradled it against his chest.

"He's Sainte Sauvage!" I yelled, but my voice was barely audible above the roaring crowd.

"Gavin is dead!" Arsenault cried. "My godson is dead!"

Behind him, the lieutenant rose from where he was examining the body. Gingerly, he picked up the joined sword Relic, still sticky with Gavin's blood. My chest twisted to see it so close to Arsenault, but I'd known I couldn't carry it with me. I'd known Arsenault was going to turn this on me. And Scion help me, running away with the murder weapon wasn't going to do me any favors.

"My lord." The soldat didn't speak loudly, but the crowd quieted as he spoke, straining to hear his words. "Why did we not see this tragedy unfold?"

"She is a fantast," Arsenault spat. "She is a master of illusions."

"Barely a moment passed—" the lieutenant murmured, half

to himself. His eyes sharpened on Arsenault, then traveled onward to me. "My lord, you're covered in his blood. And is this not your blade?"

"I tried to stanch his wound," Arsenault snapped, impatient. "She is the one who runs! Would she flee if she were not guilty?"

Still the lieutenant hesitated. His Husterri hesitated with him, waiting for a signal.

I barely saw the arrow fly. I just saw it sprout from the lieutenant's throat, fletched in red. Movement writhed through the crowd—scarlet masks pulling down over faces, blade-sharp noses pointing toward me. And Arsenault's leering face above it all, smiling as his red death spread through the crowd.

Red Masks. That's what Lullaby had been trying to say. *Red Masks.*

One of the people holding me went limp, her body crumpling to the ground. A quick fist laid the other flat on the cobbles. Slender hands circled my arm and pulled me out of the grip of another man, who was gaping at a tall beauty who laid a bare hand on his chest.

"You look tired," Oleander whispered, with an enchanting smile.

He collapsed at her feet. I turned and buried my head in Lullaby's shoulder.

"I'm so glad to see you," I whispered. "But why didn't you escape with the other legacies?"

"Billow and Haze led a contingent to where Dowser's waiting," Lullaby confirmed. "But we couldn't just leave you here."

"We have to get you somewhere safe," Luca growled, moving to stand beside Oleander.

"Where?" Worry slicked Oleander's gaze as she turned on her heel and took in the scene of violence unfolding around us. "It would seem Sainte Sauvage is calling for your blood."

Disguised wolves and Husterri had left off fighting each other and had turned as one on the Red Masks. There weren't as many of them as the soldats in uniform, but they seemed sharper—more frightening. Each mask was a dangerous blade; each body a weapon carved out of hatred and misplaced faith and distorted ideals. And they were ruthless—bystanders fell prone on the ground or were used as human shields, while both Loup-Garou and Husterri were loath to use brutal force on innocent Ambers.

The Red Masks bore terror in their wake, and I wasn't the only one who felt it—civilians and soldats alike fell away from their onslaught, fearful of the only thing they had that we didn't—a symbol.

But no—that wasn't true.

In the chaos of my confrontation with Gavin and Arsenault, I'd nearly forgotten what I'd come here to do today. This wasn't about the Sun Heir. This wasn't about the Ordeals. This wasn't about what my family thought they could steal with cunning and silence and treachery. This was about *me*.

This was about everything I'd dreamed of, in that long-ago dusk at the edge of the darkness. That impossible world—more precious, more exquisite, more radiant—than the one we had been told to expect. But radiance wasn't always sunlight. Impossible things could be wrapped up in improbable deeds. And sometimes, the things we needed most already lived inside us, caged between our ribs and buried deep inside our hearts.

We carried worlds of possibility within us, just waiting to shine light into the dim.

"We have to go back," I gasped out.

"Back?" Luca asked.

"Back," I confirmed. I straightened my shoulders and stood a little taller. "I'm not going to run from what I started. I'm not going to run from *him*."

I looked at Arsenault, pacing the podium and waving the joined Relics, yelling blasphemy at his minions. Red Masks chanted his words on repeat, a cacophony of exploited prayers as they beat and maimed and mauled their way through soldat and civilian alike.

I am the sword—
I am the sword—
I am the sword—

"We have to go back," I repeated. "I'm not done here today."

Oleander looked like she wanted to spit poison at *me*. Luca slowly nodded. Lullaby set her mouth and took my arm again, making a beeline toward the podium without a backward glance. After a moment of jostling through bodies shoving in the opposite direction, she opened her mouth and began to sing.

A bubble of glory wafted before us like a shield. People stepped away from us, smiling. We neared the platform in half the time it had taken me to escape. This close, the violence was extreme. Husterri and diamond wolves fought side by side, even as Red Masks pressed close from every angle, silent hidden faces in stark contrast to the grimaces and groans echoing from the other soldats.

We were nearly there. We took cover in the shadow of a wooden support.

"What's the plan now?" Luca growled. His hand clutched a dagger that looked too small and fragile to do much against this onslaught.

Lullaby kept softly singing, her melody like a shield around her, but I could feel her listening.

"I need the sword," I hissed, glaring at Arsenault. Behind him, Severine's hulking ambric throne glowed dully in the low sunlight. "And then I need time."

"Done," Oleander promised. Her eyes flashed, and she raised

her bare hands, stained with streaks of green and carmine. "Can I kill that bastard?"

"No." I pushed away a visceral memory of blood on bright mirror glass: This time, when I gazed into my reflection, I saw Gavin's face staring back. "I've had enough of killing. But can you incapacitate his powers?"

She flexed her fingers. "That, I can do."

The four of us rushed up the stairs toward Arsenault. I went first, and Luca and Oleander flanked me—Luca lashing out with his dagger and dancing circles around Red Masks, Oleander spinning venom from her mouth and anesthetics from her fingertips. Lullaby came last, spilling her song behind us to deter any pursuers—Red Masks jolted against it, then fell away, looking pleasantly dazed.

We crested the steps. Arsenault saw us—fury melted his features. His raised the sword in his good hand and shouted something incoherent. Luca barreled into his broken arm and sank his dagger into Arsenault's thigh. He screamed, bloody teeth bared. Oleander walked up to him, composed as always, and slid her hand around his neck. Lines of puce laddered his throat—his eyes turned black, then rolled up into his head. He collapsed on the boards, a pace away from Gavin's lifeless body.

"Go!" Oleander cried, rounding on me.

"We'll make sure he stays where he is," Lullaby promised.

I shook myself, then bent to pick up the joined Relics where they had fallen from Arsenault's insensate fingers. The sword was heavier than I expected—with the jagged kembric crown as its hilt, it weighted my arm. It was heavy with other things too—the burden of death and power. Still, I hefted it, trying to ignore the patina of blood drying along its already red surface. I drew the third Relic from my bodice—*my* Relic, the ambric sunburst I'd had since forever.

The Relic I'd touched a thousand times with hopeful fingers. The Relic I'd whispered my wishes to. The Relic that had made all my impossible dreams come true, then forced me to confront whether I wanted any of them after all.

Yes, I wanted the world I dreamed of.

No, it did not look the same as it once had.

But maybe that was what growing up felt like.

I lifted the ambric Relic to my lips. It glowed at my touch, then pulsed hard at my fingertips. A jolt of sadness bit into my heart, because I knew what I had to do. I'd known what I had to do from the moment I watched Arsenault join the first two Relics into one.

I lofted my ambric pendant. Low sunlight purred along its contours, lighting it from the inside.

I slammed it down. It fit perfectly into the pommel of the sword—its beveled edges sliding neatly between the sharp points of the kembric crown. A scrap of inky shadow slid around the hilt, welding the Relic in place. Echoes of ancient laughter and mythic blood and the forgotten scent of the Oubliettes gripped me.

Light exploded from the Relic.

It was pure amber at first, red as the sky above the palais. Then it took on the colors of a thousand skies—blasted orange and flat carnelian, sharp magenta and sheer blue. Metallic hues joined it, sharpening its curves into facets. Hammered kembric and bronze-bell hearts. Forged dristic and the sword of longing at the edge of love. And spooling through it, whisper thin, was a thread of moonlight, hard as diamond.

Abruptly, the light fell away, leaving a stunned crowd in its wake. Even the Red Masks had stopped to stare at the joined sword, which glowed a scalding, molten red. Silently, I lifted it for all to see. Slowly—just a few at first, scattered through the crowd—the Red Masks began to remove their disguises. And behind those masks they were just people—boys and girls, men and women, young and old and rich and poor. I stared down as the light from my Relics shone upon them, and tried to feel what they felt.

I stepped from the platform, sword balanced on my palms. Behind me, one of my friends made a noise in their throat. I ignored it, and took another step. Three. Four. The cobbles of the street rang beneath my heels, and I moved among the people. Husterri, diamond wolves, Red Masks, civilians caught in the conflict with nowhere to go—all crowded around me, tense as a bow with an arrow on its string.

I threw the sword down to clatter against the sun-glow street. Its light flared, then winked out.

Murmurs chased each other through the crowd.

"I am not your Sun Heir," I said, harsh. "And I never will be."

FIFTY-THREE

Silence rang loud. I stared at the Relic sword and tried to remember what I'd wanted to say.

"Four girls stand before you today," I cried. "The first is Sylvie. She was born in the Dusklands, and grew up with shadows in her heart. She was taught to love the Scion, but not herself. And so she ran away toward the light, because she thought she could find a world where she belonged. She hadn't yet learned that you belong wherever your heart lives."

I lifted my eyes to Coeur d'Or, looming pristine and impossible above us. The crowd gazed with me, caught for a moment in the spell of my words.

"That first girl came here, to this palais, and became the second girl. They named her Mirage, for she was an illusion she had created for herself, an illusion of the person she thought she had to be—an illusion she didn't dare find the edges of. She was taught that cunning and intrigue would earn her respect, and so she played their games of wits. She set traps with words and actions and laughed when they were sprung."

I took a deep breath. The crowd inhaled with me.

"Then she learned of the taint in her bloodline, the sick beating heart at the center of all she'd ever known. And she became the third girl. She had no name, but she had violence in her eyes and deadly intent in her bones. She hunted down the woman who she thought was to blame for all her pains, all her sorrows. That woman was her sister. She carved out her ribs with mirror glass, and tried not to stare too closely at her own reflection gazing back from the shining blade."

A little gasp ran through the crowd. Weight shifted. Eyes

grew hard. I bit my lip and hoped I wasn't losing them.

"And now, I am someone else entirely," I cried. "I am all those girls, and none of them. I have stolen their minds and broken their hearts and endured their battle-metal wounds. And I know now what I should have known from the beginning." I pointed a trembling finger at the Relic sword, lying untouched upon the street. *"I don't want that."*

Their silence rang with discomfort and confusion and the slightest burble of hysterical laughter.

"I mean it," I said. "Anyone who wants it should take it. Pick it up! Break it apart and sell its bits and pieces for scraps—those ores are as fine as any you'll find elsewhere, and should fetch a few livres at the least. I don't care—good riddance to the ugly heirloom."

Someone laughed, sharp. Greed surfaced in one woman's eyes, then slid away when she saw me looking.

"Or better yet," I went on, "pick it up and wield it! There has been bloodshed here today—why stop there? See how this sword flames, molten with the sun's hot warmth? That must mean the Scion himself has blessed this weapon. Use it upon your neighbor, for surely his beliefs are inferior to yours. Someone else has preached this to you, and so it must be true. Carry this weapon before you in place of kindness, and smite those who disagree with you. You will conquer the whole world with it, but in the end only you will be standing."

A young man to my right lifted an absent hand to the red mask dangling around his neck.

"But really, there is only one thing to do." I pointed at the sword, then at Coeur d'Or. "Pick it up. March through those gates—they will open for you. Claim any room in the palais—I recommend one of the big ones. Drink fine wines and wear silks and paint your face in rouge and mascara. You will be happy, for a time. But one day, you will realize—none of those things are free. They come at the price of power. And that—that is nothing but a burden."

Somewhere, a baby wailed into the silence.

"I don't want it," I repeated. A tear slid down my cheek. I didn't bother to brush it away. "My Sabourin blood has done as much to curse me as it has to bless me. Which is why I'll walk away from this—I'll walk away from this impossible dream forever, and be glad for it. But someone else needs to pick up the sword and shoulder its burden."

No one moved so much as a muscle.

"I am not your Sun Heir." I knelt beside the sword and bowed my head. The sunlight sparked on the diamonds embedded in my skin and ground them hot against my veins. "I am not my legacy. I am not my dynasty. I was forged in the dusk and tempered on failure. I am nothing but what I made myself. Every action I have taken has led me here. If I asked for this once, I asked for it a hundred times—even when I didn't know I was asking. So let me take this burden onto myself one more time. Let me be your Duskland Dauphine."

There were no cheers. If there were flowers, no one threw them. The ground beneath my knees was spattered with blood and sweat and spilled liquor. My head throbbed and my corset pinched and my throat burned with future tears. And yet—

A boy stepped forward, gingerly, as though he thought someone might stop him. He couldn't have been older than twelve, and he reminded me—with a bright sharp ache—of Gavin. Dark hair and tanned skin, with a smile lurking behind his teeth and sunlight in his eyes. He bent, and lifted the sword. It was too heavy for him, and he didn't know how to grip it properly—lines of blood burst along his palm.

I bit my lip.

He looked around, apprehensive, searching the faces of soldats and Red Masks and Ambers for some disagreement, some disapproval to let him know his instincts were wrong. He must not have found any, because he stepped closer.

"I think," he said shyly, pressing the sword into my hands, "I think it should be you."

I bit back a laugh and smiled through sudden tears. And as I climbed slowly to my feet, the crowd's murmurs turned to cheers.

Duskland Dauphine.

The sound spilled away from my feet like the cresting of a wave, rushing down the Concordat and gaining momentum as it went. But that noise wasn't just cheers.

That was the sound of hoofbeats.

An *army's* worth of hoofbeats.

Fear pounded through me, and my hand found the hilt of the sword. Its ancient power frothed up my arm, whispering thirsty calm toward my heart.

These Relics were not afraid of battle.

But I was. I peered over the crowd's head, but couldn't see anything. I turned to launch myself up the podium, but the way my friends were staring down the Concordat stopped me in my tracks. Instead of standing on their guard or looking fearful, they all looked—

Happy?

I threw myself up the steps two at a time. I reached the top, breathless, and turned.

"What—?" I gasped out.

Oleander flashed me a luminous smile. "He's here. He's late, but he's here."

Heat burned my veins. I shielded my eyes, staring along the broad boulevard. For a moment, it looked like a remnant of Haze and Shade's illusion of night. But no—the darkness that streamed up the Concordat resolved itself into black destriers bred for snowy peaks, ridden by ten-score black-cloaked wolves. The militia's commandant rode three paces ahead, his bright hair a clarion. He urged his stallion faster, toward the edge of the crowd beginning to shy away from the soldats.

"He came," I murmured.

"Of course he did," said Oleander, who had put her gloves back on and clasped hands with an exhausted-looking Luca. "De Veres don't break their promises."

But sudden panic gripped me. The army closed in on the chaos of what had once been a coronation, and I saw Husterri nervously lift lowered weapons even as the disguised Loup-Garou hoisted their own black swords and cheered for their comrades. Red Masks backed away, hemmed in on all sides by potential enemies. Ambers looked for quick exits that didn't exist. The shaky peace my speech had forged seemed on the verge of breaking. Violence still simmered in the crowd.

"But I promised to keep him from bloodshed," I protested.

"You did." A frost of pride rimed her chilly eyes. "Surely there's no harm in letting him help clean up the mess?"

"Who's that with him?" Lullaby asked.

"His wolves, I assume."

"No," she said, pointing. "Look."

I looked. Riding alongside the Loup-Garou was a smaller force—two dozen men, perhaps, or slightly more. They were clad in shining dristic armor, a streak of bright moonlight at the edge of night. I frowned at them as they drew near. Those bright helms looked familiar, the cloaks almost like—

"Are those *Skyclad*?"

"Looks like," Luca confirmed. "But why would they be riding with Sunder?"

I didn't have an answer. I picked up my joined Relics with one hand, my skirts with another, and dashed down the steps. Pushing through the crowd toward the oncoming militia, I shouted for them to stop. Confusion burst across Sunder's thunderous face. He didn't recognize me.

Idiot. I cursed myself. Of *course* he didn't recognize me—I was disguised in diamonds and illusion and wielding a giant tri-metal sword.

I skidded to a halt. Sunder reined in his snorting stallion, who stamped and frothed. I reached for the horse's bridle, trying on a smile as I looked up. Confusion and aggression gave way to a creeping recognition as his eyes lit upon my face—he took in the dristic in my hair, the diamonds studding my throat, the confection of midnight and starshine spilling from my waist, tattered now with violence and spattered in Gavin's blood. He reached down and swiftly cupped the side of my face, making sure I was flesh and blood and not an illusion wrought from moonlight. His gloves came away silver.

"Mirage?" he whispered. "What in the Scion's hell is going on?"

"It's over," I said. "Tell your wolves to stand down."

He didn't question me. He sat tall, raised his arm, and gestured to the army at his back. Swords slid away into scabbards, hoods were pushed back over light hair, pale faces softened toward peace. Around us, the crowd relaxed.

He dismounted from his destrier.

"I came here expecting a coronation, demoiselle." He looked around with bewilderment. "I'm not sure what you've given me instead."

"A different kind of coronation, I think." Impulsively, I squeezed his hand. Surprise registered on his features. "I'll tell you everything later."

I was about to say something more, but a shriek of noise twisted my head and raised the hairs on the back of my neck. A blur of blue and black sped by me—*Lullaby*. She launched herself at a man on a grey steed—the leader of the Skyclad contingent. Horror pulsed through me—why was she *attacking* him? I had declared an armistice, I had told Sunder's men to stand down.

But Lullaby wasn't screaming in pain or anger or fear—she was screaming in *joy*. She flung herself at the man on the horse, grabbing the pommel of his saddle and hoisting herself into his arms. He caught her around the waist with a grunt, laughing in surprise. And it was then—in that flash of perfect white teeth, that glimmer of mirth in an otherwise unfamiliar face—that I recognized him.

I turned wide eyes to Sunder. He smiled, and nodded.

I took two halting steps toward the boy, staring in wonder at his face. There was so much different about him. His tan had faded, and his freckles with it. His bronze curls had been cropped brutally short. He'd lost weight, carving out the hollows beneath his cheekbones. But he was perfectly, exquisitely, undeniably—

"Thibo!" I cried out.

He grinned at me around Lullaby's death grip, and winked. "In every inch of glorious flesh."

"Scion, I saw you—" I choked on words I couldn't say. "I thought I'd never see you again."

"Please." His face softened. "I have every intention of aging like a very fine wine."

"But you're not—" I was about to say *Skyclad*, but already I knew he wasn't.

No—the phalanx of soldats he'd brought with him wore

Skyclad colors and armor, but without the grim rigidity of Severine's garde. Silvery cloaks draped over insouciant bare arms, painted faces laughed, breastplates gleamed with personal sigils. Confusion hazed my thoughts.

"No," he chuckled, releasing Lullaby to the ground and dismounting behind her. "But word of your coup d'état made poorly paid Skyclad soldats very persuadable. And I am nothing if not persuasive."

"We met three days' ride from the city," Sunder supplied. "He'd heard nothing of Gavin, or the Ordeals. We decided to ride in together."

"We ambushed your wolves," Thibo corrected him, with a laugh. "And you bribed me here with promises of a bath and a half-decent cocktail."

Sunder inclined his head. Thibo strode forward and folded me into an embrace. I gripped him tight, inhaling his unfamiliar scent of dust and sweat and fading Duskland shadow.

"I looked for you." Tears threatened to choke me.

"And now," he said, "you found me."

The crowd churned restless. I looked around and nearly laughed—how many different armies clogged this boulevard? Three? Four? Uncertain Husterri and sour-faced Red Masks gripped weapons and looked for escape routes. But between the palais and Sunder's and Thibo's soldats, everyone was pinned down.

Perhaps it was time we all stopped trying to fight each other.

"Build a pyre." I drew myself up to my full height and ignored the nervous glances. "Use the wood from the podium. Any Red Mask who throws his disguise into the fire is free to leave this place of death and betrayal. Any who doesn't—"

I glanced at Sunder. His glittering eyes gave nothing away.

"Any who doesn't may leave too. They will answer to the

Scion. But I will no longer rule this city with swords and violence."

I turned and faced the broader crowd. "That goes for all of you! Husterri—you have done nothing wrong but follow orders. You are free now to do as you please. Ambers, this city has been a closed fist for too long. As of now, I declare all gates open, all trade routes resumed, all purchasing bans lifted. Everyone else—?"

I looked at my friends—my *family*. My ribs unclenched around my heart. A trickle of color spilled out to dance along my bones. I smiled.

"I think it's time to go home."

Thibo let out a whoop, and leapt into his saddle, dragging a laughing Lullaby up behind him. Horses stomped and whinnied. Oleander and Luca clasped hands and grinned. Sunder swung onto his destrier. He held a hand out for me.

"Coming, demoiselle?"

I shook my head.

"I think this is something I have to do on my own."

I turned, squared my shoulders, and walked into my palais. And for just a moment, the sword resting heavy on my shoulders didn't feel like such a burden.

FIFTY-FOUR

My new Relics roused me from sleep with a premonition of death.

I fumbled through gloom. My fingers found the edge of my circlet, discarded by the bed—the metal was cold to the touch, and I flinched away. I found the hilt of my sword a moment later. I gripped the ambric sunburst at the pommel, and it glowed—sunlit warmth flooded through my veins, and behind it strode the twin comforts of strength and rationality. I breathed deep against the bloody push of images I didn't understand.

I was beginning to intuit the power of these joined Relics. The ambric Relic had helped me earn all the things my heart desired. The dristic Relic gave my hands strength. The kembric Relic kept my wits sharp. Together in my hand, they made me stronger, smarter, and wiser. It was a feeling I wanted to lash to my bones. It was a feeling I wanted to reject. It was a feeling that made me want to take over the world.

I levered myself onto my elbow and glanced over my shoulder at Sunder. He slept sprawled on his side of the bed. His limbs kept just enough distance from me that I knew, even in sleep, how carefully he kept himself in control. I reached out, slowly, until my hand rested a hairsbreadth from his fingers. A spark zipped between us—pain lashed up my arm toward the elbow. I curled my hand away. I watched for Sunder's steady breathing, then slid out of bed and padded from the room.

The palais was silent in the hours past Nocturne. Ambric globes pulsed light into creeping shadows, and I kept to the center of the halls. No black-clad wolves stood guard at corners or doorways. In the weeks since Ecstatica, I had refused to return to the martial law I'd relied on after my coup. There had been unrest, yes, and more than a few skirmishes. And this empire would never be free of swords. Half of the Husterri had chosen to defect to my ranks, and a few Loup-Garou too. I smiled when I remembered Calvet's declaration of loyalty, his bowed head and dristic sword.

Sun Heir or Duskland Dauphine, he'd promised. *Either way, your light shines my way.*

I didn't think Sunder had minded. Much.

But I didn't want soldats posted in these halls. I'd realized they made me just as nervous as the potential threat of unseen assassins. And there had been none of those since Sainte Sauvage had been exiled to Aifir with a strongly worded missive to the high commander and a hefty dose of Oleander's legacy-numbing poison in his veins.

Besides, something told me I wasn't defenseless anymore. With each step I took, the power of the joined Relics whispered in my bones—each pulse of my heart pushed their influence deeper.

It had been generations since they'd been joined together. They wouldn't let me die so soon.

I slipped into Severine's chambers unnoticed and unseen. The room had been dimmed for Nocturne, but ambric light spilled in from the open skylight, painting the pale walls in shades of ruin. I stared at her still form, half hoping for her to finally be dead. But the bloody vision my Relic had shown me wasn't true. I had seen her death, seen her dying, yet she just lay still, captured between life and death.

Perhaps it had just been a bad dream. I sank onto the edge of her bed with a sigh and looked at my sister.

What had her coronation been like? Had she stood before the palais on Ecstatica and accepted the clamorous love of her people? Or had she, like me, opted for a small ceremony, friends and important courtiers only, to hide the misbegotten nature of her rise to power?

Had she liked the feel of that crown on her brow? Or had it felt too heavy to her too?

Had she ever woken from nightmares that gripped her heart and pummeled her soul?

I slid my hand to her neck—more out of habit than anything else. I squeezed.

Perhaps we had both been caught between worlds. She, between life and death. Me, between dark and light, hatred and love, reality and fantasy. I'd finally fought my way out of that confusion, charting a perilous course toward the world I'd always dreamed of. But Severine? She wasn't going to wake up. And if she did, it would only be to upset the fragile peace I'd fought for.

Perhaps she'd earned a peace of her own.

Lullaby's voice echoed through me: *It would be a mercy.*

Slowly, hesitantly, regretfully, I hefted the sword and laid the blade against her throat. Light from the joined Relics painted her in gory shades from collarbone to jaw.

Her pulse fluttered in her throat, then ratcheted against the blade.

She jerked, convulsed. Horror moved me to snatch the sword away, but her limp hand clutched the blade. Blood burst along her palm and drenched her unvarnished nails in red. Her pale thin eyelids slashed open; staring violet eyes found mine.

"Hello, little sister," Severine said.

Terror shoved me away. Memories of our last confrontation slicked my mind—blood and mirror glass, her hands at my throat stealing my legacy. But hiding beneath the fear was something else, something I didn't expect: a childlike wave of *hope.*

Severine began to cough violently, explosively. She seized on the bed, her torso convulsing with the force of her coughing. Droplets of blood burst from her mouth, staining her lips and splattering the pristine bedspread. She coughed until I thought she would come apart at the seams.

She wretched. Gagged. The corners of her mouth bent around something—an *object*—wedged between her teeth. She spat it out onto the mattress, choking on the spume of its ejection. I stared at it, but it was impossible not to recognize. I had seen it in my nightmares, in the memory of my blood. I had held it aloft, no more than a dream. I knew it because it had been meant for me.

It was the diamond Soul Relic. Blood spattered. Spit-frothed. Shining like a moon. Unmistakable. I stared down at it and fought the urge to snatch it up.

"You know it," Severine croaked, around a smile like death. "Of course you know it—you have brought the rest together. They called you to it as it woke. And so you came."

She choked and coughed again. This time, the cough sounded dangerous—a sound beyond illness, edging toward death.

"You—" Shock and disgust made my words slow. "You—you *swallowed* it?"

"How else could I keep you safe?" she rasped.

"Me?"

"All of you."

Old fury spangled through me. "You tried to *murder* all of us."

"Better dead than shackled with this burden," she groaned, her eyes fixed on the diamond. Her hand snapped out, tightened around my wrist. She dragged me closer. "Listen—don't you dare give it what it wants."

"What does it want?" I heard myself ask.

"It wants to take," she said. "If you let it, it will take and take and *take*. Whatever you want—whatever your soul desires—it will feed off that want and transform it into power."

Revulsion gripped me. "What are you talking about?"

"You think you can control the hunger of the Relics?" She stroked a hand along my cheek and smiled bloody. "Perhaps you can. You were strong enough to win, after all. But you were also weak enough to listen to their call. They want to be together. And you—*you* joined them."

Her eyes found the sword, dangling forgotten in my hand. Her fading gaze blazed with mad light.

"Meridian's gifts all have teeth," she hissed. "But his soul is worst of all. You think I wanted to steal? Steal lives? Steal powers? Once upon a time, I just wanted to feel what they felt, experience what they experienced. But that wasn't enough. The Relic sank its fangs into my throat and never let go." Her fingers moved to my cheek, finding the chips of diamond embedded in my neck, my collarbone. "But—oh. *Sister.* You have already tasted its bite."

I slapped her hands away, but her words had their own sharp fingernails. "Get your filthy hands off me."

She let me go. She laughed as she fell back against the pillows, and the sound sprayed blood and bile down her chin.

"Don't listen." Her eyes fluttered shut. "It doesn't matter to me now. Finally, I'm free."

I backed away as my sister died. Her chest heaved. Once. Twice. Her fingers played out a rhythm against the bedspread, and her lips moved once more. Finally, she lay still.

I choked on a traitor sob as illicit hope fell away. My hands fumbled toward my chest, but the ancient comfort of my sunburst Relic was gone. I found its light, gleaming from the hilt of the sword. But it looked suddenly treacherous, covetous, craven.

Meridian's gifts all have teeth.

I reached toward the bed, reluctant but morbidly intrigued. The diamond gleamed from the bedspread. I plucked it up, wiping it free of blood and saliva. It nestled in my palm.

Beautiful. Scion, but I didn't know if I'd ever seen something so exquisite. Its facets caught the low red glare and transformed it into moonlight. It glittered against my palm like it belonged there, and I could almost imagine it as part of myself. An extension of my own person, my own *soul*—

The edges of my skin curled up, lifting over the rim of the diamond Relic.

I threw it to the ground. It bounced, once, then rolled beneath the edge of the bed. Slowly, I bent. I rolled the edge of my sleeve over my hand and lifted it gingerly off the cold floor. I dropped it in my pocket. With shaking hands, I gathered up the Relic sword and backed out of the room.

I turned, before I left. Severine lay prone against the headboard, her mouth slack and her eyes glazed. Hatred pushed out of me like a tide. When it ebbed back in, I felt only pity. Pity for the sister I never had. Pity for the girl who'd lost everything. Pity for the woman who'd fought for all the wrong things, who had taken what didn't belong to her, who had stolen too much.

And as I backed out of the room, I knew.

My last sister was free. And I was finally alone with my burden.

FIFTY-FIVE

I stood on the roof of Coeur d'Or and let the world fall away around me.

It had not been so long ago—bare spans, no more—when I stood on this rooftop as a provisional courtier and practiced surrendering to my legacy, reveling in a power that had seemed to work *with* me for the first time, instead of against me. I'd conjured brilliant, exquisite illusions: milk-white plains beneath sharp blue peaks; sand-pale dunes rippling liquid beneath a sea of sky; wings like blades that cut the world into pieces. But mostly, I'd dreamed of a perfect city, built from the brittle glass of ancient dreams. A city lingering sharp as an unspoken wish.

I'd been so sure it existed, because I'd been so certain of my place in it. But that impossible world where I belonged by virtue of my exceptional blood? That world was dead, scorched in fire and drenched in blood. Yet I had survived, reshaped and remolded, and I knew that dream had transformed with me.

The past weeks had been their own transformation. After Gavin's death and Arsenault's exile, both Barthet and Lady Marta had rejoined my Congrès. I knew I'd need them in the coming months. Dowser had too, but recently he'd been focused on his new pet project—a school for young legacies who couldn't control their abilities. It was apparently more common than I knew.

I'd quietly stripped Lullaby's mother of her holdings in the Sousine—one château in particular, with a long sloping lawn and caves down by the sea, I was particularly keen to gift to someone else. I smiled when I thought of Lullaby there, and

Thibo with her—eating candy on the beach, wine in hand, while arguing about something unimportant.

I wished I could join them.

"Demoiselle?" The voice pulled me away from the edge of the roof and my impossible daydreams.

Sunder climbed up onto the sloping tiles, tall and lean and achingly handsome. The wind caught the edge of his white-gold hair and flung it off his forehead. He was dressed the way I remembered him best; not in the gilded fashions of court, nor the stark regalia of the Loup-Garou, but in the simple angular polish of Belsyre—boots for riding and a doublet for fighting and a thick black fur cloak to stave off the chill.

"You're going home," I said.

"I think I must." He stood close. A dull, fevered glow painted his skin shiny. "The mine at Wolf's Mouth runs deeper than we thought. Besides, our lands have been too long without their lord and lady."

His dristic-and-pine eyes swiftly tallied me up: my gown—moonlight and the edge of night, too fine to be standing on this roof; the trio of Relics hanging too heavy from my belt, the lump of cloth I held awkwardly in my palm. He looked like he almost wanted to smile. "But you didn't summon me here just to say goodbye."

"No." This close, I could see the livid lines climbing his throat—red shot through with black. "It's still getting worse?"

"It's killing me," he said, expressionless. "But it'll be better in Belsyre. I think the chill helps."

The wind sang between us.

"What would you risk," I asked, because I had to know for sure, "to take it all away?"

"All of it?" He did smile then, his gaze going wide and deep. I thought, perhaps, he dreamed of it often. "I'd risk everything."

Wordlessly, I handed him the bundle of cloth. He frowned, and unfolded the fabric with deft fingers. A circular diamond stared up at him, pristine and shining with a faint glow. He lifted his eyes to mine, confusion blurring his features.

"What is this?"

"It's the lost Relic," I said simply. "Now listen—you can't hold it for long. So before you touch it, I want you to think about what your life would be like, unencumbered by your legacy. How light you would feel without your burdens. How it would feel to be free."

"I've dreamed it a thousand times, demoiselle." Sunder's eyes went jagged. "Sometimes I can almost believe that somewhere, the boy who never learned pain actually exists."

"He does," I whispered. Quickly, I tugged off one of his suede gloves. My skin brushed his—sparks needled my fingertips. Sunder hissed, and moved to yank his hand away. "Don't."

I cradled the diamond Relic from its nest. Its power was a pull against my skin, but I slid it gently into Sunder's palm, and curled his long fingers around it.

"Now close your eyes," I said fiercely. "And dream about being free."

He obeyed. His lids squeezed shut, dark lashes streaking lines of soot on his high pale cheekbones. The wind lashed higher, frothing his hair and lifting the heavy edge of his black fur coat. A chill raced along the line of his shoulders, and his emerald eyes flew open.

He cried out. The wind fell away, abruptly, so for a long moment everything hung motionless—his fine hair, the hem of his cloak, the sound of his soul being torn apart. His voice reverberated in my heart, and I held myself tight against the need to reach for him, to comfort him, to take his pain onto myself.

He collapsed to his knees. His palm unfurled. The diamond

had already tasted his flesh, curling greedy around its facets. I snatched it away, swaddling it in cloth and shoving it in my pocket. But Sunder had barely noticed—he scrabbled at his coat, jerking buttons awry and tearing at his undershirt in a sudden, silent effort to reach his own skin. His clothing fell away. He put a hand to his stomach. Dull red light winked out. The timbre fell away into his hand. He ran disbelieving fingertips over the sprawl of scar tissue marring the even ridges of his abdomen.

He looked up with a sear of pain so deep it nearly broke my heart. But then his gaze cleared, that glacier of his will melting away into brittle ice. And when it shattered, I fell—fell soft and quiet toward bright mirrored certainty, fell from a distant hope toward a cool promise, fell like the moon toward the balm of a dusky horizon. He stood, and when he swept me into his arms, the world fell away from us like silk.

He kissed me like he'd never been kissed before, and I knew I would never know another kiss like his. The world narrowed to the space between our lips, our kisses stitching time away like thread. I tasted every unspoken secret on his breath, and told him all of mine, until we were light enough to float away. I curled fingertips in the soft hair at his nape, smelling like pine sap and snow. No fever. No blood. No pain.

Just Sunder.

Everything was perfect.

I tried to ignore the bitter scent of heartbreak rising on the wailing wind.

He pulled away from me at last, resting his forehead on mine. He closed his eyes, and whispered: "Oleander?"

I laughed, a little. To be loved by someone like Sunder was to be held precious against the rest of the world. I envied her, just a little.

"She went first," I said. "We didn't know—we didn't know

whether the rest of her would be swallowed up with the legacy. She didn't care. She said she'd give anything, and meant it."

"So she's also"—Sunder rolled the word around like he wanted to relish its flavor—"free?"

"Yes." I laughed to hide how frightened I'd been. I'd told Oleander about my encounter with Severine, and it had been she who intuited what my sister had meant: *You think I wanted to steal? Steal lives? Steal powers? Once upon a time, I just wanted to feel what they felt.*

It wasn't her legacy to steal magic, Oleander had breathed, leaping to her feet. *It was the Relic.*

I'd been so uncertain. It had felt like murder, or suicide—I wasn't sure which. But Oleander had insisted. I hadn't been able to refuse the hunger on her face when she reached for the seductive eye of the diamond Relic.

And it had worked. She'd screamed on the floor as her soul released something rooted so deep, ripping it out nearly broke her. And when she'd risen, trembling, she'd torn off her elbow-length gloves and hugged me like salvation. When we took the Relic from her palm, it came away bloody.

Let me bear the scar. Ecstasy had made her whole. *Let it remind me of all the things I've lost. And all the things I've now gained.*

But I would let her tell Sunder all of that. Now I just wanted to gaze at him—to memorize his angular cheekbones and plush mouth. His spill of pale hair and his metal-and-gemstone eyes. The way he looked through me, finding the things I wanted to keep hidden from everyone but him.

"Demoiselle?" He lifted his hand to my chin and tilted my face toward his. I leaned into his touch, basking in the utter normalcy of it—his skin against my skin, the rasp of callous a glorious imperfection. His eyes gathered shadows. "Why are you looking at me like I'm still dying?"

"Because in a moment," I whispered, around the blade sheathed in my throat, "I'm going to say goodbye to you."

His hands tightened against my jaw, then slid deep into my hair. He kissed me, hot and greedy, and then again, fiercely gentle.

"And why," he breathed against my mouth, "would you do a thing like that?"

"Because I can't let you love me." I drew away, tears scorching the back of my throat.

"In this, demoiselle, you cannot command me."

"Love would make martyrs of us all." I forced a laugh. "You and Oleander need to go home and remember how to love yourselves. And each other. And I—I need to learn how to love myself before I can ask anyone else to. I need to learn to love this city, and the mess I've made of it. I need to learn to love as the moon loves—bringing light to dark places without forcing the shadows to hide."

Sunder's hands tightened.

"Not forever?"

"No." I laughed through my tears. "I think not forever."

His gaze shifted from my face. He ran his thumb along the line of my jaw and down the side of my throat, catching on diamond splinters. He touched them tenderly, like they reminded him not of metal and conflict, but of chips of ice and frozen kisses. He smiled.

"Not forever," he promised. "And when I return, I will bring a thousand bright stars to join my moonlit dauphine in the dusk."

He kissed me, one last time, lingering over my lips and tasting my tears.

"I don't want to say goodbye." Snow fell across his alpine eyes.

"Then don't say anything," I wept.

I lifted my fingers to his mouth. He kissed my fingertips—all ten. Then he raked hair back from his face, and walked away from me.

I watched him recede down the stairs. Then I crept to the edge of the roof and watched until I saw his entourage set off along the Concordat—a line of black smearing like shadows toward the horizon. He rode at the back, Oleander at his side. And beside her—Luca, his laughter audible all the way from here.

"I don't want to say goodbye," I whispered through my tears.

He turned, wheeling his horse to face me once last time. I couldn't see his face, but his hair caught the low sunlight and shone like a blade in the dim.

And I knew—

I knew I would never be free of him. And I knew I didn't want to be.

I waited until they disappeared into the bowels of the city. I rose to my feet, scrubbed my tears on my sleeve, and climbed.

The main dome of Coeur d'Or was steep, its gilded tiles slick beneath my feet. A high wind ripped my breath from my lungs and flung it away. But still I climbed. The sword hanging clumsy from my waist spoke a metal promise—it would not let me die so soon. I fit my fingers into narrow chinks and kicked at the roof until it bore me up—up toward the pinnacle of the city I'd dreamed of, so long ago in the dusk.

I stood, clinging to my balance like a dancer. The wind whipped at my dress, unfurling shadows against the diamonds scarring my arms and throat. Slowly, my eyes found the eastern horizon. The Midnight Dominion was nothing more than a smear of dusk beneath purpling clouds, yet as moisture prickled my wide eyes, I swore I could reach out and touch it.

Thibo's words echoed suddenly in my mind. We'd gone strolling together, a few days before he left for the Sousine with Lullaby—he, thin and preoccupied in his velvet suit, and me, racked with an empire's worth of decisions. After minutes of silence, he'd finally turned to me on the Esplanade.

I'm not superstitious, Sylvie. The brutal crop of his bronze curls made his face harsh. *But I saw things in the Dusklands I can't explain. Would you believe me if I told you the darkness was coming?*

I did. Especially now, with the wind whipping strange voices by my ears and teasing nightmares from my fingertips. I ran a finger over the sunburst pommel of my Relic sword, stealing a filament of comfort from its power. I absently touched the chips of diamond embedded along my throat. I unwrapped the diamond Relic. We gazed at each other for a long, aching moment. My reflection flashed upon its surface.

My eyes were sharp with moonlight. My blade pierced the roof of the sky. Deep beneath the city, something began to move. Something with a thousand shining feet.

I tore my gaze free of the diamond. My chest ached with a thrill of something like love.

The moon's light could unveil the beauty of the dark. But it could also show your soul strange, deceptive, impossible things.

I looked down at the city spilling away below. *My* city. *My* empire. It wasn't perfect, like I once dreamed. But neither was I. I was born in the dusk, where darkness stole sunlight and shadows had teeth. And perhaps that was where I would always live, no matter how brightly I tried to shine. But I could live with that.

Despite our dire history, I believed Severine. This Relic wanted to *take*. And perhaps that was the burden of power. But I couldn't let it take anything I wasn't willing to give.

Not today. Not *yet*.

Quickly, with a length of wire I took from the armory, I

lashed the diamond Relic to the highest spire on the highest dome of Coeur d'Or. It pulsed at me, cold and angry, as I trapped it where it couldn't touch, couldn't tempt, couldn't *take*.

I stepped back. For a moment, the world seemed sliced in half. On one horizon, amber sunlight foamed, and the eye of the Scion cascaded over the city in light and color. And far away—so far I could almost believe I imagined it, beyond the line of shadow at the edge of the world—I saw an answering flare of calm, smooth light. Sunlight and moonlight both kissed my face, then faded away.

I smiled into the light, and smiled beyond it. I smiled into the darkness and knew:

I might someday need the lost Relic, the diamond Relic. The *Soul Relic*.

But until that day, I had a new world to dream.

ACKNOWLEDGMENTS

I was told sophomore novels were difficult. I should have listened. This book was a challenge for me every step of the way, and yet it is the one I am most proud of having written.

To my brilliant agent, Ginger Clark—I honestly couldn't have finished this book without your continuous encouragement. Thank you for pep talks, tough love, and chocolate-covered pretzels.

To Scholastic Press, for allowing me to tell the next chapter of Mirage's journey. To my editors, Lisa Sandell and Olivia Valcarce, for your editing sorcery—if there was any real magic in the writing of this book, it was wielded by you. Huge thanks to everyone at Scholastic who has helped and supported me along the way: Jordana Kulak, Tracy van Straaten, Rachel Feld, Isa Caban, Nikki Mutch, and David Levithan. To Elizabeth Parisi and the team at Vault49, who gave me a cover I love even more than its predecessor—you outdid yourselves.

To all my friends, colleagues, and support systems. Roshani Chokshi, you inspire me daily with your exquisite words and beautiful soul. Shauna Granger, I rely so much on your keen eye and red pen—I'm sorry if there are still incorrect fight scenes in this book. Sara Holland, Samantha C. Helmick, Nicole Evelina, Liv Rancourt, Evan Matyas, Erin Dionne, and Scott Westerfeld— I feel grateful for your contributions to my writing journey. Sonia, Lauren, Hannah, Jess, Austin & Sara, Carrie—I'm so lucky to have such amazing and supportive friends.

To my family, as it expands in all directions—all the love in the world.

To Steve, who lent these characters the Shakespearean melo-drama they deserved—thank you for everything.

And to my readers—you truly mean everything to me. Thank you for reading.

LYRA SELENE is the author of *Amber & Dusk*. She was born under a full moon and has never quite managed to wipe the moonlight out of her eyes. When she isn't dreaming up fantastical cities and brooding landscapes, Lyra enjoys hiking, rainstorms, and autumn.

She lives in New England with her husband in an antique farmhouse that's probably not haunted. You can find her online at lyraselene.com and on Twitter at @LyraSelene.